the DEMON COURT

USA TODAY BESTSELLING AUTHOR
EMMA HAMM

emma hamm

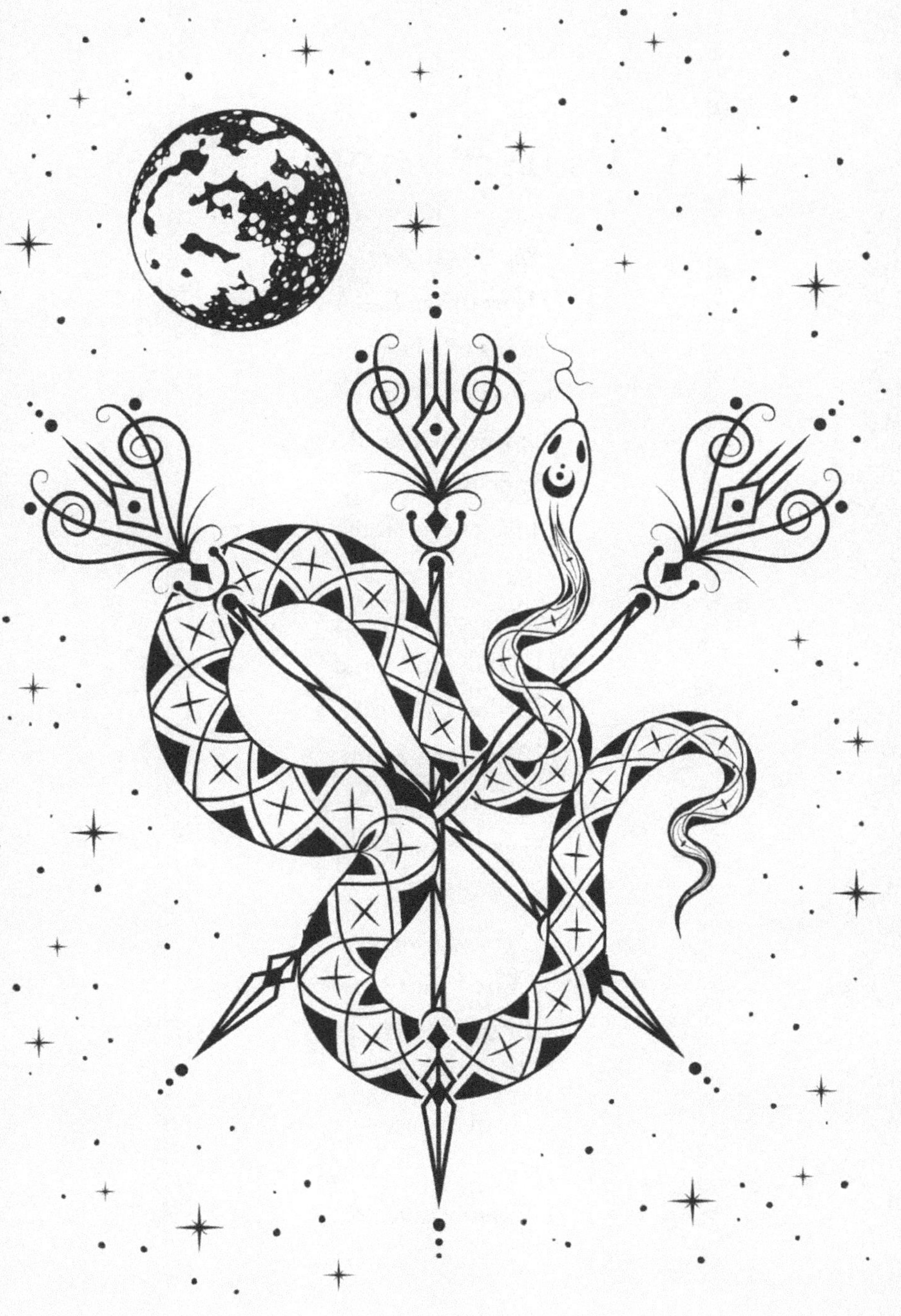

ALSO BY EMMA HAMM

The Otherworld
Heart of the Fae
Veins of Magic
The Faceless Woman
The Raven's Ballad
Bride of the Sea
Curse of the Troll

Of Goblin Kings
Of Goblins and Gold
Of Shadows and Elves
Of Pixies and Spells
Of Werewolves and Curses
Of Fairytales and Magic

Dragon of Umbrar
Fire Heart
Bright Heart
Brave Heart
Torn Heart

and many more...

For all the readers who kept begging me for more spice.

You're welcome.

emma hamm

VI

the demon court

Copyright © Emma Hamm 2022

All rights reserved. This book or parts thereof may not be reproduced in any form, stored in any retrieval system, or transmitted in any form by any means—electronic, mechanical, photocopy, recording, or otherwise—without prior written permission of the publisher, except as provided by United States of America copyright law. For permission requests, write to the publisher, at "Attention: Permissions Coordinator," at the address below.

Visit author online at www.emmahamm.com

Cover Design by The Book Brander
Dust Jacket Design by Rachel Bostick

This book is a work of fiction. Any references to historical events, real people, or real places are used fictitiously. Other names, characters, places, and events are products of the author's imagination, and any resemblance to actual events or places or persons, living or dead, is entirely coincidental.

LUST'S CASTLE

PRIDE

GREED

LUST

GLUTTONY

ENVY

SLOTH

WRATH

THE
WHITE TOWER

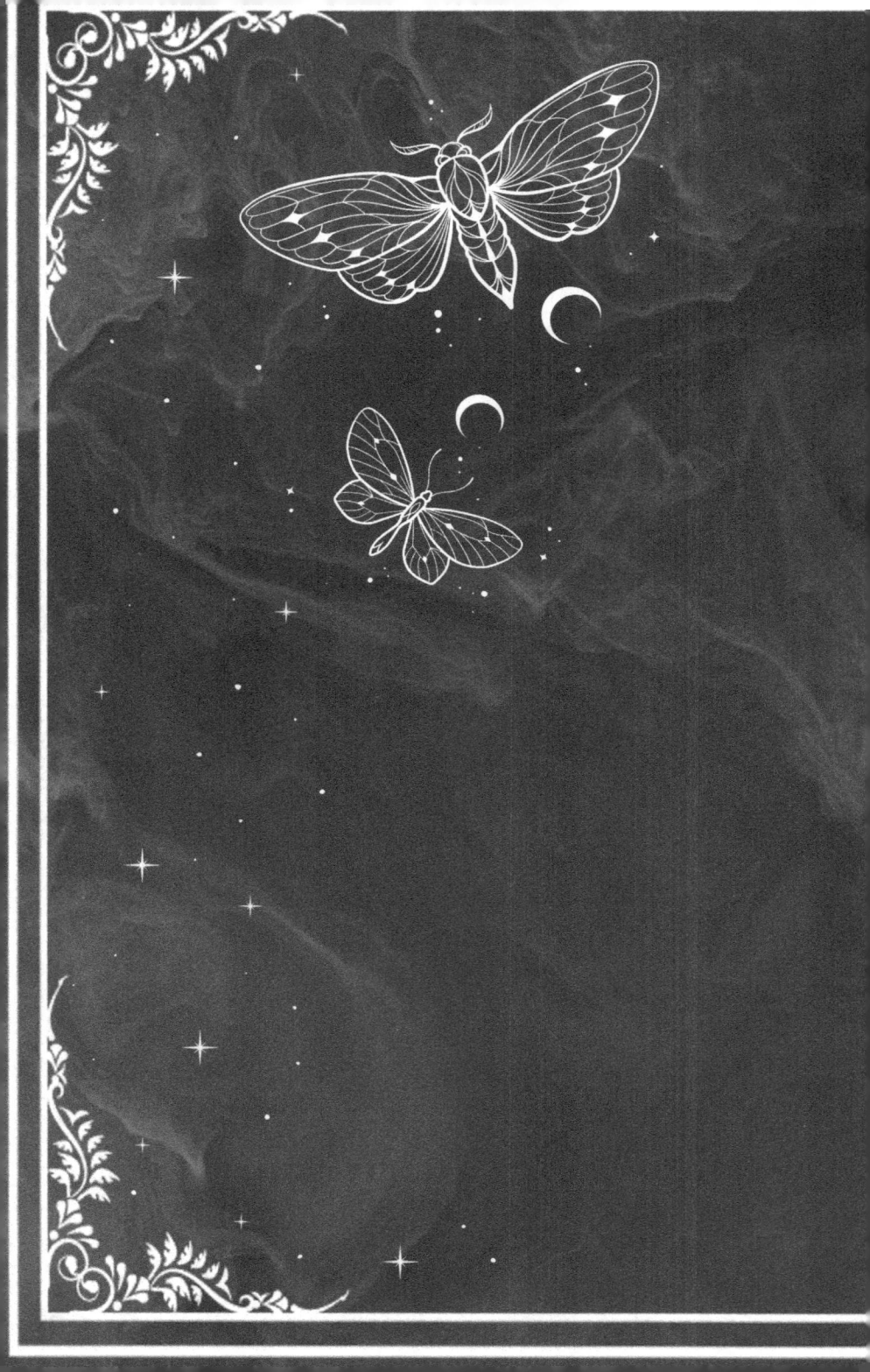

Chapter 1

There ought to be tears when plotting a man's demise. Or at least hushed whispers, quiet chambers, and secretive movements. Not the strange mixture of laughter and smiles that surrounded Selene.

But maybe this was different. They weren't plotting to just kill him, after all.

They were going to make his life miserable as well.

Idle chatter and the hushed whisper of sorceresses mingled in the air. She could pick out each voice by name. Minerva, Sibyl, Ursula, Bathilda. Mother, sister, cousin, friend. Not by blood, no self-respecting sorceress would ever have a child of her own womb, but by circumstance and necessity.

They moved around her like the undulating waves of the sea. They crested, hands rising as they wove a spell around her, then broke at the floor where they carved runes into the cold stones with knives usually used for sacrifice. Today, they were sacrificing for her.

Selene had never thought this day would come. A foundling like herself, trained to be a sorceress but not yet welcomed into the fold, was never given an important task. But she'd been born for this. Molded and shaped since the day she was left shrieking at the front door. Her mother had known what a rarity they had been given, and what opportunity they would use her for.

Today, she would tempt a demon king, and then she would bring him to his knees.

Wind whistled through her dark hair. The columns at the peak of the Tower only funneled the bitter cold ever closer. And it was always cold, this high in the mountains. The home of the sorceresses, the Tower of Silver Thread. Home to the Eternal Sisters, Wives of the Night Sky.

The white marble floor reflected the cold light of the sun, which even here cast no heat upon their home. Seven women surrounded her, for seven was the number of sorceresses. Each had their part to play in this spell that would weave her to them. Together, they would cleave Selene to her purpose forever more.

Why had she agreed to this? Because she wanted to finally be part of a family that she'd always looked at from the outside. If she succeeded, they would take her as their own. As she had dreamt of since the moment she'd been born.

The first workings of the spell thrummed through the air. She heard it, the whisper sound of a violin in the distance, screeching like a woman's scream. The spell suddenly fractured around her. Silver threads hanging in the air, suspended for her to see all the fine points of their unbreakable spell, like a spider's web woven only for her.

"Daughter," her mother said. Minerva's voice had deepened through years of smoke inhalation and prophecy seeking. The wind whipped around her, hugging close to her body and crackling with energy. That was Minerva's special talent.

As they all had a special talent.

Selene ducked her head, avoiding eye contact with the High Sorceress as she approached. In this moment, the woman before her was not her mother. There was no softness to her. No kindness in those features at all.

"You were delivered unto us as a gift. You will stand beside the Beast and you will bend him to our will. Too long has this land suffered without the hand of a sorceress plucking at the strings of life. You will be the first act in our battle to take back our land."

The first act, but not the last.

"I accept," Selene said. Her own voice had yet to suffer from the terrible misuse of spell work. Someday she would sit in that smoke filled room, chanting with her sisters as she sought her own future. But not yet.

"You will tempt him," the High Sorceress's voice weaved around her. The spell warped as she spoke, drawing closer and closer to Selene. "You will make him believe he has found a rare rose while you set roots throughout his kingdom. Every movement you make, every word you say, it will draw him to you. Like a moth to a flame."

The other sorceresses repeated her words. The spell flexed again, and then it was upon her.

Selene gasped. She'd felt the touch of magic before, but never like this. It was sticky and warm, clinging to her skin like the web it was meant to be. She didn't mean to touch it. It was a reaction her body could not prevent. One moment, she felt it touch her and the next, her pinky finger just barely brushed against it.

She didn't think anyone even noticed she'd touch it, but Selene did. She felt the tiniest of rips. One thread of that spell had stuck to her hand and when she jerked to remove that touch, it... loosened. Snapped. Gaped a little and only she knew that there was a hole there.

A weakness.

Selene opened her mouth to tell her mother they needed to do it again, but then pain struck her to her knees. Gasping through it, Selene reached for the High Priestess. One hand outstretched, her fingers curled into pained claws.

No one would help her. They all stared, eyes burning with glee, happy to see the pain settle into her because that meant they had done the spell correctly. It should hurt. Magic always did.

The sizzling ache curled up her body like she was being burned alive. It hissed through her mouth, singed her torso and seared her lips. Only to rest at the base of her neck, where spine met skull. A symbol would remain there, she knew. A symbol that only other sorceresses could read.

Cursed.

Hunted.

Burdened with purpose.

On her knees before her sisters and mother, she took a deep breath and then staggered to her feet. *There is no room for weakness here,* her mother's voice whispered in her ear. A memory from long ago but never forgotten.

She forced herself to shake off the horrible feeling of the spell. Selene squared her shoulders and laced her fingers at her waist. "I accept this purpose, High Sorceress. I will stop at nothing until our will is the command of this kingdom."

"Of course you won't." Her mother broke through the circle of runes to run her fingers along Selene's jaw. "You are my best creation, pet. Now, go to your demon and we will all watch him fall."

Now? Selene had hoped…

She didn't let the thought take flight from her mind. One of her sisters had already started drawing the runes of a portal. There was no time to waste. She knew what she had to do, and she knew how to do it.

But she hesitated. This was her home. She'd grown up here with only memories to keep her safe. The softness of the blanket Ursula had given her for her sixteenth birthday. Hugs from Sibyl after a particularly trying day. Even the stories that Minerva would tell her about a time when sorceresses had ruled these lands, long before the demons had come and destroyed all of it. These were the memories that would make her wish to return.

Selene couldn't return until she'd made a demon king bend to her whims, but she hadn't ever believed she'd be forced to be with him.

The sparking sound of a portal shooting to life made her flinch. She wasn't even dressed like herself. Selene was more likely to hide underneath long layers of clothing and thick woolen skirts. The more layers, the better. It was too cold here for anything less.

The travel clothes of a sorceress were far from what she would consider comfortable. Leather leggings encased her legs, squeezing too tightly. The corseted top stole her breath and pressed her breasts up like a serving platter. Not to mention the long gloves that covered her hands, all of it marked with protection runes. Anyone would take one look at her and know where she was from.

"You'll be back in a few days," Ursula said. Her nearly white hair swayed at her hips as she held out a small pack for Selene to hold. The smile on her dark face gleamed. "You'll lead him here after he sees your pretty face. I have no doubt at all."

"And then we'll deal with him," Bathilda added darkly. Her close cropped dark hair had only just begun to curl after she'd shaved it. She held out Selene's cloak. "Make haste, sister. We all want this over with quickly."

Selene had to bite her tongue. Did any of them think they wanted this over with faster than her? She was the sacrifice for the demon. She was the one who had to convince him she was worthwhile for his attention, and get him back to the Tower. They only had to sit here! None of them had to wonder how much a demon would compromise who they were.

But she couldn't say any of that. Her job wasn't to complain or even to point out how unfair this situation was. She needed to drag all that into the dark recesses of her mind.

Selene always thought her power felt like sinking underneath the surface of an icy lake. At first, it hurt to shove those emotions into a place no one else would ever find them. But then it felt... nice. Cold, perhaps. But at least she couldn't feel.

"Good," her mother said, coming up behind her. "You're ready."

Because, of course, the High Sorceress would feel Selene shove those emotions down. It was hard enough to swallow that her sisters would throw her to the wolves. But her mother? Selene's flair of anger should have burned through her. Instead, it was a mere spark that flew away and then dimmed into nothing.

"I'll return with the demon, Mother."

"I know you will."

And with that, Minerva planted a hand on Selene's chest and shoved her through the portal.

She hated portal travel. The pull of magic on her body that unmade and then remade her as it spat her out somewhere other than the Tower. Selene had traveled before, but never alone. Never to find a demon.

She stumbled out of the clear magic that looked somehow like water and landed on her hands and knees in the dirt. At least her sisters didn't see her stagger through. They'd have made fun of her mercilessly for it.

Shoving back the wild tangle of her dark hair, she leaned back on her heels and planted her hands on her thighs. Where had her bag gone? She needed that. There were a few outfits in there that were necessary to catch the attention of a demon.

Her eyes followed the dirt path she'd landed in the middle of. Mud ruts were dug so deep into the earth, she could only assume this was a trade route. The emerald green grass on either side of her gently rolled to the forest's edge.

Was she near Greenbank? That wasn't where she'd thought she'd end up.

Someone cleared their throat. She glanced down the path again, her pack suddenly lost to her thoughts, and found herself looking at a young man. He stood in the center of the road with a wagon behind him. An old horse was hooked at the front, happily munching on grass even though its sway back seemed to make the lean of its neck difficult. His pants were covered in mud, his white tunic yellowed with age. But he had a pleasing face and bright green eyes that glowed with amusement in the dirt smeared expression he wore.

He held her pack out to her and pushed at the dirty blonde mop of hair on top of his head. "This yours?"

"It is." She made no move to get up, though she did eye the smears of mud on her bag. "Why do you have it?"

"Well, it landed nearly on top of me. I stopped the wagon, all confused when a leather bag fell out of the sky, and then you dropped next to it."

"Neither of us fell out of the sky," she corrected.

"Where'd you come from then?"

She wasn't about to tell him. If he was so uneducated that he couldn't tell a sorceress when he saw one, then she wasn't about to inform him of it. Nevermind that she was a foundling, no one would understand what that was outside of the Tower. Besides, she didn't have time to answer questions.

The few times she'd left her home, she'd gotten the impression that the citizens of this kingdom were uncomfortable around her kind. Magic folk, she'd heard them whisper more times than she could count.

The young man tilted his head to the side, looking her up and down. "I wouldn't imagine someone with clothes as fine as that would want to kneel in the mud much longer."

Was she?

Selene glanced down and realized that the rather cold sensation on her knees was indeed mud. She looked up at the man as though he knew how to help her, before heaving a sigh. She was supposed to arrive and make an impression, not blend in with the locals.

"Unless you are needing... help? Are you hurt?" He dropped her pack—the bastard—and then rushed toward her.

Selene threw up her hands. She'd defend herself if she needed to, but really, was he so stupid as to attack a sorceress in the middle of nowhere? No one would find his body when she was done with him. But he approached swiftly, gripped her elbows, and drew her upright. Gently. All of it so gently.

Blinking at him, she felt her jaw drop open.

He flashed her a much too handsome smile. "You can pay me with a kiss, miss. If you want to keep looking at me like that."

She blinked again and felt tiny furrows deepen between her brows. "I'm not going to do that."

"Ah." The young man released her and rubbed the back of his neck. "Sorry 'bout that. I've just always wondered what it would be like to kiss one of those clean ones, you know? The untouchables."

"Excuse me?" She had no idea what he was talking about, but he'd already turned around and picked her pack up out of the mud.

"You'll be going to the Festival then, yeah?" He climbed onto his wagon, not looking back at her at all. "They all come here for the Love Festival. Maybe you'll get lucky and Lust will pick you to go back to his castle."

Lust? Another name for the demon king who ruled this land. But why was the man saying his name with reverence?

"Where are you going?" she asked, planting her hands on her hips. "You have my things."

Another bright grin. "I figured you'd be needing a ride into town. We're a ways out yet."

She shouldn't. She should walk, because who knows what this young man might be planning? He could drag her to his home and she'd have to burn his eyes out to get away.

Or... Not. He might actually want to help.

"How far?" she asked, suspicious.

"At least a day's walk. You'll miss all of it if you don't get a move on." He made a show of pursing his lips and holding a hand out to his brow as though staring off into the distance. "But you could follow the signs, I suppose. Might not get lost."

He had a good point. Selene hadn't traveled to Greenbank in years. She stomped toward his wagon with a curse on her lips that never quite made it out into the air.

The hairs on her arms stood up. Her entire body clenched with something unnamed, although the young man's gasp made her realize what it was. Lust. Quickly, she gathered up all the emotions in her body and dunked them into the icy water of her magic.

Bury it, Selene, she told herself. Bury it deep.

She was still frozen, cold as she always was, when the carriages started past them. Gold and gleaming in the sunlight, they were more like children's toys than they were practical. Even the mud didn't stick to those wheels.

And she swore for a moment, when the middle one rolled by, there was a face in the window that looked at her. She only caught a small glimpse of him. High cheekbones, golden hair, bright blue eyes.

Then they moved past her as though Selene and her new found companion never existed.

It took a while for either of them to make a sound. The young man blew out a long, steady breath. As though he were counting the length of it before he shook his head.

"Get on the wagon if you're coming with me." His voice had deepened, gruff sounding now. Uncomfortable.

She didn't hesitate this time. Selene climbed up onto the bench in the front and dragged her pack into her lap. "You sound different."

"Not surprising." He grunted again and then reached into his pants to adjust himself.

Horrified, she swiveled her eyes to the front of the road and sat rigidly beside him. "Was that really necessary?"

"Indeed it was. Can't help it when the Lord of Lust rides by." He let out a little curse and then snapped the reins. "You're wishing you'd kissed me now, I reckon."

She didn't wish that at all. She wished she'd never left home.

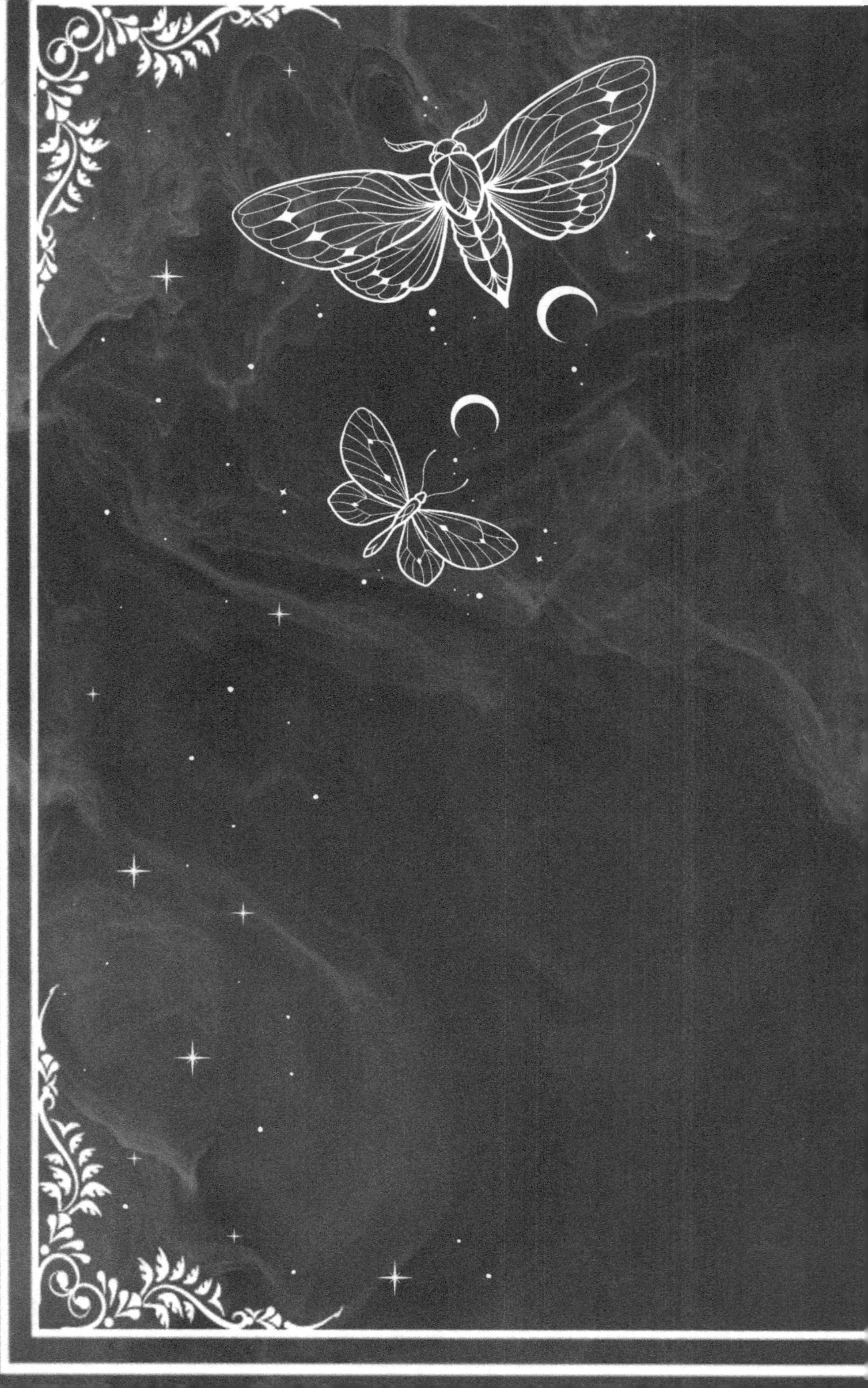

Chapter 2

Greenbank was ugly at the best of times. But even uglier during the Love Festival.

Lust never understood why he had to make the rounds every year, other than to be an excuse for their celebrations. They always wanted the king to be present during the festival season, which was why each town had a different day to celebrate. They all enjoyed being around him, and it was the only time of the year that they saw him.

But he'd already been to sixteen different towns before reaching this one. And had three more to seek out after he was done here.

Lust, although he'd never admit it, was tired. Tired of people, tired of their foolish antics, and frankly tired of the show that never changed year over year.

Why was it that every town thought they had something new for him? Some new woman or man that would make his heart race in his chest or make his eyes light up with wonder. As if he hadn't lived long enough to think every human was, frankly, the same.

He'd fucked every type of woman, man, and everything in between. He'd done it in every position, used every orifice, seen all the toys and the extras that could be brought into the bedroom. Did they think a thousand year old being could ever be surprised these days?

It made it rather difficult to be hard, if he was being honest. And he was the embodiment of lust! The king who ruled these lands and who could spread lust like pollen through the air, so he had to get himself together before he reached the fucking town or... or...

They rode past a young man and his wife. Dirt covered the wagon, and he thought there was perhaps a rather large amount of hay in it. He didn't know what was considered a large amount these days. He could taste the young man's lust immediately, the flavor bursting on his tongue. Acidic, earthy, like he'd put a handful of dirt in his mouth and then tried to chew.

But from the woman with him, cloaked in darkness, he felt... nothing.

Not a single spark of lust, or anything else, for that matter. Nothing.

Lust lifted his hand to rap it against the roof, letting his driver know to stop, but... no. He was wrong. There was too much to do today and not a chance in any of the seven kingdoms that she hadn't felt lust as he drove by. It wasn't possible. No one stayed in his kingdom unless they felt that emotion, or at least something. No one was so cold that their minds felt like dust.

He must have gotten the taste of her lust mixed up with her husband's, that was all. He'd made a mistake, as he could do, because he was tired.

Blowing out another long breath, he tried to prepare himself for what waited for him in Greenbank. And in those preparations, he put aside the thoughts of dark eyes following the carriage, locking with his own as he rode by.

The town loomed around him before long. And he knew it wasn't fair to call it looming. The buildings were well made, each a specific color designating the family that lived inside with intricate wooden patterns along the outsides. They stood on top of an emerald green hill that rolled like waves all the way down to the river beside it. Four houses had water wheels attached to them that lazily moved as the river passed by. He thought he remembered they were used for the paper mill here, as it was one of the few towns in his kingdom known for binding books.

Sitting up at that memory, he wondered if maybe today wouldn't be such a waste. They weren't the backwoods town he'd come from, even though the houses in Foxbridge had been just as fine.

His carriages halted in the center of town, which they had done up in their best fineries. Ribbons in all shades of purple hung from the rooftops and stretched to light poles above his head. They'd laid out an impressive swath of violet fabric that led up to the podium, where the mayor already waited for him.

Everyone had worn their best outfits. The men in their suits that were ill fitting but still of fine quality. Women in dresses with circle skirts that would whirl around them as they danced. He already knew their purpose. To reveal shapely thighs and secret shadows between them to the men that might chase them down later tonight.

He had business to attend to first. They all did. He'd listen to their mayor tell him all about their paper yields this year and how much money they had made. How they would send a certain amount to the castle, while keeping a certain amount for themselves. Of course, most of the gold would return home with Lust. There was a reason he brought so many carriages with him.

Sighing, he opened the door to his own carriage. No need to wait for the footman who stared up at him in shock.

He just wanted to get this over with and get home.

"My lord!" the mayor called out, stretching his arms wide as though an old friend had arrived. "We've been waiting for your return since last year with all the hopes of a good harvest. We are pleased to inform you this year has been our best yet!"

It was the same as every town. They all said it was their best yet until he started looking at their financial records and pointing out all the inconsistencies. Every year. It never changed.

Still, there were expectations, and he was loath to disappoint. "You know, Greenbank has always been my favorite to visit. The honor is mine."

Cheers surged around him, as though he'd given them the best compliment they could have asked for and not that he said the same words to every town he went to.

How he had managed to keep up this farce as long as he had, he'd never know. His brothers didn't pretend to enjoy their own kingdoms. But Lust had set a precedent, and he continued doing so year after damned year.

As the crowd continued to cheer, some of them already wearing the gleam of lust on their faces, he leaned close to the mayor. "We'll see just how successful your town has been."

"I would never lie to you, my lord. This has been a good year." The mayor's face had turned waxy and pale, though.

Lust snorted. "We'll see. You shouldn't lie so easily, Mayor, you'll find it gets all too easy to spin tales. And you won't like what I do when I find out the truth."

The human gulped, his throat moving in a rather impressive bob before he gestured for Lust to follow him.

And so the games began.

It took the better part of the day to look over the mayor's finances. Everything was a mess. All the documents were kept in individual folders, changes made to the margins, scratched out, and then rewritten in a hand that was almost illegible.

He had his brother's voice in his head the whole time. "Why are you still doing all that work? Isn't there someone in the kingdom who can do math as well as you? It's just adding numbers, Lust. For fuck's sake, there have to be better things for you to do."

And the rub of it all was that there was. Plenty of better things, and people, for him to be doing rather than sitting in a dusty office that rarely saw use. Blowing out a breath, he watched the dust motes ascend into the air and glitter in the waning sunlight that sparkled through the fractured window behind him.

He'd run out of time. For the first time in years, he hadn't finished surveying the books before he had to go out and perform at the festival.

Cursing, he stood up and stretched out the crick in his back. He reached for the jacket on the chair, intending for his suit to be completely done up when he went out, but... Well. There was no use for it, now was there?

He knew the festival would end with him wearing no shirt at all. Likely wearing nothing. They'd throw some young woman at him, a virgin, the damned things, or a whole group of women. Some towns would add a man in there for a bit of flavor to it all, but they did the same thing every year. The whole festival would turn into an orgy.

A boring, routine orgy.

Rubbing his hand down his face, he hissed out a long breath. He was tired, damn it. What he wouldn't give for a cup of tea and a quiet evening.

He left his jacket behind. Let them pawn it off for a little extra money to pad these god awful books. Then maybe they'd be able to break even this year, let alone prove the glorious investment the mayor kept prattling on about.

Lust passed by a mirror and paused. He smoothed his hair down around the twin horns on top of his head. The blonde locks always tangled on the ribbed ridges, and it made him look... mussed. It made him look like himself, he assumed. Whatever they expected him to look like. But he'd rather look a little put together before they ruined the image.

"My lord." His footman coughed into his hand. "They've been eagerly awaiting your arrival."

"I know."

"There are four women this time."

"So few?"

It took a bit for his footman to get his grin wrestled back to that nonplussed expression. "I had them whittle a few of them down. Said some of them were too young."

He squeezed his eyes shut. Seven kingdoms. He hoped they weren't throwing children at him now. "Thank you for that. And everything else?"

"Exactly as you'd expect it."

So there was food, too much wine. The people were already deep into their cups and already letting their inhibitions get the better of them. At this point, they didn't even need him to be there. He missed the early days of taking this kingdom and watching humans bend to their lustful nature. He enjoyed watching them hate what they were doing and love it at the same time.

Now, they looked forward to him coming. Like they knew they could use him as an excuse to do whatever they wanted.

"Fuck," he whispered. "And they're all here?"

"Apparently, they were waiting for one young gentleman who hadn't made it back from the market yet. Poor sod picked up some waif on the side of the road and broke a wagon wheel not a mile away from town. They walked the rest of the way with a horse that looks like a ghost beside them."

"What a tale." He couldn't care less. "Let's get on with it, then."

He strode out of the mayor's house and tossed on the persona of who he was. Should be. Usually was. It hadn't been this difficult last year, had it?

His exhausted expression smoothed out into one of complete and utter confidence. He winked at the women as he passed by, ignoring their swoons and dramatic faints into the arms of their friends. The men gave him curt nods, their eyes already hungry as they looked for the woman who would be their enjoyment tonight. And, of course, there were a few heated stares in his direction as well. After all, he was made to appeal to everyone.

Though his eyes trailed over countless figures, he didn't really see any of the people. They blended into his memory of all the humans he'd seen before and would see again. Nothing was new. It was all the same. The same pattern, the same fabric to make the same damned people.

A warm body collided with his own and gasps of horror echoed through the crowd. Not a light bump, either. Not the kind of collision that came from a young woman manipulating her way into his bed without the mayor's permission.

She hurt. She connected her shoulder with the delicate side of his ribs as though she hadn't seen him with the full force of her weight. It was not an easy bump. She struck him hard enough to make his ribs groan.

Letting out a sharp sound, she would have staggered backward and fallen if he hadn't grabbed onto her.

Too late for him to not touch her. He knew what these women did when his hands were on them. They sometimes fainted, but most times they would still, and look up at him with those big, needy eyes, and he...

He did what they wanted. Lust might not have been a good man, but there were a few things he was very good at. He knew it wasn't the same thing, but sometimes it was the only comfort he had.

She looked up at him, as expected, but her eyes widened in... shock? Disgust? Was that disgust he saw in her eyes?

It was the woman from the road, he realized. That dark gaze was like so many he'd seen before. But not the feel of her. He couldn't sense even a lick of emotion. No burst of flavor on his tongue, not even a pinprick of desire or lust or... anything.

She was as vacant as a snowy field. Nothing between him and those dark eyes that saw right into his soul.

How was she doing that?

She wasn't a particular beauty. Her dark hair had lovely waves in it, like obsidian glass, but he'd seen that color many times. He liked blondes anyway, so he could see an image of himself in them. Her skin was pale. Clearly she didn't work in the fields much. He preferred freckles. She wore a cloak so he couldn't see much of her body, only that moon-shaped face and wide, wide eyes.

His eyes dropped to her lips as she wet them. Crimson. Plush. Pretty, even he could admit that. And those lips twisted in revulsion.

Lust knew a challenge when he saw one. If she wasn't attracted to him, that was fine. There were many men for her to choose from. But few looked at him like that. He uncapped the stopper he kept on his power, letting it leak out around them until all the surrounding people gasped and then moaned with pleasure. They knew what this feeling was. The lust that poured out of him was like he seduced every person in the town square without even looking at them.

She didn't even flinch. The woman in his hands didn't move at all. She stared up at him with a question in her eyes that he wasn't certain he wanted to answer.

"Who are you?" he asked, his brows furrowed in confusion.

"The beginning of something new," she whispered. He could see something flicker in her eyes. Like she didn't quite believe those words herself.

Then someone shouted his name. "Lust! My lord!" And he looked up for a brief moment.

It was enough for her to slip through his hands. He wasn't holding her prisoner, or even that tightly, but he was surprised at the sudden lack of her.

He stared down at his empty hands for a moment, then turned to see her disappearing down a street. Dangerous, that. People were in the square for a reason. They wanted to participate in the festival, and he was careful to keep his influence to this area lest things get out of hand.

"Wait!" he called out, snarling under his breath at the damned audacity of the woman.

"My lord," the voice called out again.

"Start without me!"

Lust charged after the fool who was going to get herself killed, or worse, only to find that she'd disappeared. He couldn't find even a hint of her as he backtracked through every street and yet, somehow, she was gone. He even looked through a few windows, caught a few embarrassing sights—why would anyone treat a fruit the way that man was treating it—and couldn't find her.

Until he stepped on a small scrap of fabric. Normally he wouldn't have noticed, but he could smell her. Ice cold. Winter winds. The faintest hint of...

He stooped and picked up the small bit of dark cloth. Holding it to his nose, he inhaled deeply and finally figured out that last bit of her scent.

Peppermint.

So strange. Why had she run from him? And why couldn't he feel anything from her other than cold indifference?

Footsteps clattered behind him. His footman, no doubt, was shocked that he'd leave a festival like the hounds of Wrath were on his heels.

"My lord," the man said, wheezing from the short run. "What is... what is wrong?"

"Nothing." He straightened, but his normally smooth brows had drawn together. "What do you make of this?"

He handed the scrap of fabric over without looking back. His eyes still watched the alley, wondering if she was still here. If she was watching him.

"Your hand," his footman said. And which one was this? James? Jeremy? Jordan?

Lust looked down and saw a faint line of blood on his fingers. Not his, certainly. Hers?

Frowning, he pointed at the fabric imperiously.

His footman gulped and turned the piece over his hand. "It's, um... Looks like it has the mark of the Tower, sir."

"Silver Thread?" he asked, groaning. "Of course it would be Silver Thread. Ready my horses."

"But, the festival... my lord?" he said the last bit in a question.

"I know there's a fucking festival, Jeremiah." He pulled at his hair, hating that he had to choose between duty and his own curiosity.

But he already knew which one was going to win.

Lust turned on his heel and stalked back toward the festival. "Are you coming or not?"

"Yes, my lord." His footman bowed, but not before he heard, "Though it's Jason, not Jeremiah."

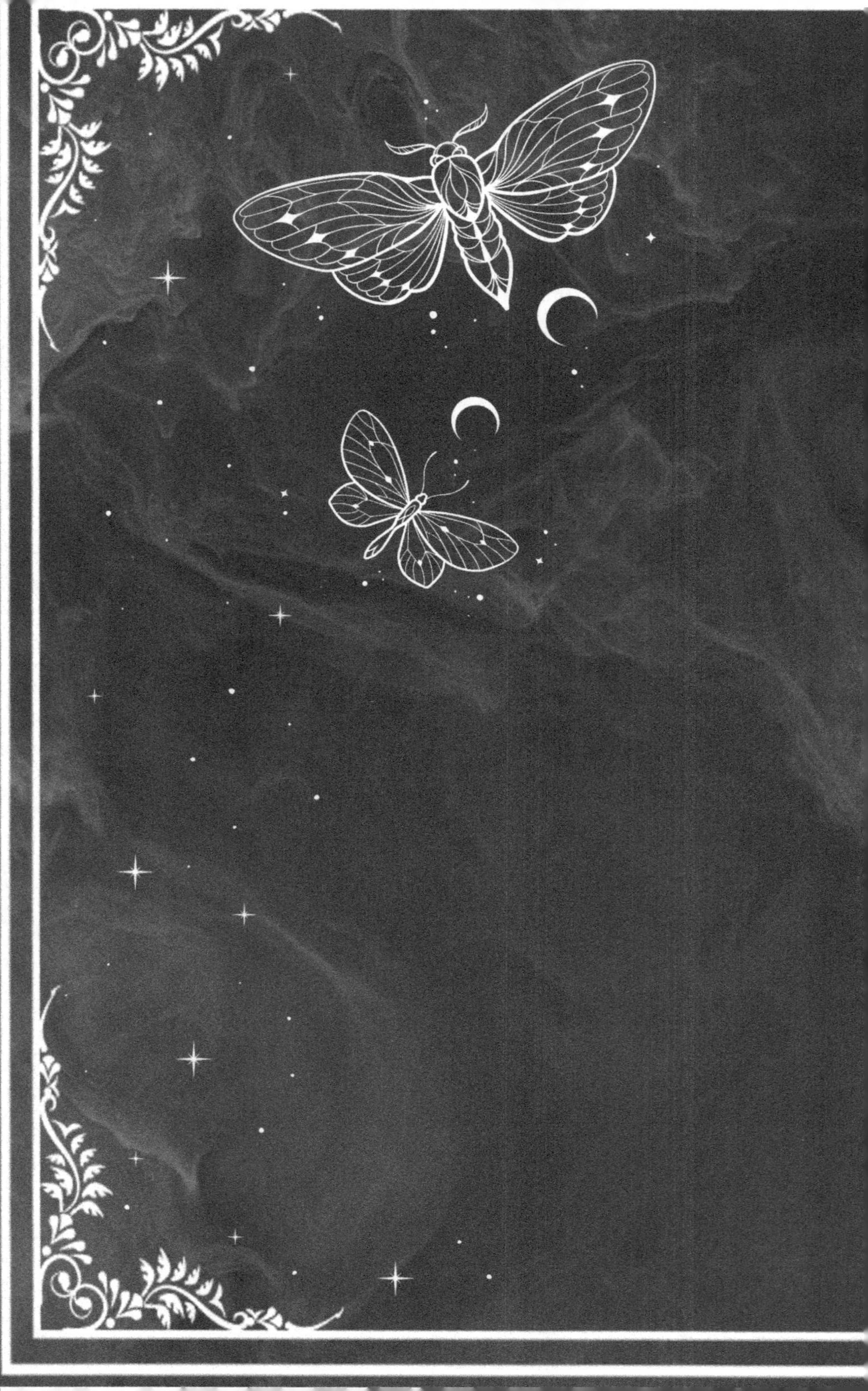

Chapter 3

"You've done well, daughter. Very well."

It didn't feel like that.

Selene could still feel his hands on her. How he'd carelessly held her shoulder, as though he didn't think for a second that she'd try to slip away from him. The confidence in that grip, the strength, had frightened her.

More so, she'd felt him use that power of his. The one that made both men and women fall onto their knees and lose all sense. She'd watched over his shoulder as the woman behind the demon had been affected. The woman's pupils dilated, and she'd grabbed at her own breast. The villager had been standing there, watching them with amusement just two seconds before all sense had fled her.

And if Selene hadn't been able to hold on to her own emotions, what then? What would she have done?

Even melting that frozen wasteland inside of her held the lingering effects of his power. As though his magic never quite dispelled once it touched her. It waited for her to thaw just a little so she could feel him again.

Shivering, she shook her head to clear it of the thoughts and then nodded at her mother's image in the small crystal ball she held. "I think a few more times for him to see me might do the trick."

"You don't think he's interested in you already?"

How was she to know? Selene had never attempted to woo a man, or captivate them, or whatever it was she was doing here.

She chewed on her bottom lip, casting her eyes out over the buildings below her. "I'm not sure. I'd rather be certain that he needs to find me. That he's compelled to come to the Tower…"

She didn't finish, but she didn't have to. The High Sorceress spoke over her. "Rather than wait for the temptation to draw him, you want him to hunt you down. Ever the intelligent one, aren't you, my dear?"

A feeling deep inside her bones suggested she needed to talk to him more. That he'd been interested in her only because, for a split second, she was different. And for a being who had lived a thousand years, different wasn't something he saw every day.

She wasn't all that different, though. His powers didn't work on her, no, but surely he'd met someone like that before. In his vast years and knowledge, there had to be someone who had been born with the same power as she.

Or maybe not. Maybe she was the first, and that was a problem.

Oh, by the seven kingdoms, if she was the first person with this power, then that would be a real problem.

"Keep doing what you're doing," her mother said, interrupting her thoughts. "Bring him here, child. Then let me handle the rest."

Selene hadn't asked what the "rest" was, nor did she want to know what would happen next. Her job would be complete the moment he walked into the Tower. "Understood."

"Goodbye, child."

Her mother's face disappeared and Selene pocketed the crystal. She thought maybe Ursula had made it, but... it was hard to know. Her sisters were all so talented, and they studied so many books on sorcery. They knew more about the magical arts than she could ever dream of. Because Selene had been born for... this. So she had to wait until her first purpose was over with before she could become a sorceress like them.

Grumbling under her breath, she tugged on her extra set of travel clothes. She preferred to be clean, and this tavern hadn't given her an opportunity for any bath last night.

She'd snuck in behind a couple who she was quite certain were actually having sex against the door, bartered with the innkeep who had asked her multiple times if she wanted to pay in "favors", and then tried not to hate herself for being here. The room was dirty. The sheets were unwashed. And she'd had to wedge a chair underneath the door in fear someone would barge through it.

If she'd ever questioned whether Lust was a demon or not, now she knew for certain. The entire town had lost their minds last night, and no one seemed the wiser.

Gathering her things, she left her dusty room and headed downstairs. She needed to get some food in her, and hopefully some freshly brewed coffee. She had minimal hopes for the former. Almost zero hopes for the latter.

But her head hurt. She was exhausted from staring at the door all night, and she still hadn't figured out how to tempt Lust any more than apparently bumping into him. Hard enough to make his breath wheeze a bit, which she was very proud of.

And so that was how she walked into the dining hall of the tavern, with a grin on her face. Memories of her first encounter with Lust being one of her besting him, ignoring the fact that they'd seen each other on the path to Greenbank, of course.

Sitting at the bar, she waited for the elderly man behind the counter to see her. "Breakfast?" he asked.

"I'd love that."

He frowned, squinted his eyes, and then burst out laughing.

Why?

Looking behind her, she saw nothing other than new people entering the tavern. New people wearing clothing that was far too nice for a town like this.

Shit. Shit, of course he would come to the one tavern she was in. "Why are you laughing?" she hissed at the bartender.

"Well, ain't you the woman who bumped into Lust last night and nearly knocked him off his feet?"

"Please stop talking about that." She didn't want any more attention than she was already getting.

"Ah, shy about it? What a shame. Seems like something that might surprise the lord enough to share his favor." The man shrugged, but then set about getting her breakfast.

Selene pulled the hood of her cloak up over her head as the sound of boisterous men filled the room. Those who had already been in the tavern were overjoyed to hear that Lust was visiting their fine establishment! And wasn't he to leave earlier? Oh, he was here for an extra night? Why was that?

She had a feeling it was because she'd left a small scrap of fabric behind and a few drops of her blood on it to boot. He might be a demon, but he was still man enough to wonder about that little mystery. A fair maiden runs away from him, bleeding? Surely that was something anyone of the masculine nature would want to hunt down.

His voice sent a shiver down her spine, even from the front door. "I have more to do here than I originally anticipated. The other towns have been informed."

The sound of him wasn't the only thing sending shivers through this tavern. A woman to her left suddenly squirmed in her seat, incapable of getting comfortable. Even the elderly man who brought her food back was sporting a tent in the front of his trousers that made her nauseous.

He saw her looking and grinned. "I love it when Lust is here. You know I haven't been able to get it up for almost ten years now?"

"I couldn't care less." She grabbed the food and placed a single coin on the counter.

"Ah, well. You young ones will understand soon enough." He leaned on the worn wood across from her, thankfully hiding his affliction now that Lust was around. "Where you from?"

Oh, they were talking? He thought this was acceptable?

If only she didn't have to avoid a scene. Selene ground her teeth and replied, "Sapphire Falls."

It was the first town she could think of, and honestly her favorite one in this kingdom. The falls really were sapphire. They tumbled down from the mountains and burst into bright white plumes that filled the air with the scent of saltwater. She'd loved it there when they visited, although the sorceresses so rarely left the Tower.

The old man frowned. "That's a long way from here."

"Been traveling a long time, and I'm afraid I'm a little too tired for civil conversation."

The gleam in his eyes only intensified. "Did you know that's the start of our lord's rounds? Every year he visits Sapphire Falls first."

She paused with the spoon halfway to her mouth. All she wanted was one damned bite. "I did not."

"My lord!" the man shouted. "We've got a town hopper here! She's been with you since Sapphire Falls, she says. Have you had the pity to talk with her yet?"

Damn it.

Damn it all. She was going to kill an elderly man, and it was a shame to end his life when he had so few years left.

"Keep your mouth shut," she hissed, only to hear the sound of approaching footsteps.

"Well, far be it from me to keep any of my adoring followers waiting." Lust sat down on the open barstool next to her, his back to the counter and his arms spread wide across it.

His hand almost hit the bowl of porridge, and she found she would have been interested to see it sink into the sticky gruel. It would serve him right to have disgusting fingers. Even for a few seconds.

But then his eyes lit upon her, even though she wasn't looking at him. She could feel his gaze lingering on her features. He reached out, slowly, as though giving her time to flinch away. And then he dragged the hood off her head.

His fingers trailed across her cheek as he did so. A scorching line of heat lingered in their wake, long after his skin had stopped touching hers.

And those emotions all froze where they were and then sank deep underneath the prison of her mind. Still. Silent. Nearly dead if she wanted them to be.

"The little one from the village square," he murmured. "I've been thinking about you."

"I'm sure you're mistaken."

"Oh, no. I'm not." He watched her, his eyes like the touch of his hand even though he had dropped it back onto the counter. "Do you know why I haven't forgotten your face yet?"

She stared resolutely at the back of the bar. Every tavern she'd been to before this one had bottles on the shelves. But not this one. Instead, they had decorated with animal skulls and hides. She wondered if they didn't have enough alcohol to display. Nothing was more depressing than seeing three bottles of rum with a tavern full of people.

A warm hand tucked underneath her chin, sliding up her jaw and then forcing her to turn her head and look at him.

So look at him, she did.

His lips were almost too full for a man. Soft and plush and oh so kissable. His features were largely undefined, so it was impossible to place where he'd come from or where his lineage might have started. A perfectly straight nose gave him an aristocratic quality, not to mention the dark slashes of his manicured brows. And at the top of his forehead twin horns coiled up his skull. They weren't large, just larger than her hand, but they had a brilliance to them that made her think he'd dusted them in gold.

She noted that his clothing was odd, even for a place like this. While the men here were happy to wear well pressed suits made of wool and fine fabric, his was made of silk. It floated around his body in a billowing white shirt that was then trapped by what looked like a corset. Instead of making him look feminine or soft, it only accentuated how broad his shoulders were and how narrow his waist tapered.

"Well?" he asked, as though he knew she'd become rather

dumbstruck by his face. "Do you?"

She wasn't dumbstruck. She was merely observing.

Selene arched her brow. "I don't think you remember me at all."

"Are you suggesting I'm a liar?"

"There is no reason for a demon king to remember a nameless, faceless woman in a town far from his castle."

That made his eyes widen a bit before a choked laugh escaped him. "Demon? Very few call me that."

"Is that not what you are?"

His eyes searched hers, confusion marring his handsome features. He hesitated before replying, "No, actually. I am Lust."

"I know who you are."

"But you are confused by what I am." He tapped a long finger against his chin, and she could physically feel everyone lean forward at that movement. The woman to her left even let out a little whine. Staring at the digit as though she wanted to suck it. Or ride it.

Selene was glad she couldn't feel anything. Not a single thing but that ice cold disappointment. "I'm not confused in the slightest. Why are you talking to me?"

"Because you left something for me to find, and because you said something that I can't seem to forget." He reached into his pocket and pulled out the square of her cloak that she'd left behind.

Of course he had it. Exactly as she'd planned.

Then he lifted it to his nose and inhaled. Taking a drag of her scent like her perfume was the antidote to a poison he'd ingested.

"I did not leave that for you." She reached out and tried to snatch it from him.

"Ah, but you did. You left it for me and you said something that you knew I wouldn't be able to ignore. Do you know what that was?"

Selene didn't offer him a reply.

"That you were the beginning of something new. Do you know how impossible that is to a being over a thousand years old?" He laughed and the entire room laughed with him. "The last new thing I experienced was well over three hundred years ago. It was a young woman from Wolf Haven and she did this thing with her tongue that down right shocked me. Never experienced that before, probably never will again," he added with a mutter.

"Am I not new?" she asked. Selene knew she shouldn't play this game, but she found the faintest twinge of annoyance breaking through the ice.

She might not be unique, but he'd tracked her down, anyway. The ice broke just enough for her anger to guide her mind toward a solution.

He grinned at her, slow and controlled. "Not at all, pretty one. You're just like all the rest."

Oh, he thought his words would sting. They did not.

She lifted her piece of toast and crunched down on it. Taking her time to chew, she finally said, "And yet you're here. Talking to me."

Selene enjoyed watching his confident expression fall into one of confusion. Wrinkles even formed on that perfect brow. How many people got to see that face? So few.

He seemed to struggle to find words, another surprising thing to him, she was certain. So Selene took her time chewing her toast and then stood.

"Thank you for the delicious breakfast," she sarcastically said to the tavern keep before turning her attention entirely to the demon spread out over the bar.

His slow, languid smile suggested he thought she had bent to him.

Maybe there was a part of him that assumed he couldn't sense her lust for some reason or another, but that she still felt it.

Selene's confidence might be lacking in certain areas, but she was still a foundling of Silver Thread. Her mother was the High Priestess, and she had trained her entire life to lure him in.

She rested her own hands on the bar, just underneath his arms and close enough to his ribs to feel his heart rate pick up. Leaning in close, she said, "And I am the beginning of something new. You might not know who I am. You might not recognize anything different about me. But I assure you, Demon, you've never met someone like me before."

And for good measure, she flicked one of his stupid horns just to see the gold dust fall off them.

"Of course. Glitter," she muttered in disgust. "Goodbye, Lust."

Selene left him with his mouth hanging open, still dramatically draped over the bar. She let herself feel for a small second, and with that came a rush of what felt like victory.

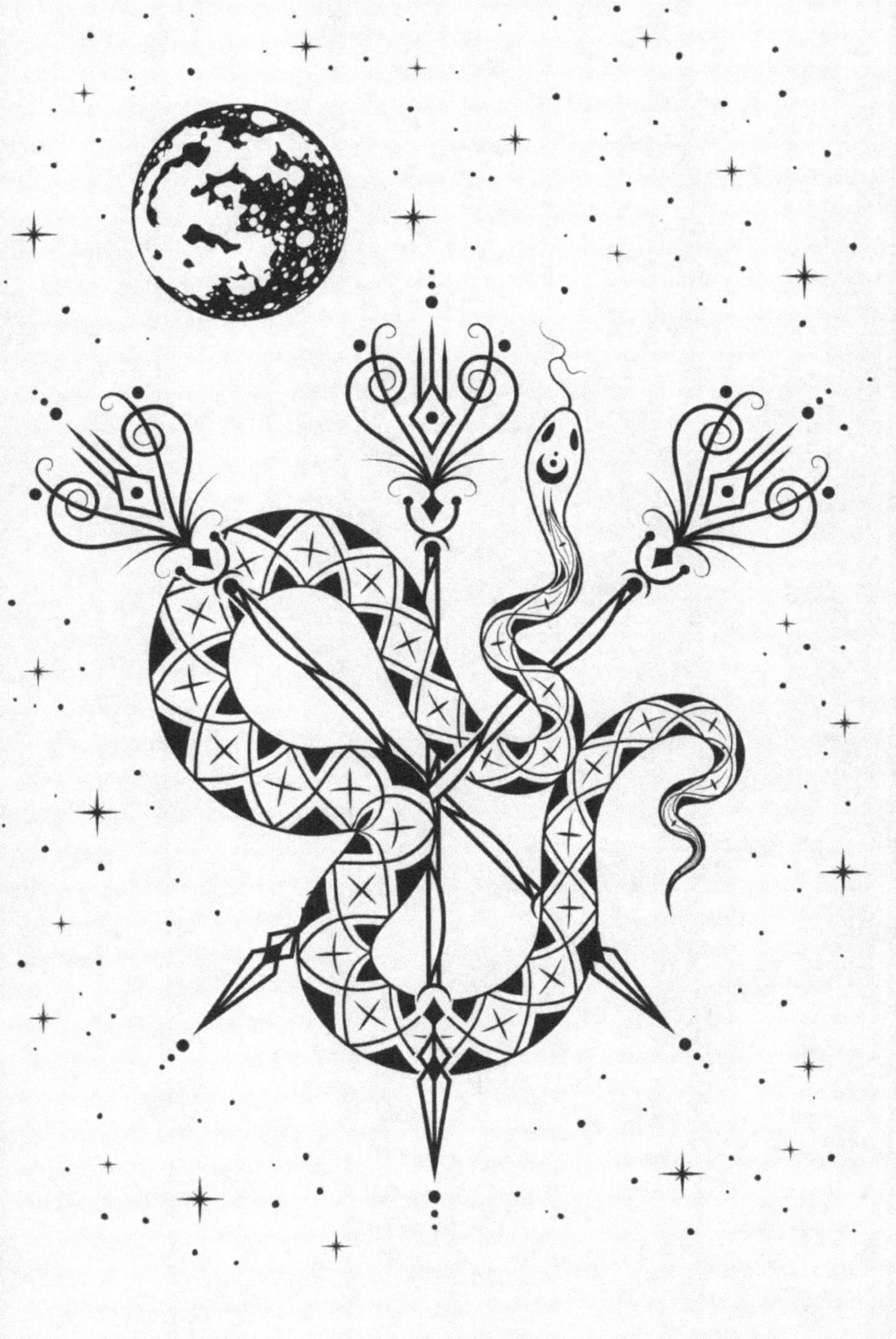

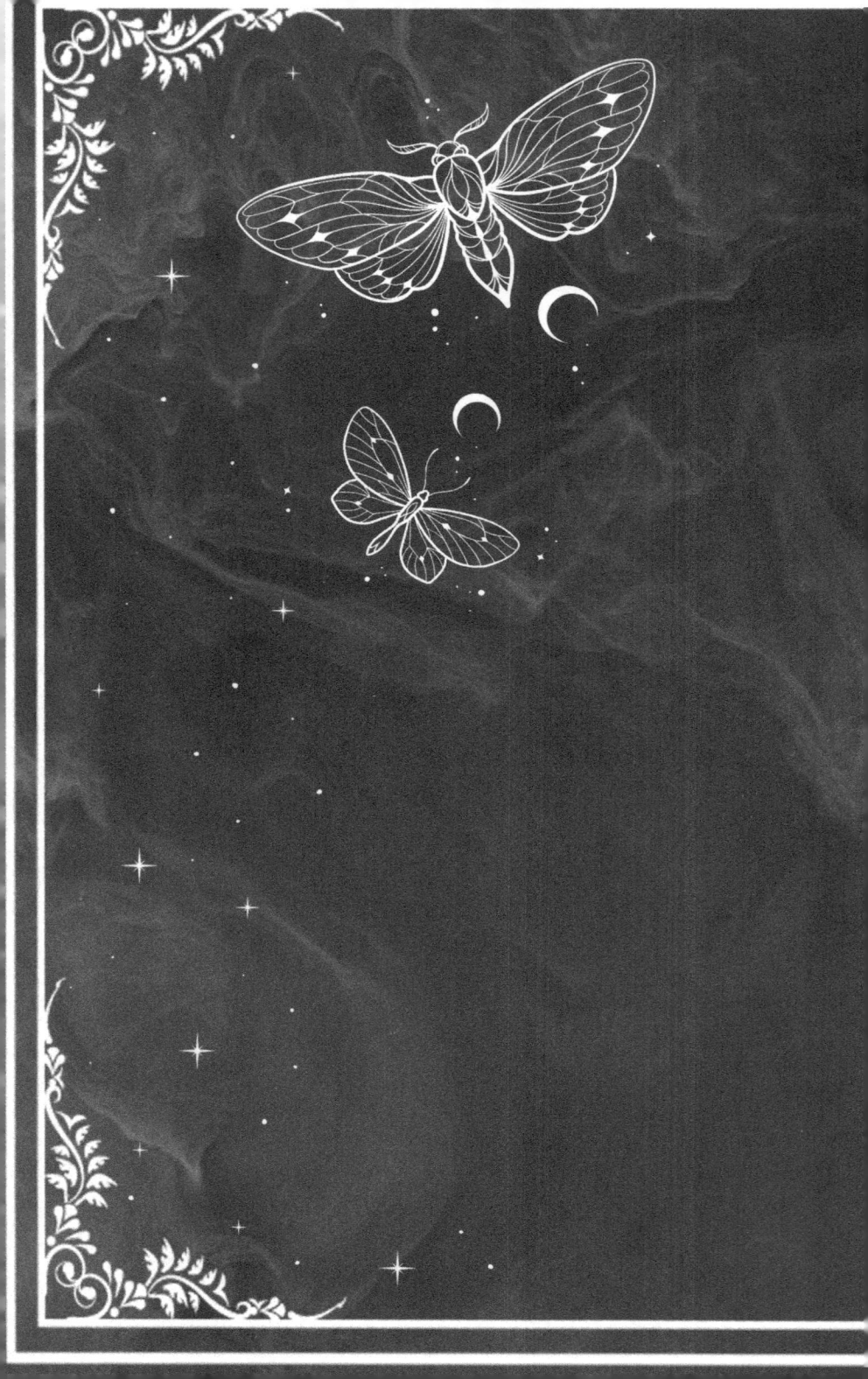

Chapter 4

He finished his tour throughout the towns with a flourish. And that was to say that he did so with an incredibly disgruntled expression and a boredom that made the other mayors wonder if they'd done something wrong.

Perhaps they had. They didn't bring him a woman like the one who had confronted him in Greenbank. Accosted, that was the correct term for it. She'd nearly struck him and then had taunted his intelligence in the middle of a busy tavern.

He'd like to say that had never happened before, and it had been a while, but alas. Nothing was new anymore. Never was.

After he'd finished with his regular business, he'd headed back home. Returning to his own castle where there was a fair city surrounding its safe walls. Only the best were allowed to live in

Lust's Castle. They were the nobility, the rich, the beautiful. People who stood out in every town that he'd gone to and thus he'd brought them here.

He might be a vain man about his own looks, but he was as equally vain about those who surrounded him. He refused to allow anyone "lesser" to grace the halls of his home. His beautiful court of simpering fools who never left him alone.

The castle itself was a work of art. He'd had it built in a glade that led up to a cliff side. No matter what room he stood in, his eyes were filled with a different kind of nature's beauty. On the eastern wing was a view of the mountain range that stretched high up into the heavens and as far along the ridgeline as mortal eyes could see. On the western wing, he could stare into forests that never seemed to end. To the south, the plains where most of the food crops were grown every year. But it was the northern wing that was his favorite. Because it had a view of the edge.

Every kingdom in this realm floated in nothing. Open air. Each of his brothers had been given their own kingdom, all of them connected through light bridges that were heavily guarded. Lust enjoyed standing at the edge and letting the wind play through his hair.

All it would take was one misstep, and he'd fall. Tumble right down into the nothingness below and learn just how little there was there. Or how much waited for him.

His brothers used to say there were creatures lingering in the depths. Monsters who had lived for thousands of years, starving in the darkness, waiting for a single person to fall. Sometimes, if he listened hard enough, he thought maybe he could hear their echoing groans.

But perhaps that was merely fancy.

An icy cold wrapped around his ankle, coiling up his body as though a freezing snake had decided to climb him.

"Affection," he snarled. "I thought I told you to leave."

The damned spirit never left him alone, however. The creature was little more than a wisp of a spirit at this point. Why it had wanted to cleave itself to Lust, made no sense to him. A spirit of affection needed to be around people who could at least feel that emotion. Otherwise, how did it feed?

This one was hard to shake, though. It didn't want to leave.

Humming low under its breath, it finally finished its journey and laid across his shoulders like a mink stole. "You've returned."

He hated how it felt wrapped around him. Its weight dampened the sensations that usually ran across his skin. As though lust had to be filtered through it before he could feed off the humans' emotions. And he needed to feed. Constantly. That was why the demon kings, as that woman had so aptly called them, were so powerful.

"Oh," Affection murmured. "You met someone."

"I did not," he grumbled in response. "I had a run in with a local, that's very different from meeting someone. I'd appreciate it if you didn't say that to anyone else."

"Hm." Its voice was higher than most voices in this area, although he thought it sounded rather melodic. Like a flute, sometimes. Other times perhaps the high strain of a violin. "So you think that was just a stranger? But you can't stop thinking about her. Can you?"

"She basically ordered me not to."

Amused, he told the spirit the entire story and turned away from the darkness below their feet. While he wouldn't mind tumbling into oblivion, the spirit attached to his shoulders was young and had much to learn. Perhaps another time he'd investigate the creatures below.

He brought the spirit back to the castle while finishing up the story and then sat on a bench just outside the northern door.

"So she's completely stumped you?" Affection asked.

"I'm not sure I would say that. She was a surprising human, yes, but that doesn't mean I'm any more interested in her than any of the others." He didn't think, at least.

Why was he so interested? She'd threatened him, proven herself to be a surly little thing, and then decided to flounce off where he couldn't find her again. He should let her memory fade from his mind like the rest of them.

"Because she was different."

"She wasn't," he corrected. "I've seen that color hair a thousand times, and nothing else was even remotely remarkable otherwise. She was just another woman who lives in this kingdom."

"But she tested you."

"And others have." He shrugged, shifting the spirit up and down on his shoulders. "It wouldn't be the first time a woman tried to gain my attention by pretending to be different from the others. Sometimes women will try to be more pushy, take charge, they think it will get them farther than the women who fall all over themselves."

"Playing hard to get?" Affection asked.

"Exactly."

"But that's not what she was doing. She told you she was the beginning of something new." The spirit moved along his shoulders, hovering in front of his eyes in a fine white mist that had some substance but was nearly impossible to see. "And you believe her."

He searched inside himself for an inkling of that emotion. Lust wanted to feel surprised again. He wanted to feel as though someone or something could make him feel something new.

That feeling didn't exist anymore, though. All he felt was a strange sort of rage that she'd tempted him at all. That she'd tried to make him believe, for even a second, that she could surprise him.

"No," he replied. "I don't believe her. I'm just disappointed that she can't do what she said she would."

The spirit hummed out a low breath, disappointment making it shake as well. "That's not fair."

"Living thousands of years was never the plan, now was it?" Lust lifted a hand and gently pet through the mist. "We were supposed to come here and live a normal, mortal life. We took these forms so that we could lead these people and then everything got all messed up."

Sort of.

They'd all made a pact, he and his brothers, that they would lead these kingdoms until they felt safe enough to leave. So they could return to the spirit realm where they were born and continue on anew. But then they'd realized what a pleasure it was to be alive. And everything had gotten muddled up after that.

Affection shook in his hands, and then he heard the faintest sound of laughter in his ears.

"Are you laughing at me?" he hissed.

"Well, you're lying, aren't you?"

"I am not lying."

"You've got her square of fabric in your pocket." It uncoiled itself from his shoulders and slithered onto his lap. Affection then nudged his front breast pocket where he did have that fabric.

"Only because I haven't thrown it out yet," he replied. Cross with the spirit, he pulled out the fabric and intended to toss it onto the ground but... Then he smelled her again.

That cold scent of peppermint struck him hard. It reminded him of the coming winter and how the first real snow always blanketed the land in silence. It was a beautiful moment. Cold and glittering and quiet.

Why would a scrap of fabric make him think of that? It was foolish. Ridiculous. A woman shouldn't make him feel like this and yet...

He lifted the fabric to his nose and inhaled deeply.

Maybe Affection was right. There was something about her that lingered in his mind, no matter how hard he tried to ignore her. She wasn't different, though. She wasn't anything new other than a woman who seemed to think rather highly of herself. He'd seen people like her come and go throughout his life for centuries now.

"Maybe," Affection started quietly. "She's not new. She's not someone that will change your mind about the world or all that you've done. But she might be entertaining for a while. You've surrounded yourself with the same kinds of people for such a long time, Lust. She might not be someone you haven't met before, but trust me when I say she might be new enough to make things interesting around here again."

Ugh, he hated it when the damned spirit was right. It always gloated for hours on end after he admitted it.

"Fine," he muttered. "I'll send out a few messengers to see if they can find where the hell she got off to."

"Why would you do that?"

"You just said you thought I should bring her back here." He stood, dumping the spirit onto the ground. "You were the one who thought up this plan, and now I will enact it. My patience has limits, Affection."

And with that, he strode back inside the castle.

He'd need to talk with the captain of the guard. The man might be a little difficult to manage, but he did his job well. Hamish had seen many attacks on the castle and had even stopped an assassination attempt all on his own. Though it might have been foolish to risk his very mortal life for a very immortal spirit, Lust appreciated it all the same. If anyone could find her, it was Hamish.

"Lust!" Affection called through the hall, slithering along the floor as it desperately tried to catch up to him. "I'm not finished!"

Yes, well, the spirit would never be finished if he let it keep talking. The damned thing liked the sound of its own voice.

The captain would need to know more about the woman to hunt her down. He had a feeling that would prove more difficult than any of them expected. She was a wily little thing, especially having already slipped away from him. First, they would start back in Greenbank.

Why she'd been there, he had no idea. She clearly wasn't a local with clothing like that. And she certainly hadn't been following him since Sapphire Falls. That was the first lie he'd caught her in, but he had a feeling it was the easiest. She'd had no idea where she was.

And she'd reacted like a tourist, he realized, slowing as he approached the captain's station. She'd moved in the tavern as though intensely uncomfortable. All the more reason to be certain she was a ploy from Minerva to get him under her thumb.

He didn't want to make a kingdom wide manhunt for her. The last thing she needed was to be dragged to this castle in chains by a group of militia who thought they were doing the right thing.

Lust supposed he could wait until the next festival season. He'd probably see her then, but that felt like a very long time. The thought was startling for him. After all, he had nothing but time.

She didn't, though.

Mortals died all too quickly, and that made him… uncomfortable.

Strange. He hadn't had that thought in a long while, either.

Tugging on one of his horns, he almost didn't stop at the captain's station at all. Maybe he should just find her on his own. Maybe he could go back to Greenbank and ask questions. They wouldn't deny him an answer to anything he wanted to know.

He stalked through the door and entered the room, where many of his leading guards already were. Apparently, he had missed an important meeting this morning, or they were all talking about how to kill him. It had happened before.

Lifting a hand before the captain spoke, he stalked to the large table in the center of the room that was carved with a map of his kingdom and slapped the fabric down into the center of it. "I need you to find this woman."

His captain stared at him with a blank expression, while the other remaining four men wore expressions of shock, horror, and intrigue. Curious, he'd expected them to all jump to attention. Not just stand there slack jawed.

"Well?" he said.

"Um." The captain shook himself free of his stupor. "Who would you like us to find?"

"There was a woman in Greenbank. My footman can tell you more about her if you need information. Dark hair, pale skin, not from the area but for some reason was there. It's lingering in my mind."

A frown creased the captain's already lined forehead. "Is she a threat, sir?"

"I'm not sure yet."

Another voice interrupted them, slithering up from the floor. "She's not a threat and you know it!"

Affection took its time rolling over the table, knocking over a few chess pieces they used when they were talking about the towns. The pieces each represented a town or a figure they were keeping an eye on.

He stared down at it in exasperation. "I told you to go away."

"Well, I would if you weren't wasting time."

"Me?" He jabbed a finger at his chest. "Wasting time?"

If Affection had a face that was easier to be seen, he swore it would have frowned at him. "Yes, you. You're missing the details that are right in front of your face! The details someone already told you!"

"What details?"

"The fabric."

"Yes, I've seen it." He grabbed it again, shifting it closer to the spirit. "Her perfume has nothing to do with finding her. The blood on it won't help us track her down unless you want to hire a sorceress and frankly, I have no interest in them."

"That's the detail!" Affection undulated in front of him, the mist rolling in a happy dance. "The detail you missed!"

He had no idea what it was prattling on about.

At least, until his captain took the fabric from him and smoothed it out. The man shifted it into the light, stretching the fabric so a hidden detail in the folds revealed itself.

A rune. Sewed into the fabric for protection. He'd seen enough of them to know how to read the sorceresses' language, but not enough to do the spells himself. That magic was entirely their own.

Groaning, he slapped a hand to his forehead and hissed out a long curse. "She's a sorceress?"

Affection leapt on the table and scattered the remaining chess pieces that were still standing. It did a quick circle along the edges of the wood before returning in front of him. "Yes! Your footman already told you that, and you just forgot."

"Silver Thread," he muttered, baring his teeth in a glare.

His captain made the same disgusted sound and then tossed the fabric onto the table again. "You still want us to track her down?"

The problem was yes.

He did.

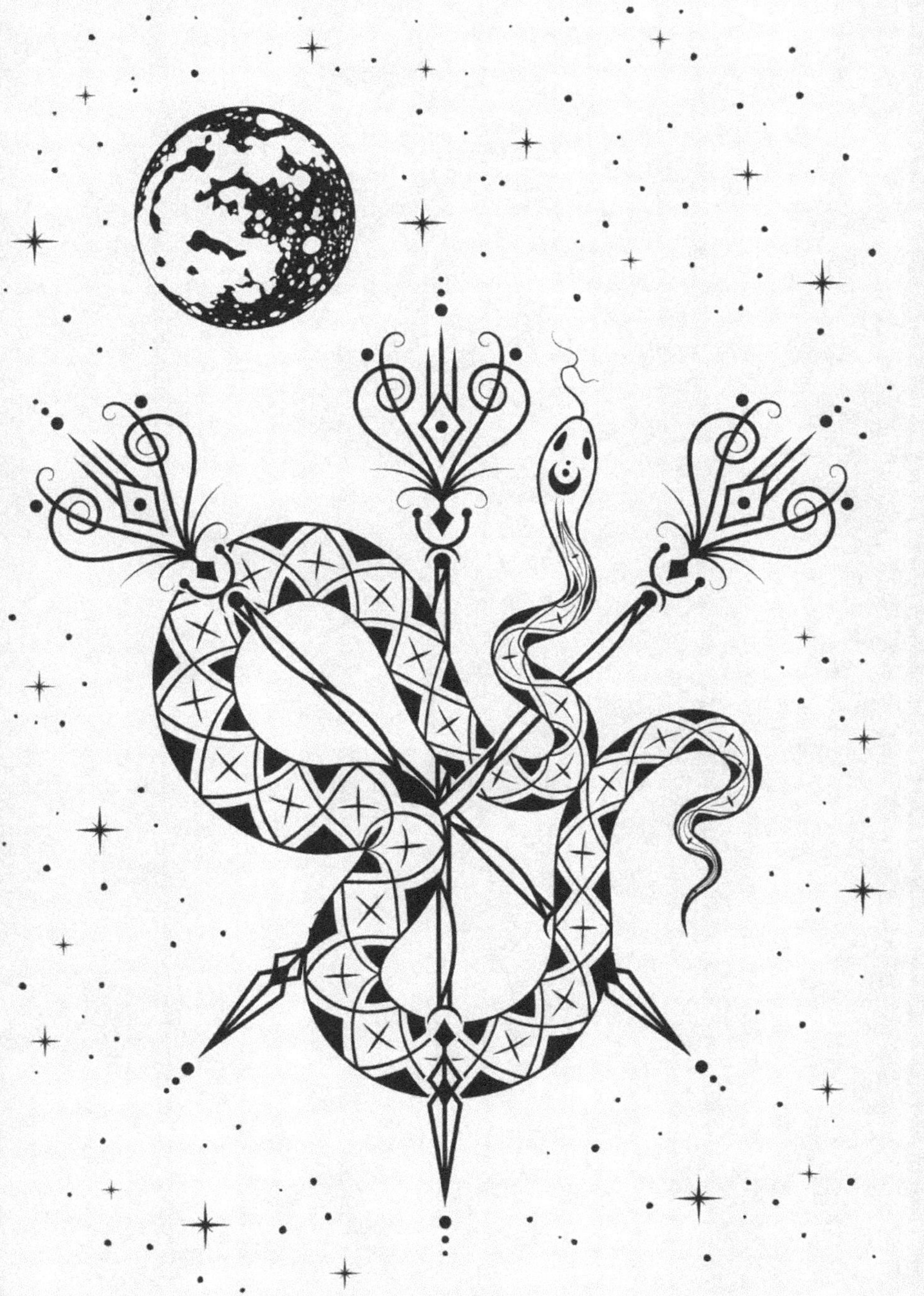

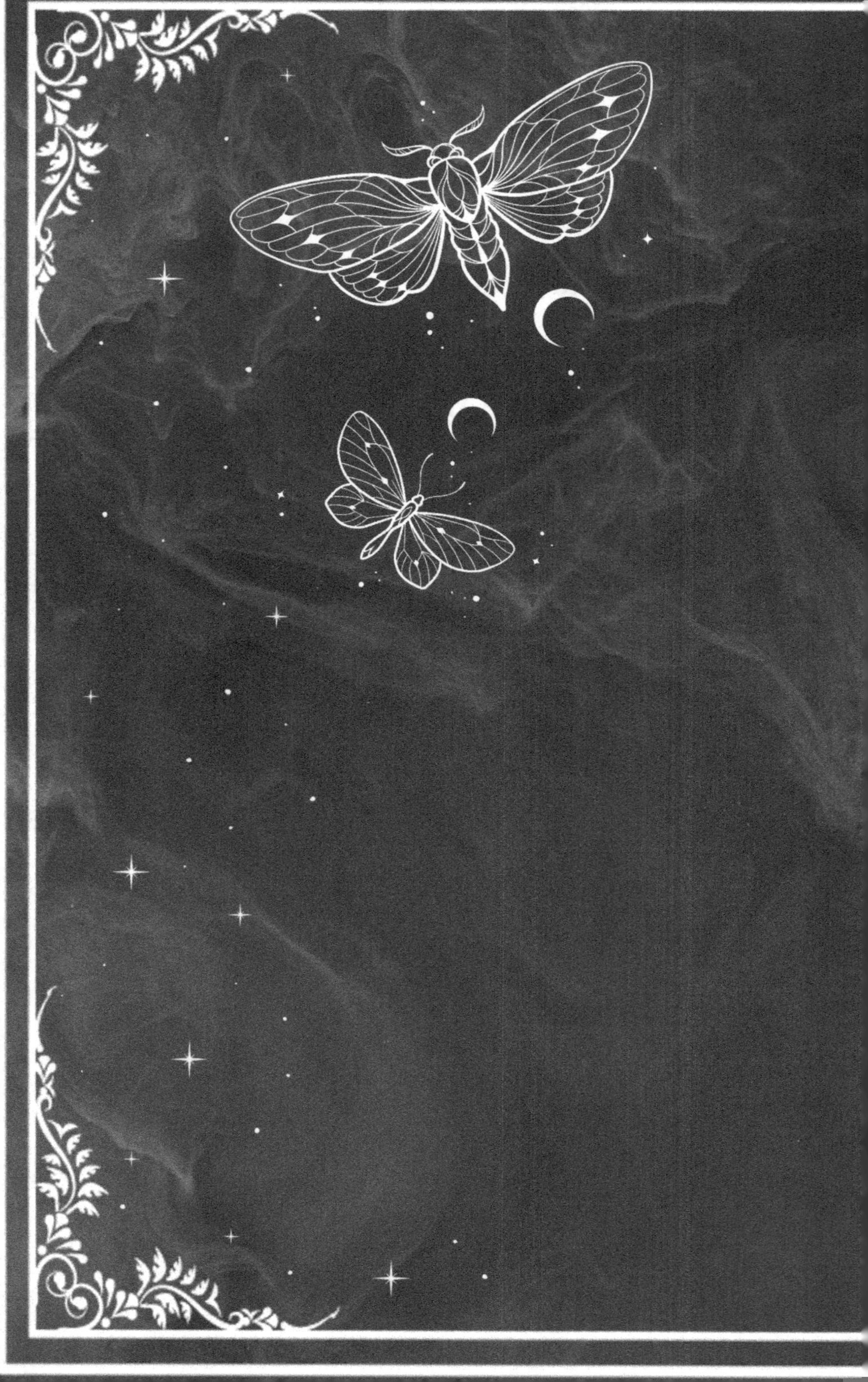

Chapter 5

"He's coming!" her sisters whispered.

The words bounced around the chamber outside her room. She hadn't heard of anyone approaching the Tower, but Selene had hidden herself as soon as coming back.

The problem with her power, or the second of her powers, really, was that she couldn't keep all those emotions underneath that icy lake forever. They had to come out. And knowing that he would follow her here had meant that she had to let it all out so there was room for more.

It was in those moments that she realized two problems.

The first was that his power was immense. She'd felt nothing like it before, and she'd encountered a few witches who were very proficient in manipulating emotions. Apparently, they were not anywhere near the talents of a demon king.

The lust that he'd poured into everyone at the tavern, during the festival, even when he passed by her on the road, all poured out of her at once. It struck her like a sledgehammer to the head, soaking her immediately and turning every touch into something horrific.

There was no pleasure to be found in that much lust. Only pain.

Wool was difficult to wear. She found it scratched too much against her skin, the sensation both pain and pleasure until it mixed into an overwhelming sensation. Her sheets touched her so much that she couldn't sleep. She couldn't stand because the wind brushed against her nipples and made the sweat cool on her body. She couldn't think other than to endure because no amount of orgasms even touched it. Nothing satisfied.

So she'd stayed in her room. Until she realized the second problem.

If she had to endure him again, there would be no safe place to purge all the build up of emotions. Was he connected to her? Would he be able to feel her lust even from his castle? And he'd been able to tell when people were affected by his magic. She'd seen it in his eyes.

So, as the lust in her body finally cooled, she knew this would be a test of her own power. Because if she couldn't keep all these emotions under lock and key in her mind, then the trick was revealed.

She wasn't the only person he'd ever met who his magic didn't work on. Not at all.

She was just another sorceress who was quite good at lying.

Ursula knocked on her door again. "Selene? Did you hear me? He's coming! You did it."

Of course she'd done it. She'd laid the groundwork for him to be interested and he was nothing if not a man who enjoyed conquest. He'd come. He'd tracked her down because she had thrown down the gauntlet before him.

Damn it. Why had she been born for this job and not to be Ursula's assistant?

"Selene?" Ursula asked again, her voice quieter this time. "Is everything all right?"

No. It wasn't. Selene stared at her reflection in the mirror and wondered just how she was going to survive this. The icy lake in her mind was completely and utterly purged. Free of any emotion she'd had to bury within the ice. But that didn't mean it wouldn't fill up again. And quickly.

How did she stop it from spilling over? From leaking, even when it should have been locked underneath mountains of ice?

Her power made little sense, even to herself. Selene had read a thousand books on magic, spent countless hours researching how to expand what she could do. She'd trained with every other sorceress, but none of them had been able to understand why her magic was fractured. Sorceresses were good at one thing. She was good at two.

Maybe it had something to do with how she'd been left for them to find. Selene's real mother had dropped her off in the middle of winter right in the front of the Tower. Minerva claimed that Selene had been outside in the cold for hours before someone had opened the door. No one went outside the doors in the winter. They were lucky anyone had thought to go outside at all.

The moment of fear and cold and icy despair as the one woman who was supposed to love her left had become her power. The sorceresses taken her in as a foundling and changed her life forever after that.

Ursula opened the door and poked her head in. "Are you alive?"

"Yes," Selene replied, straightening the brocade of her gown one more time. "Alive enough, that is."

"Oh." Ursula ducked into her room, carefully closing the door behind her as though she didn't want the others to see. "You know none of us would agree to this if it wasn't absolutely necessary. He won't hurt you, love. None of us would let him get close enough."

Of course they would. If he offered them all a role in the palace and in the running of this kingdom, every single one of them would sacrifice her. Selene knew that. And she didn't appreciate the lie.

Sighing, she shook her head and gave herself one more once over. The black gown should have been worn for mourning. A square neckline showed off her pretty collarbones, though they'd be mostly hidden by the fur lined black cloak she'd put on top of it. Steel gray embroidery decorated the bodice and down into the skirts with the vague impression of flowers, though it was difficult to see them unless the light was just right.

She'd pulled her hair up into a low bun and pinched her cheeks so she didn't look quite so pale with fear. Unfortunately, that was the best she could do, given the circumstances.

"I'm afraid," she whispered. "I hunted him down and now he's played right into our claws. What will he do when he realizes I've lied?"

"This is a blessing. Our mother has spent her entire life preparing us all to take down this demon king. Soon we will walk through the kingdom, the rightful rulers of this realm! Can't you see it? A better place for everyone. You even said yourself that the villagers were living chaotic lives. We'll make it better." Ursula walked up to her side and gently smoothed a single strand of her hair back into place. "This is a gift. You have to start looking at it as one."

A gift to condemn a demon to death? How novel. The idea made her want to vomit.

"Of course," she replied, though. Because that was what was

expected of her and nothing else. "I'm just having a moment. Is he here already?"

"He rode through the gates. Minerva is going to meet with him in the great hall before she tells us what to do next. She said there's a long conversation they need to have. Naturally, he'll be very suspicious of her, and she wants to ensure he's lulled into a sense of comfort." Ursula held out her arm for Selene to take. "Do you want to listen in on it with me?"

"You know we're not supposed to."

"One more mischief. Just like when we were kids."

They'd always called them "mischiefs" when they snuck around the Tower as children, getting into trouble where they weren't supposed to be and taking over areas of the attic for their plotting and planning. They'd take over the entire Tower someday, they'd said.

Ursula might. She'd make a good High Priestess. Maybe then Selene would be a sorceress and not just a foundling.

She set her shoulders and rested her hand on top of Ursula's arm. "Why not?"

Together, they snuck past their sisters and skittered up the stairs. There was only one part of the tower where they could survey the great hall. And that was five stories up on a tiny balcony that was meant to be decorative. Selene had the faint worry that maybe their weight would make it bend, considering they'd been children the last time they tried this.

But the two of them tucked behind two equally large green bushes that some gardener had placed to make it look more decorative and less like a mistake that a balcony had been left here at all.

They couldn't stop laughing. Both of them were breathless from their sprint up the stairs to make sure they were hidden before anyone entered the great hall beneath them. If they weren't careful, they'd be caught. And they both remembered what happened if they got caught.

"Your skirts," Ursula said at the end of a giggle. "They'll see your skirts!"

Selene yanked her skirts closer and perfectly timed as the front doors of the Tower banged open.

"High Sorceress!" Lust called out. "I know you're in here, and I believe you were expecting me."

She'd recognize that voice anywhere at this point. Those deep tones were... well. Delicious.

Ursula squirmed in front of her, eyes wide in shock as she mouthed, "Is that him?"

She nodded because she couldn't say "What do you think?". Ursula already rocked to the rhythm of his footsteps, without realizing that her body knew what his power asked of it before her mind had caught up. Even Selene could feel it.

Warmth dripped from his words and then surged out of his body. Right now, it was only the faintest hint of his power. Just the soft touch of strong hands digging into tight muscle. Hands that certainly would put her entire body at ease if she would only let him.

The feeling was a trap. She knew that. Her sister knew it. All the sorceresses in this entire place had to know it, but what were they doing? Plodding along with his magic.

He'd already gotten them under his thumb and none of them even knew it yet. Her mother had better have a good plan.

She leaned around her plant to see Minerva walking down the stairs. The great hall was actually the center of the Tower. The giant circle was bare until it reached the stairwell that wrapped in a coil throughout the inside of the building. Every room was only a small part of a larger circle, every floor proving the absolute delight of architecture within which they lived.

The white walls, ceiling, floors, and stairs were meticulously cleaned every single day. Sometimes by younger sorceresses who had yet to come into their power, sometimes by the few servants they kept on staff.

Her eyes moved to the demon king. He stood in what could have been royal regalia, or could have been his traveling outfit. A black corseted top with a black shirt underneath. Dark pants that clung to his thick thighs and tightly cupped what was between them. A gold cloak over his shoulders kept him warm from the chill, and it was metallic. It even reflected the light.

Minerva had chosen a much more classic outfit. Her black gown clung to her form. Even in her fifties, she was stunning. All hips and tiny waist and smooth steps that made her look as though she were gliding across the floor.

Selene remembered thinking she was the most beautiful woman in the world when she was young. Now, seeing her mother standing before Lust, she thought she had been right. They fit. The two of them were otherworldly in their looks, and she felt horribly drab in comparison.

"Wow," Ursula whispered. "Look at them."

She was. And she hated every second of it.

"To what do we owe the honor of welcoming our esteemed demon king?" Minerva asked, a little too close to Lust for it to be a surprise visit.

"You know why I'm here," he replied with an arched brow. "You practically laid her out on a banquet table for me."

"I did no such thing." Was she... flirting with him?

Selene looked over at Ursula and watched her sister shrug. Flirting wouldn't make sense, but Minerva knew what she was doing, so... surely this was the plan?

But then Selene felt another pulse of lust. She buried it deep, already concerned with the limitations of her power. Ursula squirmed again next to her. Her sister bit her lip, eyes focused entirely on Lust now.

"Come now, Minerva," he said, tsking his tongue against his teeth. "Neither of us has time to play games."

"And what game do you think I'm playing?"

"The woman. She's one of yours."

"Yes, and if you want her, then I'm afraid you'll have to beg."

What was her mother planning? Jaw dropping open, Selene almost stood up from behind her bush. Her mother certainly couldn't expect a demon king to beg for her daughter. Could she?

Minerva wouldn't give her up. Her mother wouldn't send her off with the demon as if she was property to be bartered? They'd wanted him here, and that was the end of what she was supposed to do.

Ursula grabbed onto her skirts and tugged her back down at the same time Lust chuckled.

"You know that's not going to happen. If I wanted her, I would have her already."

"And yet, you are here. I have her and you don't." The flash of pride in Minerva's gaze wouldn't keep her safe.

Selene braced herself at the first touch of his magic and then hissed out a low breath as it pulsed through the room. Sorceresses appeared behind her mother, ready to protect their High Priestess from his rage. But that didn't stop him. Another pulse of lust sent every woman in the room to their knees.

Even her mother. The High Priestess of the Tower of Silver Thread, a goddess in her own right, fell onto her knees before him, rocking back and forth and... and...

Moaning.

Selene shoved it all down, deep underneath that lake, and ignored how Ursula pressed her hands hard between her legs as though trying to hold it back.

"If I wanted you all to bow before me, I could make you." His eyes searched the six women who'd approached and sighed. "And yet, I do not see her."

"She was born for you," Minerva whispered, but her voice carried up into the rafters. "She arrived to us as a child and since then we have trained her for you and only you."

"A puppet," he snarled.

"No. A queen."

"I have no use for a queen."

She stood up with a snap. Her skirts billowed around her even before she realized that she was about to shout at him. She didn't want to be a queen either, and her mother had no right to trade her off. She had given her dues, and she was supposed to be a sorceress now. Not a queen. Not a sacrifice to a demon!

Selene ducked behind the bush again as his eyes glanced over at the balcony. All her bravery fled in the wake of those blue eyes. Don't see me, she thought. Please don't see me.

"You have use for her. The entire kingdom awaits your choice of queen who will rule over them. There are whispers in the streets. Whispers of how you will rule on your own forever and disregard the needs of your people."

"I have never done so," he snarled. And when she peeked out from behind the bush again, his eyes had moved back to the High Priestess. "None of us, as you so affectionately call demons, have a bride. And we never will."

"You may know what the nobles and the beautiful ones say, but you do not know what is whispered in dark places. You have need of a sorceress, Demon."

He rolled his eyes, and the light caught on his horns. More glitter, she noted with disdain.

He eyed her mother and then sighed. "I've seen this ploy before. You are not the first High Sorceress who tried to wriggle her way onto the throne. You offer me a puppet who, if I indulge in a few nights, will expect a payment for access to her innocent body. You will then try to make me bend because you believe that I care about your daughter or sorceress or foundling. When I do not allow you to cajole me into a bargain, then you will threaten her life. I will tell you I have no interest in her life, and then she will die. Your people will rebel against you because you killed one of your own with your careless actions, and then a new High Sorceress will take your place. Within two more centuries, all of this will repeat itself. Or am I wrong?"

Selene caught her breath.

Was that the plan? Was she to be thrown into his arms only for her mother to make demands of him later?

Of course it was. She saw it so clearly now. After all she'd given up, her mother wouldn't trust her with something so important as this. The truth of her mission had never been just to tempt him. It had always been to infiltrate the castle.

"You underestimate me, Demon," Minerva hissed. "We will no longer bend to you."

"Is that so?" A flash of anger made his face even more attractive.

The pulse of his power was stronger this time. Then another. And another. Over and over again, until even Selene winced.

His voice thundered around them, terrifying and monstrous in its power. "All it takes is one thought for you to drop to your knees. Another for you to know what it is to die a little death. How much more power do you believe it would take for me to end you all where you stand?"

Ursula moaned, the sound echoing with the rest of her sisters as all the women suddenly writhed on the ground.

And she couldn't take it anymore.

Selene leapt to her feet, then raced down the stairs. Her footsteps might have echoed, but who could hear them over the sounds of her sisters? Or her mother?

This memory would haunt her for the rest of her being. Finally, she reached the ground floor and stood at the top of the stairs where her mother had stood only a few moments ago.

"Demon," she called out, her voice ringing out not with lust but with anger. "You will cease this foolishness."

His eyes flashed again, another pulse of power rocking through the entire building until she feared it might loosen the stones from their base. As though his magic penetrated even the rock surrounding them.

But it didn't. And she just stuffed his power underneath the ice in her heart and glared at him.

"Enough," Selene said again. "You've done enough."

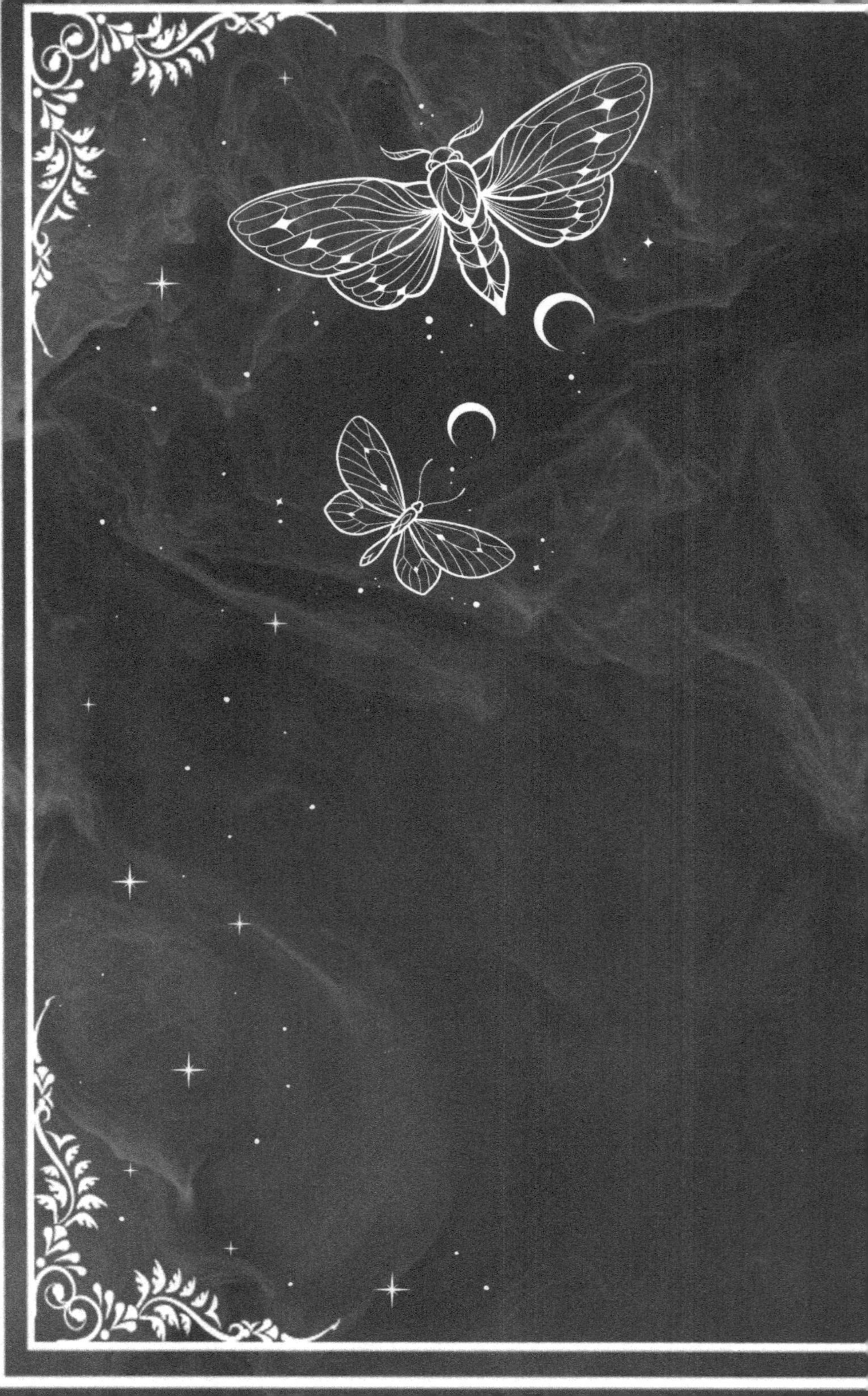

Chapter 6

He hated sorceresses. Always had. Always would.

But there was something to be said for a group of them on their knees before him. He'd never been a particularly ruthless man. Lust did not come with the desires for pain or torment, unless enjoyed by both parties. Something told him that the sorceresses would regret this later.

Still, seeing the High Sorceress without a means to an end to the pleasure he gave her made a wicked voice in his mind whisper, "Yes."

He hadn't felt this way in a long time. The victory of battle running through his veins even threatened to reveal his true form, which was much more than just the horns on his head. They were not entirely correct in calling him a demon, but the rumors had started from somewhere.

His brothers might wear those forms a little more comfortably, but Lust knew how to make himself more desirable to these humans. And desire him, they did.

Even the strongest women in the entire kingdom writhed at his feet, moaning as though they needed just a simple touch and he'd set them off. Should he? He knew the torment would linger with them. They'd hate themselves for how much they wanted his touch again.

Because his power only worked on those who still felt some form of lust for him, no matter how small.

"Enough," her voice rang out. Beautiful and clear and cold as the first winter storm.

Lust glanced toward the stairs. And there she was.

Beautiful was too common a word for her, and incorrect in many ways. He would not call her plain. That was a disservice to both her and himself. Certain features of hers were pretty enough. The dark waves of her hair might have been even close to beautiful if she hadn't flattened it to her skull in a severe bun. He supposed he could also admit the glare of disgust in her eyes was perhaps a little attractive as well.

Her glare sharpened into something close to hate as he sent out another pulse of his power, testing the edges of whatever shield she'd put up and... strangely... Nothing.

He hissed out a low breath and suddenly reacted.

His cock hardened, straining against his pants in a sudden rush of blood through his entire body. The hairs on his arms stood up and his heart thundered in his chest. That look in her eyes. The one that said she wanted to throw him across the room if she could. Why did he like that so much?

No person had made him react like this in centuries. He'd seen every woman he wanted. He'd tasted them all, been inside their wet heat, licked every possible part of their body and yet... This woman made him harden completely unbidden.

A part of him wanted to lunge for her. Surely she felt something. No one was immune to him unless they were one of those rare asexuals, but they didn't live in his damned kingdom. They moved. She stayed here for a reason, which meant she was interested in sex at least a little.

And if she wasn't interested in him, that was fine. Most of these sorceresses didn't want to fuck him. But they wanted to fuck someone. A few of them had been avoiding each other. A break up? His mind caught on theirs for a second, noticing how their emotions tangled with each other. Or perhaps a fling that had never started, but both of them desperately wanted. Their attentions were on each other, not him, but the effect was the same.

No matter. He turned his attention back to the stairs as the hard snap of her heels struck the white marble. She approached and every time that click echoed through the hall, an answering zing of electricity danced down his spine.

How dare she? How dare she think she could seduce him before she felt even an iota of those emotions herself?

"Ah," he called out, opening his arms wide as though she didn't affect him in the slightest. "The puppet."

"Easy now," she said as she stepped over the High Sorceress. "You may call me that to my mother, but I am no one's puppet."

"Eavesdropping is for the weak, you know. You could have come down and seen to me yourself." He let his eyes linger over her curves. "I wouldn't have minded."

"I'm sure you wouldn't have, but there is such a thing as self restraint." She'd even laced her fingers together at her waist like the proper little pious pet sent to the slaughter.

"Self restraint?" His nostrils flared in anger. "You know nothing about lust if you think there is no restraint in it. Perhaps you are too innocent to even understand the concept of it. Is that why your mother chose you to surrender to me? Because you're a child who has never understood what lust feels like?"

He knew it wasn't. There was more to this than any of them wanted to let on, but he wanted to see the anger flash in her eyes like it had in the tavern. He wanted to push her into doing something silly. Like flicking his fucking horns as she had in front of all those people.

"I can feel," she hissed. "I just feel nothing for you."

And she walked right into his trap.

So she could feel lust. She understood the concept, and she'd felt it before in her life. Which could only mean she was somehow blocking his power. A shield? That was the only thing he could assume, but no sorceress had ever been born with that power. No one had ever been gifted the ability to block a spirit who'd taken physical form.

They were inevitable. He and his brothers were mortal emotions turned flesh. They called out something deep inside these humans that they could not fight against because it already existed inside them.

And yet, this woman thought she could resist him.

He scoffed then and let his powers ease. With that, the women on the floor surrounding them slumped. The sound of their heavy breathing echoed through the chamber, although at least they weren't moaning any longer. That sound seemed to distress his new little toy.

Striding toward her, he kept his hands down at his sides. He knew how to approach a skittish horse, and she was little more than a filly for him to break.

He circled her, eyeing her body up and down, wanting to make her feel uncomfortable, but all he succeeded in doing was making himself uncomfortable.

Fingers flexing at his sides, it took all of his self control—restraint, as she wanted him to believe he did not have—to not pull those pins out of her hair. He wanted to see them tumble down around her shoulders. Would that dark tangle smell like peppermint? Would he find himself in a wave of that scent that made him harden even more?

Moving around to her front, his eyes traced the graceful lines of her collarbone. He didn't want to just lick her there, or even run his fingers along the shadowy hollows below. He wanted to feel how delicate they were underneath his hands. How easily breakable she was and knowing that she wanted him to touch her where it would be so easy to hurt.

"What is your name?" he asked, his voice little more than a husky whisper.

"Selene." Her throat moved in a long swallow. Even there she was like a swan, delicate and lean.

No, she was not some great beauty. But damned if he didn't want her.

"Named after the moon, under which all nefarious acts are consummated," he said. "And no doubt your mother wishes me to worship at your feet. She wants me to bend before you, on my knees, whispering sweet nothings in your ear while you command my kingdom."

Anger laced through the tight restraint of his lust. He felt his chest swell with it, his nails growing longer and the tips of his horns stretching.

"I have no desire for a kingdom or a throne," she replied. Her voice rang through the great hall and her mother's head snapped up.

Did the old bat not want her daughter to say that? Well, maybe she should have told her daughter more information about the upcoming moments then. The plan was fractured between the sorceresses. Obviously, some wanted to rule over the kingdom, and others wanted merely to rule over him.

Ah, that wouldn't do.

He needed them all to be involved in the same plan or he'd be chasing multiple threads that all led to the same knot. If that meant he had to convince this Selene that she had the same desires as her mother, well then he was just making sure the family stayed together. Now wasn't he?

Moving around to her back, he trailed his fingers over her shoulder and had to swallow his own moan. She was soft. He'd thought she'd be hard and cold like ice, but the damned woman was soft as velvet on his fingers.

"Now, here's the problem," he murmured, leaning in behind her to whisper the words in her ear. Goosebumps rose on her skin, and he had to bite back his grin. "Your mother wants to hand you over to me like a sacrificial lamb. I'm not opposed to that. When I first took over the kingdom a thousand years ago, many of your kind thought blood sacrifices would keep me appeased. I spent many nights in the arms of all those people, just like I would spend many nights in yours."

Sliding his finger up the back of her neck, he noted a small dark mark there. A rune? No. A seven-pointed star that triggered something in his memory. But he couldn't quite grasp the recollection before she bit out her words in a retort.

"I have no interest in becoming your sacrifice. If I am to go with you, then it will be as your queen."

"I have no need of a queen. And I thought you didn't want to be one." He said the words flippantly because he wasn't listening anymore.

He already knew what she was going to say.

Muttering under his breath, he whispered the words even as she said them. "The kingdom needs a queen. We've never had one, and that is reflected in every aspect of this kingdom. You have created a man's world, and it desperately needs the touch of a woman. The guidance of one such as me."

Her mother's words, but not entirely. Little Selene hadn't been listening to what her mother was suggesting. Minerva didn't care if the kingdom was led by a woman. She cared that it was led by a sorceress. So Selene didn't actually know the High Sorceress's plan.

"One such as you?" he replied, finally giving into temptation and attacking the damned pins in her hair. "You think you, a child, know how to run a kingdom?"

"I'm twenty-five years old."

"Ancient."

"I have seen enough of this realm to know how it should be run. I have spoken with enough people here to know what they desire."

"Have you?" he asked, putting a few of those pins in his mouth. No sense to lose them, they did look rather expensive. "And what did they say?"

"That their king is a fool who doesn't listen to his people. What are you doing?" she snapped. But she didn't turn around.

"I find it amusing that you claim they call me a fool. They do not. I am the only reason this kingdom still runs as it does and no one could ever deny that." It was getting more difficult to speak with all the pins in his mouth. Why had she turned herself into a pincushion?

"Because my hair is thick and needs more pins to hold it together."

Oh, had he said that last bit out loud?

Lust spit the pins into his palm and then let them fall onto the floor. Their tinkling sounds struck again and again, and as he watched, more of those delectable goosebumps rose along her neck. Fascinating. So she enjoyed sounds, even if her mind refused to believe it.

He could work with that.

Finally, he pulled the largest pin and let the long waves of her hair free. Just as he'd imagined, the peppermint of her scent overwhelmed him. His eyes rolled back in his head at the first waft of that ice cold threat of magic and power and woman.

Ah, but she was a pretty little thing. A block of ice that needed to be chipped away until it revealed the crystalline sculpture beneath.

"You want me to believe you feel nothing," he whispered in her ear, so close he could feel the shiver that trailed through her body. "That the sight of me disgusts you."

"I'm not trying to convince you of anything. I want you to see what is in front of you."

She could talk all she wanted. But her body didn't lie. He trailed the backs of his fingers down her arm until he gently lifted her wrist. Her arm laid atop his, all heavy brocade and scratching embroidery. "When you come to my castle, you will be covered in silks. You will wear clothing that is fit for your form until I can see all of it. You will sleep in my bed. I will be the first and last person you see every day and I will never stop tempting you. Do you really think you can suffer through that?"

"You are not as tempting as you think."

But she'd leaned back into him. He wasn't sure she even realized she was doing it. Selene shifted her weight into her heels, just slightly, enough so that he could feel her pressing her back against his chest. Not enough to nudge his painfully hard cock, but enough to tease him with the fabric that covered her.

He chuckled low in her ear and knew even then that he'd broken through. Her faint gasp, along with a slight inhalation that made him grin.

He couldn't taste her lust like he had the others. He couldn't even sense that she was affected.

But she was.

He rumbled a hum in her ear, just to feel that shiver one more time, before he muttered, "I'm going to enjoy breaking you."

And then, because he could, he stepped away from her and let the cold rush of air replace him.

She stumbled, as if shocked. Or perhaps trying to put space between them because she refused to let him try to break her as he claimed he would.

It would be the sweetest seduction, he realized. But that would be the challenge of it. Even if he was walking right into the damned sorceresses' trap.

Turning on his heel, he glared down at the High Sorceress. "We leave today. If you want her in my castle, then get her ready. I will not come back a second time."

The High Sorceress's jaw dropped open. "That is not enough time to prepare her, let alone pack her things."

"Excuse me?" Selene snapped from behind him. "I need to say goodbye to my family. I haven't packed, and I certainly am not prepared to leave now. A week is not that long to wait."

He didn't turn to her when he replied, "I have no wish to wait a week." Then he crouched in front of her mother, who had at least gotten onto her knees and tilted her chin up to him. "And I don't want you to wriggle your way into her mind anymore than you already have. You've had twenty-five years to brainwash her into your puppet, Minerva. Now I will see how strong the bond between mother and daughter really is."

He sneered at the last sentence. Mother and daughter. He knew the tendrils of control when he saw them, and Minerva was no mother. She'd seen an opportunity, and she'd taken it.

Minerva bared her teeth. "I think you'll find my daughter is loyal to her family, Demon."

"Ah." He nodded and then stood. "Because your family is so loyal to her. You're feeding her to a demon, after all."

He turned without looking at anyone else and stalked toward the door. Damned woman had gotten him all tense again, and he'd have to take care of it before he put that little sorceress in his carriage or who knows what madness he might try. Like getting on his knees and begging for a taste just to see if she was as icy between her thighs as she appeared.

"You have two hours!" he called out, his voice bouncing off the marble. "I won't wait any longer than that."

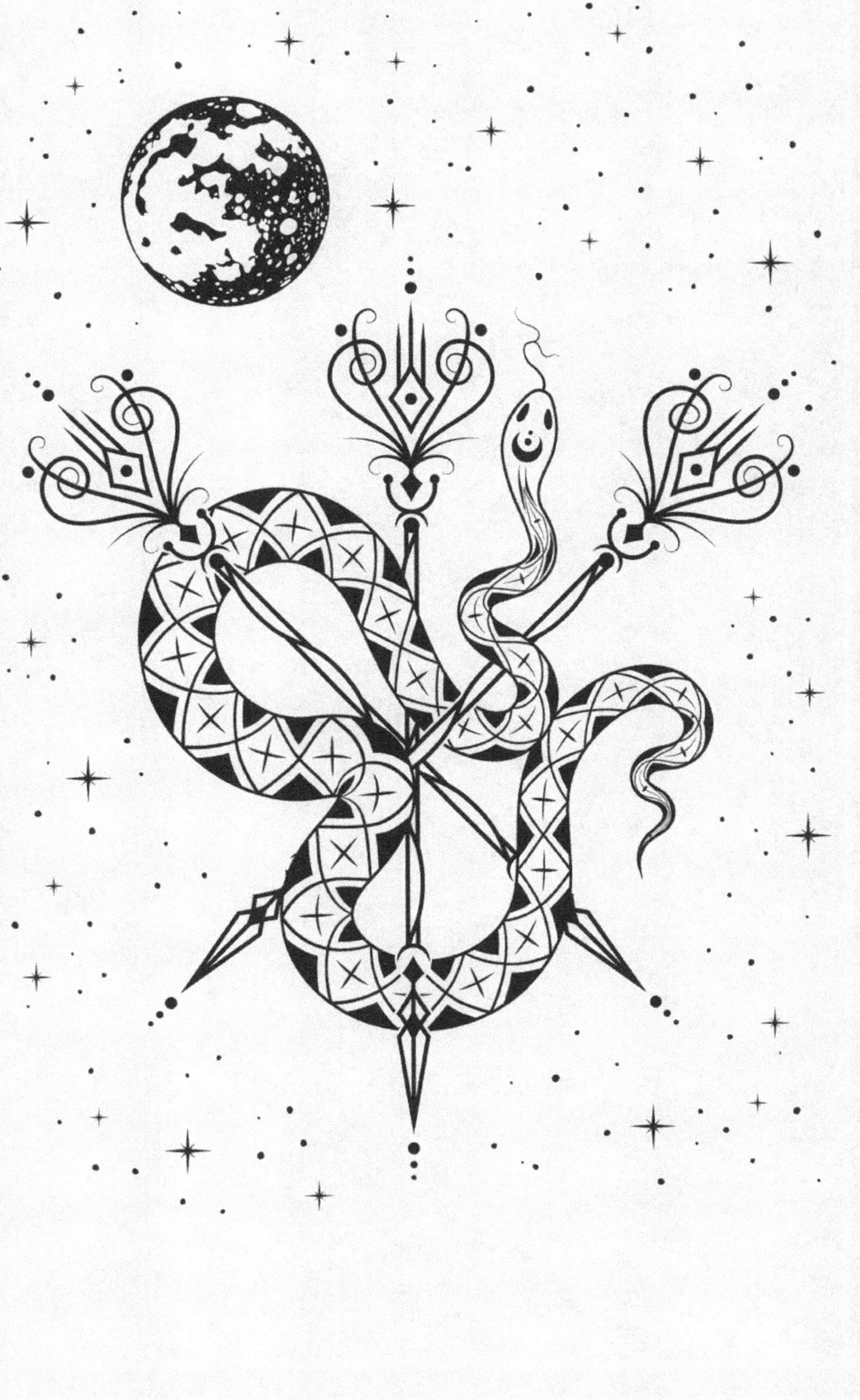

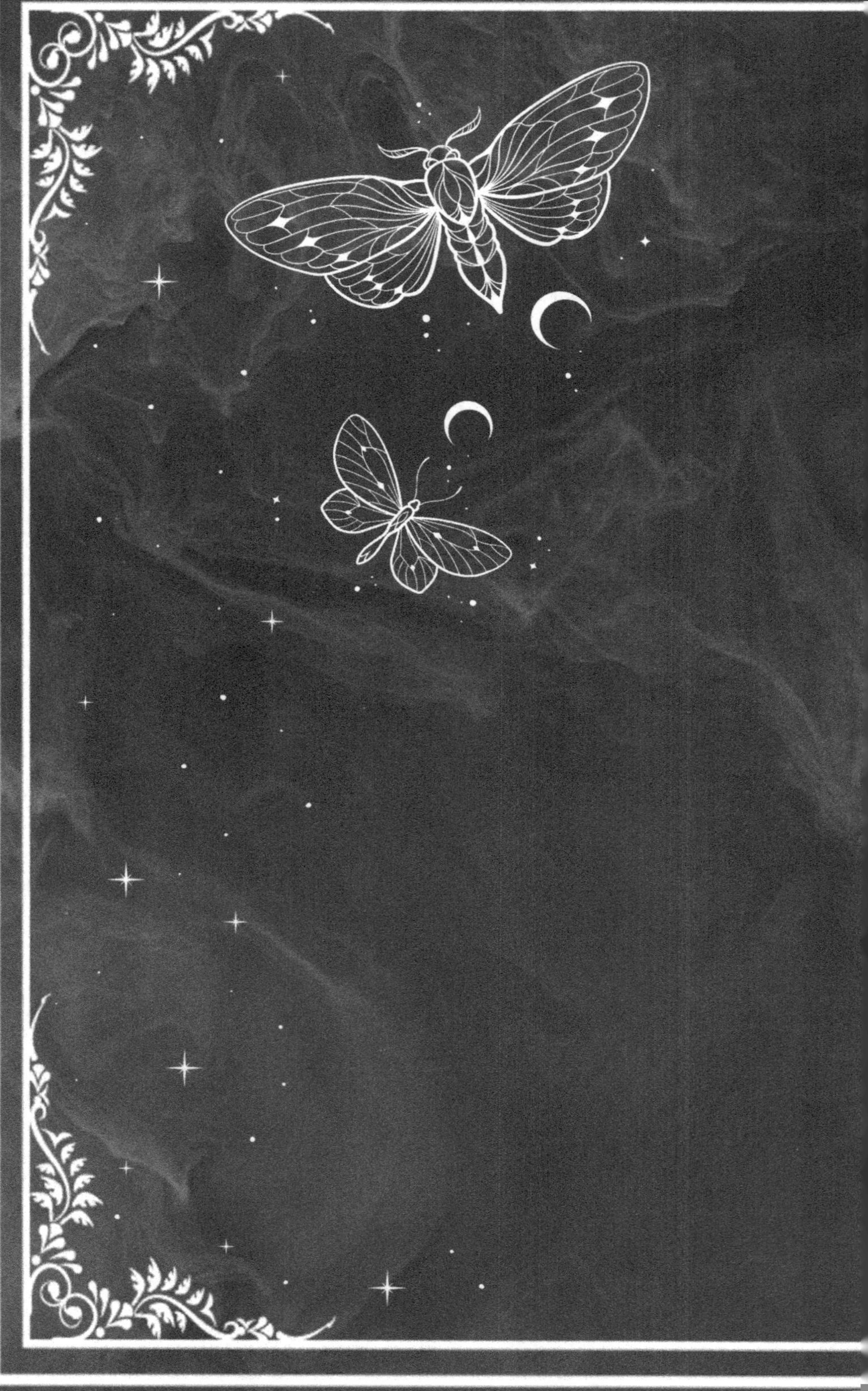

Chapter 7

Four of her sisters packed up her entire life in the matter of an hour. Selene stood in the center of her room, staring off into space as she faced the fact that she was leaving. She would no longer be one of the sisters. A man wanted her, and now he'd taken her.

She'd never forgive him for that. Already a fire bloomed in her chest because, damn it, she wanted him. She still wanted to touch him, to see if that warm, golden skin was as smooth as it looked. Then she wanted to slap him, to wipe that knowing smirk off his damned face, because how could he know that she wanted him?

Selene could barely feel the lust that he'd sent out into the room, but she could still feel the belated interest. It was like looking through the world underwater. The sensation of his magic was dull enough to be aware of but not feel.

Why was this happening to her when all she'd ever wanted was to be here?

She glanced around her comfortable bedroom one last time and sighed. This was her purpose. She was meant to be the person who would lead her family toward a better future. That's what her mother always said.

But of course, her mother wasn't even here to say goodbye.

Minerva had sent Bathilda to tell her the plan. Since they could not trap the demon with the spells they had unearthed deep in the library of the Tower, they needed to go to the second plan. She would go to his castle and she would find whatever information she could to take him down.

Selene would report back to the Tower at every moment she could. They would keep in touch with her through spells and portals, letters if they had to. And that was how they would destroy the demon king. From the inside.

It was her sisters who walked her through the gardens and out the front door. The gate gaped open, an unusual sight for the Tower as they never left the doors open lest someone wander in while they were practicing magic.

For some reason, the sight of it made her stomach turn. Would she ever come back here? Likely not. He'd find her out and then he'd kill her. Perhaps he'd send her head back as a gift for her family.

Ursula pressed a book into her hand and smiled. "For the ride. I thought maybe you would need something to distract yourself, considering... Well..."

The words were left unsaid in case one of Lust's people overheard what they were saying. It wasn't a problem, though. There was still enough space in the deep well of her power to hold more of whatever he threw at her. For a while, at least.

She pulled Ursula into a hug. "I'll be fine."

"Are you sure?"

No.

She couldn't be sure. She'd been sold to a demon king.

"I'm sure," she whispered against Ursula's shoulder. And then she turned to hug the rest.

Only Bathilda had tears in her eyes. Or maybe that was a trick of the light.

"I miss you already," Selene called out as she turned to walk through the gate. But some part of her soul whispered that she might not miss them for long. They were her family. Her comfort, of course. But they'd never satisfied her need for adventure. Adventure, which now waited in a gilded carriage.

A footman hopped down from his seat near the roof to hold the door open for her. He grinned, his face overly friendly as she reached for the small handrail to help pull herself in. Selene didn't look at him. She couldn't.

Instead, she looked at the interior of the carriage and made a face. Everything inside stank of luxury. The violet pillows glistened in the waning sunlight, likely silk as he threatened to dress her in. Tiny amethyst chips decorated the interior walls as though they were seated inside a geode. Lust reclined on one of the cushions, leaning on his elbow with his leg up, as he nearly laid down on the entire cushion. He took up an entire bench.

Clearly, he meant for her to sit on her own. And that suited Selene just fine.

She clambered in, fluffed out her skirts as she sat, and opened the book in her lap.

She could just barely see him out of the corner of her eye. He'd stiffened the moment she opened the novel and then bared his teeth in frustration. Had he thought their game of wits would continue while they were in the carriage?

It would not. She was angry at him, and the last thing that Selene had any interest in doing was entertaining a brat. He'd rushed her goodbyes, forced her to come with him far sooner than she wished, and she would not fall into his trap to start an argument.

He had to realize there would be punishment when he tried to walk all over her. And yes, that bloom of heat in her core immediately suffered the same fate as any other emotion. She imagined tossing it hard and the resulting numbness that came after gave her little sense of satisfaction. She shouldn't enjoy the idea of punishing him and yet, there it was.

Stupid man.

She hunched a little over her book, leaning harder against the back of the carriage and trying to make herself look utterly horrid. Perhaps if he thought he'd brought a gremlin back with him, then he'd leave her alone long enough for Selene to get her head on straight.

He struck the top of the carriage hard, and then they were moving.

Away from her home. Away from everything she knew.

Sighing, she staunchly stared down at the pages and ignored Lust after that. He tried his best to get a reaction out of her, though. Because what immature child wouldn't?

First it was just little sounds. Grunts, angry sighs, all of which eventually turned into a mockery of lovemaking as he tried to get her to look at him. She did not. Then he adjusted himself in his pants, multiple times, as though by touching himself he would scandalize her. Considering he didn't whip himself out and flail his cock around, she did not move her gaze from the book. Even when he started talking, she simply continued reading the novel that Ursula had handed to her.

Not that she'd absorbed a single page with the man child in the carriage. But that was another matter entirely.

Finally, he let out an enormous pulse of his power as though that might break through her magic. She mused that he must think she had a shield or something similar, and if he used enough of his power, then he might break through it. He must not have ever come in contact with a power like hers.

Curious.

She merely turned the next page. He frowned at her and then let out another massive burst of lust that made ripples form on the icy sheet covering her lake. Not good.

Finally, she looked up from her book and said, "Can I help you?"

"That didn't affect you at all, did it?"

"No. But I do request that you stop or your carriage driver will take us off the road. I'd rather not be traveling in the dark." She glared at him. "You're acting like a child."

He ignored the jab and leaned forward. With his sleeves rolled up to his elbows and his forearms braced on his knees, he was altogether too close. She could see violet flecks in his eyes and wondered if they changed color with the seasons.

"Are you asexual?" he asked.

"What is that?"

"Do you not find yourself attracted to anyone at all?"

She arched a brow. "I find myself attracted to some men, but not all of them."

"So you've felt attraction."

"I'm interested in men, yes." When she wanted to be. But Selene didn't enjoy the sensation and hid those emotions the older she got. "I'm just not interested in you."

He leaned back again, legs spread wide and confusion marring his pretty expression. "So you do feel."

"Yes." Selene lifted her book into the air. "If that's all?"

"It's not."

"What a shame," she muttered as she turned back to the story in her lap. "One might think you were getting angry with me."

"I am."

"If only I was listening." Selene then ignored him for the rest of the ride, no matter what he did. If he wanted to make his driver's mind break, then he could. She would not care in the slightest.

It took the better part of the afternoon to get to the castle, but they moved faster than she expected. Perhaps he had his own roads, so he didn't have to worry about other carriages with broken wheels or wagons with aging donkeys trying to pull them. Her thoughts drifted, and she turned the pages as though she were still reading.

Still, it was too soon once the carriage rolled to a halt in front of the castle. Lust always had a flare for the dramatics, and this building was not any different. She stared up at the gleaming columns, pointed peaks, and the thousands of windows that let in all the natural light, and sighed.

If only a fraction of that money had gone to the rest of his kingdom, what would it look like?

He got out of the carriage by himself and held out his hand for her to take. "I know that look."

"What look?"

"The one that says you think this castle is too extravagant and that it should go to the rest of the kingdom. I've seen it a hundred times before." He grinned, even though that should have been an insult. "In case you haven't noticed, every town is very well funded. They don't all live in a castle like myself, but they live comfortably."

Not according to what her mother had said, but Selene didn't want to get into another argument with him. She needed time to figure out a plan, and he hadn't given her that on the ride here.

Ignoring his hand, she stepped out of the carriage on her own and followed him as he turned. Considering the stiffness in his spine and the pout on his lips, she had a feeling he was more insulted that she hadn't let him touch her.

Let him be insulted. She had a job to do here, and it was to tempt him or find information. He'd never had a woman do what she was doing to him, and, if she was reading the situation right, he couldn't stop thinking about her.

Besides, she didn't like him. This was fun.

The front doors of the castle were easily three men tall, if not bigger. Gilded like everything else Lust owned, they gleamed in the sunlight. So beautiful it made her eyes hurt to look at them. And then they opened to reveal what was beyond and it made her breath catch in her chest.

The entrance hall stretched far into the distance. Tall pillars held up a second-story balcony that wrapped around it, and each pillar was carved to look like a giant. Women with gowns falling off their shoulders, men in various states of undress with rippling muscles and handsome faces. Massive chiffon curtains hung from their shoulders and hands, gently swaying in the breeze from the windows open all around them.

Down the center of the hall was a long, narrow pool of water. Lily pads floated on top of it while golden fish swam underneath them.

A thick heavy carpet laid on either side of the pool, decorated with pillows here and there in case someone wanted to lay beside the fish or feed them. All this pointed toward a dais that held a massive golden throne.

Selene hadn't realized she'd stopped to look at it all. She could only imagine her eyes were enormous as she tried to soak in all the luxury that surrounded her. But goodness, this was... impressive. Colorful. And surprisingly comfortable.

She should have guessed comfort would be important to a demon of lust.

He'd stopped to look at her, his hands tucked behind his back and a soft smile on his face. "Does it suit?"

"Excuse me?"

He gestured around them. "Does this satisfy you?"

"I don't see how it matters if it does or does not." She didn't want to admit that it did. All of it did. This was so much more than the blank white walls of the Tower. So much that it was almost overwhelming.

"Because you're supposed to be my queen. Wasn't that the deal?" Although the sarcasm in his voice didn't sound like he considered her his queen. Not until he walked over to her did she realize his intent.

"Absolutely not—" she started before he tugged her into his arms.

She was suddenly pressed against him. All of him. She could feel the thick trunks of his thighs as he wedged one between her legs, the hard bulge of his cock pressed against her hip, though he did not grind himself against her as she thought he would. Instead, all he did was wrap a tendril of her hair around his free hand and look at it in the light.

"You really aren't that pretty," he breathed. "So, why did they choose you?"

"Perhaps because they knew I wouldn't like you," she hissed and shoved at his shoulder.

"No, it's not that. Dislike makes for rather explosive lust. You aren't supposed to fall in love with me, darling, you're just supposed to want to rip my clothes off. That doesn't require liking a person at all." He hummed out a low breath and then shook his head. "What is your power?"

The swift change in subject made her head swim. "My what?"

"Every sorceress has one. An innate born ability, if you will. What is yours?"

She stared up at him, wide eyed. He shouldn't know about that. No one knew that sorceresses were born with their magic. They'd taken care to cultivate rumors that had become truths. Sorceresses knew magic, all kinds of magic, and even he couldn't know...

Lust tucked a finger under her chin, then stroked it along her jaw and down to the sensitive skin of her throat. "You can answer me or kiss me. One or the other."

"Light," she hissed. "I can make light."

"Such a weak power."

She ground her teeth together at the insult. "A power is only as weak as the person who wields it."

"Such wisdom for someone so young." He trailed his finger lower, pausing at the square neckline of her gown. "This dress is ugly."

"I did not choose it for you."

"Clearly. You would have worn something softer if it was for me. Something more comfortable and less... stifling." His lip curled in disgust. "I will never understand you mortals choosing to wear something uncomfortable when you could wear whatever the season calls for."

"You don't need to be touching me to tell me all this."

"Oh, but I do." The grin on his face turned into something wicked. "I own you now, Selene. Your mother sold you off to me like an heirloom she couldn't wait to get rid of. And that means you will attend to me in all matters. You will do whatever I wish."

She stiffened in his arms. Not because she was afraid of those words, but because she was... intrigued by them. And she hated that.

"Don't you worry. I'm not so much a monster that I will force you to do anything you don't want. You will always have the ability to say no." He leaned closer, inhaling at her neck. "But I don't think you'll want to say no."

She trembled in his arms, as though she were some weakling who needed him to hold her up. How dare he make her feel like this? She stuffed the emotions away. Fist fulls of them until she could breathe without wondering if he could scent the lust on her. Finally, she replied, "You'll have to work a lot harder to convince me that I want someone like you."

His warm, wet tongue traced up her neck and a tendril of desire almost escaped. Almost.

"Your lust will taste all the more sweet for the battle to earn it." Then he released her, letting her stumble back as he shouted for a servant to bring her to her quarters.

Selene stood there, waiting for someone to guide her, legs shaking and her heart hammering in her chest.

She'd almost ruined everything when his tongue had touched her. And it was then that she realized how difficult this was going to be.

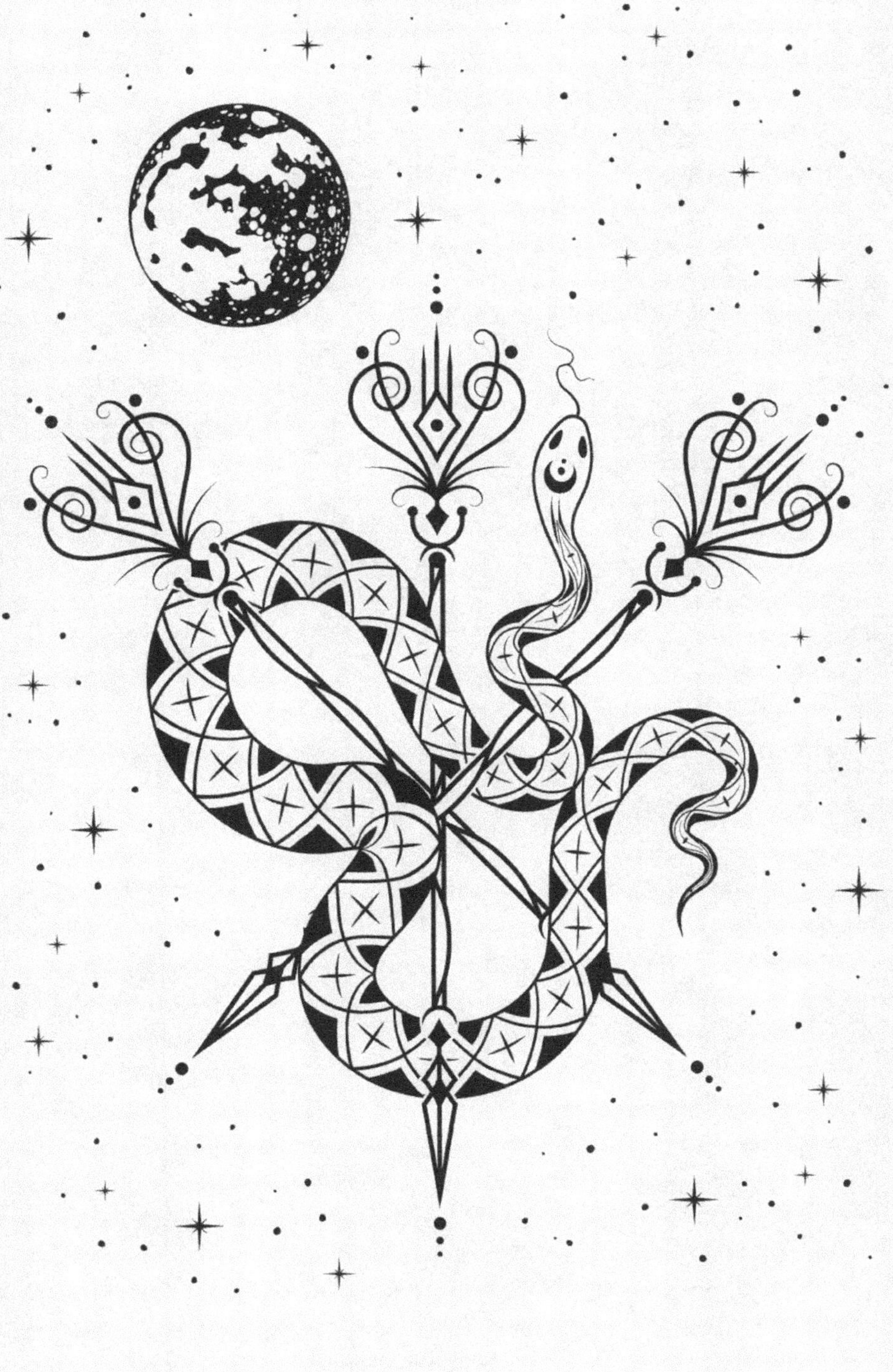

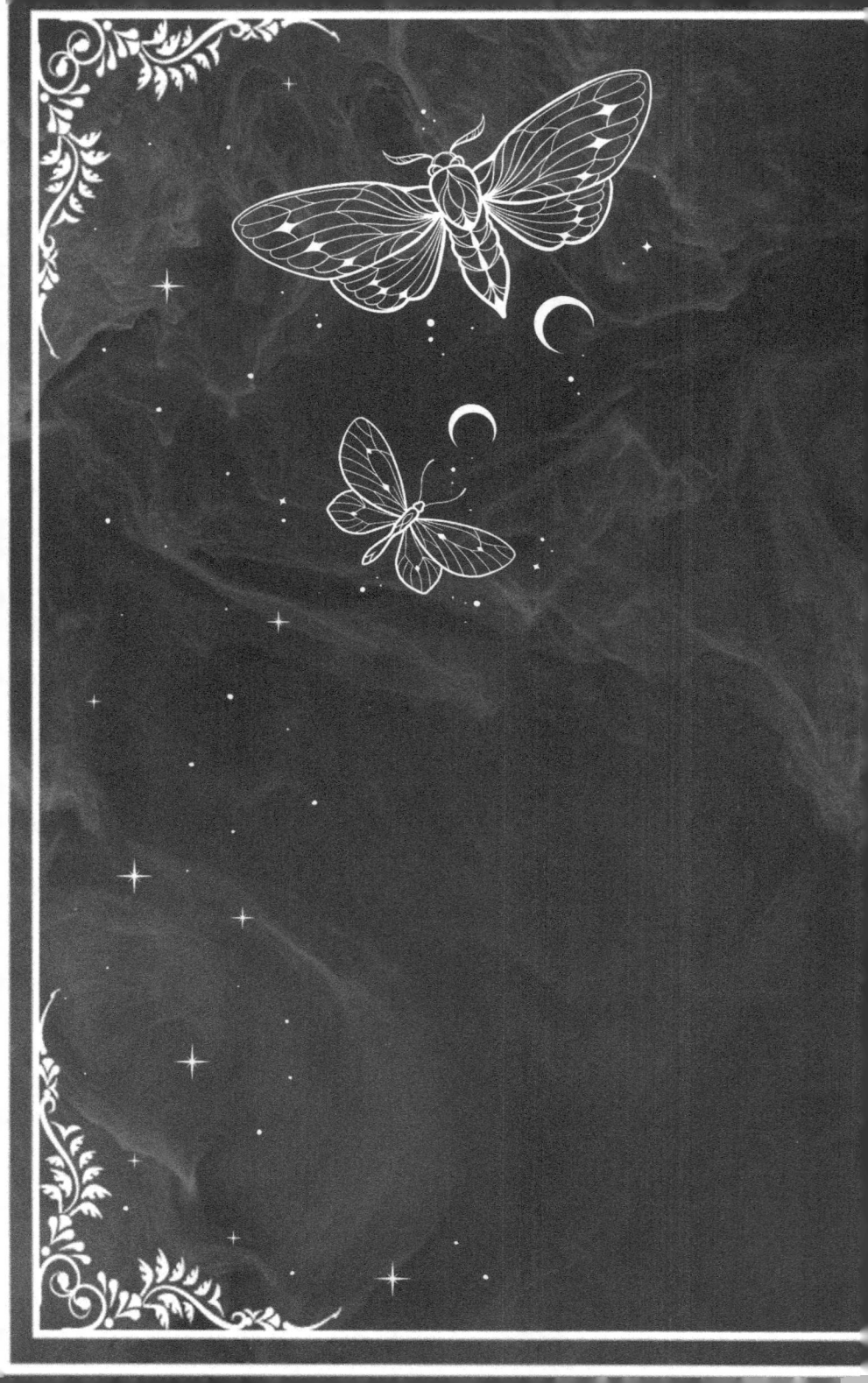

Chapter 8

He let her get settled in, not because he had no idea what to do with her and certainly not because she'd turned his world onto its side. She could suffer in any way that she wanted while in his castle. And ignoring her would only make that suffering all the worse.

Except he knew he was lying to himself. This strange little woman had turned what usually was his sanctuary into a rather terrifying place to be. He worried that he'd run into her in the halls. What he'd say if he did see her.

What he'd do.

No woman had ever resisted him this long. He'd always been the one that they all wanted. Lust was an easy emotion for mortals to feel and even easier for them to bend to. They wanted to indulge in that particular feeling. He just gave them what they wanted.

Except her. She didn't want to bend to lust, or she had some strange ability to avoid it entirely. And he hated it.

It made him feel weak, and he hadn't felt that way since he'd taken on his physical form. The feeling became so uncomfortable that he didn't want to look at her. Or even think about her. So he went about his day as though nothing had changed.

Until he couldn't anymore.

Lust walked into his office, an austere room filled to the brim with gold accents and plush, velvety pillows. The long curtains at the window moved with a gentle breeze, the gauzy fabric making the entire world look white. Like snow. Like her.

Damn it, he couldn't even work without bringing her into it somehow. He'd only just sat down when his door burst open and some insane thought whispered maybe it was her. Maybe she'd decided that she couldn't wait any longer, because she felt his lust pulsing through the castle as only he could make it do.

Lust sat up straighter, only to slump back when he realized it was only one of his nobles, followed by a very familiar misty spirit.

"My lord," the man said, bowing until the top of his head almost touched the ground.

Theo was a good man with good intentions, but he simpered far too much and frankly, that had become rather annoying of late. He was, unfortunately, an extremely good noble, and that made it hard to hate him. Even if he would lick Lust's boots clean.

Pinching the bridge of his nose, already annoyed, Lust asked, "What is it?"

"I came to congratulate you on your bride."

He could have heard a pin drop in the silence that followed from that statement. Affection peered around Theo as though it were looking for whatever expression might then show on his face.

A bride must mean that Affection would be fed soon. He blinked at the little spirit and saw it had not changed in the slightest. Therefore, there was no proper amount of affection in this castle. As he'd expected.

He swallowed hard, hearing the audible click in his dry throat as he asked, "What did you say?"

"Your... bride?" Theo's face burned bright red. "Everyone is talking about it. In the castle, in the streets. I'd be surprised if the entire kingdom wasn't aware that you'd taken a bride from…"

The man trailed off as he saw anger blooming in Lust's features.

Lust expected his horns had suddenly grown because he wanted to put his damned fist through a wall. He flexed his hands on his thighs, claws suddenly digging through the fabric.

"Those fucking sorceresses," he snarled. "Meddling bitches. Of course, they spread a rumor. Why didn't I anticipate that?"

Affection rolled toward him, its mist undulating in tendrils that reached out to comfort. "Because you were so caught up in your new bride?"

"Do not touch me."

"Because you wanted to make her more comfortable and forgot to announce to the kingdom that you'd found someone who was important enough to put at your side?" It reached up a tendril, slowly stretching toward his knee.

He moved. "Stop it, Affection."

"Just a taste."

"There is no affection between myself and that lying little witch who has hidden in her room since the moment we got here. She is an enigma I am trying to understand, and a little lie between myself and the High Sorceress. That does not mean she will be queen!" He slammed a hand down on his desk, nearly breaking it with the force. "Why didn't I see they would try to force my hand?"

Theo cleared his throat. "Well... I should let you know that the entire kingdom is waiting for an announcement."

"An announcement?"

"They are expecting to at least... meet your bride." Theo shuffled his feet and then tucked his hands behind his back. "My apologies. I thought this would be a happy occasion, not one of strife."

"It's not your fault," he ground out through his teeth. "It's the monstrous fools I allow to stay in their Tower while the rest of my people work for their food."

He had to figure out a way around this. Minerva had played her hand already, and he hadn't expected her to turn his entire kingdom against him this quickly. If he didn't show off his new bride, then he would look as though he was trying to hide her. And why? The rumors would fly, soon becoming a wave that he could drown underneath.

But if he fell into the sorceress' trap, then he really would be forced to marry her. He couldn't take Selene out into his kingdom and introduce her to his people, only to then say she wasn't a good enough fit. Minerva knew this.

Of course she did. The old woman had more guts than he'd given her credit for.

The only person who could help him get out of this was Selene herself. She knew what her people were planning. She knew how to get around them as well, he had a feeling. All he had to do was trap her in the right way. Get her to be uncomfortable enough to tell him anything he wanted, and he knew just the way to do that.

Glancing down at the mountain of paperwork he was about to leave, Lust sighed and stood from his desk. "Send for the woman.

Have her delivered to my private quarters."

"My lord?"

"I'll answer no more questions, Theo."

Lust stalked from the room, back to the same damned place he'd just left. This couldn't wait, though. He had to nip these rumors in the bud, which meant he had to throw another fucking party after he'd just finished up the festival circuit.

Could he not rest? Or catch up on all the work he'd gathered along the circuit?

He couldn't contact his brothers. They always made sure the other kingdoms were still doing well, or at least well in the way they wanted to run it. He still had to connect with all of them to...

Fucking hell. He wouldn't be able to sleep for a month if he wanted to get all this done on time.

Lust made it to his rooms and picked up a pillow from the floor. Shoving his face into the soft, decadent fabric, he screamed into it until he got himself under control. At least a little more than he was moments ago.

He needed his wits to battle with the sorceress he'd foolishly let underneath his own roof.

In the time it took her to arrive, he'd made sure everything in the room was in place. Everything from the thick cushions near the fireplace, the plush carpets covering the floor, to the desk in the corner where he sometimes worked late into the night. He closed the door into his bedroom. No need for her to see that just yet, and then he lounged on the cushions before he heard the tell tale clacks of her shoes.

Those damned heels would be the death of him. Just the sound of them made him want to know what it would feel like if she put them on his throat. The gentle pressure, the knowledge that all it would take was one twist... He hissed out a low breath.

No. He was not going into this fight already wanting her. He refused.

The door opened and a lilting voice from the other side called out, "My lord. The lady Selene."

Lady. As if she was worth the status of that title.

"Enter."

If he made sure that his body was laid out a little more comfortably, that was only to ease his muscles before they tensed. Not because he wanted her to see him from his best angle.

She walked through the door like a fucking nightmare. Those heavy woolen skirts that must be too hot, even for this late in autumn. The wide square neckline that both covered everything and somehow made her throat all the more exposed. She wore long gloves that even covered her fingers. Even her hair was severely smoothed back from her head and twisted into that awful bun.

She glanced around his room, unaffected by the splendor, and instead focused her attention on him.

A flash of something burned in her eyes. Not quite lust, but the start of a similar emotion, until it fizzled as though she'd snuffed out a candle with her fingers. Curious, but exactly the battle he was looking for.

"What do you need?" she asked.

"You."

She visibly flinched, but stood her ground as he rolled onto his feet. Lust prowled toward her, knowing the firelight glinted off the skin revealed by his unbuttoned white shirt. He had made certain he was a temptation.

Why was she so easily able to brush him aside? It was maddening.

"Your mother has already made problems for us," he snarled.

"Oh?"

"She's told the entire kingdom that I have taken a bride."

"That was the deal." She folded her hands primly at her waist. "Unless you wish to make a liar of yourself."

"You seem to think I always lie." Lust stalked around her, attacking the pins in her hair. "Now, you are going to help me."

"My loyalty is to the Tower."

"If you are to be my bride," he leaned down and dragged his nose up the side of her neck, inhaling deeply. "Then you are loyal only to me."

She couldn't hide her little shiver or the creaking sound of her gloves as she curled her fingers into fists. "And how am I going to do that?"

"Strip."

Her breath caught in her throat. He'd managed to startle her, at least.

She growled, "What did you say?"

Oh, but he could get used to that sound. The surprise in her voice mixed with a heady combination of indignation and a slight tinge of fear.

"I already told you," he whispered against her skin. "I am not a monster. I will not force you to do anything you do not desire. But your mother has made a problem for the both of us. We need to remedy this by allowing some of my people to see you, but not the entirety of them."

"I fail to see how I need to be nude for this."

He hummed low under his breath. With quick fingers, he plucked the last of her pins and then gathered up the heavy length of her locks. "You have very long hair for a sorceress. I have seen few of your kind who keep their hair as long as yours."

He knew that a change in subject threw her off her guard. Lust twisted the strands into a long braid, waiting for her answer. She'd soon find he could wait for a very long time.

Finally, she snarled, "I've always kept my hair long. It's a personal choice."

"I like it." Finishing the braid that nearly reached her hips, he wrapped it around his fist twice before tugging her head back. Hard. "But your clothing choice offends me, little moon. If you do not remove them, I will."

She hissed at him like a cat. Teeth bared and eyes flashing, he almost took the warning for what it was. A threat.

Instead, he scooped his hand underneath her chin, tilting her head back even more with the rope he'd made of her hair. "Your choice, Selene."

The defiance in her eyes threatened that she would never let him forget this. Good. He didn't want to. Just seeing the long line of her throat bared to him made him hard as a rock while a growl vibrated through his throat.

He released her before he became even more of a liar. He'd never forced a woman before, and he never would. No matter how tempting she was, or how the hate in her eyes made him burn.

Lust strode away from her, heading to his bedroom, where he knew a dress waited. Not for her. For anyone, really. But he suddenly didn't want to see anyone else wear it ever again.

The sound of heavy fabric hitting the floor filled his ears. A heavy throb between his legs was the only answer to that sound, and for fuck's sake, he already needed to scream into another pillow.

He needed to call one of his favorites over tonight, he decided. He couldn't suffer with this pent up feeling any longer.

Snatching the gown out of the closet, he stalked back into the room like a man going to war. He'd battle with her again. Lust had no question about that. She wanted to claw his eyes out, and he wanted to throw her onto his bed and... and...

His mouth went dry.

She stood in the middle of his living quarters in nothing but small scraps of cloth. All that smooth, pale skin that had never once seen the light of day. He loved freckles, loved kissing them, and finding their secret hiding places, but this woman... By all the seven kingdoms, she looked like a marble carving come to life.

Selene glared at him, ever defiant, with her hands at her sides so he could see every inch of her. His eyes trailed up her long—fucking long—legs to the pale stomach with a single dark mark next to her belly button. She was lean but soft, every bit as strange as her personality. Graceful arms, full breasts hidden with a strange binding that wrapped all the way around her. But so pretty they made his mouth water.

A chuff of breath escaped him before he remembered what he was doing.

Gruffly, he rasped, "Come here."

"Why?"

He held up the dress in his hands. Like an idiot who couldn't talk at the sight of her, but he... Shit.

She lifted a brow. "What am I supposed to do with that? It's just a hunk of fabric and rope."

Right. She didn't get out of that Tower much, and he could guess she hadn't seen what most of the higher born people in his kingdom wore. He needed to pull himself together. She was just another woman, like all the others he'd seen before.

Lust approached her, gesturing for her to turn her back to him. And that was a stupid choice.

He stared down at the round curves of her ass, the tiny hollow in her back where twin dimples waited for his tongue. His hands flexed at his side and he had to close his eyes for a few heartbeats. Steeling himself for a battle that shouldn't be so fucking hard.

Rope first. Lust reached underneath her arms, winding the rope around her waist, her ribs, then up and over her shoulders. Intricate knots went between her breasts, pressing that binding closer to her skin because he damned well wasn't taking it off. Not when this much of her skin made him a drooling idiot.

He needed to fuck someone else. That would help. It had to.

Neither of them spoke for a while as he tied her up. It was just clothing, he kept telling himself. He wasn't making these intricate knots, so she was easier to grab, or to tie her up to his bed, or the hooks in the wall. She was innocent. She was a woman who couldn't handle all the things he wanted to do. All the things he'd started doing because everything else bored him.

He could control himself. He was a thousand years old! No one made him feel like this anymore, and this was merely confusion because he couldn't feel her lusting for him as well.

Lust bent down to grab the fabric from the floor and gently glided his hand along the outside of her thigh. A sharp intake of breath made him pause, reaching out for the lust he would surely find, but… nothing.

The red fabric dripped off his hands like blood. It turned from black to crimson, the ombre meticulously dyed by the finest of artisans. This he secured to the ties around her neck, covering her breasts with pleated layers that criss-crossed over her chest and then bound at her back. Another two strips of fabric hung from the knots just underneath her ribs, and then at her waist. It left a small diamond shape of skin and rope just beneath her breasts, while her sides remained completely bare.

Because he knew she wouldn't want that much skin showing, he gave her another layer around her waist so she had somewhat of a skirt. And then finally, he attached two gossamer pieces of crimson fabric to her wrists with heavy golden bangles, threading the fabric through the ties at her back so they wouldn't drag on the floor.

Tugging pieces of hair free around her face, he left the rest in the heavy braid.

"There," he said, palming her hip with a too familiar hand and dragging her shoulder blades to his chest. "I've always found dressing someone to be far more intimate than undressing them."

"I don't want any intimacy between us."

"That's a shame." He pressed a kiss to her bare shoulder, then sank his teeth into the flesh at her neck. Hard enough to leave a mark, but not break skin.

She froze underneath him, hissing out a long breath again. And for a moment, he swore he felt something. Not a wave of lust like she should have felt, but... something. No taste on his tongue. No scent in the air. But it was a start.

Lust laved his tongue over the red mark on her lovely swan-like throat. "You're to be my bride, little moon. Your mother made sure of that. Intimacy will only grow between us. From now until our wedding."

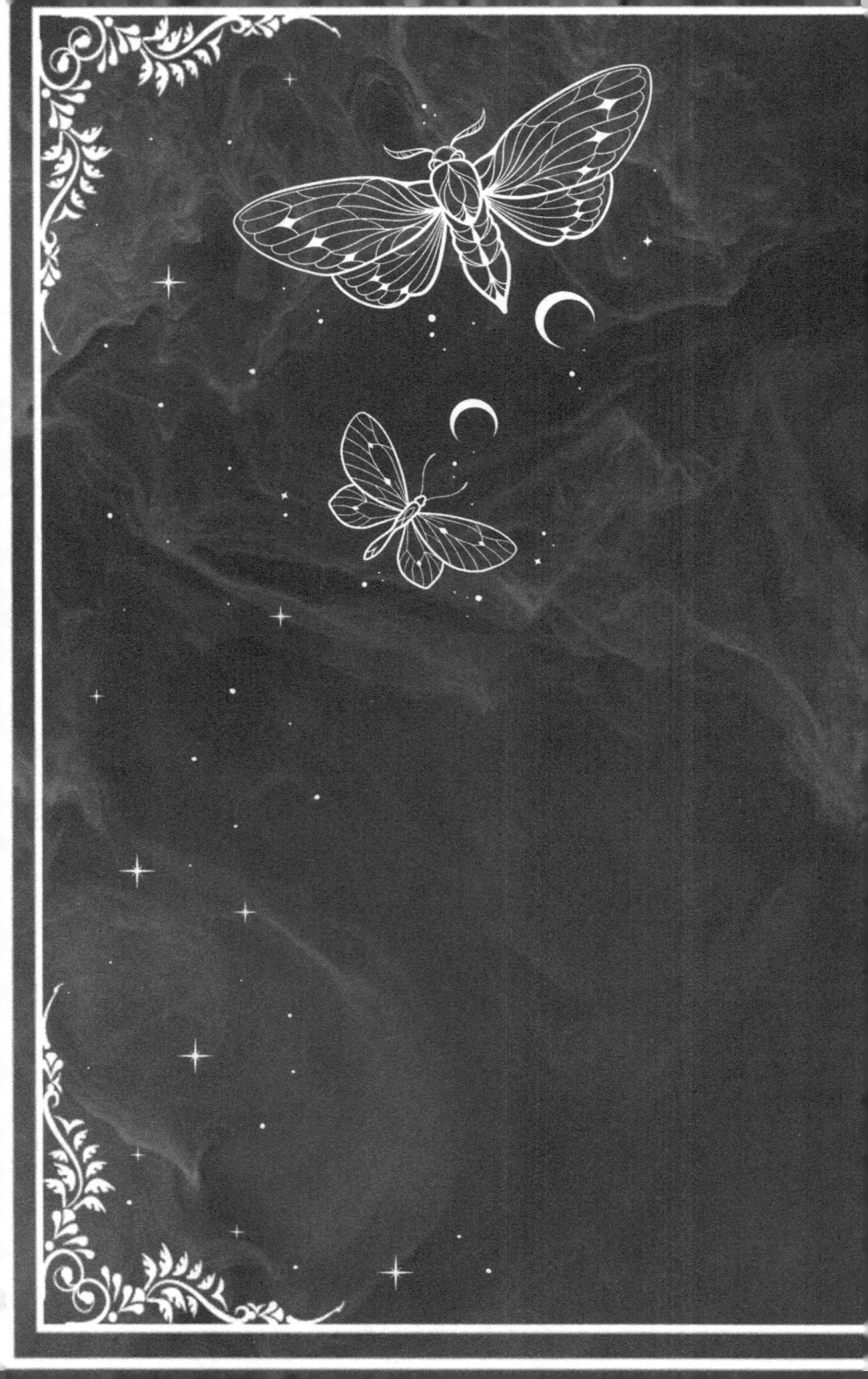

Chapter 9

She'd known the moment the magic protecting her emotions had cracked. But how was she supposed to not react when he'd bitten her neck? Selene hadn't realized such an action would send tendrils of desire rushing through her body.

The warmth of his hand had sunk through her skin. She'd wanted him to touch more of her. She'd wanted him to drag his hand up her thigh, move it around her hip, and delve it into the place that desperately needed to be touched.

He'd find her wet if he did so. He'd realize how much she wanted him, even though he couldn't feel it. Her body couldn't lie, regardless of the feelings she'd buried so deep.

Already, in just a few days, she needed to release the pressure that built up. If she didn't, then the entirety of the prison she'd built for her emotions would overflow. He'd feel it. All of it.

And yet, there was nowhere safe for her to do so. He'd put her room too close to his. She'd have to wait for him to go down to the great hall, or even better, out of the castle.

Oh, she was so screwed. He'd send her packing back to the Tower once he knew she didn't actually have any special abilities to avoid his advances. But he hadn't even been using his power on her when she was in his bedroom. And he'd seemed unaffected other than the slight surprise that she'd stripped without arguing.

Then he'd dressed her and...

A low moan escaped her lips before she could catch it. The demon had been right. Dressing her was somehow more intimate than undressing. She'd felt more bare in this dress than she had in her woolen skirts.

Although she was much cooler. Her flushed skin at least could thank him for that.

Sighing, she glanced at her bedroom door again. He'd said he would invite everyone who was anyone to the castle for the evening. Of course, she'd thought it was impossible to plan a party this late, but he had insisted it was the easiest way to do it. And from the sounds in front of the castle, everyone had arrived, even after such a late invitation.

Lust had claimed it was up to her, whether she wanted to meet his people or not. She'd prefer not. The nobility in this kingdom were less nobles in the common sense and more the favored beautiful ones who surrounded Lust. They did nothing. They had no responsibilities or jobs; they were just pretty, so they were well kept.

Selene understood why so many people in the towns stayed in their homes. Moving between kingdoms was costly. They had to remain or lose their life savings. But these nobles? They chose to be here.

She'd rather have nothing to do with them if they wanted to be around Lust more than they were forced to be around him.

"Are you not going?" a soft voice whispered from the doorway.

But... no one was there.

Tilting her head to the side, Selene tried to see through the veil of magic as her sisters had taught her. No magic obscured someone in the doorway, nor had the door opened. Instead, all she saw was a faint mist that pooled underneath the gap between the door and the floor.

"Hello?" she asked hesitantly.

"Sorry. I didn't mean to interrupt your thoughts, but there's a whole party downstairs dedicated to you." The mist seemed to congeal on the floor, gathering up into what looked like a blob of... fog. Kind of.

Selene had no idea what she was looking at. "What are you?"

"A spirit."

"Like a ghost?"

"Oh no, entirely different from that." The mass of mist or smoke gathered itself up a little more and then two eyes blinked open from the center. Not physical eyes. Selene didn't think she'd be able to touch them, and she could see straight through them. But they were there. "Is that better?"

"Not particularly." Selene slid off the chair in front of her vanity and sat down on the floor so she could get a better look at the creature. "You said you were a spirit?"

It bobbed up and down. "I am."

"But not a mortal spirit."

"No." She swore there was confusion on its face before it pooled closer to her and whispered, "I'm a spirit of affection."

Confused even more, Selene asked, "What is that?"

"What is that, she asks!" The little spirit bobbed again. Apparently the movement was one of anger. Or perhaps disbelief. "She's a sorceress, and she knows nothing about spirits. What are you doing here, then?"

"I... don't really know." Was she supposed to learn about spirits? Selene had heard of them before. Ghosts that lingered after someone's death. But this clearly wasn't what she'd come to think of in relation to hauntings.

The mist rolled closer to her and then an icy touch pressed against her hand. "Oh," it squeaked. "You have quite a lot of affection in you."

Selene furrowed her brows, too stunned to speak for a few moments. "How do you know that?"

"I can feel it." The spirit patted her hand with a tendril that felt a little more solid than a few moments ago. "Spirits are all around us, all the time. Some of us want to take more physical forms, most never even think beyond their own emotion. But I am a spirit of affection and I can only feel that."

This was so confusing.

"Are you saying you're a spirit of an emotion?" she asked.

"There are many of us, yes." It bobbed again in front of her, although this time it looked a little more like a nod than anger. "You've never met one of us before?"

"No."

It giggled. "Yes you have!"

She definitely hadn't. Selene didn't think there were any creatures like this in the Tower, and she'd never come across one in person. She'd have remembered smoke talking to her like a person.

"What are you doing here?" she asked, then gestured around them. "This isn't a place for spirits of affection. I imagine there's very little of that in the castle."

Although her words may have stung, the little spirit only sighed. "I know. It's so hard to live here sometimes when people are so fleeting. But I do so feel that it's the place to be. Does that make sense?"

Not at all. But Selene didn't want to hurt the little one's feelings anymore. For some reason, she was rather fond of this spirit already. It was an innocent beacon of light in an otherwise dark place.

She turned her hand palm up. "You were worried that I wasn't going to the party?"

"Well, it was prepared for you." The spirit coiled up in her palm, anchoring itself with tendrils that wrapped around her wrist, and sighed. "Oh, so much affection. Who is Ursula?"

She stiffened. "Can you read my memories?"

"A little."

"Please don't."

It hummed, paused, and then said, "Too late. She's quite lovely."

And just like that, tears burned in Selene's eyes. She hadn't wanted to get homesick this early. But being away from her family already toyed with her emotions. "She is."

"I didn't mean to make you sad!" The little spirit patted her arm restlessly, looking around the room for something to help. "Make it come back, please. Don't let you missing her make the affection go away. It's not nice anymore."

Sighing, Selene shook her head. "It's hard to not let those emotions get out of control. Why don't we go see what is happening in that party and that will help distract me?"

"It will!" The spirit bobbed up and down in her hand as Selene got to her feet and left her bedroom.

She hadn't explored the castle much. She'd been terrified and shut up in her room, away from everyone. Though she told herself it was to hide herself away for a better plan, Selene knew she was just hiding. It was so different here. So vibrant. All those colors almost hurt her eyes.

And then she was meant to gather information, but from who? From where? She glanced down at the mist pooled in her palm and wondered if she was heartless enough to use this little being. Surely the creature knew the secrets of this castle and its king. More than anyone else, perhaps.

The spirit was all too happy to play her guide, and it directed her through the halls with ease. Selene's gut twisted as she asked questions, knowing that the spirit couldn't guess her deception.

"How long have you lived here?" she asked as they turned yet another corner in the labyrinth of this place.

"Something like six hundred years."

Selene paused in her walk and then blinked. "Six hundred?"

"I'm very young for a spirit to have even this corporeal form." It bobbed again, almost as though agreeing with her shock. "Some spirits just get lucky. Like myself."

"Six hundred years old," she repeated and then shook her head. "How marvelous. And what do you like to be called?"

"Affection."

"Yes, I know that's what you're the spirit of, but what is your name?"

"Affection. It is my name and the emotion that I came from."

A thought bubbled into her mind and she flinched. She didn't want to ask it, but the words were already out of her mouth before she could control them. "Then is Lust…"

"Similar to me, yes. He was once just like me, in fact." Affection sighed happily. "Someday, I wish to take a mortal form like him. I think feeling affection in that form would be much stronger. Is it?"

"I don't know how you experience it through me," she murmured, although her mind was already whirling with the implications of what the spirit had said.

Were the sorceresses wrong? She'd grown up knowing that the kings of all seven kingdoms were demons who must be purged from the land. But if they were spirits of emotions, then... Did that complicate things?

She wasn't all that certain. If her sisters were aware that these were actually spirits, who seemed rather harmless now that she held one in her hand, would they want to fight against Lust so viciously?

Oh, her thoughts were all tied up in knots and she didn't know what to do. Perhaps that was why, when she stepped back into the great hall, she didn't notice as much as she should.

Instead, her breath caught as she looked up at the ceiling. They'd opened the glass ceiling to let the night pour in. The stars glittered above her and the clouds had gathered low. Some even slipped through the glass to hover above their heads in fine, glittering mist. Even the stars had pulled from their places in the sky to gently rain down upon her. Glittering faerie lights danced the moment her eyes lit upon them.

The torch light, which should have been warm and cheery instead, had taken on a bluish hue. It turned the entire world into something like midnight come to life. The sway of the pale curtains turned into the quiet sound of snowdrifts on a winter's night. The carved people who held up the second floor had been draped in midnight blue velvet that pooled on the floor in icy heaps.

A few other lights glowed in the depths of the pools, though they were warm. The golden glow bounced and flickered off the scales of the fish that swept past them. Gilded and lovely, drawing her toward the pool like a moth to the flame.

The music in the air was quiet. The faintest strum of a guitar and a violin that sang along with it. Quiet, lovely, so peaceful she didn't quite know what to do with herself.

Until she saw the bodies.

Countless people, all wrapped up in each other. Some of them were draped over the pillows, the red velvet exchanged for blue. Some of them were pressed up against the columns, skirts around their waists, and men already well underneath them.

A couple closest to her were halfway through their first act of sex. The woman's breast was bared, and the man slowly dragged his tongue across her pebbled nipple. The woman's moan cut through the relaxing sound of the violin.

"Oh no," Affection whispered. "You don't like this."

"Not at all."

"But this is... this is the castle. Is this not normal?" The little spirit grew agitated, obviously growing more upset the more uncomfortable Selene became. "We should go back. We shouldn't be here."

"No, we shouldn't." But she was no fainting princess. She wanted to make her displeasure known.

Picking her way through the bodies, she stepped over countless people locked in embraces. The closer to the throne, the more debauchery was revealed. Multiple partners, multiple people all plunging into whatever warm, welcoming hole was available. So many people that they were all tangled up together into one mass of limbs, so threaded that she'd never guess how many were there.

The sounds of their pleasure made her cheeks flame, but she refused to back down. Not when she knew this was his plan all along.

And there, sitting on his throne as if this were the most normal thing in the world, was their absurd king.

Lust had forgone his usual corset. Instead, a pale shirt was split wide over his muscular chest. Tight velvet pants hugged his thighs and did little to hide how affected he was by the display before him. But he cushioned his head on a fist and the expression he wore was decidedly bored.

That is until he saw her. She knew the moment their eyes made contact how her presence affected him.

His nostrils flared. His pupils dilated. He even sat up straighter in his throne, leaning forward as if to come to her, only to settle against the back once more. A young woman rounded the throne with a tray of wine and two stemmed glasses. She poured the red liquid into a glass, ignoring Selene, who was the only person standing in the entire room.

"So you came after all," he said, his voice ringing through the atrium. "I thought you'd hide away in your room all night."

She lifted the hand that held Affection, even though the little spirit tried to hide from his gaze. "I made a new friend."

His eyes narrowed on the spirit. "You have other duties tonight."

Selene watched as the young woman sat down beside Lust's leg and dragged her hand up it. Dangerously close to what should have only been Selene's if they were actually going to be married. She knew what the other woman was trying to do. And she didn't care.

"I have no duties here," she replied, her voice like the lash of a whip in this otherwise splendorous room. "You've made that very clear."

His eyes flashed with anger. "Have I?"

"I will take no part in this."

"This is how we celebrate in the castle, little moon. If you want to be their queen, you will do well to remember it."

Affection was trembling so badly in her hand that it had lost all shape. It kept slipping between her fingers, trying to pool onto the floor and sneak away. But Selene just gathered it back up like a strange slime and held it in her arms. "I am not from this castle, nor do I have any wish to linger in this kingdom. You took me from my family. You made me come here even though you know I wished to remain in the icy north, within the safe walls of my Tower. And now you think I should endure what happens here? No. I think not."

He planted his hands on the arms of his throne, then froze when her voice snapped out again.

"Don't get up." Selene curled her lip in disgust. "I have no desire for your presence."

And with that still echoing throughout the hall, she turned and made her way back to the door that would lead to her quarters. She held her head up high, a foreigner in this strange world where people performed public acts that should remain private. She wore a gown that wasn't hers. She was engaged to a man who would never truly desire or love her.

She didn't let a single tear drip down her cheek for even a moment. No one would walk away from that party saying that the would be queen of Lust's kingdom was weak.

But she heard their words before she closed the door. Strange. Odd. Unnatural.

It was the last word that broke through the layers of her armor. That frigid lake inside her crackled, popped, and then released a deluge of emotions that flooded out the moment she reached her bedroom.

She'd thought what would come out would be a massive amount of lust, desire, and sexual frustration. But instead, it was only loneliness. A bitter, bone deep loneliness that made her skin feel icy cold and her heart brittle.

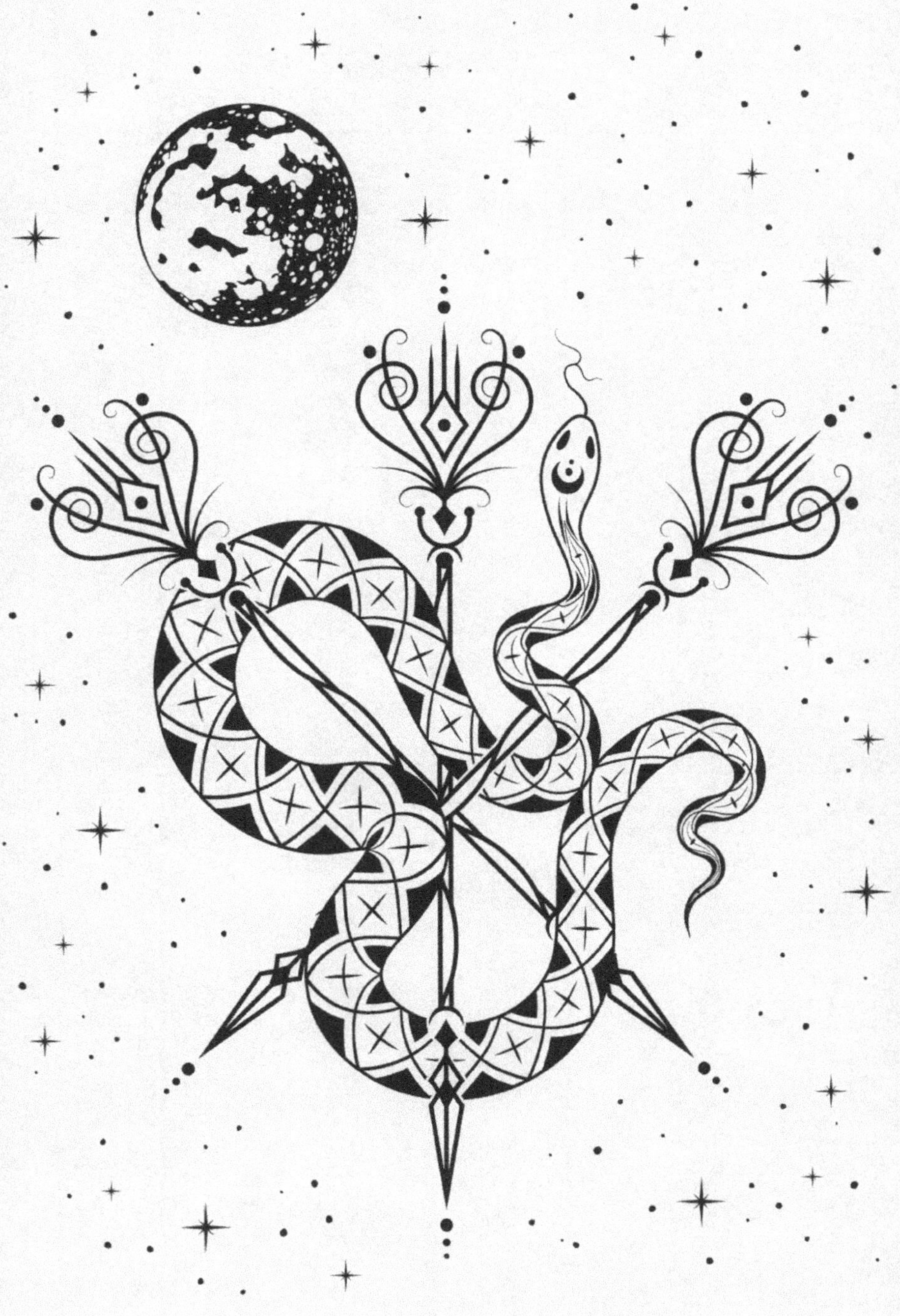

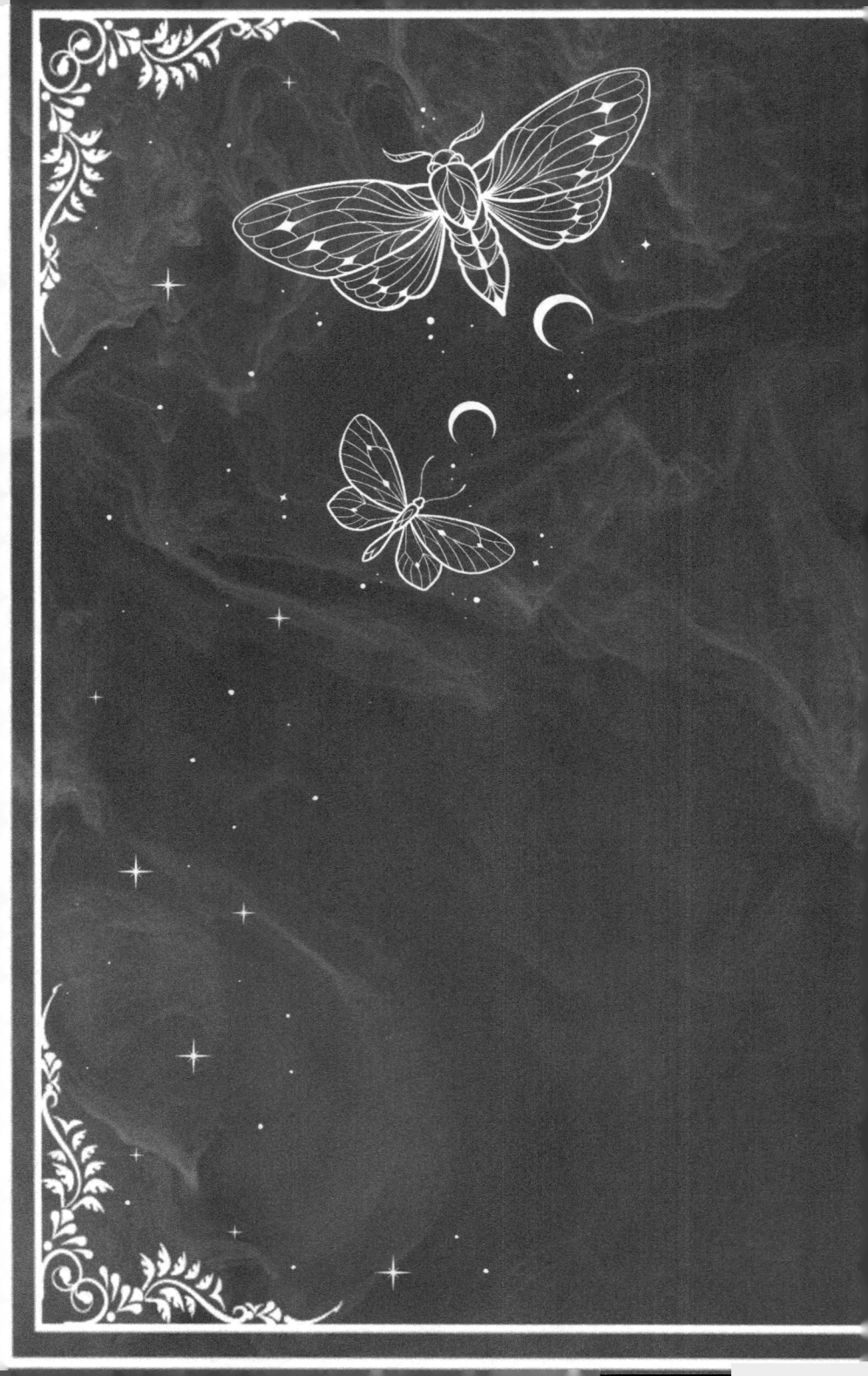

Chapter 10

He'd known this would shock her. In fact, Lust would admit he'd been counting on it.

His people enjoyed the way he ruled them. No matter what the sorceresses said, there were plenty of people in this kingdom who were grateful for his rule. Even enjoyed it. The nobles certainly did, and he knew for a fact that no one in the room was complaining right now.

Lust gave them a time and a place to indulge in their senses. They didn't have to feel guilty about their desires for each other or in a single night of indulgence. They could do what they wanted and he wouldn't judge them for it.

But Selene?

She walked into the room with her nose held high, disgust on her features as she walked past people who had been performing these acts since before she was born. Past high born nobility who had come here in safety, knowing they could do whatever they wanted.

And she'd judged them. Harshly.

He found that infuriating. His people were here because they knew they were safe and cared for. She'd taken that thought and dashed it onto the ground.

Rage already bubbling in his chest, he'd watched her look down her nose at him and then dismiss him. In his own house. In his own court! She'd made it very clear to all the nobility in the room that she didn't want to be his bride, that he'd taken her by force, and that he'd gone against his own rules. No one was here without wanting to be. No one was forced to partake in any action without desiring to participate.

She'd made a liar out of him in all but a few moments before she walked out with her head held high. Like the hero she clearly thought herself to be.

He wasn't proud of the anger that coursed through his veins. It made him sick to think he'd thought about hurting her for even a moment. He had, though. The thought ran through his mind of turning her over his knees and spanking her until tears ran down her cheeks.

But then the woman at his feet rubbed her hand over his thigh. "It's all right, my lord. She's new. She'll... learn."

The hesitancy in her voice made him pause. Lara had been with him for years now. A faithful servant, a lively bed partner, a kind woman who had a child somewhere, maybe working in his kitchens. Not his, but well cared for now that she was in his employment.

Who was Selene to cast her doubts upon a woman like this?

Gently threading his fingers through her hair, a dastardly plan bloomed in his mind. One he'd never have entertained if he wasn't so embarrassed and angry.

"Will you help me with something?" he asked, his voice gentle. "You do not need to if you have other plans."

"My nights are yours."

As they always had been.

He patted the top of her head, then stood and helped her up. "My new bride has proven... difficult."

"I saw." Lara furrowed her brow and glanced toward the door. "Almost as if she was unaffected."

"That is what she would like me to believe. But I have to admit, I wonder if it is because she's not interested in men." He scraped a hand down his jaw. "There was a time when you—"

She lifted a hand to interrupt him and gave him a soft smile. "It would be my honor to bring pleasure to the woman who will be our queen. You needn't ask twice, Lust."

Oh, but he should. He had a feeling his bride to be, as they were calling her, would fight against them with every step. But he had to be certain. He had to know this one last detail to see if she had been sent to him as a test. He would waste no more time trying to seduce her if she was only interested in women.

Perhaps it would be easier that way. At least then his pride might not sting so badly, and that was his brother's domain.

"Come," he ordered.

Together, they walked through the tangles of people who tried to salvage the night. Ruined. All of it was ruined because of the careless nature of a prude.

Shaking his head, he pulled his shirt off as they went. Something had to tempt her. She'd claimed to be able to feel lust, but that she didn't feel it for him. Time to put that to the test.

Selene gasped as he shouldered her door open without knocking.

She stood in front of her vanity, staring down at the knots he'd tied around her torso as though they were an enemy she had to battle. Two of the skirts he'd wrapped around her waist were already on the floor in a ruined tangle.

His tongue stuck to the roof of his mouth at the sight of her long, pale legs. Strong legs. Legs that would wrap around his waist in a vise grip, and thick thigh muscles that he'd kill to feel clenched around his skull.

Blowing out through his nose, he gestured for Lara to help. "Your mistress has never worn clothes like this. Perhaps you wouldn't mind assisting her."

Selene's eyes widened. "I don't need help."

Not to be deterred, Lara laughed. "Even I need help to get out of those. Lust ties knots like he wants them to stay on for weeks. Let me help."

Jaw clenched, Lust reclined in one of the chairs beside her fireplace. He avoided the bed, knowing just where his mind would go if he watched his mistress undress this wicked sorceress before him. Those thoughts needed to stay dormant. He wanted to watch. He wanted to see the emotions in her eyes, to know if she reacted to the touch of a practiced woman.

She didn't. Selene stood frigid as a pillar of ice as Lara ran her hands over her. His servant was quick, but he noticed the lingering touches she placed all along Selene's body. Light touches, meant to tease and tantalize as only women knew in the seduction of each other. Hidden areas that could only be teased with a feather light graze.

Nothing.

Not a single reaction. Just a stoic discomfort as Lara tried her best to rouse his bride from the dead.

And when she stood in her underclothes and knotted rope, he saw the first bit of emotion flicker in her eyes. Fear. Not the emotion he thought he'd see in her eyes with the touch of another woman running over her.

Anger burned through him. Suddenly he wanted to take Lara's hands off for ever making Selene uncomfortable. He wanted to hand them as a gift to the sorceress, proof that he'd never do this to her again. But then he remembered that he wasn't her savior. He was the demon king who had kidnapped her from her home.

Just what did she think would happen here? He would not make her fuck his servant, she was just supposed to enjoy it.

For fuck's sake, could she enjoy nothing? Maybe the woman really was dead.

"Get out," he muttered.

Both women looked at him, and he could see the confusion on both of their faces.

"My lord," Lara murmured, ducking her head. "Would you like me to finish untying her for you?"

The poor thing thought he was displeased with her. This whole night had royally fucked everything up.

He pinched the bridge of his nose as though that might hold back the horrible migraine that pulsed between his eyes. "No. I have no need for you to finish. I can take care of the knots myself."

"But I thought you wished for me to—"

"Enough, Lara." His voice boomed a little too loud, a little too frustrated.

Her eyes widened again before she ducked her head and stepped away from Selene. It didn't escape his notice that the sorceress's shoulders curved in on herself, as though he'd forced her to endure something horrific.

He waited until Lara closed the door behind herself before he spoke. "Go on, then."

She looked up at him, silent as ever.

"You want to yell at me, I can tell." He waved an imperious hand, giving her permission to start. But she didn't. She only stood there in her underthings and that damned rope, her hands flexing at her sides. "You'll never get me to believe for a second that's all you had to say in the throne room. Clearly you wish to argue with me, so spit it out."

Selene took a deep breath until her ribs showed through her skin in deep hollows. "I would appreciate not being touched by another stranger. At least for a few more days."

The pang of answering guilt in his chest had him hissing out a breath. He had no right to do what he'd done. Every day with her in his castle made him step further and further toward the monster she thought him to be. And he hated it.

Standing, he approached her with his hands up in peace. "If I had thought you wouldn't enjoy it, then I never would have invited her."

Lust expected a flash of anger. For that glare he was becoming rather fond of to slash at his face. Instead, she stood silent. Selene stared off into the distance as if she wasn't even in the room with him.

He gave her that time to think. She'd earned it. Instead, he moved around behind her and started working on the knots. But that silence quickly turned into a tension that he couldn't stand as he let the rope slide from her body and hit the floor.

One last time to provoke her, that was what he told himself. Then he'd leave her alone.

Lust whispered in her ear, guttural and deep, "I didn't think it would be so easy to break you, sorceress."

the demon court

There it was. The stiffening of her spine and the hatred that swallowed her up. She glared at him as though he was the scum of the earth and damned if it didn't harden his cock.

"I am not broken," she hissed. "You took my body, fair and square. My mother gave me to you and I am loyal to my family. I will do what I must. None of that requires me to give you my mind or my loyalty."

"Ah, but you will be loyal to me. You have no one else." He stroked the backs of his fingers against her velvet soft cheek, surprised to see she didn't lean away from him. "You are alone here, little moon. Soon you will come to me for comfort."

"Like I said in the throne room, I have no use for you." She turned her face from him and then he saw her retreat again.

He'd never seen someone do that before. Oh, he'd helped people after awful things had occurred. He'd brought them back into a realm of sexuality that was safe and comforting. But he'd never seen someone just... disappear.

There was always a hint of the human beneath the mortal flesh. A flavor of them always existed.

But she withdrew. No hint of who or what she was. No mortal in front of him at all, just a darkness and a blank cold that wriggled underneath his skin.

Oh, this wouldn't do. If this wasn't breaking his little sorceress, then it was something much more terrifying and he refused to watch her fall apart. Not because of him. Not when it made his stomach twist and his heart thunder in his chest. Like he'd lost someone important.

Dragging his knuckles underneath her chin, he forced her to look back at him. "What would it take?"

"For what?"

"For you to feel something, little moon. I don't want to see this husk of a woman in front of me. It hurts." He tilted his head to the side, eyes tracing over her lovely lips and those cold, dead eyes. "You are a vibrant woman. The warrior I met in the tavern had more emotion in her than she could keep still. It overflowed from you, did you know that? I was made to feel only lust from humans, but I could feel everything from you. Your anger at me for being in the tavern. Your pride at having bested me. The amusement you felt when you flicked the gold dust off my horns. All of it."

Her eyes had opened a little wider with each word he said, and he knew he had captured her attention. Even now, he could feel that fleeting flicker of interest.

But it wasn't quite enough to get her to look at him with that anger he so adored.

Leaning so close he could feel her breath on his lips, so close the barest movement would have shifted them into a kiss, he whispered, "Now where is that sorceress? She was far more tempting than this one."

"I don't want to tempt you," she replied.

"But you do all the same."

Those dark eyes saw too much. They sliced through his very soul as she peered into his gaze. Searching for something? She'd find no pity or remorse in his eyes, not when he knew he was doing the right thing.

Finally, he felt a long sigh brush against his mouth. "Trust."

"What does that have to do with anything?"

"If you want me to feel something, you must give me a reason to trust you."

"There are many who trust me, and I have never had to win their affections."

At the word, she arched a brow. "Clearly you are wrong. Lust has no need for deeper levels of trust. They have to know you won't hurt them, but so few people want to hurt others. A friendship, a relationship, that all grows from much deeper trust. Trust that grows like the ancient roots of a tree. Everything but lust requires a certain level of it, and you do not know how to make people trust you. Only to desire you for a few moments and then leave."

The words struck harder than he'd expected them to. He even took a few steps away from her, wincing as he rubbed his chest. They struck him like a knife between his ribs. And he didn't know why.

"Then I ask again," he growled. "What does it take?"

"To make me trust you?"

"Yes." Why did this matter? It didn't, but oh it did.

She shrugged, her limp arms dangling by her sides. "Well, this isn't going to help."

"Being comfortable with each other?"

"Being bare in front of a man I have no interest in. A man who has taken me from my home and forced me to see sights I am nowhere near comfortable with."

He waved a hand in the air. "Yes, I know. That was a mistake. The past cannot help me win you in the future."

"Is that what you're trying to do?" Her words hung between them, shocked and surprised.

He realized that was exactly what he was trying to do. He wanted to win her. And win her trust. "Yes," he replied after a few moments of hesitation. "I believe it is."

She looked at him, brows furrowed and teeth chewing at the inside of her lips. "Then... Then I suppose you have to understand that trust takes time. It takes effort."

"That does not explain how."

"Time. With me. Spend time with me, get to know me and who I am. Where I came from, know what my story is, or what my favorite color is and my favorite food." She shrugged. "Care that I exist rather than only look at my body for what it can give you."

All of that was confusing. Why would he waste that much time on a single person when so many of them needed him? He could go back to his room right now and dive straight into Lara's comforting body without having to worry about any of this work.

But his stomach twisted, and he found himself asking, "What is your favorite color?"

She stared at him, dumbstruck before stuttering, "B-blue. Ice blue."

Of course it was.

Snorting, he turned and walked out of her room. Leaving her and her confusing theories about trust behind.

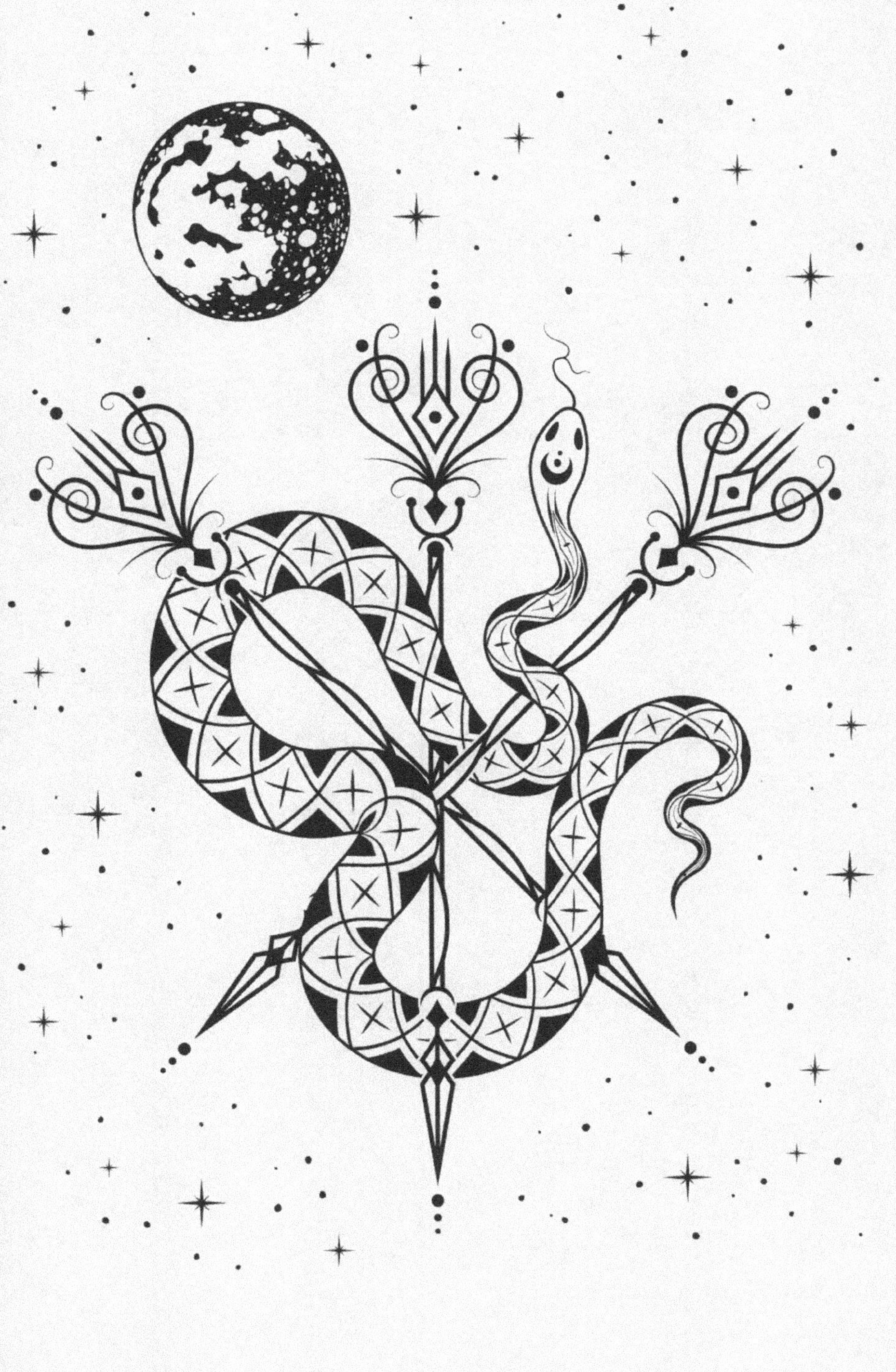

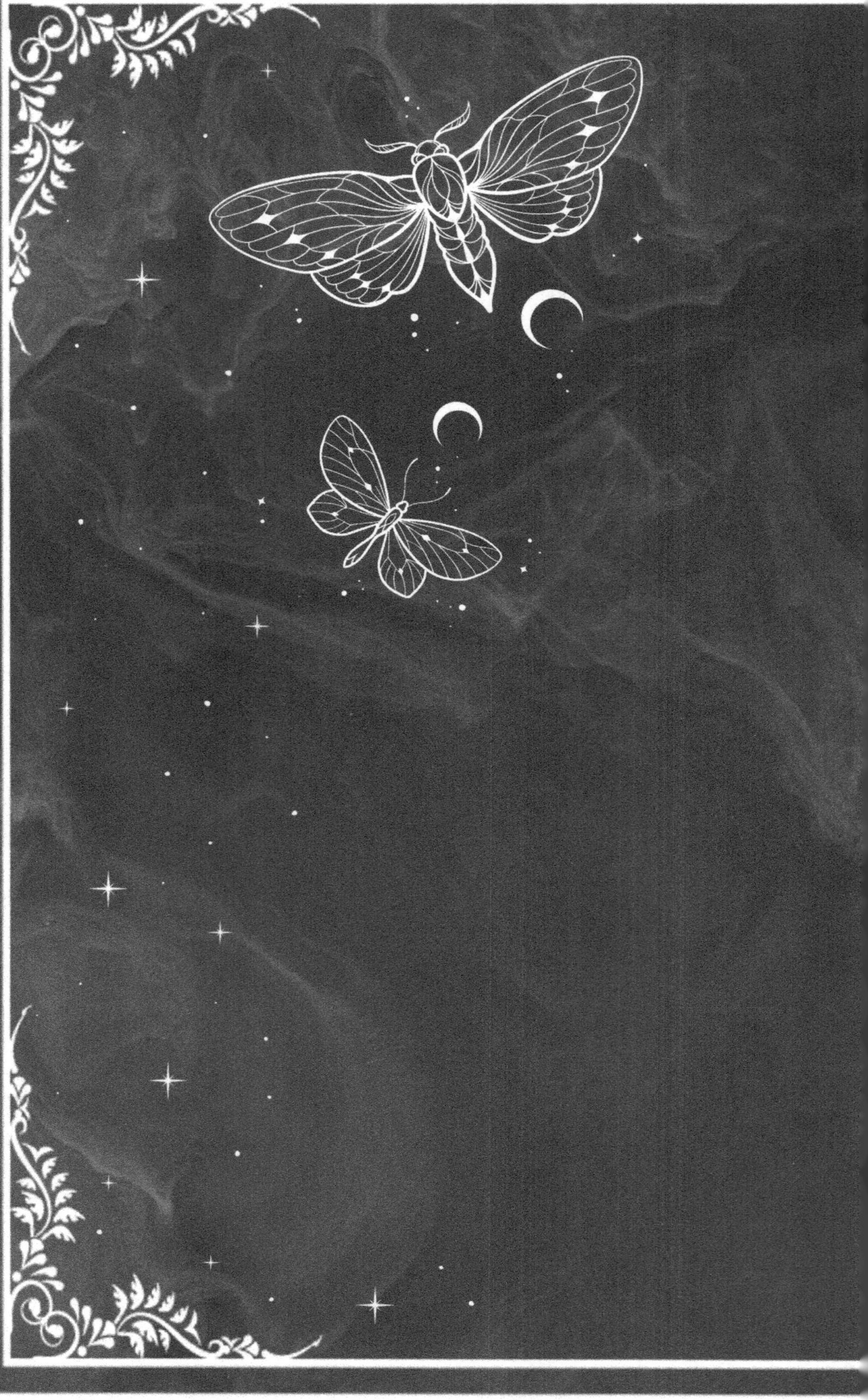

Chapter 11

Though she'd thought this place would be a bit more of a prison, Selene realized that no one cared if she moved about the castle. The sorceresses had led her to believe that this place would be terrifying. Full of dark corners, cobwebs, straps to hold women down so that men could have their way with them.

But that wasn't what Lust's castle was like at all.

In fact, most of it was wide open spaces and natural light. The amount of windows on every wall was worth enough to feed the entire kingdom for two years and there would still be some money left over for more windows.

She thought it was a frivolous expense when they could have just had the small slits in the wall like the Tower had. Sure, cold air got in during the winter, but...

Well. She'd admit it was pretty nice to be warm in the sun even when the winds were a little cold outside.

Maybe there were a few benefits to living in the castle. But she hadn't explored every corner yet, so there could still be some dungeons in the bottom that she'd missed.

After their conversation, Selene had poked around. The rumors about this place were ripe with decadent sins and monstrous delights. Only the most wicked would come to this castle and indulge in what Lust could offer them.

She'd gone right to the depths of the castle the day after their talk. Someone surely would stop her if they were hiding horrible secrets, and she was certain that someone would. The only thing she'd found were the kitchens, full of a ridiculous amount of servants all bustling about, preparing dinner for what looked like a massive amount of people.

They'd shooed her out of the larder, suggesting that if she was hungry, she should call her servants and they would get her whatever food she wanted. Everyone gave her a strange look, as though she was some poor country dear who didn't know how to wander about a castle.

She wanted to shout that they had servants in the Tower. She knew how to be a proper lady. What she was looking for had nothing to do with the food in the kitchen and everything to do with a trapdoor that led to the dungeons where poor women were tied up while men in masks looked on.

Except, try as she might, Selene couldn't find any trap door.

Every day went by where she looked for yet another lie that her family had told her. Or proof of the truth. Everything was so muddled up in her head and it was far too soon for that to be happening.

Her mother had warned her that Lust could turn her mind in a heartbeat. That she needed to be strong for the sorceresses, for her sisters, for her mother. The kingdom needed them to rule. That was why Selene was here.

Maybe she needed to go visit other towns. Her mother had been so adamant that the kingdom was suffering. Their purpose was just and true. Selene wouldn't have been sent out into a prospering kingdom simply because her mother wanted power.

She paused while brushing her hair, staring into her own reflection in the mirror. She had more conviction than this. A few weeks in a castle should not change her opinion of her own people.

A knock on the door interrupted her thoughts. She hadn't called for anyone to attend her, but these servants were incessant! She knew it was because Lust had allowed her mother's rumors of their upcoming marriage to spread. Why, she had no idea. Her dismissal of him had embarrassed the man in front of all his people.

If that hadn't gotten him to reconsider all this, she didn't know what else would.

At some point soon, she needed to find him. To apologize and simper and do all the things that her mother would tell her to do. After all, she'd been the idiot who had angered him when she was supposed to be getting him under her thumb. Or at least getting him to ignore her so she could snoop around for the truth.

He just made her so angry! Why did he seem to think it was acceptable to startle her rather than welcome her?

"Come in," she called out.

She watched in the mirror as the door slid open, but no one stood on the other side. Frowning, she twisted around and searched the floor for a misty substance. Affection had been visiting her often, although the poor thing had only gotten more weak lately. It refused to explain why it was having a hard time even rolling across the floor.

"Affection?" she asked.

She heard the faint sound of someone clearing their throat, but... What was going on?

Standing, she smoothed her hand down the dark bodice of her gown. The high neckline was stiff with gold embroidery, trailing down into long sleeves that almost covered her hands. The tight waistline accentuated the hourglass of her shape and draped in lovely, stiff pressed lines all the way to the floor. It was one of her favorite gowns, and she wore it only because Lust would hate it if he saw her.

Gathering up a handful of her hair, she twisted it over her shoulder as she sighed and walked toward the door. "I told you all, I have no need of assistance. Thank you for offering, but I'm perfectly capable of dressing myself."

She meant to slam the door shut and lock it. Curiosity, however, had other plans. She should stuff that emotion into the lake with the rest of them, but she still poked her head out and glanced to the left down the hall. Nothing. Of course not.

Yet again she heard someone clear their throat and she looked the other way. Lust leaned against the wall next to her bedroom door. He had his ankles crossed, broad shoulders leaning against her wall while he completely ignored her. He stared down at his fingernails, then splayed his hand wide.

"What are you doing here?" she asked.

"Hmm?" He looked over at her, pretending he had no idea she was there. "Oh, there you are."

She wanted to grind her teeth. Unfortunately, this meddlesome demon was a little too aware of everything around him, and he'd notice. Instead, she forced herself to smile. "I take it you were looking for me?"

He looked at her, and his eyes widened in shock. "Oh, that's a terrible expression. Stop doing that."

"What?"

Lust waved at her face. "Whatever you're doing with your face."

"I'm not doing anything odd. I'm just smiling at you."

"That's a smile?" He curled his lip. "Stop it. Right now."

"I'm not..." She sighed and let the fake smile drop. "Fine. What do you want?"

"We're going. You're dressed well enough." Though his eyes skating up and down her body clearly said otherwise. "I suppose you'll be... warm."

"Oh, please. You hate the dress, that's why I picked it." Selene crossed her arms over her chest. "Where are we going? I dislike surprises."

"Of course you do. You're no fun at all." He held his hand out for her to take. His fingers were long and stronger than she'd thought they would look. Lovely hands, really. "You were the one who said I needed to work on you trusting me. And now I am asking you to do just that."

"You have given me no reason to trust you."

"And I have given you no real reason not to, either." He waggled his fingers. "I promise not to shave your head, force you to remove your clothing, or otherwise startle you. Not today, at least."

"Somehow I doubt that."

Selene glared down at his hand. But the hand wasn't the problem. His sudden change in demeanor was. Why did it matter to him if she trusted him? He had a hundred, probably a thousand, other women who were happy to warm his bed.

He didn't need her at all. But right now, she'd caught his attention, and that was exactly what she was supposed to do.

So even though it made her skin crawl to touch him, she slid her hand into his and nodded. "Fine. But not for long."

"You have appointments, I take it?" He grinned and that damned expression made a shiver travel down her spine.

Not a bad shiver, either. Angry at herself, she snarled, "No, I just don't want to spend much time with you."

"Ah, the sorceresses sent me a snarling wolverine for a bride. And here I was thinking your mother sent you to me planning to seduce the demon king." He tucked his finger underneath her chin and forced her to look at him. "Is that what you're trying to do, little moon?"

"Seduce you?" she snorted. "That's the last thing I want."

Confusion rippled through those expressive eyes. "That's what I thought you'd say. How strange. Never you mind, though. I would like to spend time with you, and the idea of seducing you is rather abhorrent to me as well. Follow me, and I promise to keep my hands to myself. Unless you ask me to touch you."

"Not going to happen."

"Never say never, darling." He winked at her again, only to then drag her through the halls.

He said nothing after that, and Selene had to rush to keep up with his long legs, so she was rather quickly out of breath. They raced through the castle like someone was chasing them. She couldn't understand why, but it made the entire situation feel rather uninhibited.

No, that was wrong. He made it feel like they were breaking the rules, and her heart raced at the thought.

What was he doing to her?

She kept her mouth shut until they left the castle and approached the edge of the kingdom. She'd known that it existed near his castle, but she hadn't thought it was this close.

The edge of their home plummeted into the darkness. Into

nothing. She could feel that oppressive madness that lingered beneath. That feeling was the reason so few people ever got close to the edge. A part of their brain knew something existed deep in those shadows that wanted to devour them.

And Lust was continuing closer and closer.

She couldn't take it anymore. Selene tugged hard on his hand, and her fingers slipped through his grip. She immediately took five enormous steps away from the devouring darkness. "Are you going to throw me off the edge? Is that your idea of an afternoon well spent?"

He looked back at her. The smile that split his face didn't make her feel any better. "While I'll admit, throwing you off the edge would end my problems, that was not my plan for today."

"I have no interest in getting closer. I know what waits at the bottom."

"Do you?" He arched his brow. "I was under the impression only my brother knew the answer to that. So go on then. What do the sorceresses know is at the bottom?"

Her heart pounded in her throat, panic clawing its way up her throat. "Darkness. Madness. It has many names. But it is hungry, always hungry."

Lust almost looked disappointed. "Ah, so the same old rumors everyone else knows. I'll admit to being as curious as the next about what is actually down there. And Wrath is so tight lipped, he'd never tell me. He barely wants to share how his kingdom is doing, let alone the secrets of the realm."

It was the first time she'd heard him speak of his counterparts. She realized this was her moment. If she could keep him talking, then maybe he would reveal some innate weakness. All it would take was for her to poke at this moment and see just how much he'd reveal.

"Wrath?" she asked. "Is he your older brother?"

"Older?" Lust's chest puffed up at the question. "We're all the same age. You mortals are so obsessed with years, but after a thousand of them, they stop mattering so much. We came into our physical forms at the same time. Five seconds doesn't matter."

She bit her lip to stop her smile. "So you are younger than him."

"Five seconds," he snapped. "It's not enough to make him older than me."

Oh, she couldn't help herself. Selene tilted her head back and laughed. The idea was so ridiculous that he'd argue when it shouldn't matter at all. He and his brothers were hundreds of years old and they somehow still argued about who was older?

And when she stopped laughing, she saw he had the strangest look on his face. It had softened him. His eyes slightly crinkled at the corners, his lips parted, his gaze looking at her not with hunger but with something else entirely.

"What?" she asked, breathless from her laughter.

"It's just..." He shook his head. "Nothing."

"No, I want to know. You're giving me a very strange look, Lust. You were the one prattling on about gaining my trust. You can't then keep things secret."

She held her breath as he looked back at her. Why was this so important? It felt like she had to know the answer, even though there wasn't a proper reason for her to push him.

He shook his head and muttered, "You're rather pretty when you laugh. It took me off guard."

Now she was the one who was speechless. Who was supposed to be seducing who, here?

Selene licked her lips and then gave him a little nod. "Ah. I... Well."

He stared at her a few seconds longer before seeming to shake himself free from his thoughts. "Come. It's not much farther, but I did want you to see the edge."

"Why is that?" Selene would take any distraction at this point. She didn't want to think about why her palms had turned sweaty or why her face had reddened at the mention of how pretty she was. She wasn't, she knew that. He'd already made it very clear that he thought her plain.

Lingering on these thoughts wasn't good for either of them. She needed to keep herself separate from her emotions.

"I was researching how to trust people, and the book I read specifically mentioned that a good trust building exercise is doing something that both excites and frightens you." He held his arms out wide. "There is very little that I fear, and certainly less that both of us fear together. The edge seemed like the obvious choice."

"Ah, right. Obvious." Selene rolled her eyes, but then slowly walked over to the edge with him.

Someone had set up a small quilt blanket with a bottle of wine, two glasses, and a little wicker picnic basket.

"Lust," she said as they approached it. "I think we're interrupting someone. We should go."

"Indeed." Ignoring her words, he sauntered over to the quilt and lifted the bottle into the air. "It is a good vintage, though. Would you like a taste?"

"Not of someone else's wine," she hissed. "Put that down."

"It's already opened." Twisting the cork, he poured himself a glass and then lifted it up toward the sun. "And it's a rather lovely view. Wouldn't you agree?"

She took a split second to look at the view and realized, yes. It was.

Though the edge was right there and terrifying, there was also a lovely view of the other side of his kingdom. The island wasn't a perfect circle, and the warped perimeter meant she was looking right at a jagged wall of bright pink roses that grew haphazardly into oblivion. Even the air smelled of roses as a soft breeze toyed with the ends of her hair.

Oh, but it was lovely here. A perfect place for a secret meeting between two lovers sneaking away from their duties in the castle. The romance of it all wasn't lost on her, and she didn't want to ruin this moment for anyone.

"It's beautiful," she whispered. A strand of her dark hair blew in front of her face before she glanced back at him.

And there it was again. That expression was as though someone had struck him before he shook his head. "Good, I'm glad you like it. Now, would you enjoy a glass of wine, or should I pull out whatever the servants packed?"

"Are you saying..." She gestured at the picnic blanket. "Did you do all this?"

"Is it that surprising?"

"It is surprising. You hate me." Selene also pointed at the quilt. "And that looks handmade. You're more the type to drag out the best silks and velvet pillows, not caring how you ruin them in the dirt."

"Yes, well. The quilt, I'll admit, was Affection's choice. Not mine. It looks moth-eaten and drab. But Affection assured me that you would appreciate the effort." He looked away from her, out over the darkness toward the nearest kingdom that floated in the distance. "And I don't hate you, Selene. I don't think you're here for the right reasons. But your words made me realize that while you don't trust me, I don't trust you either. If we are going to be stuck with each other, then we should work on that."

"But why?" she asked again, the question burning in her chest with a need to understand. "Why does it matter to you?"

He opened his mouth, closed it, then rubbed one of his horns with his palm. "I haven't gotten that far into it, really. It's a gut feeling, that's all."

And she supposed that was good enough for her. Selene sank down on the quilt and gestured at the bottle. "Pour me a glass, then. What are you expecting from this afternoon?"

"Conversation."

"About?" She took the offered glass and tried to guess what he wanted to know.

"What's your favorite food?"

Why did he... She snapped her jaw shut and answered, "Cherries."

"Cherries," he muttered. "Of course you'd like a food difficult to find this time of year."

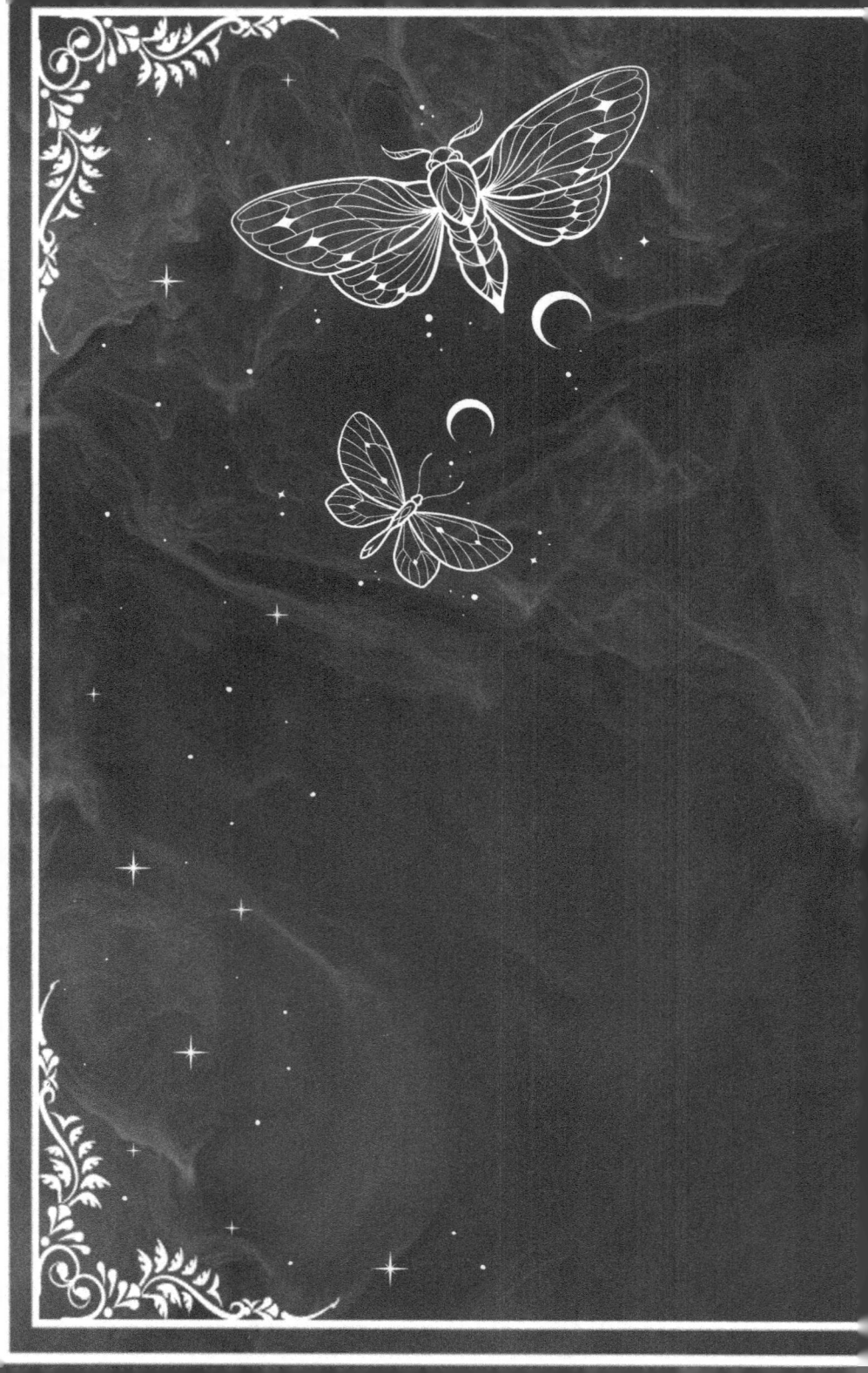

Chapter 12

Lust sat in his office, running a finger over his bottom lip as he mused on his afternoon with Selene. It had been a rather lovely afternoon, although not an ounce of it had been sexual in nature, which was frustrating to no end. Every time she'd sipped her wine, he had wanted to run his tongue down her throat. And every time she'd popped a grape into her mouth, he'd wanted to whisper how lucky it was to have her tongue upon it.

Of course, he didn't say any of those things. They were working on building trust with each other, and everything he'd read in his books stated that sexual advances were not helpful during this period of growth.

If anything, those philosophers had mused that sex did the opposite of build trust. Without trust, sex was more likely to drive a person away.

Which was ridiculous. He'd seen many people who were drawn

together by sex. So who were these philosophers to say a word about how damaging lust could be to a relationship?

The door to his office opened and Lara walked through with a plate of food. Apparently, they'd already reached lunchtime, and he'd wasted almost an entire day thinking about an afternoon that had happened a week ago now. A waste of time. But also he couldn't stop thinking about it.

Sighing, he looked over at Lara as she put his lunch out on the table. She worked efficiently, and never once interrupted him from his thoughts. She'd been with him long enough to know that there were times for her attention and other times for her to remain in the shadows.

Most days, he didn't even see her walk in. He was busy enough with his own work. The last thing he needed was for someone to break him out of his train of thought.

But right now, all he could think about were those damn books and how sex ruined trust.

Sighing, he pinched the bridge of his nose as she scurried away. "Lara."

She paused in front of the door. "Is there anything else you need, my lord?"

The faint sound of hope in her voice used to annoy him. Now, it just made him feel a little guilty, and he couldn't understand why. "Yes, I have a question for you."

She folded her hands at her waist and waited for his question. Lust took his time planning what he wanted to say. Instead, he looked over the curves of her breasts, barely contained in the sheer gown she wore. How her hips had grown over the years and there were faint wrinkles around her eyes that he didn't remember. Lines on her forehead that showed she wasn't the young woman he'd brought underneath his wing all those years ago.

She'd been his favorite then, and was still his favorite now. Of all the women in this castle to serve him, she was the only one who had done so simply because she liked him. Or at least, that's what he'd always assumed.

If sex ruined trust, then she was the one to prove that wrong.

"Do you trust me?" he asked.

Her jaw dropped open before she could catch it. Stammering, she forced herself to pause, cleared her throat, and then said, "With my life."

"I knew it." Lust slammed his fist onto the table to punctuate his words before realizing how strange that sounded. "My apologies, Lara. I'm still musing over something that was said a few days ago."

"Was it perhaps the young woman you've brought to the castle?" Lara knew better than to pry, but she could tread the line easier than others.

Sighing, he shrugged. "I suppose I can admit it. She seems to think that trust cannot be grown when one is embroiled in lust."

"That's silly. I have no question you will do whatever you want to my body, and that you know exactly what I want. Even if I cannot tell it to you." She made her way over to his desk, skirting the edge to sit down in front of him. Her legs gracefully parted, offering him what he normally would have taken. "I've known you long enough to be certain of that."

It was the last sentence that made him pause. If she hadn't said it, he might have indulged both of them in an afternoon distraction.

And yet... "So you agree it takes time?"

"What?" Her eyes went wide. "What takes time?"

"To build trust." He glared and kept his hands to himself. "She seems to believe that trust requires not only time to grow but also knowledge about the other person. You seem to agree with her."

"I... I don't..." Lara shook her head. "Trust should be freely given. I trusted you the first time you had my body, and I continue to trust you now."

But was that the same kind of trust that Selene wanted between them? He pinched his lower lip, lost in thought for a moment, before another bloomed. He met Lara's confused stare and promptly asked, "If I wanted you to give me your daughter for a few nights, would you?"

All the blood drained out of her face. "She's only eight, Lust."

"Yes, that doesn't matter. I'm not interested in children. But if I asked for you to give her to me, would you?"

Surely that would prove to Selene that others trusted him. What would be more symbolic? Women were most protective of their children, above even themselves. Lara would loan the child—what was her name?—to Lust, and then he would bring the child to Selene. The sorceress would know what to do with a little girl, and he could make a point.

Easy. It was a good plan.

Except then his attention drew back to Lara as she slid onto the floor in front of him. Her hands on his thighs, fingers shaking as she begged. "I will do whatever you wish, my lord, my king, my god. I will lick your floors to keep them clean if you wish it, but my daughter remains in her home. Away from the castle. Away from here."

Now this was confusing.

"She is just a child," he murmured, running his fingers through her hair. "Surely I cannot do anything to break her? There is no safer place in the kingdom than this castle."

"I do not wish her to be like me," Lara whispered. Her eyes dropped to the floor between his feet as her hands slipped off him. "I am not ashamed of what I do to keep her life comfortable, but it is my choice that she not end up here."

"Fuck."

Lust leaned back in his chair, biting his lip as he realized two very important things at the same time. First, Lara didn't really trust him. Perhaps to pleasure her, but not in any way that was important. And second, she thought he wanted her daughter to serve him as she did. And that made her ashamed.

"Fuck," he said again, leaning into the word.

How had that damned sorceress wriggled into his mind this easily? He'd been happy without her question mark hovering over his head and making him question every aspect of his life.

To make the day even better, a golden orb floated in through his window. An orb that could only be one of his brothers attempting to contact him.

"Go," he said, waving Lara away. "I have other things to attend to."

Her face somehow paled even further. "Home, my lord? Do you not wish..."

"Fucking—" He stared up at the ceiling. "Go back to work, Lara. You have done nothing wrong. I am not angry with you."

She pulled herself back together. He watched as she reeled all those unraveled and unnecessary thoughts back into herself and then smiled at him. "Thank you, my lord. If you need anything other than your lunch, please have them send for me."

He watched her leave with a sense of confusion burning inside him. Could all women do that? She'd seemed eerily similar to Selene in those moments. Maybe it was a female thing he would never understand.

No, that couldn't be it. Even as Lara closed the door, he could taste her sense of disappointment that he hadn't taken what she'd offered.

But she still didn't trust him. And that bothered him more than he'd thought it would.

Slumping back in his chair, he waved his hand at the orb that hovered over the chair on the other side of his desk. The magic in it pulsed, brightening for a moment before a cascade of golden lights burst out of it. They gathered up to make the vague impression of his brother, sitting in a chair, likely at his own desk.

"What is it?" Lust growled.

"Angry today, are we?"

"I have other things to do than entertain you, Greed. What do you want?"

His brother was looking rather peaky. Not a good look for a man who already had very little self control. The plume on top of his head was longer than Lust remembered, and it looked like he'd cut the sides a little closer. That hair right now looked golden, but Lust knew it was bright red as the flames Greed surrounded himself with.

He wore nothing but a leather vest and leather leggings, the broad expanse of his chest bare for all to see. He looked like a warlord who had just gotten back from a conquest. Considering his kingdom was full of desert, sand, and more desert, Lust wouldn't be surprised if he'd made himself into a warlord.

Greed eyed him with a feral smile. "Oh, hush. I can't check in on my baby brother?"

The memory of Selene's laugh when he'd gotten frustrated over that term flashed in his mind. And somehow, that memory made it a little easier. He hated that she'd eased the sting with the riotous memory of her laughter.

Instead of arguing, he calmly replied, "No. Not usually. Most of the time, you ignore that I exist."

"We both know that's not true." Greed leaned forward, eyeing him with no small amount of suspicion. "Why aren't you fighting back?"

"Because I find you boring, Greed. We both know you have something to say, so get it out."

And also because Lust wanted to go back to pondering the horrible realization that even his closest lover didn't trust him. Not entirely. She'd place her body in his hands, but anything beyond that, she wouldn't. Was it because she didn't care what happened to herself as long as everyone else remained cared for? That was a horrifying thought.

Greed leaned back in his chair and sighed. "I did want to check in on you, and needed to know how you were doing. I know leading a kingdom can be exhausting, and you like it to be more exhausting than half of us. Always better than us, you were. You know, sometimes I wonder if you're a little too soft for this. Less of the demon and more of the angel, yeah? Until I heard a little rumor that you were getting married and I had the thought, maybe he's just going to corrupt this new bird on another level entirely."

There it was.

"You've heard wrong." Lust lifted his hand to dispel the magic. "Thank you for your concern, brother. But I have everything handled."

"By getting married to a human?" Greed lifted his hand to mirror Lust's, effectively stopping the spell that he would have cast. "No, you're going to talk to me about this. Have you lost your mind? A mortal remaining for any longer than necessary cannot end well for either of you."

"I'm not marrying anyone."

"Really? That's not what everyone else in the realm is saying, so I have to tell you brother, I question it."

Lust rolled his eyes. "And when have I ever cared about what the rest of the realms say? I say I'm not marrying her, and that's final."

Lust had no intention of fulfilling whatever the sorceresses wanted him to do. He also knew for a fact that Selene didn't want to marry him, either. And as he'd told her, he was not a monster. He'd not force her into anything she would regret.

"Then why is she there?"

As if he had an answer for that. Not one that Greed would like, at least. Sighing, he shrugged. "The sorceresses of the Tower are trying to grasp for power again. They wish for me to marry one of their own, thinking that would make me easier to manipulate."

"This is not the first time they've tried to do so. What makes this time different? You've never even entertained them. Not even the last time when they cast spells over your kingdom. All you did was go around and unmake them, even though you knew damned well they would keep casting those spells." Greed tilted his head to the side. "And there is something different about this one, isn't there? You aren't going soft on us."

No, he wasn't. He wasn't going soft in the slightest. He was trying to figure out this woman's mind because she was stranger than any other he'd ever met.

Newness made him uncomfortable. He'd grown complacent, knowing how everything would go and how everyone's thoughts ran.

The last thing he wanted was to tell Greed the truth. But he had no one else to talk with this about, and he found himself begrudgingly admitting, "It seems she is immune to my power."

"Hilarious. Why is she actually there?"

Lust stared at his brother with his brows raised. "That. That is why she's here."

"So she's asexual. We have plenty of them here in my kingdom. Send her my way and you'll be rid of her."

"She isn't immune to lust entirely. She's just immune to it with me." Seven Kingdoms. He hated even admitting that. It made him seem weak. Like he was losing control over his power.

Greed paused, then his expression shuddered into something terrifying. "You're joking, of course."

"I am not."

"We've never seen anyone immune to our powers. We are spirits of our emotion, the strongest of our kind. Demon kings, they call us, because we can manipulate them."

"Yes, I lived the stories."

"We have ruled these lands for a thousand years and never has a single mortal been born with a power to resist the compulsion of our powers."

Lust hissed out a long breath. "I'm aware of that, brother. Do you think I am not? I know how it is, that's why I brought her here! She is under my supervision until I understand what is going on."

Greed tapped his finger against his chin, shaking his head in denial of it. "Change is what's happening. And I don't like it."

"Neither do I." Lust had barely slept since she got here. Even now, he only slept in fits when he knew there was someone out there who he couldn't control.

"You know we need to tell Pride about this."

Their most meddlesome brother? The one who thought he was the true ruler over all seven of the kingdoms? "Absolutely not," he snarled.

"We will not tell him a single thing about this."

"Then Wrath."

The eldest of their brothers, and arguably the most dangerous. Lust already knew what Wrath would say, and that was to kill the problem.

"No," he said again. "We keep this between the two of us until we understand what has given her this strange power. I need your word on this, Greed."

But his brother was staring at him with the expression that meant he was about to make trouble, and Lust didn't have time for that.

"Whatever you're thinking, stop," Lust said, pointing his finger at Greed. "My answer is no."

"But it has been so long since I've visited your kingdom! Too long." Greed's grin split into that feral expression again. "I should meet this woman myself. Another pair of eyes might see something you do not."

"You are not welcome in my kingdom after what you did last time." Lust didn't want him here, anyway. Greed collected unique objects, weapons, places, and people. He hoarded them like a miser, like a dragon, and if he saw with his own eyes how different Selene was, then he would try to take her from him. Even if that meant kidnapping her in the middle of the night.

He couldn't let Greed visit. He wouldn't.

"No," he repeated. "You are not coming here, Greed. She's not another pet for you to view."

"Oh, but I don't need your invitation. None of us need one to visit the other, now do we? Besides, you keep far too many pets to yourself." A flash of that grin was the only warning he had before the spell was severed.

Damn it.

He held his head in his hands, grabbing onto his horns with a punishing grip. Everything was falling to pieces. All of it was wrong, wrong, wrong.

"Fuck!" he shouted, clearing his desk of all items and listening to them shatter upon the floor. Even that could not satisfy the sudden rage that burned through his chest until he couldn't even breathe.

He could lose her. So easily. And all before he figured out the answer to the puzzle she'd presented him.

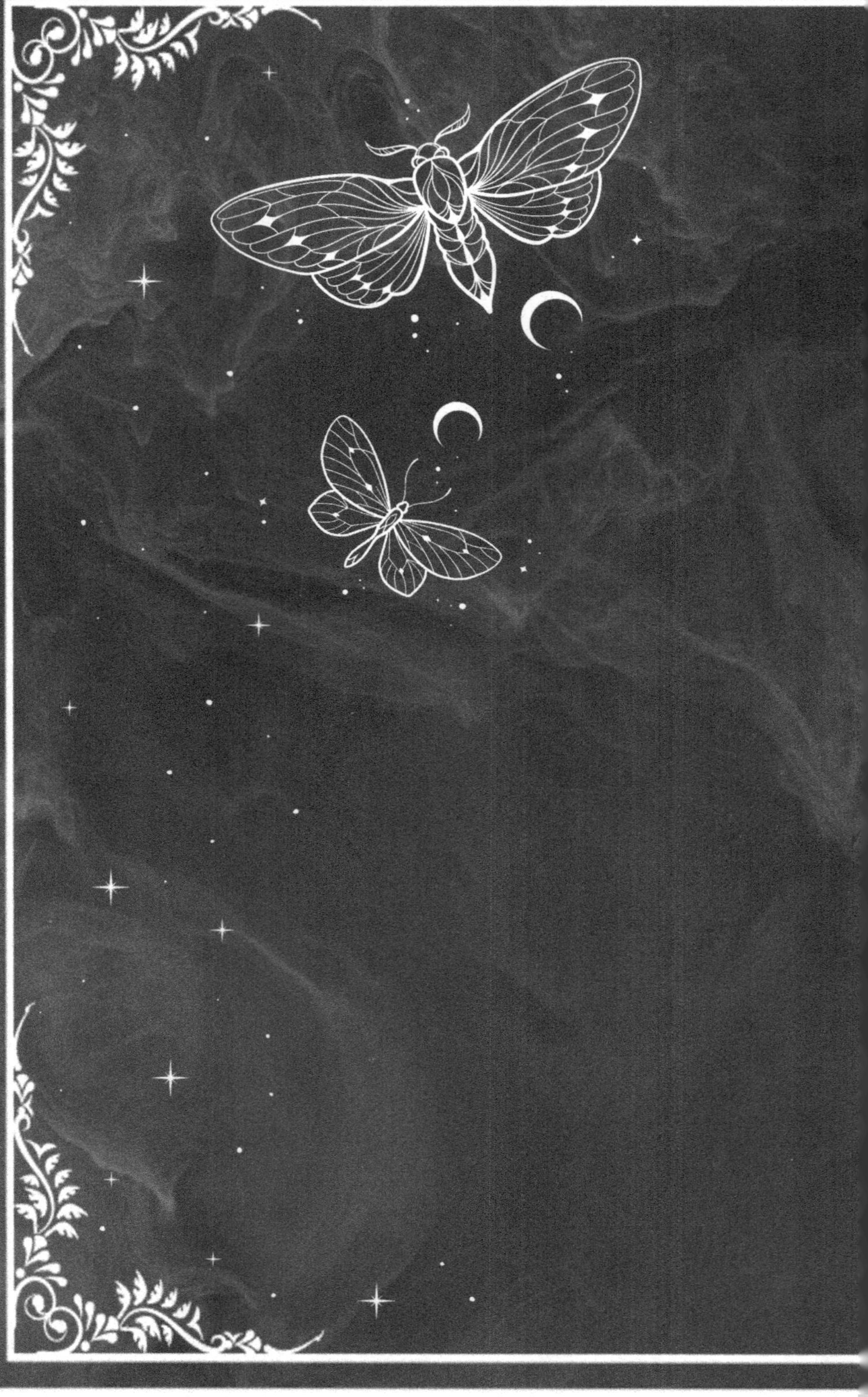

Chapter 13

"Affection," she scolded as she chased the spirit underneath her bed. "You have to go."

"I don't want to go."

"I know you don't want to go, but I want to go to bed." Selene had thought the nightgown would suggest how ready she was for sleep, but apparently the little spirit had no intention of leaving.

It had come into her room for a conversation, or so Affection had led her to believe. In fact, the spirit had stalled for hours on end until it was well past either of their bedtimes and it was still here.

She wouldn't mind if Affection wanted to stay overnight in her room, but it didn't stop talking. Ever. It just kept prattling on and on about all the people it had felt affection from, where that affection had come from, how utterly decadent it had felt.

And sure, she'd enjoyed listening to all the stories Affection had to tell. Namely, because it made her wonder just how much of this applied to Lust.

He'd been in a physical form for a thousand years, or so he claimed. Did that mean he wasn't the same as the rest of the spirits without a body? She could only assume he'd have changed in all the time since he'd taken a body. Being mortal must affect the spirits that took them on. What if he was just like her, and she had missed a very important part of understanding him?

The jumbled mess in her head was almost too frustrating for her to handle.

She had to tame him so the sorceresses would have some claim to power. But the longer she was here, the more she thought maybe the sorceresses were wrong. Then she got homesick because she missed her sisters so much, and the predictability of her life in the Tower. But inevitably her mind drifted back to the afternoon she'd spent on the cliff with Lust and how hard he'd tried to understand her. He'd made her laugh, and he had called her pretty.

Surely that meant something?

"Come... here..." she grunted, waving her arm underneath the bed as she tried to grasp onto Affection's long, wispy tail.

Frankly, she would prefer to work through these thoughts on her own. It made her nauseous to think she might have softened a bit toward the demon king who wanted to destroy their kingdom. It also made her sick to think her mother and sisters thought so poorly of him when he was trying to do a decent job of things. He was just a damned spirit of lust and nothing about being human made sense to him.

Affection pressed against the wall right in the middle of her headboard, far out of her reach. "I'm not leaving!"

"You can't stay here."

"But you're thinking such delicious thoughts, and what if I told you about them? We could talk tonight about that afternoon in the sun at the edge of the world—"

"We're not going to do that," she interrupted, shoving her shoulder against the bed in frustration. "Get over here, Affection!"

The door to her bedroom slammed open and Selene froze where she was crouched. Whoever stood in that doorway was getting a full view of her behind as she wedged herself underneath her bed, and she knew just how sheer this nightgown was. All her clothes kept disappearing from the room every time she left it, and this was the only nightgown left.

Pale, gauzy fabric clung to every suggestion of a curve, even where she didn't have them. The material tied around her neck, leaving her back completely exposed all the way down to her hips. It wasn't warm, and it clearly wasn't meant for warmth.

She intended to bring this up in another argument with Lust while she tried to figure out how to manipulate him into revealing sensitive information about himself, but... Well. She didn't mind the nightgown. It was rather comfortable and smooth against her skin.

A choked sound erupted from the doorway before she heard Lust mutter, "Under any other circumstances, I would greatly enjoy this."

Selene tried to stand up, forgot she was underneath the bed, and hit her skull so hard against the frame that she saw stars. Gasping in a breath, she wiggled her way free and turned so her spine was pressed against the side of her massive bed. "What are you doing here?"

"I live here."

"This is my room."

He stood in her doorway, silhouetted by torchlight behind him.

From this point of view, he looked even larger and every ounce the demon her mother claimed him to be. Those horns glinted in the dim glow, as though they were metallic and sharper than she'd thought. His broad shoulders blocked the entire entrance to her room, and she'd never noticed how thick his thighs were until this moment. He was... Terrifying. And she had to hide her emotions before her mouth watered.

Damn it, she wasn't supposed to lust after him. She should be terrified of him or hate him. Those were the only acceptable emotions to feel when he walked into a room.

She hadn't thought he would do this to her so quickly. A demon would try to wear her down, of course. He'd toy with her, force her to endure the constant barrages of his lustful power. But he had done none of that. He'd only taken her on a picnic and asked what her favorite food was.

No. This wouldn't do. She could not be having these thoughts while he stood there, staring down at her with a similar expression on his face.

"It's not your room anymore," he said gruffly. "Get up."

Her jaw fell open. "What do you mean, it's not my room?"

"You're being relocated."

"Where?" Selene grabbed the edge of her bed and yanked herself upright. She didn't care if he could see too much of her. This was the space he'd given her and she quite liked it. "I'm not going to a new room. This one is fine."

Something in his expression hardened, and a man she'd never seen before took his place. Lust suddenly stalked toward her, his head lowered and his shoulders stiff. He didn't even look at her as he pinned her against a post on her bed while a wall of servants entered her room. Not a single person looked at her as they began to pack up all her belongings.

"Lust?" she asked again, trying to sound at least a little quieter. "Why are you taking all of my things?"

Was this the moment that he threw her into the dungeon? She knew she shouldn't have trusted him. The bastard had lulled her into a false sense of security and now she would see the real him.

Lust continued to herd her further away from the others. Her spine struck the wall, and she glared at him. He'd left her no choice but to hope she could save herself from whatever dastardly plan he was now enacting.

"I'm fine in this room," she repeated. "I don't need to move."

His head tilted, like a falcon sighting its prey. He stared down at her, and she noticed that his eyes had changed. They were entirely black, no whites in them at all. A demon watched her and a thread of realization wove a new tapestry within her soul.

She wasn't afraid of him. She didn't have to stuff that emotion anywhere, because she'd never feel it again. Even with him hulking over her, his shoulders heaving, his horns pointed directly at her, and his eyes black as night, she wasn't afraid. She couldn't fear him after she knew there was a sensitive man in there who found her laugh pretty.

Maybe she was a fool. Maybe she would put herself in even more dire circumstances if she followed her gut. But she couldn't stop herself.

Those black eyes called out for her to see him. To understand that something had happened, otherwise he wouldn't have walked into her room like a storm and ordered her around. He'd promised he wouldn't do exactly this.

Selene dared much to lift her hand between them. She gently placed her palm on his chest, feeling the thundering of his heart underneath her touch. It felt very much like calming a raging stallion who could stomp her out of existence with his hooves.

"Trust," she whispered quietly, so none of the servants would overhear them. "Remember? We're working on trust."

Those dark eyes deepened, and the faintest swirl of violet danced inside them. "This has nothing to do with trust," he rasped.

"It has everything to do with trust. Tell me what is happening, Lust. You cannot barge into my room, take all my things, and not tell me where I'm going or why I'm leaving. I need you to tell me what is happening."

He shook his head, those horns moving dangerously close to her face. "He is coming, and I cannot keep you safe this far from my own rooms."

"Who is coming?"

"It does not matter," he snarled. "You are moving."

She'd gotten a bit out of him, but Selene wanted more. She needed more to understand why he was so angry, and she didn't know if she wanted to see what would happen if she pushed him.

Why not? Why not take the risk? Maybe this was the leap they needed to take before she could get through that thick hide of his.

Selene wasn't kidding herself. She wanted to touch the rough bristles of day old growth on his jaw. Her palm ached to feel if it would abrade her skin and spark fires that trailed throughout her entire body.

She moved her hand up, past his throat, ignoring how he seemed to arch into her touch for a moment before glaring at her with even more power in his gaze. Then she placed her palm against his jaw and gently spread her fingers. Selene scratched at the rough beard while letting out a low breath. All these riotous feelings had to go. She had to hide them away from him.

It was as if he knew. Lust tilted his face into her palm, his eyes shuttering closed as he pressed a soft kiss to her skin.

"Tell me," she urged one last time. "I cannot help you if you do not tell me."

"You cannot help me at all, little moon. You will remain safely hidden away while my brother visits, and he will not see you."

"Your brother?" A flicker of unease made her stomach churn. "Which one?"

"Greed." He inhaled deeply at her wrist, and she had to grit her teeth against the flood of warmth that burned through her body. "He wants to see you. He's heard that I may get married, and of all people to find out, he is the worst one."

"Why?" It took everything in her not to snatch her hand away from him. His kiss felt too good. His beard scraped against her skin so delicately and it... it...

Lust's eyes opened again, flashing to hers with an intensity that stole her breath. "Because he will take you from me, sorceress. You are unique. The only one of your kind to ever be unaffected by our power and so he will want you. He will steal you away, and I will let no one do that."

Oh.

When had anyone wanted her that much? Her mother had always made it clear that Selene wasn't to leave, but not because her mother liked her. In fact, Minerva didn't like anyone but herself. She'd made Selene stay in the Tower because of her powers, nothing more than that. Ursula might have wanted her as a sister, but she'd still let her go. Everyone let her go when there was nothing left to wring out of her.

Everyone except him. And it made her shudder to know that someone wanted to keep her. Her soul lit up with a thousand fireworks, but it was wrong to feel this way for him. She'd have to keep this close to her chest. If he knew how she felt when he said he wanted her?

Selene worried he'd never let her go if he knew how much her body ached to hear him say that again.

"You don't even like me," she said, trying to cover up what was happening, or she'd lose herself. Right here. Right now. "Having someone kidnap me would be the answer to all your problems, wouldn't it?"

He met her gaze, and she felt as though he'd stabbed her. The anger radiating through him shook her palm. "You're not getting out of here until I answer the questions I have about you, little moon. Don't think you can appeal to my brother's good nature and leave this place. I can assure you, the life he would give you is nothing like the life I offer."

"And what do you offer me?" She swallowed hard. "A life of captivity? Of you telling me what to do and how to do it?"

He brushed the backs of his fingers over her cheek, that horrible black color draining out of his eyes. "I offer you all that you've ever sought. Luxury, comfort, and pleasure so deeply felt that your being will unravel in my arms. All you have to do is let me."

If he knew what a temptation that was, Selene feared what he might do. She feared what she'd let him do.

Instead, she pulled them both back to reality. "We both know that will never happen. I'm not interested in you. And you are not really interested in me."

"You speak for me?"

"I do. You are only intrigued by who I am because of what you cannot compel me to do. I stand apart, as something other, and that makes you wonder what you missed. Where you went wrong. How all that power of yours could possibly be denied by a little slip of a sorceress who has no more power than the mere ability to conjure light. You are interested in me for what answers I can give you, not because you care for me or who I am."

The words were meant to be an arrow into his chest, but she found her own heart hurting. It was the truth, though. They both knew it.

He sucked in a deep breath and then took a step away from her. The space between them filled with ice. He jerked his head toward the servants. "They are bringing your items to my room."

"Your room?" She shook her head, stuttering, "I-I don't think I'll be staying there. We aren't even married yet."

"And for all you know, we never will be."

A few of the servants looked at him with that declaration. Their eyes lit up with the potential for gossip before they quietly went about their work. All her items were already packed or filling someone's arms to take elsewhere.

To his room.

"No," she replied. "I will not stay in your room with you. That is hardly appropriate, and as I said, neither of us are really—"

He pointed at her, and the words died on her lips.

"You do not speak for me, sorceress," he snarled. "You should have been in my room from the very first night here."

"That would have been barbaric of you." She tilted her chin up, wanting him to see her defiance. "I deserve my own space. A refuge."

"From me?" He placed his hand over his heart, fingers spread wide, before a grin spread across his face. A grin she didn't like at all. "You do not get refuge from the man you claim you wish to marry, sorceress. You will be in my room every night. In my bed. At my side. And you will learn your place in this castle once and for all. Do I make myself clear?"

Fingers twitching at her sides, she gave him a nod.

He imperiously held out his hand and then twitched his fingers for her to follow him. "Then come."

Lust left the room so confident she would follow him into the candlelight and flickering shadows that he never looked back. If he had, he might have noticed how she stooped one more time beneath the bed to gather up a suddenly exhausted little spirit before venturing into the dark halls.

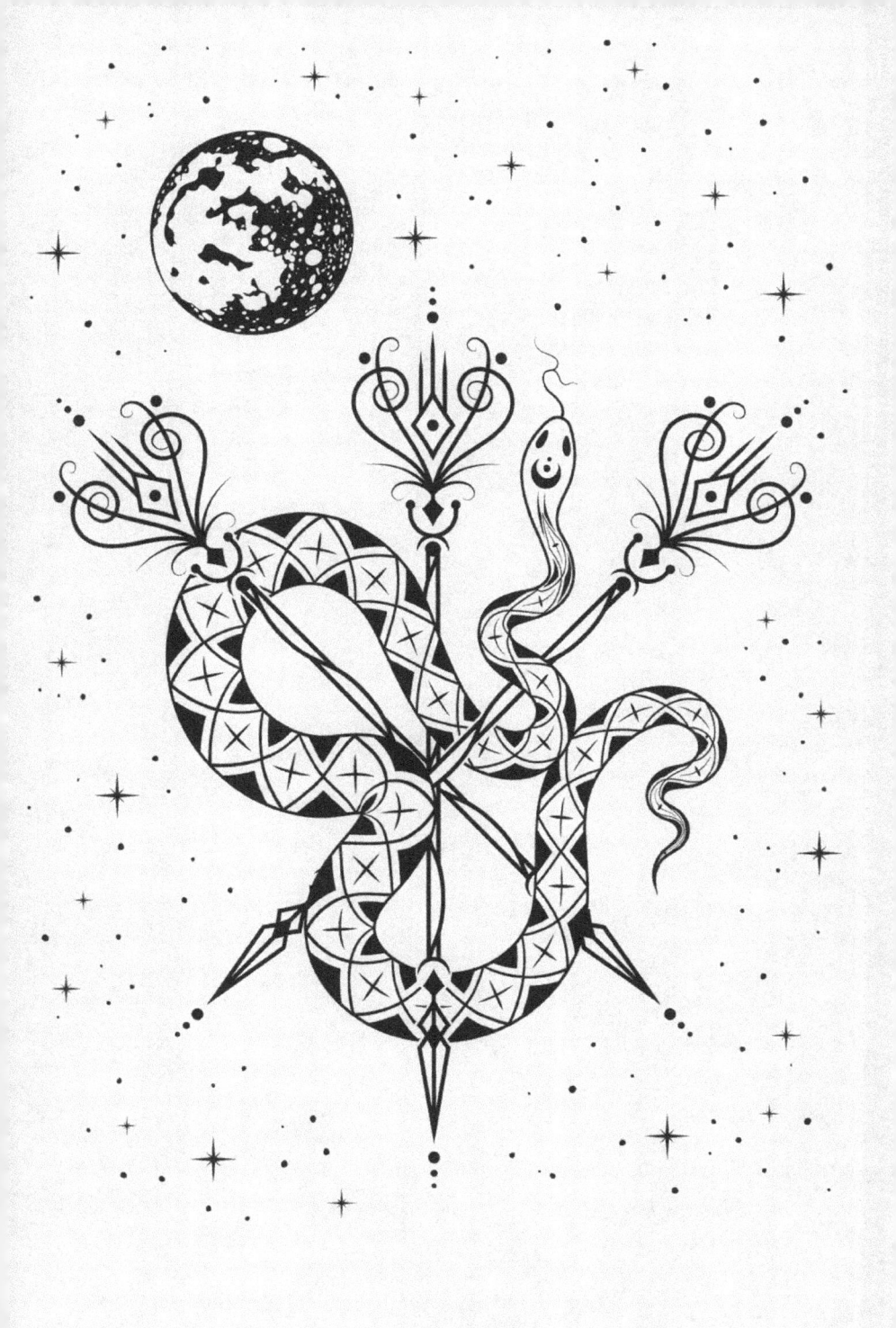

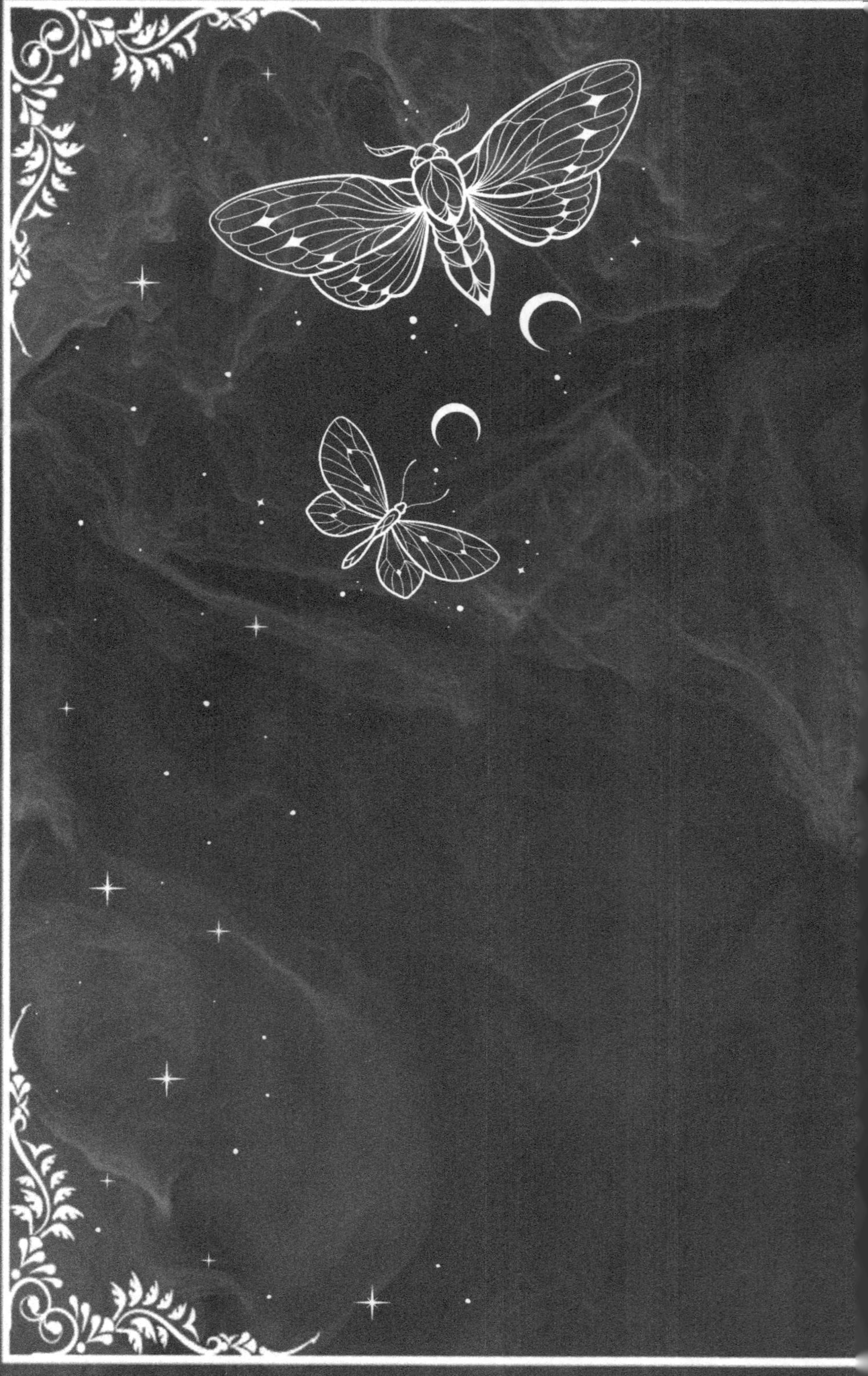

Chapter 14

He'd meant what he said. Lust could not protect Selene if she was hidden away in her own room, where his brother could sneak at any point. Greed could find her anywhere, but his brother was not likely to take a woman out from under his nose.

And damn it, he'd wanted her in his bed since the first moment he'd seen her on that street. Let alone when she'd challenged him in the tavern.

If he wanted to slide his hands over those smooth thighs, or test the weight of her breasts, or lick his way between her thighs to see if she tasted like sweet honey or if she was as icy there as everywhere else, why should he not? He was lust incarnate. He was meant to desire and for others to desire. But this foolish little mortal had tested everything he believed and he couldn't get his head wrapped around it.

Running his hands through his hair, he stalked through the halls toward the dining room. He hadn't returned to his own bed for the better part of three nights while he tried to piece through his thoughts.

He'd stood outside the door a few times, though. Staring at the wood as though he could see through it and peek into the scene beyond. Was she sleeping in his bed? Did her dark hair spread out across his pillow, leaving the sweet scent of peppermint all throughout his sheets?

The thought made him impossibly hard. It made him want to knock down the door and slip underneath the covers with her.

And that was why he hadn't gone back to his own bedroom. He couldn't. What would he do if he did?

Lust knew his own limitations. He knew she didn't want him there, and that by forcing her to move into his room, he'd overstepped the lines of trust they were trying to build.

But he didn't know why that trust mattered to him!

He could get himself together. He'd be perfectly charming during dinner, proving to her that he was a good man with good intentions, and why should she be afraid of her king? She should fear demons. But he was a spirit of lust, a blessing upon these lands.

Setting his shoulders and a fake smile on his face, he opened the doors and stepped into the candlelight beyond. The servants had removed what was a normally massive table with at least twenty chairs around it. Instead, they'd filled the room with flowers. Bright bouquets with splashes of pinks, reds, and purples had rained petals onto the floor. As he stepped, their scent rose from the delicate petals he crushed beneath his heels.

They had changed the large table out for a smaller round table, still large enough to seat six, but with only two place settings and mounds of food upon it. Candlelight glimmered all around them, hanging from the ceiling on silver threads that were almost invisible to the naked eye. As such, the lights hovered around them, flickering and swaying with the slightest breeze.

And then there was her. His little moon goddess sitting in the chair on the opposite side of the table with a glass of wine in her hands. She eyed him, clearly not sure what to think of the banquet he'd thrown for the two of them.

"Good evening," he said, his voice catching in his throat.

Embarrassing. He had seduced queens before. Women who were actual goddesses that graced these lands for only a few moments before they returned to their own realms. Lust knew how to make a woman swoon and fall at his feet with desire.

But not this one. He had no idea how to convince this woman to spend time with him. No, that wasn't right. He didn't know how to convince her to fall into his bed. That was all. Spending time with her was merely an enjoyable side benefit.

He wanted to hit himself. Enjoyable wasn't the right word either. They argued, she belittled him. There was no enjoyment in their time together other than the chase.

Yes. That was better.

With these thoughts in mind, it was easier to walk over to the table and drag his chair from the opposite side to sit next to her. He sat down with his legs spread wide and relaxation in every single muscle of his body. She did not wriggle underneath his skin at all. He languidly looked her over, as though she were nothing more than a puzzle for him to figure out. In fact, he was so unaffected that he even crossed his ankles.

She eyed him with the same suspicion as always. "Why am I here?"

"I thought mortals needed to eat."

"We do. But you and I have never eaten together." She lifted her glass to her lips, and he watched the graceful movement with rapt attention.

Her neck was so thin. Delicate. Easy to wrap his hands around if he wanted to, and he did. Lust could already see the red marks he'd leave on that pale skin, the purplish bruising of his mouth where he would latch onto her as she screamed out his name.

Damn it.

She lifted a brow as she set her glass back on the table. "Is something bothering you?"

She knew. Of course, the sorceress knew that she'd already woven him into her web. He hated it, but had no idea how to struggle his way out of this one.

"You mentioned trust," he said, reaching across her for his own goblet of wine. Pouring the red liquid, he steadied himself by watching the light dance off the wine. "Is this not a way to build trust?"

"Did you read that spending time with each other over food might inspire trust to develop?" she asked.

He had, but he wouldn't admit it. "I just wanted to spend time with you. No book is required for that."

"I don't understand why you would want to spend time with me. We clearly don't like each other." Selene's eyes saw too much. They narrowed at him, as though she were trying to peer into his mind. "But that's what you expected me to say, isn't it?"

"You are very perceptive for one so young." He drained his glass of wine in a single gulp before pouring another. "I've taken an interest in you, little moon."

"Why is that?"

"For the reasons you already know."

"Yes, because I somehow can't feel your power." She shrugged. "That's not a reason for you to be so interested. There are others like me, you said. Others less plain."

"Perhaps it is because your mother sent you to me like a sacrifice. Minerva made it very clear what her plan was for you. Come to the castle. Seduce me. Get me under your thumb so I fall head over heels for you, place you beside me on the throne, and then you will bring the sorceresses here. Together, they will all either overwhelm me with magic or I will follow along like a puppet while she threatens me with your death." He lifted his wine goblet to her. "And yet now that you are here, I find you to be stubborn, obstinate, and very much avoidant of even being around me. I find that curious."

Her eyes had widened with every word he said. Lust felt better, knowing he controlled the conversation. He'd startled her, and Selene didn't seem to battle as well when she was jarred off her pedestal.

"I..." She hesitated before swallowing a mouthful of wine. "I am not my mother's puppet, as you claim me to be."

"So you were listening in on the conversation before you surprisingly showed up." He grinned. "Listening from the eaves is rather devious, don't you think?"

"I have no interest in serving anyone but myself." She seemed uncomfortable even saying the words. "My mother has taught me since I was a child to serve her, and that my purpose would be to tempt you. You are correct in that."

"And?" He waited for her to respond before gesturing with a hand. "You were trained for this. Why are you so bad at it?"

Her eyes flared with anger. "They weren't even upset that I was leaving. They saw my enslavement to a man who they proclaimed to be a demon as something good for themselves. I miss them. I miss my home every day. I think about them when I walk through the halls of this place and wonder if they are thinking of me. But I know the answer to that question. They do not. And if they are thinking about me, then they are only wondering if I have succeeded and if they should pack their things so that they can make a new life in this castle. I fear the moment they come here, they will forget about me again. Set me aside like a little doll who they can pull out when they want me to make a show of it. Is that enough for you? Is that enough of a reason for why I have been struggling here to understand first what you want with me and second why I was even sent here or if I wanted to be?"

She took a large breath after that purging of her fears, before her eyes widened. Perhaps she hadn't expected to be quite so honest with him.

It was more than he'd expected as well.

Lust licked his lips, taking his time as he started on his second cup of wine. He watched her chest heave with her emotions, her eyes flashing with a challenge for him to catch her in a lie. But she wasn't lying. She was just as confused as he was, for different reasons.

"So what do you want?" he asked. "Deny the Tower. Throw away what you were trained to be or do. Who are you then?"

Her eyes widened before she met his gaze with nothing short of horror in her own. "I don't know."

"Do you want to know?"

"I... I'm not sure."

"Then, as I see it, you have two options." He set down his wine and started filling a plate for her while he talked. "You can continue down the same path you've been walking. You can do what Minerva and your sisters want you to do. It is familiar. I don't think anyone would blame you for choosing the comfortable option. Or you can deviate from that path and carve out something new. Try whatever you want here. That is the basis of what lust is." He handed her the plate full of food, keeping his hand on it even as she grabbed it. He made her look him in the eye. "Lust is about indulging yourself. Whatever gives you pleasure, do it. Take it. If it does not serve you or please you any longer, let it go."

She picked at the food on the plate, obviously giving his words a thought. He'd rather she agree than to ignore him. After all, she was in his castle.

The idea of tempting her with whatever she wanted? Seven kingdoms. It did something to him that he hadn't felt since he first took a physical form. He wanted to see that newness through her. He wanted to watch her experience the world and all its decadence while he feasted on her emotions.

Lust would give anything to feel that newness again. He was ancient. He'd forgotten what it even felt like. This was as close as he'd get.

She rolled a strawberry in honey, not looking at him as she popped the red berry into her mouth. "I don't know what I want. No one has ever asked me that before, and yet you seem to think that I will be able to ask for something that I do not know exists."

He almost groaned. But somehow, he held himself together, leaned forward, and forced her to look at him with a gentle hand under her chin. "Then let me. Let me offer you the world on a platter, Selene. If you do not like what I offer, we will throw it away. Trust me to know what you need."

Her lips parted with a soft inhalation and he almost kissed her. Almost tasted her bitter anger on his tongue, and he knew her lips would burn him. He wanted that, he realized. He wanted her to scorch him, destroy him, tear everything he knew from his flesh until he was remade in her pleasure.

But Selene was not a simple woman. She licked her lips and then replied, "I'll think about it."

Disappointment flooded through him. Damn it, he thought he'd had her. But Lust was not one to be beaten that easily.

He inclined his head and replied, "That is all I can ask."

Then he reached for her hand, her fingers still coated in honey, and licked the sweetness from her skin. He took his time. Swirling his tongue around every single digit, knowing she should be flooded with an answering warmth. He seduced her as only a demon could, then let out a pulse of his own power to encourage lust to grow within her.

Nothing. Not even a tiny hint that she'd felt a single thing from his touch.

Sighing, he dropped her hand and slumped back in his chair. "Absolutely ridiculous. Are you a block of ice, woman?"

She laughed.

Shocked, he watched as she tilted her head back and burst into laughter. Her long throat worked, her eyes squeezed shut in mirth, and her dark hair tangled down her back. Loose. Unbound as he had wanted it to be the first time he'd seen her.

The sound was better than any he'd heard in his life. Lust had never been fond of laughter. Usually that was insulting in the bedroom, but now he wondered what it would sound like in the dead of night. Selene would try to keep herself quiet because she wouldn't want to wake everyone, and he would keep teasing her until she burst out like this. Laughing too loud for a lady, but she wouldn't care if someone heard her.

This was Selene, he realized. These were the moments when he got to see the real her. Not the Selene who had been cultivated by the sorceresses or told how to act. No one had ever tried to change her laugh or told her how to find humor in moments like this.

He found an answering smile on his own lips as he sipped at his drink. "What is so funny?"

She shook her head, wiping tears from her eyes. "You really are very unlikeable, do you know that?"

"No one has ever said that to me before."

"I wish you were less charming. It might make it easier for others to see what I do." She shook her head again, still chuckling. "You've never had to work for this, have you?"

"Work for what?" Lust leaned forward, curious about what this strange human would say.

"To make someone like you. Getting them to trust you just to spend time with them. You've always had relationships handed to you because someone wanted what you could give them." Selene hadn't stopped smiling, so her words had a little less bite. "Perhaps we are good for each other, demon king."

"Perhaps." He set his wine down on the table and placed his hands on his thighs. "Are you really not attracted to me? Not even a little?"

She looked down at the alcohol before responding. "It's probably the wine talking, but yes. I am attracted to you. I told you before, I feel attraction. And you were clearly made to be attractive to any and everyone."

Lust preened. "I knew you had to feel something."

"But I need more than physical attraction to be interested in someone. I stand by what I said. Trust is very important to me, and not because I want to trust someone before I get close to them. I don't think I ever trusted anyone worthwhile in my entire life. The longer I'm here, the more I realize how sad that is. And I don't want to be sad anymore."

The words were sobering. He could feel his expression softening even as he stood. Lust gave her a small bow before reaching for her hand again.

This time, he noticed she didn't tense up when he pressed a kiss to the backs of her fingers. "I will do everything in my power to make you happy here, little moon. All I hope is that you trust me to offer you what you want. Or perhaps what you need."

"I haven't given you my answer on that yet."

"Then think about it while you finish dinner. I will leave you to enjoy the banquet on your own, as you have made very clear." He didn't tell her that he had plans to make.

Plans to seduce a woman who could not be seduced.

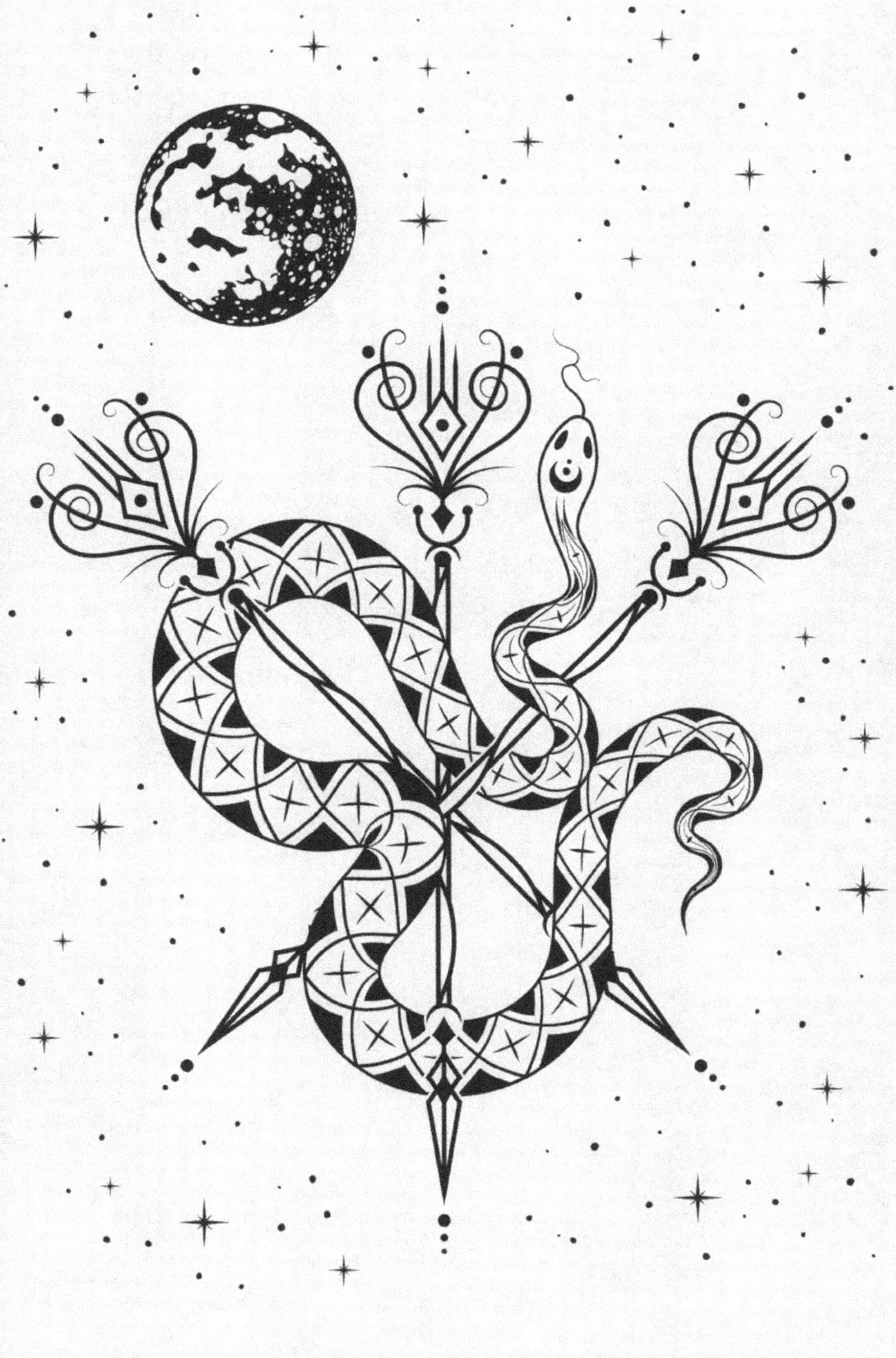

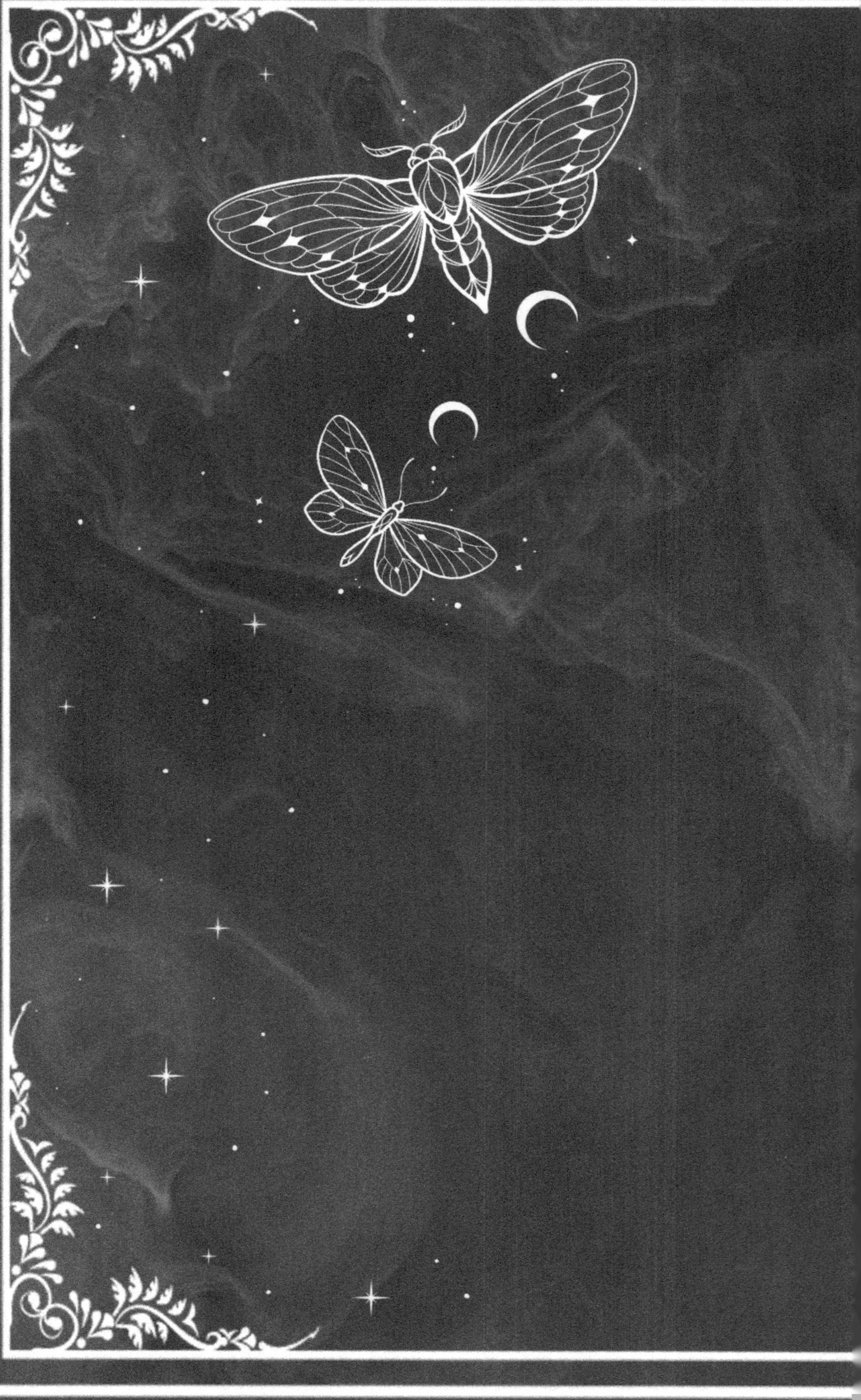

Chapter 15

He gave her much to think about. More than Selene really wanted, if she were being honest.

Lust made her want to try things she'd never even thought about. He made her consider if she liked her life with the sorceresses or if she'd have chosen something different given the chance. These were not thoughts she'd ever been permitted to consider. Her life plan was already mapped out the day her birth mother had left her in front of the Tower.

But now she wondered what she wanted. Minerva had always made those choices for her, and now... Well, now she thought maybe she wanted to make those decisions for herself.

The thought was daunting. How did one go from not knowing to knowing? She could put all that power into Lust's hands, but that seemed like a terrible idea. He was sweet now, but there was a demon underneath all of that. He hadn't earned her trust enough to let him run wild with her life.

Still, his offer was tempting. To experience the world without the lens of the Tower in front of her? To know what it felt like to indulge her senses in whatever pleasure she sought?

She could do that here. Her mother and sisters would never know until the time came for her to betray him. And she would. Selene had spent her entire life training for this moment. She wouldn't let guilt make her falter in this purpose. He would fall, and she would let him.

Or maybe not. Her thoughts were all jumbled. She hadn't been lying when she said she didn't like the man. He was unlikeable. He made himself so when he satisfied his own desires before others.

Still. He had a softer side that she could see buried underneath all that selfishness. Maybe he could change.

Just the thought made her snort. He would not change. He was a spirit of lust and Affection had confirmed her suspicions. Spirits were not people. They didn't grow and change and learn. They were here as guardians of their emotion. Their one emotion.

Lust wouldn't change any more than Affection would. Even giving him that quality turned him more into a man than a spirit, and she already knew that wasn't the case.

Sighing, she put her brush down on the vanity they'd moved into Lust's room. It was nicer here than in her old room. Much larger. And the plush bed in the center of the room constantly called out to her. She'd been enjoying snuggling into the plush velvet blankets that were satisfyingly heavy while also not being too hot. She'd have to ask him how they did that.

Selene had almost convinced herself to retire early until she felt the tug in her belly. The hard pull that guided her out of the room and toward an abandoned closet where a small bird waited for her on the floor.

It was a goldfinch; she thought. Bathilda was very good at summoning them for messages, though the poor things died after their message was received.

She hated it when she got a bird. Minerva knew that. Ursula certainly did. All of her sisters had seen her cry when the tiny bird burst into a puddle of feathers in her hands.

And still, this was how they sent her a message. This was how they contacted her after weeks of silence.

Gritting her teeth, she picked up the tiny finch from the floor. "I'm so sorry," she whispered and caressed her finger down its chest.

The bird tilted its head to the side, perhaps confused by her reaction before it opened its mouth and allowed the image of her sisters to float up into the air.

"Well?" Bathilda asked, her words curt and short.

"Well what?"

"Do you have him under your thumb yet?"

Selene wanted to scream. Instead, she ground her teeth so hard she heard a creak inside her mouth, then replied, "It's only been a few weeks, Bathilda. No, he is not yet under my thumb."

Her sister had the nerve to look disappointed. "Really? It's been quite a while. Do you at least have information about his weakness?"

"And he's a thousand year old demon who has many years of experience. Give me time. It will take a while if you want to get the results that you're expecting."

The magic shifted hands to that of her mother. Minerva glared at her in a way that still made shivers dance down her spine. She knew that look. It was the face of a woman who wanted nothing to do with her daughter right now, but also of a woman who would suffer through this interaction. Minerva knew how to cut Selene to the core.

"Daughter," her mother said. "Do you remember what I told you about the day you were delivered to our home?"

How could she forget? "That no one wanted me. That my real mother had left me because they did not understand my power. They feared me, just as the kingdom fears the rest of our kind."

"We took you in. We gave you the home that your own parents did not want to give you. We led you out of that darkness and into the light. I could have left you out in that cold and watched as your tiny body froze. It is not a terrible death, though it is slow."

She knew what a horrible death it was. Minerva had made Selene go outside when she was twelve to see a baby they hadn't taken in. The frozen blue lips and frosted eyelashes would haunt her for the rest of her life.

"Yes, I know," she whispered. "You gave me a life that would otherwise have been taken from me."

"Life, Selene. I think you may have forgotten that is why you call me mother. I gave you your life. And your sisters? They were given life by my predecessor. Those before me were kind enough to see the use in their lives, even when no one else did. You need to remember that."

And though the words were clearly wrong, Selene felt them deep in her heart. She was here only because of her mother's kindness. That was all. Otherwise, she would have died in the cold.

Gritting her teeth, she hardened her expression and nodded. "I will do my best, Mother. You trained me well. He has a fascination with me, of that there is no doubt. He's moved me into his bedroom as well."

"Then seduce him."

She felt the blood drain out of her face. "Everyone tries to seduce him. He is Lust. There is a better way of gaining his admiration than by trying to be like all the rest."

"Do what it takes. I see little movement thus far."

And with that, Minerva severed the connection. The little bird in her palm stared up at her with bright, dark eyes, and then it burst. There was no blood. No gore. Just a pile of feathers in her hand where there had once been a vibrant creature.

"Oh," she whispered. "That's why they sent you."

Her mother had wanted to remind her how fragile life was. And she wanted to viscerally make that point.

She reached underneath her hair and gently touched the black mark on the back of her neck. The spell they had cast was supposed to protect her. But would it? Could magic like that protect her when her mother's intent to threaten was so clear?

Mist pooled underneath the door and a little spirit soon joined her in the room.

Affection had gotten a little larger since she'd seen it last. There was a faint hue to it now as well, a bright yellow ball that collected in its center and stretched as it moved.

"There is no affection for that woman in you," it whispered, gathering around her feet. A single feather drifted down through the air and landed on its head. "She is not kind."

"No, she is not," Selene agreed.

Her mother had never seen the use of kindness. Selene had barely even realized kindness existed until they'd started having their outings. She was only allowed out with the older girls at first, and then she'd realized there was another type of person out there.

Bending down, she sat on the floor with her back to the wall and gathered Affection into her arms. The mist felt a little heavier today, much easier to hold.

"When I was little, I remember the first time I saw a mother with her daughter. They were in the Sapphire Falls market. I don't know if you've ever been. But the entire town is surrounded by waterfalls. Her daughter had fallen into one of the pools at their base, and the little girl was crying because her new dress was wet. It was horrible to see, and I knew that her mother would scold her. I hated being scolded." Selene smiled, staring off into the distance like she could still see them. "Instead of yelling, her mother waded into the water with her and sat down in the cold. They splashed each other, and suddenly the little girl lit up like nothing bad had happened."

"How wonderful!"

"It was. And I wanted to feel the same way. I went home with my mother and sisters that night and tried to see if I could get my own mother to play with me like that. She didn't want to." The happy feelings from the memory faded into the bitter cold of the Tower. "But every time I went to any of the markets, I always made sure to recognize the kindness there."

Selene had kept all those memories like precious gems. Locked away for a time when she was alone and could feel without fear.

The frigid lake inside her was near to bursting from her afternoons with Lust. But if she opened it up just a little, maybe it wouldn't all come rushing out.

One by one, she pulled the memories and their emotions out of that frozen state inside her heart. The affection from those memories filled her up with warmth and a bubbly happiness that she'd almost forgotten.

Affection's eyes, deep in that mist, grew wider. The yellow coloring spread throughout all of its mist until it turned into a little glowing ball in her lap. "Oh, my. There's so many of them!"

"I know people think I'm cold," she whispered, smiling down into the golden light. "I know people think I can't feel. But I can. And I do. I feel very deeply and I remember every memory that makes me feel like this. I keep them all, you see. Tucked away for moments when I cannot see anything but darkness. These are the memories that bring me back to the light."

Not her mother's grace or her life in the Tower. None of those memories made her feel anything but the icy cold that always tried to lock her up again.

Affection enjoyed her memories, it seemed. It babbled in her lap as it flicked through each and every one of them.

"You saw a circus?"

"I did," she said with a soft chuckle. "It was a long time ago, but the performers were so talented. My favorite was the—"

"Fire-eater!" Affection interrupted. "His flames stretched up to the sky like a dragon, and his throat glowed. He winked at you, and it made you feel like the only girl in the crowd watching him. He was so impressive!"

"He was."

Again, the spirit moved through her mind, and strangely, she didn't care anymore. It didn't feel as though the spirit was forcing itself into her, as her mother had always warned her with hauntings. Affection was respectfully peering into her mind so it could experience something new. Or perhaps only what it looked for.

Selene let the little spirit have its fun. It didn't get to feed often, or at least, that's what it said. And she could easily imagine that affection was hard to find in a castle like this.

Lust? Certainly. But affection took time and energy.

She could have stayed there all night, remembering only the good in her life. In her mind's eye, she could see all the memories hovering around them like glittering orbs. Before she'd met the spirit in her lap, she always imagined the orbs as windows. Glass balls where she could see through them. Now, every orb she'd pulled out had the faintest hint of yellow in it.

Maybe that was influenced by the coloring of little Affection, but... the magic in her whispered it was much more than that. Affection was yellow. The color was right, and she didn't have to understand why.

The closet door opened up and a spear of torchlight flooded into the room where they hid. Selene locked her memories back underneath the magic inside her body so swiftly she heard Affection groan in pain before it slunk out of her lap.

A woman stared at her with wide eyes. Her face was familiar, although the outfit wasn't helpful. This time, the woman in front of her wore a gauzy fabric dress that was tied at her neck. The same outfit that most of the maids wore, but not the same fabric.

The woman had been laying at Lust's feet during the orgy, she realized. This woman was one of Lust's favored ladies, or whatever it was the maids called them.

"Oh," she said, standing and shaking out her heavy skirts. "I didn't realize anyone used this closet."

The woman's eyes flicked between her and the spirit. "What were you doing in here?"

Selene couldn't tell her that she'd been talking to a magic bird that blew to bits in her hands. "Visiting?"

"With Affection?" The woman looked down at the spirit with a frown. "He'll be angry about this, you know."

The spirit huffed out a breath. "He knows we visit."

"You aren't supposed to talk to her."

Why would this woman know anything about what Lust wanted? Ah. Right. Because she was most likely spending a decent amount of time in his bed, and from what she'd heard, bedtime talks were how most secrets were passed around.

Selene suddenly felt awkward. She was not the fair haired beauty that stood in front of her. Nor did she have the natural curves that drew men to her side like this woman did. She was stunning, whereas Selene was... dark and sullen.

"I'll get out of your way," Selene said, skirting around the woman. "I didn't catch your name before. I'm sorry."

"Lara." The woman eyed her with no small amount of disdain before rolling her eyes up to the ceiling. "Be careful with him, would you?"

"Affection?" She tried to find the spirit, but it had already slunk away. "I don't think it could hurt me if it tried."

"Not Affection. It's harmless." Lara met her gaze this time with a hardness that marred her pretty face. "With Lust. He might be an ancient, but you're doing something to him that cannot be changed. He's alive too, you know. Lust has lived this way for a thousand years, and you think you have a right to change that? I just hope you know what you're doing."

Then she grabbed a broom out of the closet, a handful of towels, and stomped away from Selene.

What in the world?

She didn't have the time or the energy to think about that interaction. Selene felt all the energy seep out of her until she was nearly a puddle on the floor that Lara would have to mop up. This evening had been too much, and she was so damned cold again. Like always.

Selene weaved through the halls back to Lust's room, ready to sink into that bed and forget anything had ever happened tonight. Maybe her dreams would be better.

But as she closed the door behind herself, she heard a faint sound from the bed. The shifting of skin against silk, a longer, leaner body than her own, making the sound. A match struck, glowing bright in the darkness until Lust was revealed holding a lit candelabra. He placed it on the nightstand, the long muscles of his form flexing with each movement.

He sat at the foot of the bed, shirtless, with a mound of blankets and silk pillows surrounding him. He'd placed a pile of pillows on the floor between his legs, and he pointed to them with a slow, sensual grin.

"Come, sorceress. I thought of something you might find pleasurable."

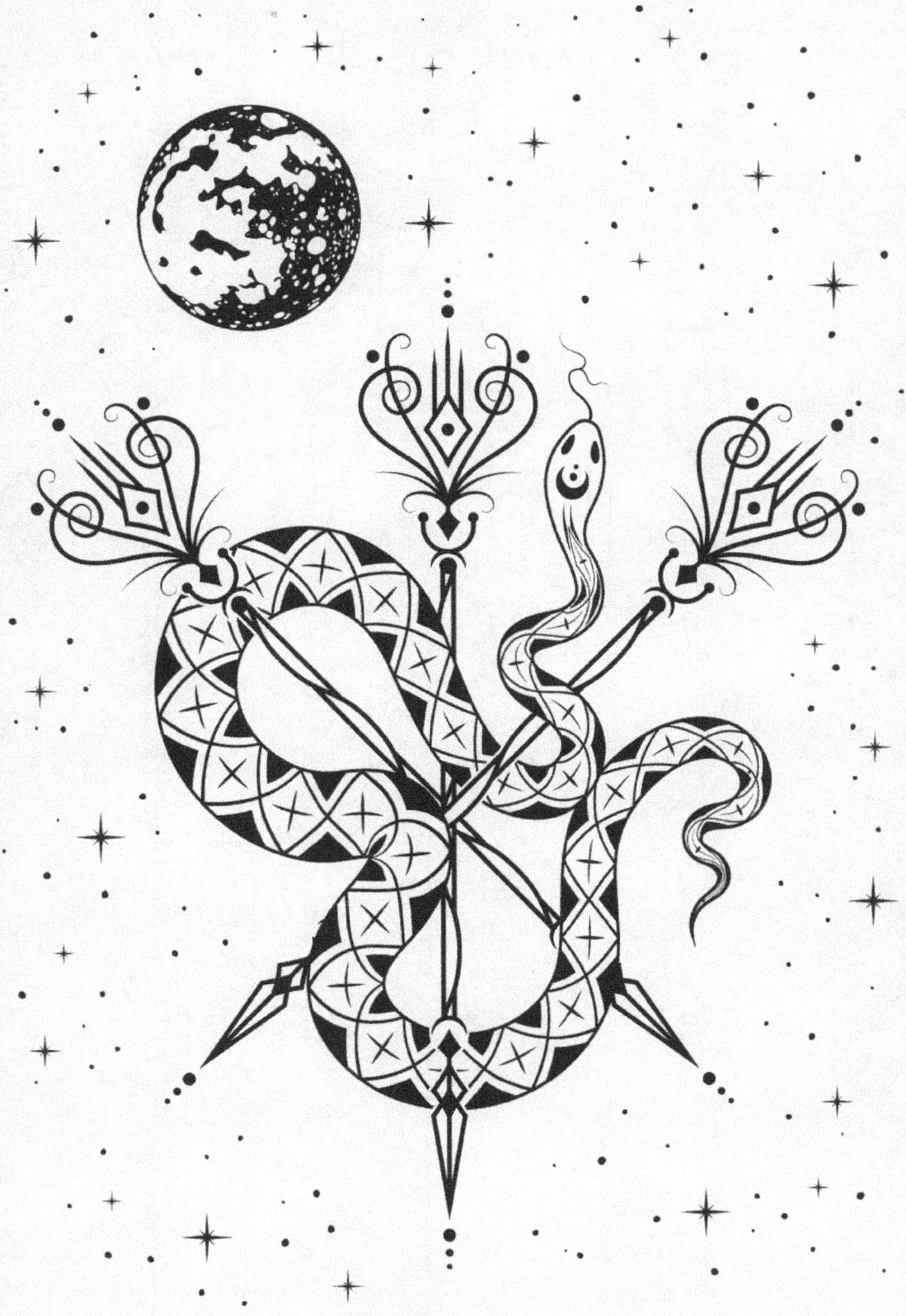

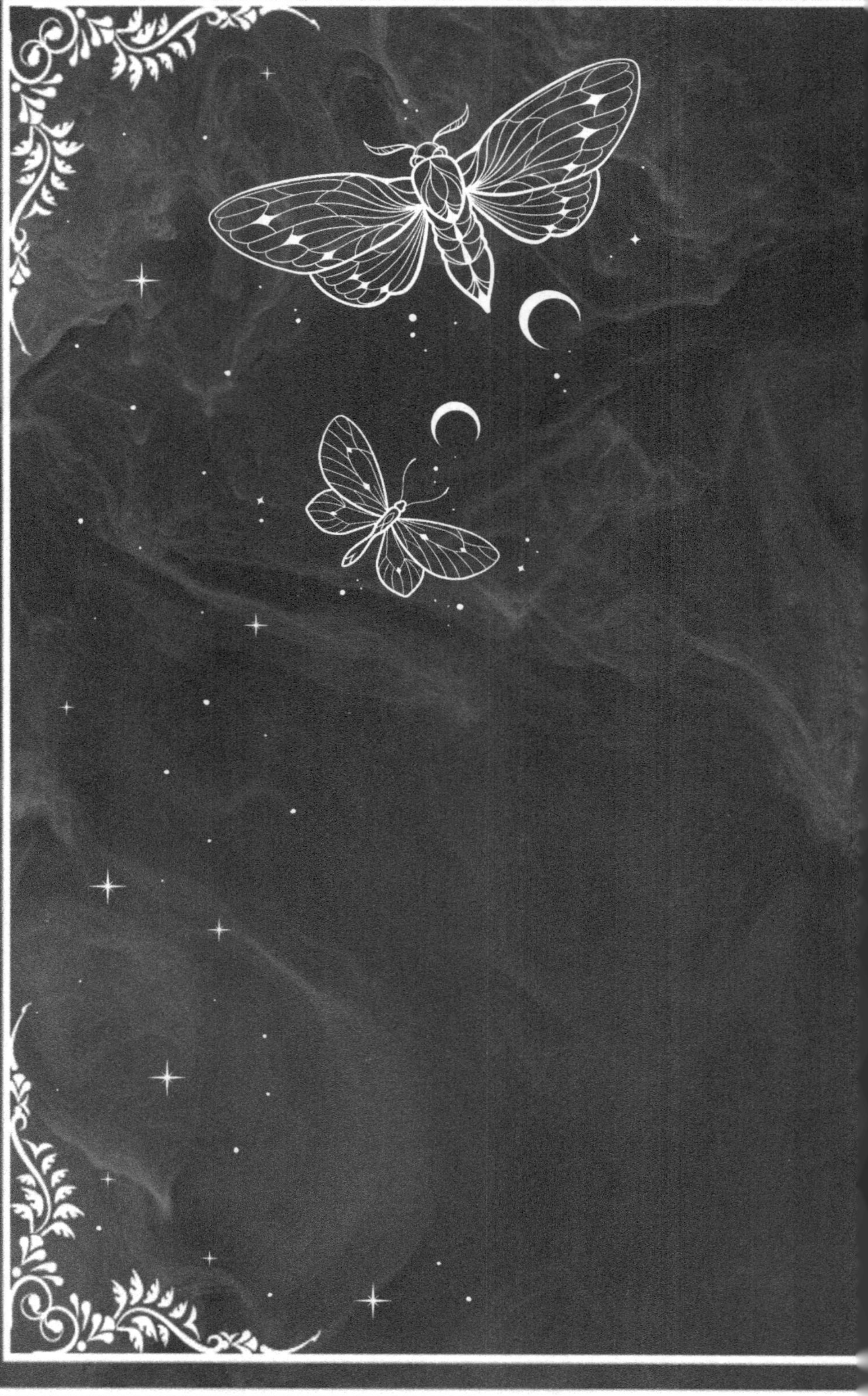

Chapter 16

Lust knew better than to tempt fate like this. Neither of them had to rush any quicker than they already were. She was just beginning to trust him, and he had proven that he would take his time. Even become friends with the woman regardless of how blinded she made him to everyone else.

But he'd had a very long day. They were preparing for his brother's arrival. Tomorrow. Greed would show up with a hundred of his own people, all of them likely armed to the teeth. They needed to figure out where he was staying in the castle. How much food they needed to bring in. Dignitaries from the royalty had to meet with the others.

He had prepped everyone on what to expect. Lara was planning a party unlike any the castle had seen in a hundred years. He'd personally spoken with the cooks because there was no one else to do all this in the absence of a queen.

And it had made him think. He'd realized that perhaps there was some use to a queen after all. A partner to help him in moments like this. Lust had to shake those thoughts away, because he also recognized them for the folly they were.

Having a queen once every hundred years to make a single day easier were the thoughts of an immortal, not of humanity. Though he would remain for years to come, whoever he married would not.

Spirits were not fleeting things. Spirits of lust even less so. His kind rarely died because humans felt the emotion more strongly than any other.

The entire day was stressful, full of aches and pains and annoyances. And by the end of it, he hadn't even thought of going to his own bedroom. He'd trailed along behind Lara, who kept giving him secretive glances and lustful stares that swept up and down his body.

She tempted him. He'd thought about losing himself in her for a few hours, or even all night just so he didn't have to think about tomorrow. Dread filled him every time he thought of Greed walking these halls, completely untamed because this wasn't even his own kingdom. Greed cared little for what he changed or affected here. He would take because it was in his nature and Lust could say nothing.

He'd stood in the doorway as Lara undressed. He'd let his eyes linger on all the curves he remembered so well, like she was an extension of his own body. Arms braced on the door frame, he'd even leaned inside just a bit before some thread tugged backward.

A thread that was tied to Selene. A thread that whispered he'd rather be somewhere else. With someone else.

Without a word, Lust had left Lara alone in her room, heard a glass smash on the ground from something she'd thrown, and made his way back here. He had thought to return with Selene already warming his bed. Instead, he'd found it cold.

Lust had circled the bed, dragging his hand along the silk sheets. Just that slight movement had released some of her scent. Peppermint floated up and filled the air with a wintery scent. Cold. Detached. But ever so lovely all the same.

So he'd sat. And waited. He didn't know how long it took her to get back to his room, but those soft moments of quiet had given him time to plan. When she stood in the doorway, surprised to see him, Lust already knew what he was going to say.

"Come," he repeated, gesturing with his hand for her to sit in front of him. "I won't bite."

"You've already bitten me before." Her eyes flicked to the door as she considered running, but then she seemed to set her shoulders against the thought.

Did she believe this was her duty? That her mother would... what? Disown her if she didn't do whatever Lust wanted her to do?

Minerva wouldn't pawn her daughter off to a demon unless she thought the girl could bring him to his knees. He tried to see what the High Sorceress had seen in Selene, but he couldn't. There were a hundred women who looked just like her, and yet, this one had made him turn down an evening of lust for yet another of frustration.

How was she doing it?

And then she wandered toward him, her hands folded primly in front of her hips and those heavy woolen skirts shushing around her. Then he knew what it was that Minerva had seen.

The woman had a spine of steel. She might do what others wished her to do, but never once did she yield. He could picture her as a child, defiantly looking up at her school teachers as she refused the homework or argued that they were wrong in their teachings. And he could just as easily see her bloodied, glaring up at a torturer and willing them to do their best.

No, she was no ordinary woman. He just hadn't seen it because he looked for the extraordinary in the physical. But she was far more than her body.

Selene sat down on the pillows in front of him, her spine straight as a board and her hands curled into fists in her lap. "What do you think I will enjoy?"

"First of all, not being so tense." He picked up her hair, letting the dark waterfall trail through his fingers. "You haven't been wearing this up lately."

He heard a sharp gulp, her surprise bleeding through all the stiffness in her body. "You seemed to hate the bun. You took my hair out the very first time we were alone here."

"You didn't leave it down for me, did you?" Because he could not resist the temptation, he leaned down until his breath would warm her neck. "I find it hard to believe you would choose to do anything for me alone."

A little shiver trailed through her and goosebumps rose where his breath had touched. "Maybe I like having it down."

"Ah, there it is. The honesty I was looking for." Lust had pity on her and leaned back. "This is an easy game, Selene. I will answer any question you have, and in return, you will let me touch you. Depending on the question, I will touch certain parts of you."

"That seems more like a game of lust."

"Ah, but you are not interested in me. We've already been over this. And I am only interested in you because you do not desire me." He rolled his eyes, knowing that she couldn't see him. "However, this game is not about bending you to my ways. You said you could feel lust, and that you did not know how to ask for what you wanted. I will not force myself on you. All I ask is that we explore what you might like together."

"That sounds as though you're asking to touch me in places I do not wish you to touch."

"I will avoid such places if it makes you uncomfortable." His soul screamed at him not to make that deal. Already his fingers itched to trail over her curves, to stroke between her thighs and see if she was as wet for him as he hoped. As if that would prove she wanted him.

The stiffness in her spine eased. Just a little. "If you will avoid places such as that, then…"

The hesitancy was the opening he needed. Because while he still wished to touch her, he also would take whatever he could. Even if that was little more than her hair.

"Ask your first question," he whispered, licking his lips as he let her long locks trail through his fingers again. "Whatever you have been yearning to know."

She looked over her shoulder at him. "Yearning?"

"It is in my nature to hope that you at least yearn for information. You are frigid, Selene. Let that ice break a little for me." He trailed the backs of his fingers over her cheek and watched as her eyes widened a bit at his words.

What had he said? She almost looked like she would bolt at any moment before she turned her head back to the front of the room. Swallowing hard again, she finally nodded.

But she didn't ask questions. Was she testing him? He could sit here keeping his hands to himself for as long as she needed him to, even if that meant he would go insane.

Lust flexed his hands on his thighs and then forced them to remain still. He waited for what felt like hours before he felt her melt against his leg. She leaned against him, startlingly warm for a woman so cold.

"What did it feel like taking a body for the first time?"

His mind skittered toward sex before he realized what she was asking. "How do you know—"

Though his words had trailed off, she seemed to understand what he was trying to ask. "Affection. It talks a lot. Mostly about things I suspect you don't want me to know."

"It wasn't supposed to tell you about any of that," he grumbled. "Affection knows better than to reveal the secrets of spirits."

"It didn't tell me about you, if that makes it any better. It only told me about itself. The rest I pieced together, considering your name and all the rumors." She stilled as his fingers threaded through her hair, but then relaxed against him as he gently massaged her scalp. "So?"

"So what?"

"What did it feel like?"

The question was one he normally would have exacted a great price to answer. But as his hands trailed down her neck and dug into her shoulders, he found this was pleasing enough. To feel her relaxed and pliant against him, it was rather nice.

"It felt strange. Being a spirit is freeing. There is no physical form to feed or water, and the mist that is our form is easier to slide into places that require much more effort when we are like this." Lust waited a few moments as her head lolled to the side for him to dig a little deeper into her neck before he slowed his movements, trailing his fingers lightly down the column of her neck. "But a spirit can only live our emotion second hand. We rely on humans to know what it feels like to be angry, afraid, happy, sad. To be in a physical form and to know what lust actually felt like. It was... sublime."

"I can only imagine such an existence is at first very confusing."

"Oh, not confusing at all." He moved his fingers around to her back and then gently undid the first buttons of her dress. "You never forget your first. Isn't that what mortals say? And I certainly won't forget that memory."

She shifted a little before clearing her throat. "Were you always a spirit of lust?"

"That's a question that will require much more touching." He leaned and hummed in her ear. "Are you sure you want to pay for that one?"

As he asked the question, Lust eased his fingers underneath the heavy back of her gown. She wore another layer underneath it, damned woman, so he couldn't feel the smooth skin of her back. But somehow, the thin cotton only made her feel all the more fierce.

He waited to see if she would answer, but she didn't. Instead, she seemed to hover in that place of not knowing. What would he do? What was the price for the question?

Gently, he eased his hands along her ribs. His fingers brushed the sides of her breasts. Their softness was even warmer than the rest of her body, but he did not push for more than he knew she would give. Instead, he lingered on the narrow feeling of her ribcage, how delicate and fragile she was.

Her soft inhalation gave him the answer he searched for. She liked feeling small underneath his hands.

Lust pressed each of his fingers tighter against her, one by one, until he felt the softness of her breasts above his thumbs. It was enough of a touch for her to gasp, not enough to be entirely inappropriate. Still, he heard her hiss out a breath.

No need to rush, he told himself, even as he hardened to the point of pain. They were working on trust, and she'd asked him not to touch certain parts of her. But that didn't mean he couldn't tease the rest.

He leaned over her, too large for this space, but knowing it would only make her feel even smaller. "Well?" he asked again, rumbling in her ear. He hardly recognized the depth of his own voice. It had turned so guttural. "What price will you pay for that question?"

Lust trailed his fingers down her ribs, moving across the flat plane of her belly that flexed against his palms. The top of her dress shifted with his movement, gaping forward and revealing enough of blushed skin that he had to look away from the sight.

Wincing, he continued his blind journey. He lingered on the sensitive sides of her torso, to the arches of her hip bones. Her little gasp as he trailed his fingers past them made him hesitate. How far did he want to push her? How far did he want to push himself?

He stopped, the tips of his pointer fingers just inches from where he hoped she was warm, and soft, and wet. "Well?" he asked. "How much do you want to know the answer to that question?"

"Enough," she whispered. "But not as badly as you want to answer it."

Confused, he saw movement in the corner of his eye. And that's when he realized there was a hand-held mirror on her vanity that wasn't set face down. It angled toward them, just enough for her to see him and all his reactions.

His eyes met hers in the reflection. And oh, if she didn't look more beautiful than he'd expected. Her eyes glowed with triumph, as though she'd caught him in a lie. Her cheeks were already flushed, her lips slightly parted, and they looked decadently wicked together.

He loomed over her, the candlelight bouncing off his horns. So large compared to her that his outline swallowed all the light. His hands disappeared into her unlaced dress as she wantonly leaned back into him. It was a painting that a prophet would use to warn young women of the monstrous demons, who wanted to take away their innocence.

Lust bared his teeth at her in the reflection, knowing before he saw them that his canines would have grown sharper and his eyes would flash with desire.

He'd never looked like this with a woman. He was meant to be desirable, alluring, a man that none could resist. But in this moment, with her, he looked like the demon she expected him to be.

And she looked like she enjoyed it.

He kept their gazes locked as she placed her hand over his. The thick brocade of her gown separated them, but he moved his palm with her as she guided one of his hands up toward her breast again. She stopped just underneath it until he was almost cupping the soft swell.

"You think this will scare me, but it does not. I knew what I would have to pay to serve you, and I was never afraid of it." She shifted his other hand lower, his middle finger just brushing her heat.

A low growl escaped his lips, and that feral expression seemed to sharpen even further. Peppermint filled his nose on an inhale and somehow that made him feel as though he could lose control. He'd drag her up onto the bed with him, roll her underneath him, and devour her lips. He'd sink his fingers between her legs, into that warm, tight pussy. He'd suck her nipples until she begged him to stop, until he'd left marks all over her body in bright bruises from his tongue, his teeth, and his lips.

Lust wanted to do all that and more, but he would not do so unless she begged for it.

And Selene begged no one.

"Is this how you want to remember this moment?" she whispered, her voice a little breathless. "A transfer of information? A payment made?"

"No," he rasped. "This is not how it will go between us."

She slowly lifted her hands from his, leaving him to make the final choice. "Then I will get ready for bed. And you—"

He interrupted her before she could finish the sentence. "Will be waiting right here for you."

Though he knew it was foolish, he intended to spend the night with her. If only to bury his face in those pillows and fall asleep with her scent in his nose.

"What?" she whispered. "No, you will…"

"Stay here. In my room. In my bed." His fingers flexed one more time against her stomach, shifting a little lower, dragging the cloth against her clit, until he felt the buck of her hips against him. He grinned and then withdrew his hands from underneath her dress. "I promised I wouldn't touch you in any way you don't want, little moon. Scared that you'll reveal yourself in your sleep?"

"Impossible. I do not desire you," she whispered, but her eyes were bright with worry.

And perhaps something else.

He nodded and then shifted up onto the bed, knowing she'd seen how affected he was by their little exchange, and not caring how wide her eyes got before she looked away. "Then get ready, Selene. I find myself wishing for dreams."

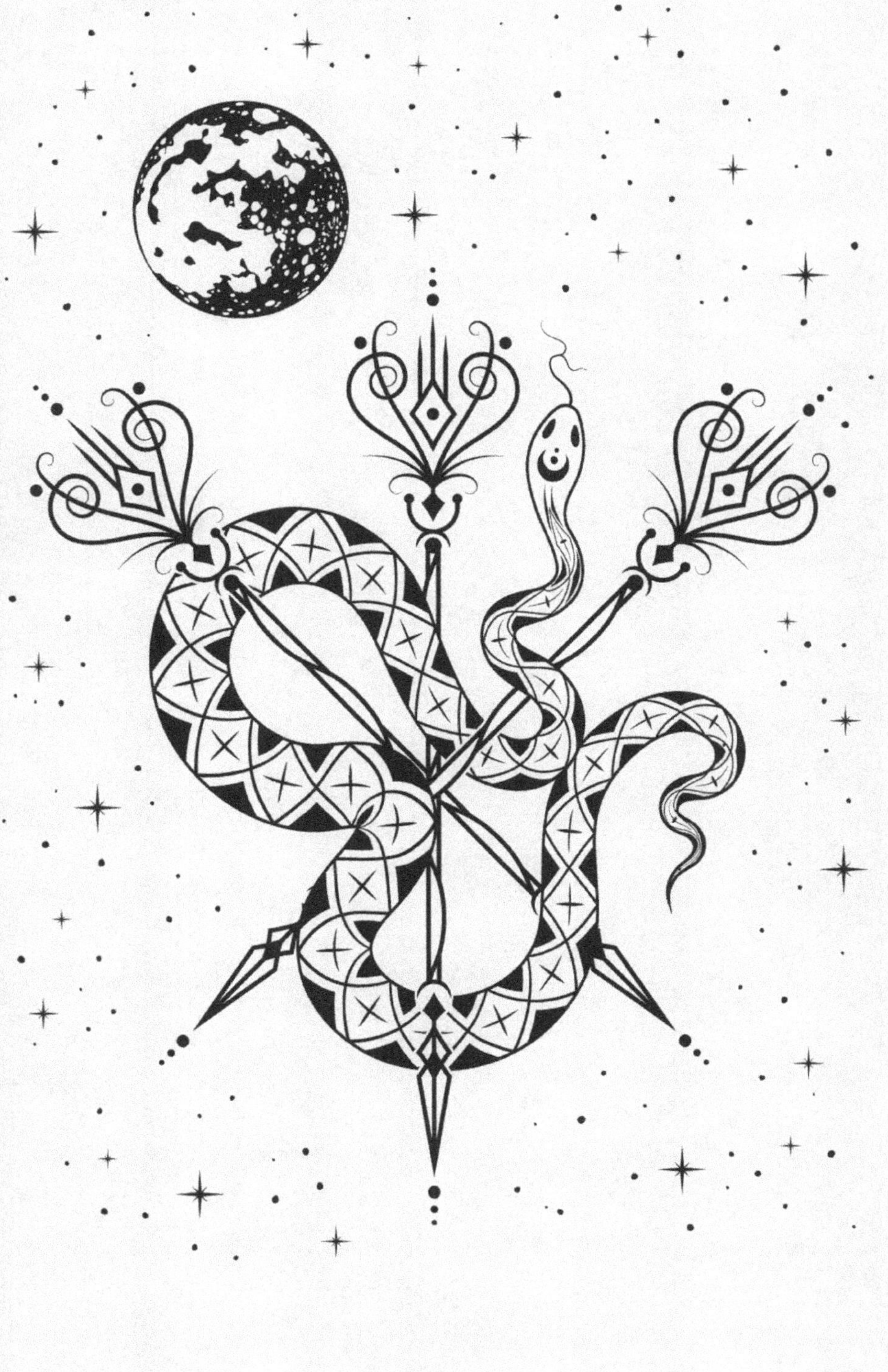

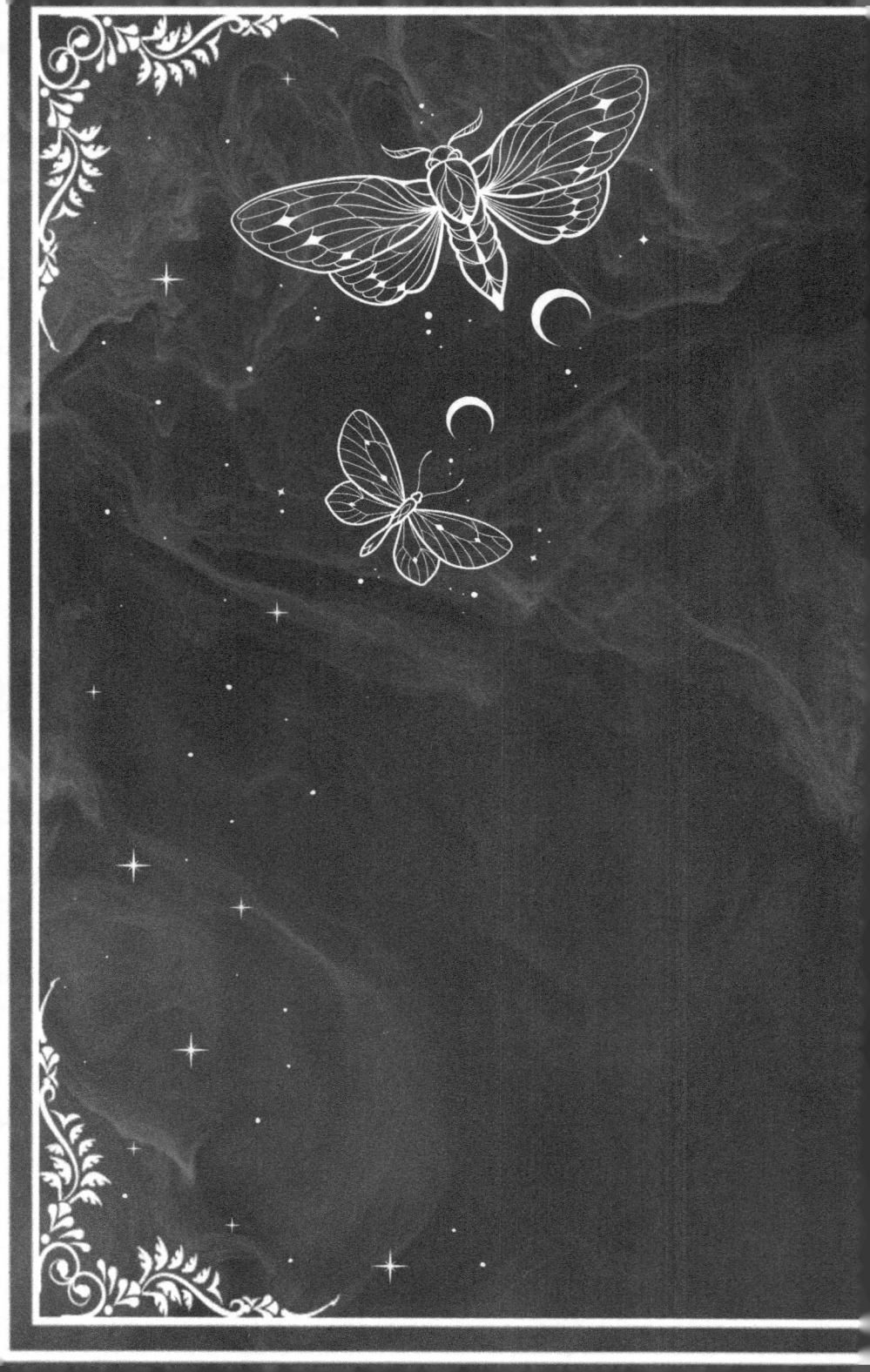

Chapter 17

Her dreams were filled with touches and soft gasps. The sound of masculine growls and the feeling of silk sheets sliding up her legs, tangling between them so she could finally find some sense of relief.

But that was not reality. Not in the real world where she knew to caution herself. Even in her dreams, she had fought back against the sensations, knowing that if she didn't stop them that she could never come back from this moment. She'd be his, and she wasn't meant to be anyone's but her own.

The dawn woke her. The soft beams of sunlight shifted through the gauzy fabric covering the balcony door. They drifted in the breeze, and she watched them for long moments from underneath heavy lids.

Selene felt as though she hadn't gotten a lick of sleep. She needed another three hours to feel more like herself, and she'd need her wits about her today. Lust's brother would arrive soon and she needed to stay hidden away. Or maybe she needed to impress him. She hadn't, really...

A warm, thick arm tightened around her waist for a moment before it relaxed again.

She forced herself to remain still, just in case her movement had nearly woken him. But the heaviness of his arm stayed very still again. Almost too still.

Selene suddenly realized how tangled they were together. His arm was around her waist, one thick thigh wedged between her own. His breath was heavy against her neck, slow and deep as it could only be in sleep.

He was wrapped around her like a second skin, and she didn't know when that had happened.

Last night, she'd wanted to turn around and let him have his way with her. She'd wanted to feel his lips against her skin, to know what it would feel like to ride that impressive hardness that he had made no move to hide in the slightest.

He'd wanted her. That much was very clear. But she also knew that he wanted everyone and everything he could get his hands on. He was a spirit of lust! As much as she disliked his favorite bedmate, the woman Lara had a point.

Selene was trying to change something that had been around for ages. He was a spirit who couldn't change, or at least, she didn't think he could. The price he'd wanted for the answer to her question was a little more than she was willing to give. But in the moment, with those broad, thick hands delving closer and closer to where he'd find her soaking wet...

She felt herself grow slick against his thigh, even at the thought. And damn it, he was pressed against her clit so firmly all it would take was a few wiggles and she'd probably explode against him. That's all it would take, and that was embarrassing enough.

This man was dangerous. Not just for herself, but for the entire kingdom. She had to remember that. She had to...

He made a soft sound in his sleep and then moved to disentangle himself from her. His thigh shifted first, dragging against her until she had to muffle the sound that came out of her mouth. Then his arm, his palm and fingers sliding over her nipples. Was he awake?

But she looked over her shoulder and saw he was still deeply asleep. His eyes were shut, his blonde hair stuck to his horns in a bird's nest of tangles that made her want to pick them all apart. And his bare chest moved with deep, slow inhalations. Rising and falling.

Even the sun played on that golden skin. The rays touched him all over, as though the element couldn't resist itself, and she hated that.

How was she jealous of the sun?

In sleep, his features were much less harsh. She could see how people would find him attractive, even more so than just the legendary Lust who ruled this kingdom. But there were laugh lines around his eyes and mouth, the marks of a man who had found much happiness. His high cheekbones and full lips were vaguely feminine, but his strong jaw made them somehow even more masculine. At least through her eyes. Perhaps if she were a man, she would see it the opposite way.

He was a creature made to tempt. That was certain.

But in this light, he also looked less intimidating. All that tangled hair hanging off his horns, the slackness to his jaw that suggested he might snore on some nights. It was endearing.

Oh, she hated to even think like this. She hated how her hands itched to brush that hair off his forehead.

But why shouldn't she?

This game they played was dangerous for the both of them. She'd seen the way his face had twisted as he moved his hands over her body, trying desperately not to touch what she'd said was off limits. Almost as though it was physically painful for him to rein himself in.

He'd done it. She was certain that a demon like him wouldn't be able to keep his hands to himself. But he had. He'd respected her wishes.

Seven kingdoms, she'd wanted him to touch her. And she'd wanted to touch him.

Maybe it was the dreams still lingering. Maybe it was her own madness coming through because she wouldn't have done it without the perfect circumstances, but she eased his hair off his horns, smoothing the strands back into place.

For a crazed moment, she let her guard down. She had to feel everything, eventually. The lake inside her was filled to the brim, and she feared it would overflow. Or worse, it wouldn't let her hide any more of her emotions within it.

He was asleep. Surely he couldn't feel anything. She would open the floodgates all at once, feel everything for a few moments and endure. And then, when the lake was halfway empty, she'd close it again. Ready for whatever Greed might throw at her.

It was a crazy thought, but she still did it. Selene let all those emotions out at the same time, letting them swell over her head and crash down. All the fear, the desire, the heartbreak and homesickness. It came out in a strange sludge, a mixture of emotions that should never be together. Her stomach twisted, vomit rising in her throat and then subsiding as the better emotions overwhelmed the bad.

She'd survived this long with them, she supposed. They lived inside her, likely spreading their poison in a way she could never outrun. But all at once, they were horrible and wonderful, nightmarish and a dream.

Even this was like a dream. Lying beside him, her heart in her throat and desire burning so deeply through her that she couldn't even think straight.

And then, with the sunlight glittering off the lilac and sapphire chips of his eyes, he blinked awake to stare at her. The lazy haze in his gaze made him appear harmless, a thought she'd never expected to link with the man lying next to her.

"You stayed," he said, his voice deep and thick with sleep.

She slammed the walls shut so hard she felt the answering ache sear through her body. But she couldn't let him get even a hint of that power inside her, nor could he know that she wanted him so badly that it made her shake.

Her breath catching in her throat, she watched him for any reaction at all. "Where else would I go?"

"Poor moon," he whispered, shifting a strand of her hair away from her face. "All alone in this place, with nowhere to go but the bed of a demon."

"It's a comfortable bed, at least."

"It is." A small frown wrinkled his brow and his lips set in a firm line. "For a moment there I thought I felt—"

Panic made her move. She grabbed his wrist, holding it against her to force his attention back to this moment. "You felt nothing, demon king."

"Oh, but I am almost certain that I did."

He rolled over her, the silken sheets slipping from his body like water as he fit himself between her thighs. The weight of him pressed her against the mattress, so decadent, so heavy. He pressed against her, his hard cock wedged so tightly between her legs that she nearly choked on the pleasure of it. He rocked against her, once, twice, brushing a tender part of her body that nearly made her moan.

Selene set her jaw, grinding her teeth and glaring up into that beautiful face. He had his eyes squeezed shut, his face the picture of rapture as he moved against her. And it almost broke her. The way the golden light highlighted the flexing muscles of his shoulders, the tense set of his jaw. He was so handsome and so dangerous.

But then he sighed and slowed his movements, easing to a stop that pressed the perfect spot and far too wrong. She needed him to move. She wanted to feel that pressure again because she was so fucking close and...

Selene was thinking like a fool. He was not some handsome man she'd met who didn't mind a quick afternoon with her. He was a demon king, and the wrong person for her.

Somehow, her hands had come to his forearms. She squeezed the muscles there tightly, breathing hard and staring up at him in shock. He had yet to open his eyes, though the muscle of his jaw ticked as he ground his teeth.

Finally, he blew out a long breath and opened those lovely eyes. He looked her over, seeming to make sure that she was all right.

She was fine. She just didn't know what to say. If Selene opened her mouth, she was afraid she'd ask him to continue. That she'd ask for him to move and ignore all the feelings between them. That it was all right if she couldn't look at him the next day, because all she wanted was to feel him rocking against her again.

But neither of them could do that. She knew it. He knew it. That was why he'd stopped.

He tilted his head to the side, staring down at her with that frown still on his face. "The thought of your lust is enough to drive me mad, Selene. I want to know what it tastes like. What you taste like. The thought seeps into my dreams and even in sleep, I think about taking you. About driving you to the very edge of madness before I let you come wrapped around me. It's enough to make a man lose his head, but it is not what I promised you. For that, I apologize."

And then he rolled off her and stood up from the bed.

The lack of him made her feel strangely... empty. She wanted him back, and she wanted to tell him to do exactly that. Fill her to the point of pain, make her scream his name as she let herself feel what he wanted her to feel.

His words echoed in her mind. He claimed to know what she wanted even if she didn't. No part of her doubted that he would make sex enjoyable for her, even without Selene telling him what to touch or where to taste. His amount of experience would only make his claims even more possible.

And she wanted that. Oh, how she wanted it. But she had to be the one to deny him because if she didn't, then she'd lose herself in him. Selene feared she'd never find her way back to herself.

Gathering up a handful of the sheets, she held it against her chest even though she wore a nightgown that covered her from wrist to neck. It didn't matter. She always felt like she stood in front of him, naked as the day she was born.

"Are you getting up now?" he asked. He moved about the room without hesitation, lithe and confident in his movements like he wasn't rock hard and tenting his pants, so it was impossible to look anywhere else.

"I—" She tried to clear the jumble of thoughts in her head. "Do

I need to?"

"Not precisely. I imagine you will have to meet with my brother, considering you're largely the reason he's coming. But I wouldn't mind taking him around the castle a few times to ease his natural tendencies before he sees you. While I understand you may be immune to my powers, it would be absurd to think you could deny all of us."

The thought made her question what to do. She could ignore all of their powers if she wanted. Selene could stuff all those emotions away for a later time, although she feared what two powerful demons would make her do. After all, she was just one woman, and they were an overwhelming amount of emotion if they wanted to be.

But it would look suspicious if she could avoid all of their powers. She should probably let Greed influence her, but that was terrifying in its own rights. She didn't know what she would do if she let his powers swell inside her.

Would she steal? Absolutely. She used to steal cookies when she was little, and she didn't doubt that she'd do it again here. And what about with Lust? Greed was very similar in its desires. Greed had people take what they wanted, no matter the cost. And she wanted Lust.

More than she'd ever wanted anything else.

No, she couldn't let Greed influence her. But she could put on a good show that would make him believe he could.

"Whatever you think is best," she murmured, looking down at her free hand in her lap. She tried to make it look relaxed. Why did her fingers keep coiling into that fist as though preparing for a fight? She wasn't going to battle. She didn't have to protect herself.

A warm hand slid underneath her chin, cupping her jaw and forcing her to look up at him.

Lust stared down at her with worry lines between his eyes. And that was something she'd never seen before. "I won't let him take you, Selene. You know that."

"I do," she whispered. "But that doesn't mean he won't do other things."

"I know you believe all of us to be demons, and that your mother made it seem like we were all evil to a fault. We are not. Besides, what would Greed even make you do?" He snorted before releasing her. "There's nothing here that you want."

Except there was.

Him.

Lust gathered up an armful of clothes before sauntering toward the door. "I'll get dressed in another room, considering it takes a village to prepare me. Take your time, little moon. Greed will be here by the time the sun hits its peak in the sky, but I won't expect to see you until dinner."

And then he was gone. Leaving her alone with her feelings that already threatened to drown her.

She didn't know how long she stared at that door until a little misty being slipped underneath it. Affection looked at her with bright eyes, and that darned yellow glow cast shadows on the wall. "Oh! You don't think he's that bad anymore, do you?"

Growling out a frustrated breath, Selene landed flat on her back on the bed again. She dragged a pillow over her face and screamed into it.

Because the spirit wasn't wrong. She thought she might actually like the bastard after all.

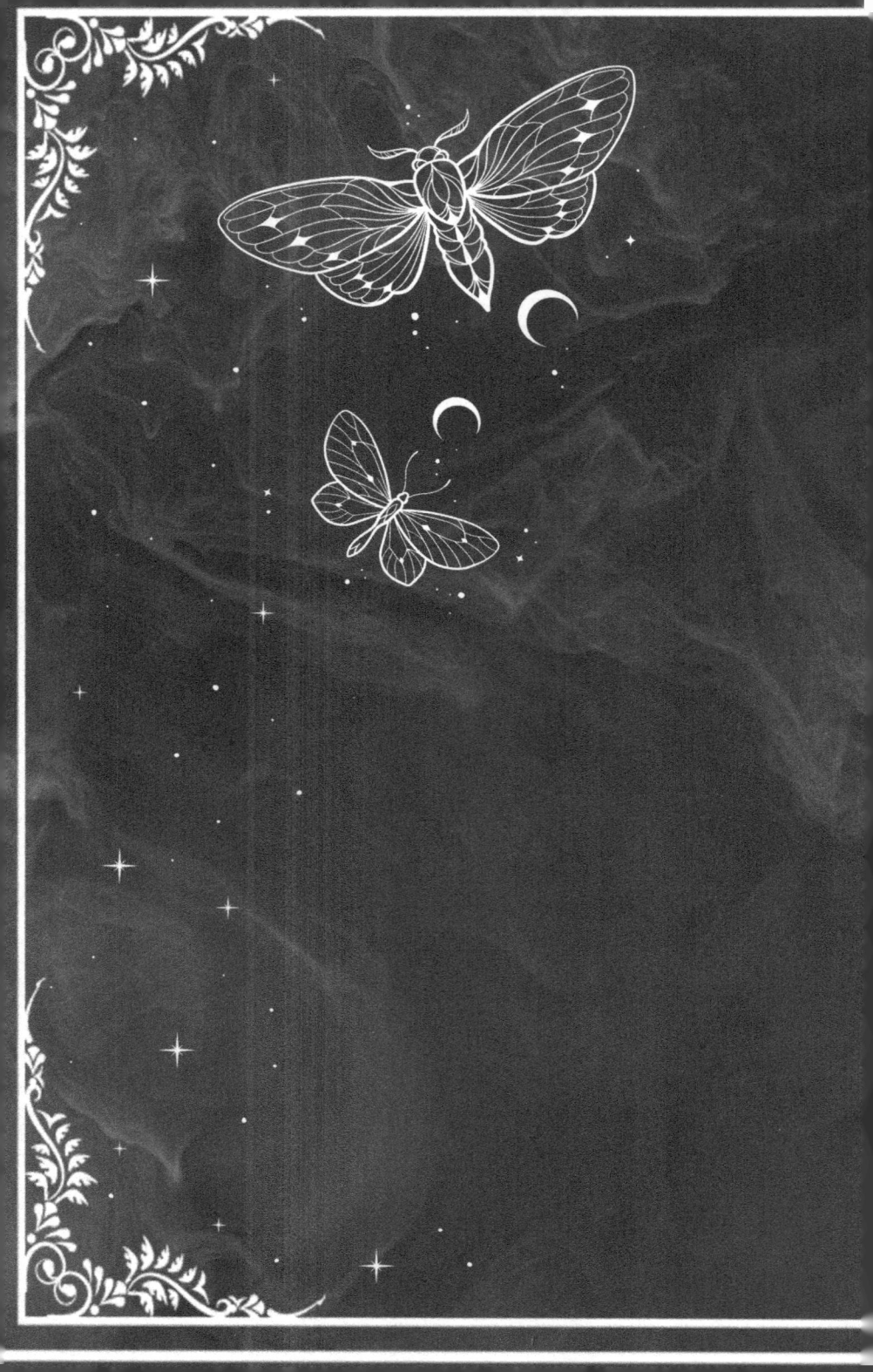

Chapter 18

Though he was nervous about seeing his brother and feared what he might do, Lust also found he was excited. It had been nearly two hundred years since he'd stood in the same room with any of his siblings.

They all were drastically different. None of them looked blood related, and in a way, they weren't. But they had fought together for years as spirits, learning and growing stronger until they could take on physical forms. They'd helped each other scare off spirits that would have stolen their power. Their feasts. And now, they were the seven creatures who ruled these lands.

Greed had always been closest to Lust. They were two sides of the same coin. Greed took what he wanted. Lust also did the same. Although their wants were usually very different.

He stood in front of his castle, waiting for the gates to open.

If there hadn't been a certain distracting someone in his bed, then he might have met Greed at the end of the glistening bridge between their kingdoms. But the bridge could only be traversed by one spirit at a time.

Mortals had a hard time on it. The substance looked like glass, but bent at the slightest touch. Some of his lovers had once meandered across, coming from different kingdoms to provide him with something "new". He remembered them saying the sway felt as though they were standing on top of a bubble that at any point could pop.

The magic wouldn't. He knew it swayed because it must, not because it was weak.

As it was, he hadn't met his brother at the bridge, as was customary. Lust hadn't wanted to wake up. And when he did, he hadn't wanted to leave the bed. Seeing her there, watching him as though she thought he was asleep? It was... sublime.

Maybe he'd fallen asleep again in her arms after she'd fixed his hair. But the tenderness of her light fingers slipping over his features, so careful to make sure that didn't wake him, it stirred something in his chest he'd never felt before.

A curious feeling. He'd need to confer with his brother about what it might be. Perhaps Greed had felt it before, and would know how to cure him of the ailment.

The doors before him swung open and shouts came from the top of the castle's walls. He was here. They were here.

Greed's entourage came rushing into the doors, their whooping calls echoing up into the sky. They were the warriors of the kingdoms, those who reveled in the fight and trained until their dying breath. They took what they wanted, by force or in battle. Greed and his people had tried to start rumors that they were the most terrifying in all the kingdoms.

Wrath only laughed when he heard those rumors. But his kingdom in the underworld was and always would be, set apart from the rest.

A grin split his features, and he descended the stairs into the courtyard below. Greed's people wore leather and furs. Some were in dark colors, most were in the natural tan hide of the beasts they killed each season. Furs decorated their shoulders and war paint covered their faces in streaks of white and gold. Some rode beasts that were similar to horses, but their skin was leathery and without fur, their bodies thin and appearing emaciated until one saw how fast they could ride. Their mouths were full of sharpened teeth, and he'd never thought to ask if Greed's people filed them, or if the beasts were born that way.

In the very center of all of it, his brother rode. His mount was covered in golden hand prints that sparkled in the sunlight as if they were branded into the beast with gold. The closer he got, the more Lust thought that might be exactly what had happened to the creature. Even its ears were pierced with rubies dangling from countless holes.

Greed looked well, though. His brother's chest was even broader than the last time he'd seen him. Greed's flame red hair was shaved on the sides and a wild riot on top. His eyes were ringed in dark kohl, and the sarcastic grin on his face made him look downright wicked. Skin burnished by the sun, his only flaw was how many freckles covered his body. For a man who had chosen the desert for his home, his skin was made for fairer climates.

His brother swung off his mount and patted its side before approaching him with wide open arms. A long lion's tail flicked behind him before stilling. "Brother!" he called out and then wrapped his arms around Lust's shoulders. "It has been too long."

Indeed. Lust gathered the other man up in a bear hug, the two of them clinging to each other. The brothers were always affectionate, even those who had fought in the past. Neither of them knew if it would be another two hundred years before they saw each other. Spirits knew to make time count.

They were the only people in this realm that understood what it was like to claw their way into a physical body. That history ensured they were closer than those even bound by blood.

"It has been far too long," he repeated, then pushed Greed away to really look at him. "You've gotten bigger."

"Well, I actually have to fight to stay alive. Unlike some of us who are happy to stay in a castle and let everyone else do the fighting for them." Greed laughed, though, and the sound softened his words. "This place! I cannot say you have gotten bigger since I last saw you, but your castle certainly has."

Lust turned with him, an arm over Greed's shoulder to look at his home. And it had gotten bigger. In the last two hundred years, they'd added two additional wings and almost three hundred servants.

Of course, he filled Greed in on all of that, knowing it would satisfy his brother's baser urges.

"You've taken what you wanted, then," Greed said with a sly grin. "I thought that was my curse, not yours."

"Ah, it is no curse. You live well and you live often."

"Indeed, brother. We are the conquerors of this land, that is for certain." Greed gestured toward all his followers. "I take it you have room for them all? I did not know how many servants you'd want in your bed, but I brought enough to satisfy us both."

"I have no need of them in my bed." Although he was ashamed to admit there was a time when he would have taken them all to his bed throughout the trip and asked for more.

His brother eyed him with a grin before he shrugged. "That's fine. Whatever lies you want to tell yourself. Regardless, you can keep them all, yes?"

"Of course. There is plenty of room here."

"Good. I even brought a few of my people who are similar to your... problem." He pointed to three of his tallest followers. The two women who were almost as tall as Lust and Greed, and a man who towered over them all. The three of them were muscled beyond reckoning, their eyes watching everyone pass by them with a glare on their faces.

"Impressive," Lust muttered, eyeing the women as though they might break him.

"Oh, not her." Greed pointed behind the tallest woman. "That one."

Another woman stood behind her, spectacles on her nose and a tablet in her hands. She was much smaller, not an ounce of muscle on her, and leaner than any woman he'd ever seen. So slight, he worried a breeze might topple her over.

"Well, Selene might be more comfortable talking with her than the giants you keep company with," Lust muttered.

"Selene, is it now? This nameless woman has been plaguing my thoughts. She has you wrapped around her fingers already, I see."

"She does not."

Greed opened his mouth for another jab, but then snapped his jaw shut with a sharp hiss. Lust already knew what he saw. Still, he turned around slowly so he could savor this moment.

Selene walked down the steps toward them, graceful and measured as always. She was no great beauty, but she stood out among all the rest for the clothing that she wore. A black brocade gown covered her from neck to toe. The intricate runes sewed into every inch made her appear to glisten with magic. She'd bound her dark hair back into a bun, and his fingers already itched to pull out those damned pins. He knew without a doubt that her hair would fall so lovely, and that he'd be hit with a wave of her scent.

Damn it, just looking at her made him react. He hissed out a long breath and turned his gaze to his brother so no one would see his embarrassment.

But what he saw on his brother's expression made every muscle in his body tighten.

Greed's eyes were glowing, like chips of gold in his head. They only did that when he saw something he coveted so utterly that he could not help himself. He'd take what he wanted. And right now, he wanted her.

"Easy, brother," he snarled. "You've only just gotten here."

"You told me she was a sorceress, but you didn't tell me she was powerful." Greed's voice changed, deepening into something rough and draconic. A man without a soul spoke back to him, and Lust knew how dangerous this circumstance was. "You made it seem as though she were just another woman, Lust. But that right there is no common wench."

Selene stepped into the courtyard and made her way toward them. Much of the talking and whooping calls had ceased. Greed's people parted for her like a wave, their eyes lingering on the strange woman who meandered through them without an ounce of fear.

She looked... He hated to admit it, but she looked like a queen.

She walked through the madness without fear or worry. The serenity on her face seemed to spill out to everyone surrounding her. They calmed, ceasing in their antics to watch her.

Lust hadn't realized how she could command a room without

saying a single word. But he supposed he had seen it before, even at the party. Those who were lost in the throes of passion had paused to watch the strange woman who ignored them all. No one would ever guess what she was thinking or feeling. Her face, like the rest of her, was smooth as ice.

Once she reached them, Selene dipped into a low curtsey, her eyes on his brother's feet. "My lord Greed. Welcome to our home."

My lord? Lust felt his anger billow up through his body at the words. She never called him that, so why would she address his brother with such respect?

Greed laughed in response, the sound far warmer than it should have been. "My, my, our home she calls it. The little witch already sank her claws into you. She claims this place as her own, Lust. Do you hear that?"

"She's not a witch," he growled.

"Ah, sorceress, priestess, witch, they're all the same, aren't they? Promising impossible deeds, claiming that they have the nature of the elements at their fingertips." Greed shrugged. "It's all smoke and mirrors."

Lust was insulted on her behalf. His brother knew how powerful this little sorceress was. She could ignore Lust's powers as though they didn't exist! No one had ever done that before.

And, as Selene's eyes flashed to him, he realized that she was insulted, too. She was far too polite to say anything, besides it wasn't her place to argue with one of the kings, but he wouldn't let it settle the way it had. None of this set right with him, and Lust had never been someone's champion before.

He supposed there was a time for everything.

"Yet you said she was powerful," Lust mused, turning slightly so that he was standing at Selene's side.

"Powerful enough for a sorceress, but there are some in my company who are more powerful." He pointed to the giant. "He can make the winds come at his bidding. His twin can scream so loud it makes people's ears bleed. Your little one is merely able to ignore a little lust. So can my people, sorceress. Lust just surrounds himself with those who enjoy their baser instincts."

"Baser instincts?" she asked, her voice clear and ringing in the courtyard. "But greed is not one of those?"

His brother's grin flashed, his sharpened teeth glinting in the sunlight. "Oh it is. It's just more useful than fucking."

That was it. He would endure his brother's jests, but Selene did not need to stand here while the man insulted both her and this kingdom.

Without a thought, Lust unleashed his power. The rolling waves of lust that pulsed out of him sent almost every single person in Greed's entourage to the ground. They writhed, their moans filling the air as they flattened to the ground. Hands rushed for belts, fingers delved into warm, soft places, and fists quickly rushed to take care of the urgency. They would find no release, though, no comfort, not until Lust wanted them to find that.

"Weak?" he asked. "Baser instincts? Perhaps. But they are useful all the same."

Greed rolled his eyes. "Please, brother. Was that necessary?"

"I'm making a point."

"And your little one is still standing, yes I can see. How valiant of her." Greed waved a hand to his guards, still standing behind him as well, looking decidedly bored. "As are they."

A small flicker of doubt grew within him. Was she like them, then? He swore he'd felt her reaction, but she claimed she hadn't. He feared maybe he'd kept her here when all she'd wanted was to be left alone. Did she despise his touch? And all the touches of those he'd offered? Those who had come before?

The thoughts twisted in his stomach, rotting and poisoning his very veins. Lust prided himself on letting those go who did not want him. He'd never taken someone by force. He'd never touched someone with force and maybe he'd... he'd...

Selene's bitter voice interrupted his thoughts. "If you believe yourself to be so strong, Greed, then surely you would be able to affect me. Even your warriors are not immune to greed. Or are they?"

His brother narrowed his gaze upon her. "No one is immune to greed, mortal. It is inevitable and undeniable."

She tilted her chin. "Prove it."

What was she doing? Selene would fall to his brother just as all the others had. She'd only make herself look more weak. He should stop her, he should...

Greed allowed his power to roll across the courtyard. Those who were pinned to the floor whined, wincing as more emotions rolled through them. The tangled mix of greed and lust was a dangerous cocktail, and Lust grit his teeth, pouring more power into them so they would all stay put and not start fucking each other without realizing it. The mixture could quickly turn dangerous.

To his shock, Selene stood through it all. Unaffected. Cold and icy as always, with her face impossible to read. How? He did not know.

Someone staggered toward a woman who was pinned on the ground. Selene's gaze flicked toward the man with a wide-eyed, horrified stare as he started unbuckling his belt. Greed and lust together created a combination that was dangerous for mortals, and regrets would be had if this didn't stop.

"Enough," she called out. "You have tortured your people for long enough. Both of you."

Together, they released their power. But Lust knew something had changed. There was a person standing before them who could ignore both his and Greed's power. It was... unthinkable.

Greed appeared to agree with him. Even his brother's face was pale, the powerful being shaken by what had been revealed. "Not so weak after all."

"My power is light conjuring," she replied. "I am no different from all the other sorceresses."

"Oh, well, we all know that's a lie," Greed replied, and he gave Lust a meaningful glare. "I trust we'll figure this out while I am here?"

"As promised."

Lust gestured for Greed and his people to follow one of his own until it was just him and Selene standing in the courtyard. Her hands were neatly folded at her hips, her eyes staring off into the distance.

"What was that?" he finally asked, his voice the crack of a whip through the air.

"A miscalculation," she replied, not even looking at him. "One that won't happen again."

"Have you been lying to me? You said your power was with light, and you claimed the same to my brother, but—"

"I have not lied to you. I can create light." She lifted her hand and a small sizzle of magic bounced between her fingers, like the tiniest bolt of lightning. "Like I said, Lust. It was a miscalculation. I did not enjoy hearing him insult you, but I have learned those arguments are not mine to fight. I put myself at risk to defend your honor, and that was foolish. You're powerful enough to do that on your own."

She was insulted on his behalf? When she was the one maligned?

Selene curtseyed and turned away from him. "I will be ready for dinner when you call on me."

And Lust didn't know what to say to stop her from walking away.

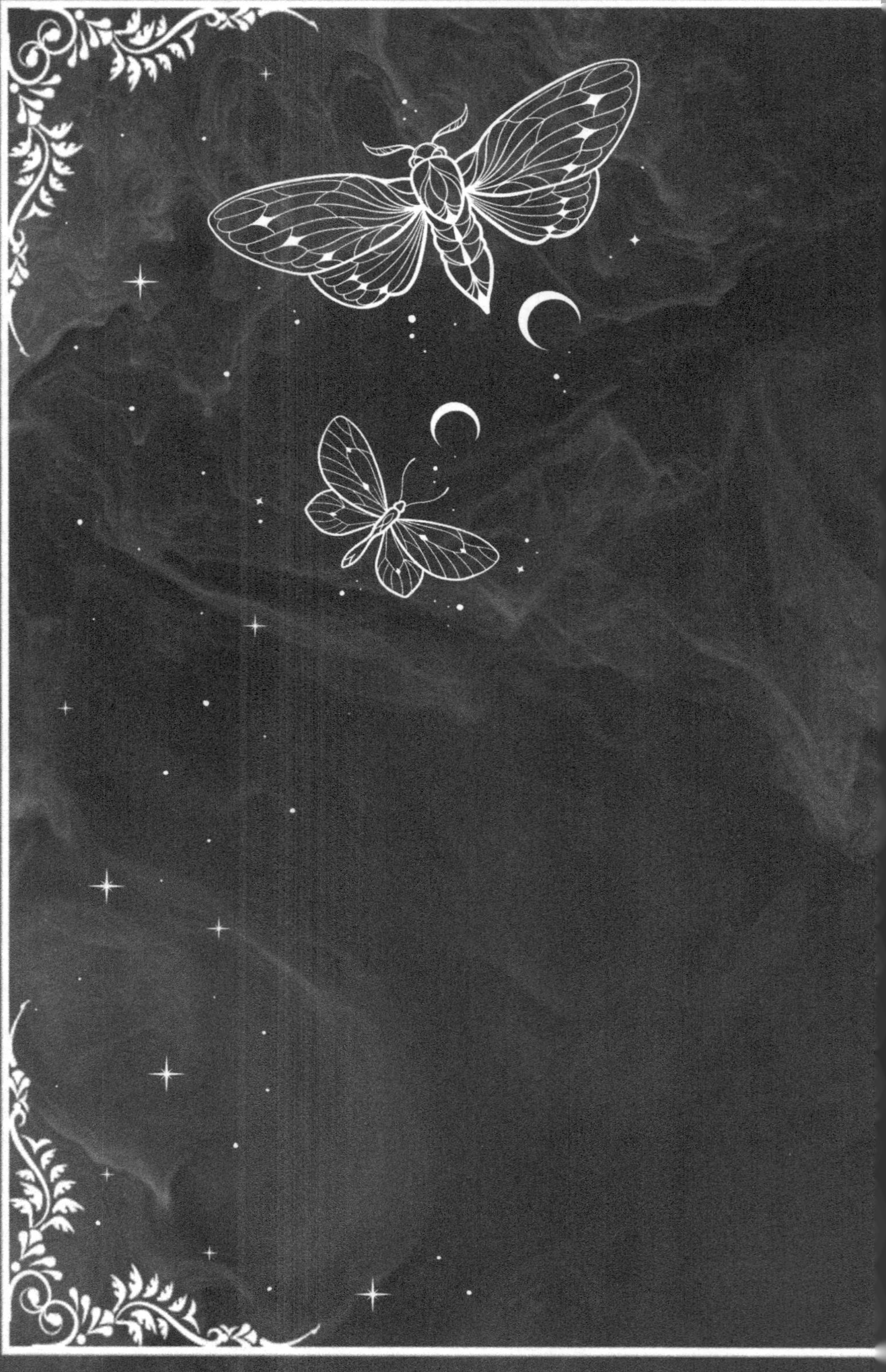

Chapter 19

This is a terrible idea. He knew it. Lust had never thought for a second that he could have his brothers around with a favorite pet, let alone a woman who was rumored to become his wife.

And Greed was the best of them to be around her, which made his skin itch. His brother was only likely to kidnap her. To keep her in a golden cage for all to look at in his realm. The Bride of Lust. A novelty for his people to come and gawk at. The others? They'd do much worse if they ever found out about her.

Considering Greed already knew, he could only imagine the others would soon contact him.

He didn't understand why any of this bothered him. Selene was little more than a new toy. She was fleeting in the long years of their lives, and she would disappear into a realm of death where he could not follow. It was no use getting attached to people like her. Lust had done so early in his years, getting soft around another young woman or man who enchanted him.

They were the true firsts. They were the people who had surprised him with their talents, their wants, their needs. He'd become enamored with their newness and how lovely it felt to experience the world through their eyes.

But he'd already suffered through the best and the worst that humanity had to offer. No one surprised him anymore, not even Selene. So why did this bother him as much as it did?

Sighing, he ran his fingers through his hair and stood in front of her door. Steeling himself for whatever feelings would burst the moment he saw her in the doorway. His brother had insisted on a party, and Lust was never one to back down from a request such as that. His castle could throw together a party with the best of them, and Greed would be satisfied.

Usually he enjoyed the rush of planning something so last minute. He got high off the lust that built in the nobility, even now he could feel it swelling through the castle. Two parties in such a short amount of time? They would soon glut themselves on each other's bodies, and he would grow bloated with power from their emotions.

Except... He didn't want to. All he wanted was a quiet night in his bedroom with the strange creature who had captivated him. He wanted to stroke her skin, see if she would let him touch more of her this time. To listen to her soft intakes of breath when he skated over particularly sensitive parts of her arms, her sides, her breasts.

Lust wanted to talk with her, too. He wanted to discover what made her tick and why, for the love of all that was holy, why was she the way she was? How did she resist him? And his brother?

Was she not human? Was she something that they had yet to encounter, but that threatened the very status of all their kingdoms?

He had too many questions, and he knew he would get no answers from her. Selene was, and always would be, a locked chest of knowledge that he wasn't privy to.

He lifted his hand and knocked on her door, smoothing a hand down the steel boning of his corset. He had dressed as everyone expected the ruler of this kingdom to dress. The dark black corset ran down his ribs, flattening his waist and torso into a smooth line that broadened his shoulders even more. A wine colored silk shirt underneath the corset billowed from his shoulders, leaving his collarbone free for eyes to trace. Black pants hugged tight to his legs, hiding nothing and everything from the imagination.

As tradition, his horns were dusted tonight as well as his eyelids. The silver sparkle caught in the torchlight any time they flickered, and he knew it gave him an otherworldly appearance. He was a creature who had stepped out of male and female dreams, both masculine and feminine. Both soft and hard.

It was a blessing and a curse to be so attractive to both sexes. Right now, he could only hope that he stole her breath.

Her door opened a mere inch. "Lust?"

"We're late," he reminded.

"Are you sure this is what you want me to wear? It's a little..."

"Opulent?" Lust leaned against the wall beside her door, grinning down at his nails as he filled in the words he knew she didn't want to hear. "Beautiful? Seductive? I bet it's delicious on that pale skin of yours."

"I was going to say revealing," she growled. "Hardly appropriate for an official event."

"You live in my kingdom, little moon. If I wanted to parade you in front of my nobles wearing nothing but my hand around your throat, they would think it divine." Lust leaned his head back against the wall and made a little hum in the back of his throat. "And what a lovely picture that paints. It's not too late to change your mind, you know. We could give this kingdom a spectacle they'd never forget."

"This is fine," she rushed to interrupt him and the door opened up to reveal the dress she complained about.

Lust tried to control his laughter at her words, so he was grinning when he looked up and saw her. The smile on his face fell immediately.

The white gown was one he'd never seen before. A high lacy neckline wrapped around her throat, cut away at her shoulders so it appeared only as a small necklace where all the silk was attached. Strands of white draped over her breasts and were woven into a pattern at her hips, the intricate weaving threaded with braided fabric cords. Her entire torso was nearly bared to his view, from collarbone to naval, her breasts only hidden by strips of fabric. She wore a delicate chain, a single strand extending from the hollow of her throat to join with others that wrapped around her ribs. More fabric fell from her hips to the floor, though her long legs were entirely visible to his hungry eyes.

He forgot how to breathe. How to think. They'd left her hair unbound and as she shifted in discomfort, he could smell peppermint floating through the air. And damn it, he wanted to kiss her.

He hadn't kissed anyone in hundreds of years. The intimate act was too personal, but he wanted to know what her lips tasted like. He wanted to see if he could get them to ease beneath his, rather than be stuck in that tight line. As if she knew what he was thinking, she pressed them together even harder.

"I can't even move in this," she hissed. "How am I supposed to sit?

I'm not putting my bare ass on anything."

He opened his mouth to tell her that she'd sit just like everyone else, but rather than the sarcastic words, what came out was, "I've seen countless beauties throughout my life, but never one who rivaled yours."

And then that was out in the open. It wasn't a lie. He wasn't trying to control her or convince her of anything. All he said was the truth. He didn't see her as plain anymore. Not like this.

Selene blinked at him, her mouth opening and closing in surprise. Then, she finally replied, "That was rather sweet, Lust."

"I can be sweet if I wish to be." He held his arm out for her to take. "You haven't had the opportunity to see it yet."

"And why is that?"

The moment her hand slid onto his forearm, he wanted to moan. Her skin against his was an electric pulse that went straight to his cock. Hard, heavy, aching, she made him want nothing more than to throw her back into that room. His brother be damned.

But he had to struggle through this night and ignore Greed's not too subtle barbs so they could get back to their room. Then he could explore this new emotion further.

Maybe she'd let him touch her again. A trade for information. Maybe she'd be willing to pay the price for her more prying questions.

He sighed and shook his head. "You aren't very sweet yourself, Selene. Why should I put in all the effort in this relationship?"

She snorted. "Right. Effort. Why do I feel like such a thing is a foreign concept to you?"

"Because it is. I've never had to fight so hard for an ounce of attention from a single person. Why is that?"

As he guided her down the hall, she blinked up at him with a soft expression on her face. It almost made him trip over himself.

"Because we don't like each other, Lust," she said, her voice as sweet as her expression looked.

"Is that true?" He stroked the back of his fingers over her cheek, watching as the skin underneath his touch burned a pretty pink. "I think you like me more than you wish to admit, sorceress."

She swallowed hard. And then they were in front of the great hall. He wanted to continue this game. But there were guests to entertain and his brother did not like to be kept waiting.

Giving a slight nod to his servants, the doors opened, and they strode into the hall.

The pools had been filled with glowing yellow orbs that lit the water as though they were molten gold. He'd changed out his banners for golden fabric that looked equally liquid, and already people were tangled in the pools of soft silk. Some of those who had indulged early were his people, others were Greed's. No one seemed to wish to wait for their indulgence.

With Greed here, there was plenty of food as well. Mounds of it heaped upon tables that were filled with everything from fine bread, to fruit, to tankards of wine that sloshed onto the floor in careless hands. Most of Greed's people were already well on their way to being drunk, though Lust's people were less likely to indulge in that way. Whiskey dick was no way to enjoy oneself.

However, Greed's people seemed to enjoy their drunken escapades, so who was he to question it?

Lust picked his way around a particularly drunk couple, who weaved in front of them. The man tripped over his own feet, his tankard of wine sloshing dangerously close to the pristine white of Selene's dress.

With a snarl, Lust grabbed the wine and dumped it down the man's shirt rather than hers. "Watch yourself," he said, his voice a low rumble. "You are a guest in this house, but I can still tear you limb from limb."

"Brother!" Greed's voice rang through the crowd. Laughter erupted from the dais where Lust usually sat. "Go easy on the man! He's been here for hours while you only just arrived with your... bride."

He cared little for what Greed thought. Lust turned and ran one of his hands down Selene's arm, making sure she was all right. Any other woman would have been shaken, or at least appreciative. But not his sorceress.

She surveyed the crowd with nothing but apathy in her expression. Glass-like and smooth, her eyes saw everything and reacted to nothing. But he felt the slightest tremble in her shoulders that made him frown.

Perhaps his ice queen was not quite so unaffected by everything surrounding her.

He laced his fingers through hers and pulled her away from the crowd toward the dais where only a king should sit.

Greed reclined on a throne they'd brought out for him, the entire behemoth clearly just made. Gold coins were stacked on top of each other, some of them still visible where they hadn't quite melted all the way through to make this golden throne. Two women reclined at his feet, their hands caressing their thighs as he let them drink from his own cup of red wine. One of them had spilled it between her breasts, clearly vying for more of his attention than the other.

Greed looked pleased with the circumstance, but his tail flicked behind him in annoyance. A sign he wasn't as happy as he appeared.

"Took you long enough," Greed said, then flicked his fingers at the ladies in front of him. "I thought you wouldn't mind if I took a few of your women for entertainment while I waited for you."

Lust looked them over to make sure they were fine. Though it shouldn't surprise him that they were, he felt a flicker of discomfort. Greed wasn't always gentle with his bedmates, but these women looked like they had yet to be touched.

What other plan did Greed have?

Frowning, he sat down on his own throne. "I do not mind if you find yourself entertainment. We are not that late, either."

"You're very late. We've all been here for hours."

Selene stood beside him, and he sensed her discomfort. She apparently waited for a chair of her own, but no one would bring her one. And though he could have ordered them to, Lust saw her fingers shake for a brief moment before she curled them together. Still nervous, then. Still uncomfortable.

He reached for her, wrapping his fingers around her wrist and tugging her into his lap. Her eyes widened in surprise, but he didn't let her go. She was forced to perch on his knee, as far away from him as she could get, all prim and proper and so damned uncomfortable.

Greed snorted into his drink. "I don't think she likes you, brother."

He trailed a finger down her spine, watching the bare skin pebble up at his touch. "Oh, she likes me well enough. She just doesn't know it yet."

Selene stiffened, but kept her mouth shut. She watched the people around them with cold eyes, and he wondered what was going on in her head. Did she see what he saw? Did she see a room full of people finally released to do what they wanted, or did she see depravity and foolishness?

He leaned back on his throne and enjoyed the view for a while. The next hour passed quickly. They drank, they ate. Greed told him more about his kingdom and how the drought had taken his people low. They were suffering more than he cared to admit, but that was partially a reason why he was here. If Lust could spare the water, he and his people would carry the barrels back. Of course he would, and he had no issues sharing what his kingdom had.

All their conversation was quiet beneath the revelry that grew louder with every drink that passed between hands. Soon there was nothing other than the moans of those enjoying physical touches and the answering groans. Even Greed had started petting the two women at his feet, his fingers caressing their necks, delving down into the shadows between their breasts before stretching up again.

Through it all, Selene remained ramrod straight on his knee. His leg had started to go numb from the hard bones pressing into his muscles. He'd thought she would at least loosen up a bit, but it appeared she only got more and more tense as the night went on.

When there was a lull in his conversation with Greed, he leaned forward. Lust slid his hands down each of her thighs and cupped her knees in his palms, so his arms bracketed her against his chest.

"Is it not up to your standards?"

"This?" she asked, nodding her head toward the writhing bodies. "No, it is not."

"They enjoy themselves."

"They could do so in private. Nothing says they have to stay in this room. There are plenty of beds."

He pressed his lips to the long line of her shoulder, her velvety skin nearly making him groan. "They are allowed to enjoy themselves in public here. And if they want to, why waste the time finding a room?"

"This is not my world, Lust."

"You judge them."

"Judgment is not necessary to be uncomfortable. I can recognize they are enjoying themselves at the same time, I know I would never do what they are doing." Another shiver went through her, but he knew it wasn't because of his lips. It wasn't revulsion, either. It was... fear.

His spine stiffened. "Why are you afraid?"

Those dark eyes turned toward him, an endless swirl of emotion, like the night sky on a clear evening. "I don't want to be here, Lust. You made me come here. You made me watch all this and I endure it because I am expected to. I am here. I am seated before all your people in the most nightmarish room that I've ever been in. Your brother and you can talk politics while those two women and I try to pretend we haven't heard it all, like little dolls for you to play with. What more do you want from me? You've taken my dignity tonight, and I fear there is nothing else for me to give."

But that wasn't... That wasn't his intent. He hadn't wanted to take her dignity or anything else, for that matter. They'd sat on a throne together! His people weren't even looking at her.

A flash of anger seared his throat before he felt another shiver shake through her, though he'd never have noticed if he wasn't touching all of her.

Fear had never been his intent. Though he did not understand it, and her fear felt like an insult, he also knew when to admit he was wrong.

He leaned back, trailing his knuckles down her pale back before nodding at his brother. "We'll talk more tomorrow."

"Ah, is that the way of it, then?"

Lust didn't reply. Instead, he stood with Selene, ignoring the pins and needles in the leg she'd sat on for an hour now. He placed his hand on her lower back, ignored the way she tried to flinch away from him, and drew her around the throne.

"Where are we going now?" she asked.

He noted the dark circles under her eyes now that he could see her face. The hollow way she stood before him, like there wasn't even a soul inside her anymore.

He'd pushed her too far tonight. This was his fault.

"There is another way to get to our bedroom." Lust scrubbed a hand down his own face, suddenly exhausted as well. "We don't need to go through the crowd. Come, little moon. Let's go to bed."

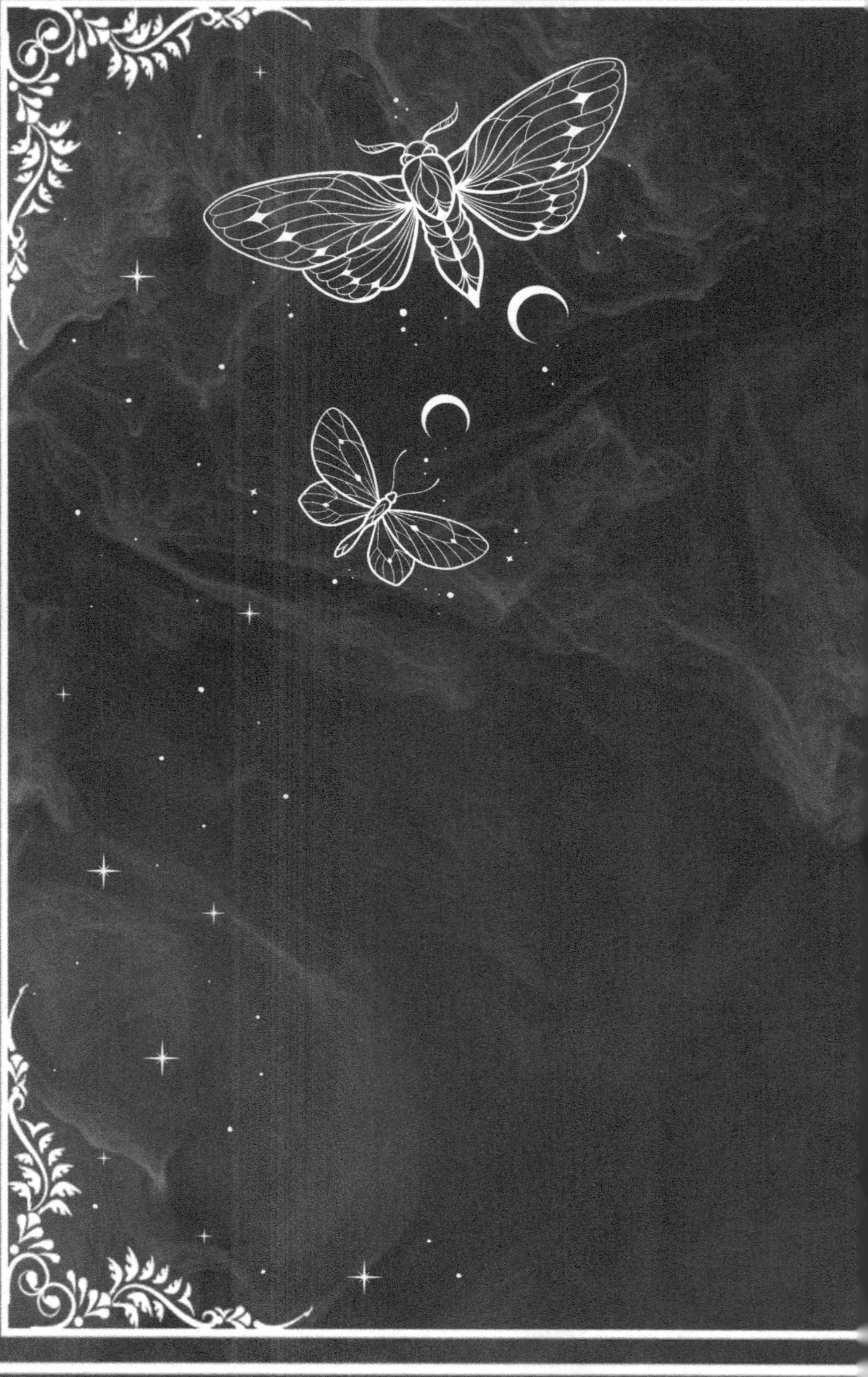

Chapter 20

The closer they got to his bedroom, the more Selene noticed he changed. Lust went from exhausted and almost sad to vibrating with anger. His usually soft mouth twisted into a dark line and his eyes flashed with another emotion she could not name.

He looked different. More so than she'd ever noticed.

But the bunching of his muscles and the way he kept flexing his hands at his sides warned her not to mention anything. Maybe he needed some time to himself. The evening had been busy, she supposed, and having his brother here didn't make him happy. But it seemed more that his anger was directed at her.

Was he going to start a fight with her over this? She didn't want to be in a fucking orgy, nor did she want to sit there and watch one happen in front of her. It was too much to ask!

So, by the time they made it to his bedroom, they were both angry. Perhaps a little too upset to even be safely in the room together, but Lust apparently didn't care in the slightest. He slammed the doors open and snarled at the two maids who were cleaning the room.

The women froze like rabbits before a wolf. They looked at her, then at him, their eyes widening with each frozen moment.

"Get. Out." His snarled words slapped through the air and both the women rushed to do his bidding.

One of them stumbled as she passed Selene. The woman reached out as though to brace herself, but her hand never touched Selene's arm. Lust had lunged forward so fast that Selene didn't even see him move. One moment the woman was reaching and the next, Lust had her wrist in his hand and the woman was dangling from it. He yanked the maid upright and nudged her toward the door.

He wasn't rough with her. But there was no way anyone would hesitate after that. He'd made his point.

No one was to touch Selene. Not a man already well into his cups. Not even the maid.

Even angry at her, he wouldn't let anyone get close. And in some way, that was... sweet. Just like how he'd said she was the most beautiful woman he'd ever seen.

She hated herself for softening towards him. He was an ass, and he'd ripped her out of that room after making her endure an hour of discomfort. She shouldn't care that he had a softer side. It didn't matter. None of it did.

And yet, she needed him to trust her so she could find his weakness. So she could betray him. Selene watched his heaving shoulders as he glared after the maids, and she thought that maybe she'd succeeded already. He certainly was protective enough over her.

Perhaps this wasn't the best moment to test that theory. The door slammed shut behind her and they were alone. Those molten eyes turned to her and the force of his anger pinned her in place.

Not just at her, she thought. He glared at her like she was the heart of his problems, and maybe she was, but he never once moved toward her. Instead, he just stared until her entire body felt like it was on fire.

Damn it, she wanted him. More than she'd ever wanted anyone or anything. She wanted to touch him. To be held by him. But right now, she mostly wanted to slap him and then kiss him until he stopped looking at her like that.

She had no idea how long they glared at each other with the sexual tension running so high she could almost taste it. Eventually, he ran his hand over his face and turned his back to her.

"I am in no mood for servants," he said, his voice still a snarl. "You will have to attend to me."

"You can sleep in that ridiculous outfit," she replied.

"Selene."

There was no arguing with that voice. The hissed start of her name that ended in a growl. He knew she would never do what he asked unless he ordered it, and so he ordered it with a single word.

She didn't want to attend to him. She didn't care if he was uncomfortable or if he spent the rest of his days bound in that damned corset. All she cared about was getting out of this dress, covering herself up, and forgetting all the embarrassing things she'd seen tonight.

If she saw another pair of breasts being groped, or another dick that gleamed with a wetness she didn't want to name, Selene thought she might explode. And not in a good way. She'd conjure up a damned sun to keep them all away from her.

Sighing, she strode up to his back and grabbed onto the ties. "Fine.

I won't be gentle about it, though."

He jerked back at her first hard tug, and then a low groan echoed from deep in his chest. "Oh, I'm counting on that."

Why did that sound so... sexual? He shouldn't want her to hurt him. He shouldn't feel better because she tugged the ropes so hard they would leave a mark on his skin.

But it took a while to get him unraveled, and she found it was impossible to be gentle. Whoever had laced him into this corset had done so as if they were tying him in for life. This corset was tight. Tighter than she'd ever worn hers, and she was no stranger to making herself thin. Minerva loved a waif-like waist, and Selene had seen some of her sisters test the limits of their own corsets. This one was laced so tightly she feared he hadn't taken a single deep breath all night.

The act of untying was almost like weaving, and the tension in her shoulders and arms eased. He didn't say a word as she worked, but she could hear the music still filtering up from the open balcony.

The quiet moment was almost... nice. She could let go of her frustration with him for a few moments to luxuriate in this domestic scene. Selene could almost imagine that they'd just returned from a ball, although she didn't know many men who wore corsets and knew even less who went to balls. Lust's kingdom was not a home for such fineries, not without sex somehow involved.

She let the corset fall in front of him, not even attempting to stop it from hitting the floor. "You are free," she muttered.

"The shirt as well."

"You can take off your own shirt."

"Selene, do not argue with me." The barked order was yet another one she knew she shouldn't ignore.

Her fingers flexed at her sides. Why could he not undress himself?

She knew he was capable of it. He'd done it since he moved her into his own bedroom. The fool was making her feel even worse, and he knew what he was doing.

Did he have to force her into the status of servant along with everything else?

All while grumbling under her breath, she tugged his silk shirt out of his pants and yanked it up over his head. He was much taller than her, and the fabric caught on his horns, but she didn't care. The delicate silk ripped as she pulled and his head jerked with it. He snarled, the sound inhuman and dangerously deep.

Selene froze just as the maids had. Her body knew the sound of a predator, even if her mind didn't. Heart hammering in her chest, she watched him for any movement other than the jerk of his neck from her movements, but he remained where he was. Muscles locked in place, bulging where they were far too tense.

Her eyes trailed down his shoulders, only for her breath to catch in her throat. He was beautifully made, she knew that. She'd seen the way his back flexed with his movements and the long tapered shadows that led to his waistband. Selene knew how much she wanted to press her lips against those muscles and feel them move against her.

But she'd never seen the deep red lines left by the corset. The welts already raised on his golden skin, crimson and angry and appearing so painful she couldn't help herself.

She trailed her fingers over one line, ignoring the faint hiss of air from between his lips. "Lust…"

"If the next words out of your mouth are not 'fuck me', then keep your lips closed," he snarled.

Another way to scare her, and yet she found not an ounce of fear remained. She touched another mark with her other hand, infinitely gentle as she followed the lines down his ribs. "Why do you wear them if they hurt you?"

Some of the tension eased out of his body. He let out a long breath and when he spoke next, he sounded tired once again. "Because I enjoy the pain, Selene."

"I don't know anyone who enjoys pain."

"There is a certain pleasure in torture, and it is not pain that scars or lasts. Perhaps that is why I find myself liking you so much, little moon."

The words made her stomach seize, and something deep inside her fluttered. "You think being around me is painful?"

He turned, and she had to take a step away from him. Lust was simply so large like this. Overwhelming. His body took up so much room, but it was more than his broad shoulders and all that smooth, golden skin. His eyes glowed with emotion, the blue turning violet almost immediately.

He prowled forward, forcing her to continue backing away until her spine pressed against the door. He flattened his hands on either side of her, caging her with his body. "Yes, being around you is painful. How could it not be? You claim I have taken your dignity by forcing you into a room while our people enjoyed themselves, but you deny what you have done to me. I was happy before you came here, Selene. I knew what the world was and now you have made me question everything."

Selene flinched as he snarled the last word. But she never took her eyes off his face.

She wouldn't hide from him, not even when he was like this. If he wanted to yell at her, then he needed to do so while seeing the emotion on her own face. He needed to look into her expression as he screamed.

But he wasn't screaming. Not really. Every word made his voice deeper, lower, more intense as he stared into her eyes and willed her to see the world the way he did.

She couldn't, though. They were two very different people who had seen so many different things. He saw humanity as flawed and simplistic, while she knew they were teachable. Those were not opinions that were easy to change.

"Did you not need to question your life?" she asked. "You say you have lived this way for hundreds of years, but in that time, you have become complacent and bored. Don't you want to experience something new again?"

Pain flared at her question. "There is nothing new left for me to experience, little moon."

"Is there really not?" She dared to lift a hand between them and skate her fingers along his jaw. "Or are you just afraid to experience it?"

That flash returned to his eyes as he narrowed them at her. "I've never been afraid of any experience."

Her mother's voice whispered in her head. That she could use this moment to reel him in, to really get him under her thumb. And weeks ago, she might have. She would have teased him, flirted until he was on his knees before her and then she would have felt the guilt later on. But right now? She didn't want to manipulate him. She just wanted him to understand.

"I think you're afraid of a lot of things," she whispered, so close she could feel the heat of his lips on hers. "I think you're afraid of me."

"You?" He laughed, and the air breezed over her face, smelling of sweet wine. "A slip of a woman with no power?"

"Who offers you something new. Neither you nor I understand it, but we both felt it the first time we bumped into each other. It's been changing since I came here, growing and warping into something neither of us can deny. Hasn't it? You've felt it. There's a change, and that's terrifying to someone who has lived the same way for centuries."

"You don't know what you're talking about."

"But I do." Of course she did. That's why it scared him so much. "Like I said when we first met. I'm the beginning of something new."

A low sound rumbled through his throat. For a second, she thought she'd pushed him too hard. But then he searched her gaze like he was looking for something important. Something that would change this moment for the both of them.

Selene didn't know which one of them moved first. She only knew that one moment she was staring up into his eyes and the next, she'd wrapped her arms around his neck. Their lips crashed together, not gentle at all but a biting, crushing meeting of lips, teeth, and tongue. This was a punishment for two people who had denied themselves for far too long.

His mouth slanted over hers, his tongue sliding against hers in a delicious glide that made her moan into him. His hands remained pressed against the door, his muscles locked underneath her palms. Selene kept her own locked around his neck or she'd press them to whatever warm skin she could find. But she remembered what his back felt like. She remembered the flex of his muscles underneath her touch, and how strong he felt.

Lust let her lead them for a few moments, and she'd thought they were kissing each other. Until he finally kissed her back.

He stole her breath from her lungs. Lust devoured her with every stroke of his tongue, every bite against her bottom lip, and every guttural groan that he poured down her throat. He kissed her like a man who was starved for any attention from her, as though he'd been waiting for this for years.

She clung to his shoulders, trying desperately to keep up. But he didn't seem to even want her to participate. His kiss was meant to punish, to show her just how much she wanted him, even if she didn't know it yet.

It took everything in her not to moan again as his tongue thrust against hers, the slow movement mimicking what she really wanted him to do to her. Her stomach clenched, her whole body seizing up as though it knew what was next.

Her pulse thundered in her throat, between her thighs, all over her body in little pulses that she had to thrust underneath the frozen lake inside her even though she wanted to feel them, damn it. She wanted to feel this. Hiding those emotions felt like she was denying what was between them, and that was the last thing she wanted to do.

They parted, and she felt the swelling of her lips and the strange sensation between her legs. She was already dripping for him, so wet she could feel it slicking her thighs. If he would just place one hand there, he would know. It wouldn't matter how much she hid her emotions. He'd be able to tell, to feel, to release her from this lie.

His fists slammed into the door. Once, twice, three times. She never flinched at the sound, even though her heart quaked in her chest.

Lust drew back, his eyes blazing with anger. "I cannot feel you. I still cannot feel you! Why can I not feel you?"

A pulse of his power rocked through the room, rattling the door behind her, but she still had to endure it. To shove all those emotions until the power inside her nearly overflowed, but she didn't dare let him know how she felt. She didn't dare let him realize how much control he had over her.

Lust's chest rose and fell with rapid, angry breaths. As he raised his hand, she thought his grip would leave bruises. But he scooped his hand underneath her hair and cupped her neck with such infinite gentleness that it almost brought tears to her eyes.

He pressed one more kiss to her lips, long and lingering and ever so heartbreaking, before he swung her around and left.

The door closing behind him felt like the snapping of heart strings.

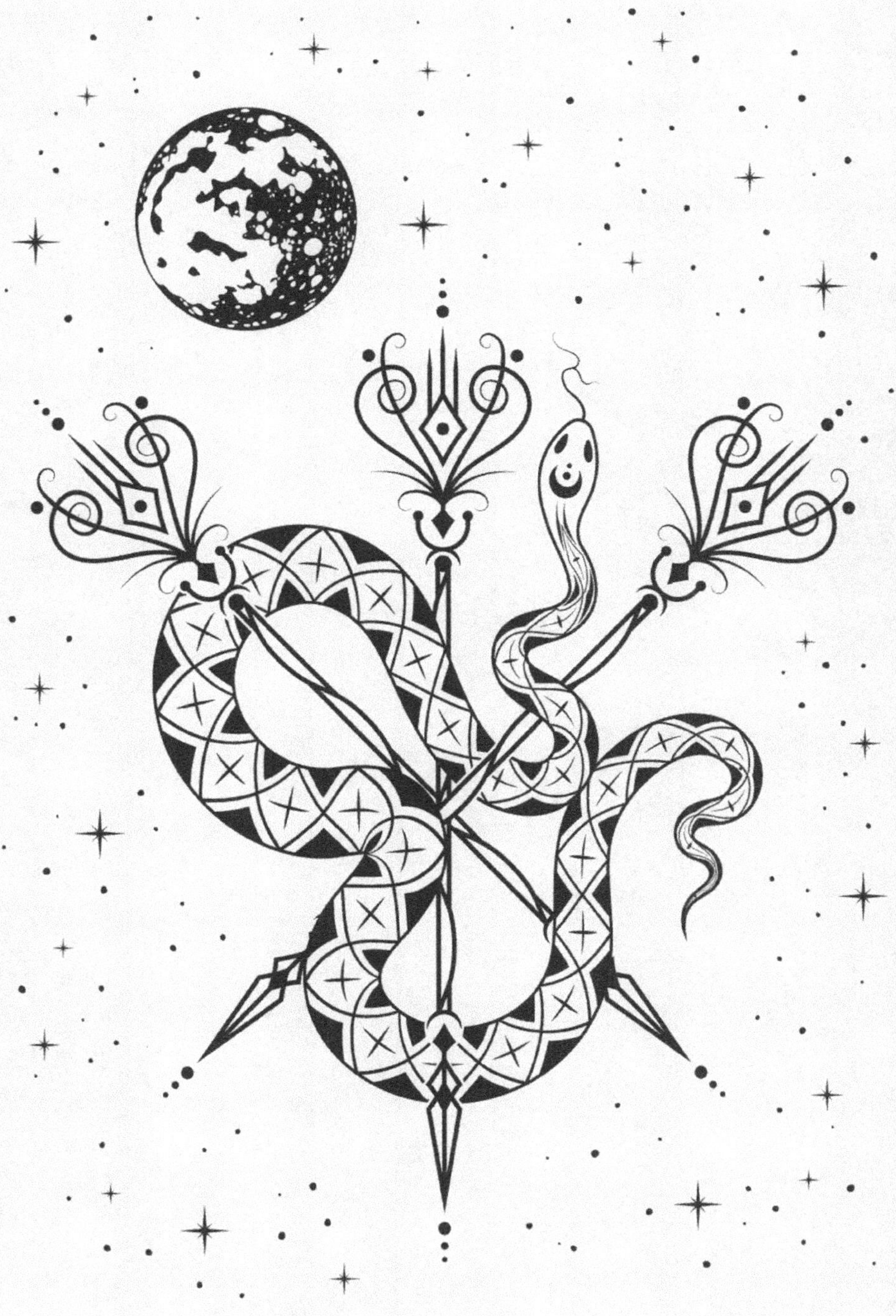

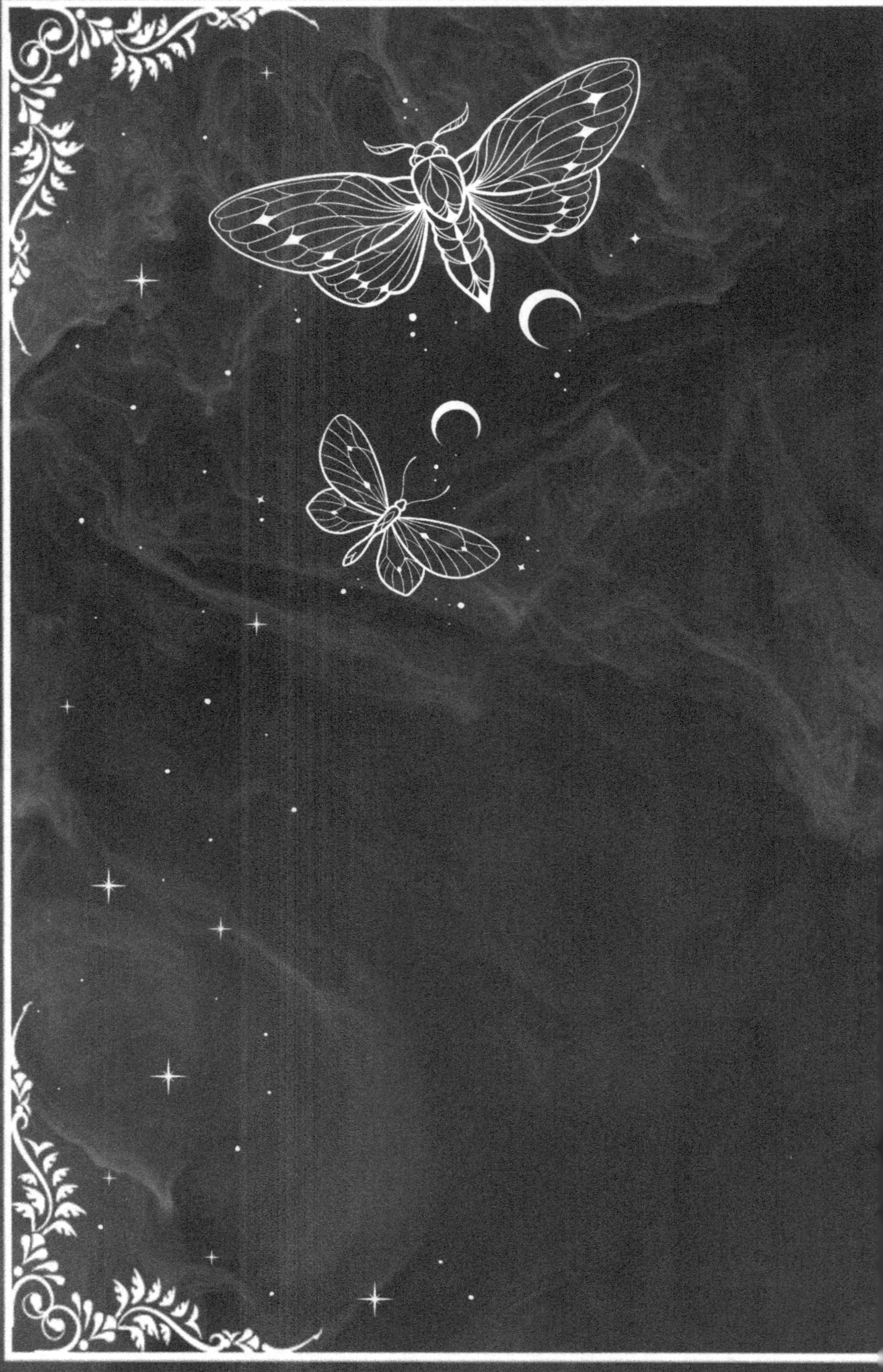

Chapter 21

Lust knew he had no right to be angry. He'd done all that everyone asked of him. He'd hosted a feast for his brother. He'd brought Selene there for all of his people to look at, even though she'd embarrassed him the last time he'd done that. And he'd suffered for as long as he deemed necessary before bringing her back to their room.

No one thought he would do more than that. No one expected more from him, and yet it felt as though the weight of all their expectations rested on his shoulders. Heavy enough to push him flat onto the ground.

Greed wanted him to take what he wanted, no matter the cost. Selene wanted him to be a softer version of himself, to bend to her whims even if it cost more than she was willing to pay. His people wanted what they had always had, and they did not desire to see that change.

What did he want?

He stalked into the room that he used as a temporary bedroom when he needed it, now that he'd given his own space to Selene. Tugging at his hair, he nearly pulled it out at the roots while he thought.

What did he want? Lust had never thought he'd have to ask himself that question. He took what he wanted. He did what he wanted.

Kings of their kingdom did not have to ask themselves what pleasure they wished to indulge in. He could have whatever he wanted. Women, subjects, food, wine, all the necessities of life.

So why did it feel like he was suddenly lacking?

Frustrated with himself and the direction his thoughts were taking, Lust stared at himself in the full-length mirror on the opposite side of the bed. He was Lust. The king of this kingdom and the emotion incarnate. No one told him what he wanted or how he was supposed to feel.

Selene had wriggled her way underneath his skin, that's all. She was a nut he wanted to crack open to taste the delicious, flavorful insides. And then he was thinking about spending an afternoon with his tongue deep—

Snarling, he turned away from the mirror before he could see how she affected him. The damned woman! She had no right to get into his head like this.

Why did it make him so angry that he couldn't feel her lust? He knew she was affected. He'd felt the way she melted against the door at his kiss. How she let out a little sound in the back of her throat that she couldn't quite catch and hoped he wouldn't hear.

She'd enjoyed that kiss. Perhaps as much as he had, although he had a hard time imagining there was more pleasure than what he'd felt in that moment.

She was... soft. Everything about her. Soft. And she wasn't asking for more than he wanted to give. She wasn't expecting him to be the best she'd ever had, shake the foundations of what she knew sex to be, nor did she think he was some god slithering into her bed.

No. She'd simply enjoyed his kiss because it was him kissing her.

And that wasn't something he knew how to deal with. People wanted from him. They wanted his body, his touch, they wanted to feel what only he could give them. That was how it went. He'd experienced that since before he had taken a physical form. It was natural for humans to desire something they could not have.

She wanted nothing he could give her, and that was frustrating. Perhaps that came from being a spirit before, however. He wanted to serve. He still wanted to give humans what they were looking for, even if that meant he was sacrificing himself in the process.

Tugging at his horns now, he seethed as he realized she was right. After all of this, she was something new. And he hated it.

"My lord?" The quiet knock on the open bedroom door interrupted his thoughts.

A brief flash of hope sent him spinning toward the feminine voice. Had she come to him of her own accord? Perhaps now she would finally relent to him. Let him kiss her more while she stopped whatever spell hid her desires from him.

But it wasn't Selene standing in the doorway.

Lara shifted, letting the warm candlelight play through the thin fabric that barely covered her body. A blatant observation in the back of his mind noticed how lovely she was. How the curves of her waist had once fit his palm perfectly, and how she'd come to him many times like this when he was angry.

He could lose himself in her. Lust had before. He could find what little peace she offered him and then disappear for a few hours. Perhaps the entire night if he wanted to keep her up that long.

And yet... It was wrong. He didn't want to lose himself in another woman when she didn't have hair as dark as night, or the blackness of oblivion in her eyes. She didn't look at him with distrust, even as she tried to keep herself away from him. It wasn't the same. It wasn't the fight he craved or the submission that he knew would happen no matter how hard they both fought it.

"Lara," he growled, letting his hands drop to his sides. "What can I do for you?"

She slipped into the room, hips swaying as she tried to tempt him. "You know what you can do for me. And what I can do for you, my lord."

All he knew was that he wished women weren't so complicated. Men were easy to understand, and yet these creatures were like another species entirely. Their tumultuous minds were a labyrinth of thoughts and dreams and ideas, so convoluted even they seemed to get trapped in their own minds.

For now, he wanted to be left alone. His thoughts were far too complicated to deal with Lara while she stood there looking at him with expectations, planning for him to give her a reason to stay the night in his bed when she knew that he'd brought home a bride.

"Lara, you should not be here," he sighed, keeping his gaze locked on her face. "You know that."

"You have always been in my life, Lust. Always. One woman wandering into the castle won't change that." She reached up and flicked the sleeve of her gown lower, letting it slide down her smooth shoulder. "I know every part of you that makes you groan with pleasure. You have lingered inside my body for hours on end, so much so that I am shaped to you. You are mine. Just as much as I am yours."

"We are neither to each other." He frowned at her, realizing for the first time that perhaps he'd kept her a little too close. She truly believed this. She believed they belonged together?

The small smile on her face said she didn't believe him. Lara approached and smoothed her hands down his bare chest. "You didn't have to take your corset off yourself. You know I enjoy doing that for you."

Her hands were... wrong. They weren't the hands he wanted on him, and he gently took her wrists to move them away. "I did not take my corset off myself."

"You had another servant?" Her eyes flashed with anger before she pulled herself back together and nodded. "I understand you have other favorites. You're allowed to, after all."

Still holding onto her wrists, he tilted his head to the side at the strange lilt in her voice. "Am I? Why is that?"

"Because you're our king."

No, that wasn't why she thought it. She was still wearing that strange expression that made him hesitate. He might never understand women or humans, but he could see when there was something off about this one.

He squeezed her wrists lightly, ignoring the way she wriggled in his grip and moaned. It was a fake sound, anyway. "Why should it matter if I am your king? You do not allow kings to do whatever they want, or there would never be a rebellion or people who wished to overthrow me. And we both know those people live even inside these walls. So what is the truth, Lara?"

When she didn't answer him right away, she tried to distract him. She shifted her shoulder until the dress slid off the other side as well, buckling fabric revealed her breasts and caught at her elbows.

He had no interest in her tonight. Instead, he squeezed harder. Until he felt her bones creaking inside his fist and her lips parted in a gasp that was not faked for his enjoyment. "The truth."

She hissed out a long breath, her eyes flashing with anger. "Because you are a demon, Lust. You can take whatever you want, whenever you want, and you should not be ashamed of it."

Tsking with disappointment, he tossed her wrists away from him. Lara flung herself away from him with the movement, exaggerating how hard he'd tossed her aside while she rubbed the red marks he'd left behind.

"Humans," he muttered as he turned away from her. "I am not a demon."

"You are, and that is not something you need to hide from me. I accepted who you are long ago." She glared at him, though, and he knew her words were a lie. Still, her lust perfumed the air. Even though she thought him a demon, a monster, a creature of nightmares, she wanted him through it all.

"Leave, Lara. I do not wish to argue with you tonight." He sat down on the edge of the bed, frustrated with the entire evening that had taken place. "Get out."

She didn't argue this time, but she did pause before opening the door. Her eyes on the wood, facing away from him, she whispered, "It wasn't another servant who removed your clothing. Was it?"

"No." He didn't hesitate to tell her the truth. "She did. And she will from now on."

"She doesn't want you," Lara replied. "She doesn't want to be here,

the demon court

or respect your people. All she wants is to change what all of us love."

And therein laid the problem. The longer she was here, the longer he stayed around her, the more he wondered if any of this was love after all. If any of his people even knew what that meant.

Pinching the bridge of his nose, he waved his hand. "Get out, Lara. I won't say it again."

The door opened and closed quietly behind her, and then all was still. He could breathe again without the cloying scent of her desire.

When had he thought of lust as cloying? It was the scent he'd craved his entire life. From the moment he'd sparked into existence, he had wanted to feed off it. Encourage it. Cause it to bloom between others and then only for himself when he'd taken a physical form.

Lara was right about one thing. Selene had come here to change everything. And unfortunately, he feared she might have.

"Oh," the lyrical whisper filled the room. "You're in here! I looked for you in your bedroom, but Selene is there and you are not. Curious, don't you think?"

He didn't stop holding his face. "Affection, I do not have the patience for you tonight."

"You rarely have the patience for me, and yet, I am still here." The smokey creature coiled around his ankle and sighed happily. "You've never sent me away, and I do believe that is because you like me."

"I do not."

"Maybe a little bit."

"Not even the smallest ounce. You are an annoying creature who refuses to leave this place, no matter how many times I tell you to. All you're doing is starving yourself in a castle like this." Though, he could admit to himself that he was fond of the little one. It was nice to have another spirit around. At least Affection knew what it felt like to live as he once had.

The mortals apparently thought he was still a demon, even though he knew he wasn't. They thought of him as a terrible creature of myth because it made their own emotions seem easier. They were not giving in to the lust they already felt. They were suffering the plaguing effect of a monster.

He opened his eyes and stared into his reflection one more time. And seven kingdoms, he looked tired. There were dark smudges underneath his eyes, his shoulders pulled in toward his chest, as though even the action of staying upright had taken its toll.

He'd never felt tired before in his life. He ruled this kingdom and feasted as necessary.

When was the last time he'd eaten?

Affection hummed. "You are looking rather thin, Lust. I thought you were feeding off Selene?"

"I am not. She does not feel lust." He scratched the back of his neck, sighing as disappointment flooded through him. "And I am ashamed to admit that others no longer taste the way they had."

"Disgusted by it, are you?"

"Not disgusted. I can no more be disgusted by lust than I am by myself." He shook his head for good measure. "My brother terrified her. This kingdom makes her uncomfortable. All of it is not what will make her happy."

"And you care to make her happy?"

"Of course I do. I'm not a monster, I'm..." He paused as he looked down at Affection. "Are you bigger?"

The little spirit was larger than the last time he'd seen it. Affection was usually a mass of mist that could fit in his hands, but now it was more like the size of a toddler. Still smaller than most spirits should be, but much more solid. The golden light inside it spilled out and illuminated the floor, his leg, even parts of the ceiling when he glanced up.

And it had eyes now. Eyes that looked back at him like big golden orbs that blinked up at him with no small amount of innocence. "Am I?"

"Yes, you are much larger." He reached down and gathered it up. Holding the spirit out in front of him gave him a small sense of shock and satisfaction. "Why? Why are you larger?"

"I think you know."

He shook his head in denial. "Absolutely not. You are not feeding off me at all, little one. It's impossible for spirits to feed off each other."

Just as it was impossible for him to feel any emotion unless it somehow related to lust. He was made simply, just as the rest of the spirits were. But if Affection was growing larger, that meant it was feeding somewhere in his castle.

Narrowing his eyes, he asked the question that burned inside him. "Where have you been? I haven't seen you in a while."

"I've been around you. I just didn't want to interrupt." It bounced up and down a bit before settling in his grip again. "I'm always near you."

"So that means you're also near Selene?" She was rarely far from him, at least. Even on the days when she'd thought he had left her alone, Lust had never been able to convince himself to go very far from her. Which meant...

"Are you feeding off Selene?" he asked.

Affection's eyes went wide. "No, I told you—"

He interrupted the little spirit before it could lie. "I know I didn't want anyone to feed off her or encourage emotions. I set that rule long before I realized what would happen. You are larger because of her feelings?"

He set the spirit down as he stood, stalking back and forth along the room as he continued. "She must be feeling some sort of affection toward me, then. Or this castle? No, it wouldn't be that. She's never liked it here, and it's very different from her home. Perhaps she feels it a bit toward you, but we both know that kind of feeding is more difficult, especially when you are in your spirit form. So that must mean..."

She felt it toward him. Lust.

Slumping, a slow smile spread across his features. "She enjoys my company, then."

"She does," Affection agreed, though it was slow to respond. "I think she likes you a bit more than you might think. But I'm not supposed to—"

He held his hand up for silence as he basked in the thoughts racing through his mind. She liked him. She enjoyed his company. Selene didn't think he was a monster like the others, nor did she pander to him because she thought him to be this all powerful demon.

Perhaps there was something to earning her trust after all. If he was lucky, and continued in the way she'd told him to, maybe she'd see him for something other than what the humans in his court already did.

She might see him as a man. As a real man, like he'd always wanted from the day he took on his form.

No longer a spirit. Just... him.

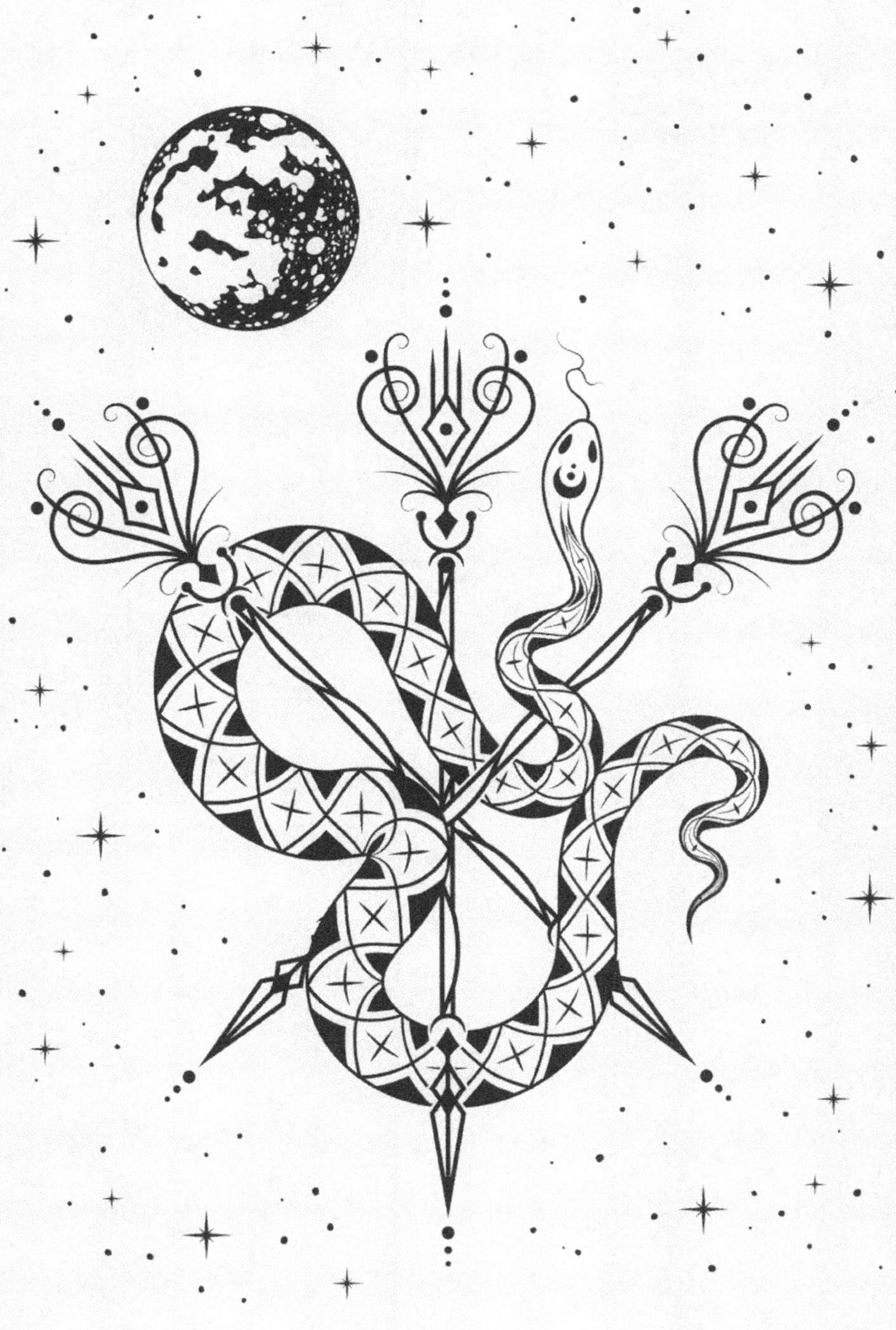

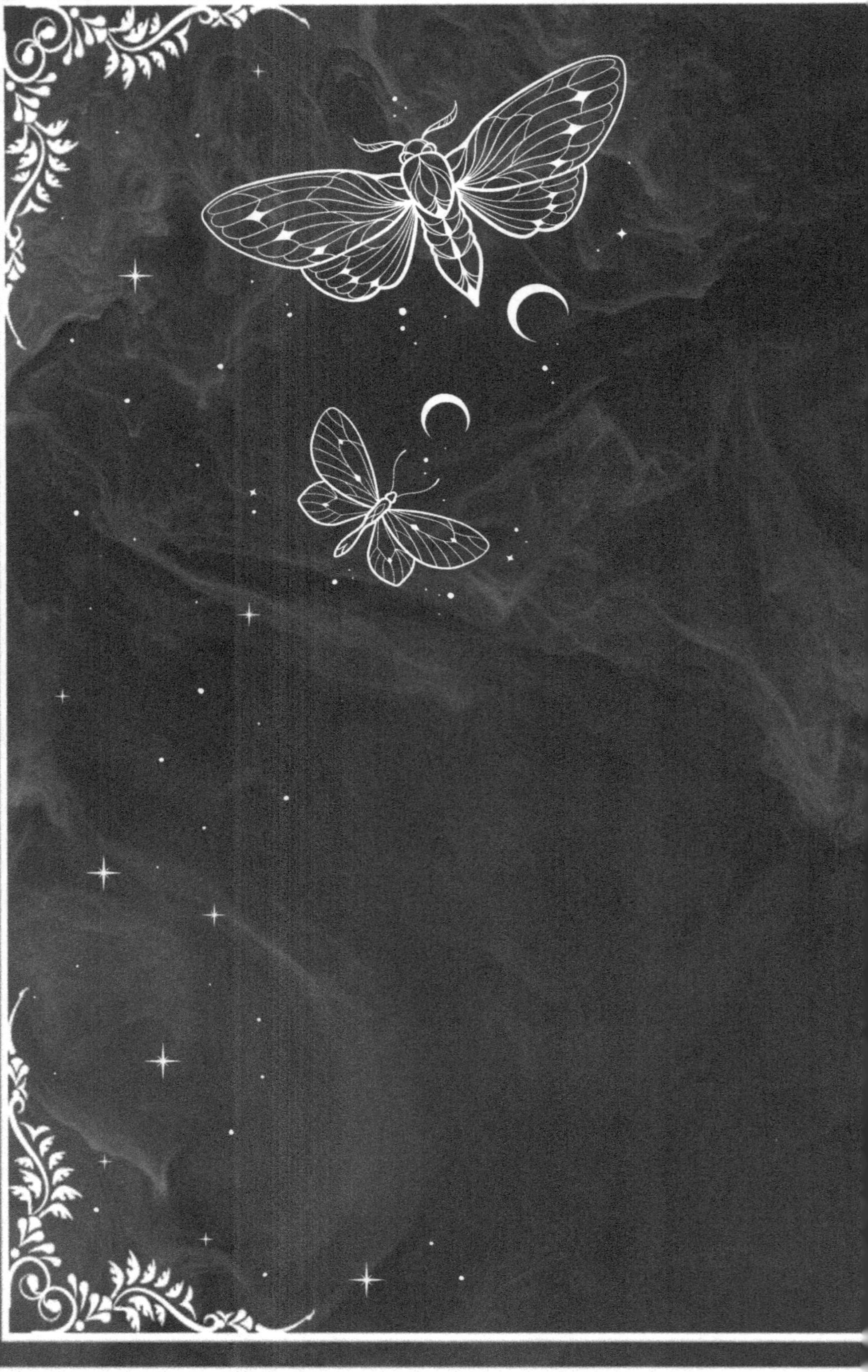

Chapter 22

Selene sighed as she trailed her fingers over warm skin. She had no idea how he looked like a bronzed statue, but it didn't matter right now. The red welts up and down his back called out to her.

Running her fingers through the grooves between twin marks, she hissed out a long breath. He shouldn't let himself get hurt like this. And even though he'd said he enjoyed the slight pain, it made her wince to see the welts.

Unlike the first time they'd done this, Selene didn't feel the need to stop herself.

She stepped closer, her fingers trailing down one line before she pressed her lips to the other. His deep groan was the same as he'd made when he kissed her. The sound echoed through her mind until she couldn't think of anything else.

His reaction made her entire body turn inside out. Lust didn't hide what his emotions were. He let her know that he wanted her. He stood there, holding onto a post of her bed, waiting for her to do whatever she wanted with him.

And by the seven kingdoms, she wanted to do everything. His warm skin against her lips encouraged her to move further. She pressed her palm flat against his ribs, holding him steady as she trailed her tongue down the marks. He tasted like whiskey, bitter and biting but oh so warm.

Her fingers skated over his warm skin, too warm, but she didn't care. His back flexed underneath her touch and he shuddered as though holding himself still for her. Exactly how she wanted him.

Selene hadn't realized how desperately she needed to be the one in control. He overwhelmed her. Made her feel like she was losing bits and pieces of herself every time he touched her. But now, she was taking from him.

Slowly, she tucked her fingers underneath the waistband of his pants. They were flush against him, leaving marks of their own on his waist and lower as she moved her fingers against the round globes of his ass. He tensed, and she refused to stop playing. Selene moved her fingers underneath the tight waistband, skating her fingers over his hip bones to the muscles that pointed right where she wanted to go.

She pressed her front flush against his spine, moaning at the heat that coursed through her body. "I've wanted to know what this felt like since the moment I saw you," she whispered, pressing errant kisses through her words against his spine. "There are rumors about you, you know. That you change your form to please every woman who sleeps with you. That you have unnatural control over the... appendage you use to bring them pleasure."

The first time she'd heard those rumors, Selene had found herself in her own bedroom with her fingers between her legs. She'd bitten down so hard that she'd tasted blood when she came at the thought of a man who could fully satisfy her, no matter what her preferences might be.

His stomach flexed against the tips of her fingers, so muscular, so smooth. Not a hair on his body even as she dipped her fingers lower. Would she find him hard? Of course he was. Iron hard and aching for the touch she had denied him for so long.

The button of his pants was icy cold, and then she drew her hand deep to find—

A crash of something metallic outside jolted her awake. Selene sat straight up, her hair cascading in front of her vision as she tried to get control over her breathing.

Had she really almost orgasmed from a fucking dream? A dream of him?

She could feel the slickness between her thighs. She was soaked, desiring him as she'd desired no other before, and even in her dreams. And damn it, she ached for him. For his touch. For someone to touch her other than her own hand, which had been lacking lately.

Instead, she thought about his long, lean fingers like the talented digits of a pianist. He probably knew all the places to touch a woman that would bring her to a blinding orgasm, and she knew nothing in comparison.

But then she thought of his hand between her legs, that stupid, sarcastic grin on his face as he watched her come apart around those long fingers and...

"Fucking hell," she hissed as she laid back down and pressed the heels of her palms against her eyes.

She was not doing this right now. She wasn't. Selene did not care that he was handsome or that she was having sex dreams about a certain demon who had no right to slither into her mind.

Maybe that was what he'd done. Demons could sneak into people's heads while they were sleeping. Perhaps he'd done the same to her. She didn't know that he was there, nor did it feel like he'd somehow possessed her, but demons could. He'd gotten into her dreams. That was his new tactic to wear her down.

But damn it, why should he have to? Her mother had practically told her to seduce him, so why was she holding out?

Rubbing her eyes again, she sighed as she admitted to herself that she enjoyed being the only person he couldn't seduce. She liked seeing the frustration on his features, but now that frustration had bubbled over into her own mind. She wanted him. He wanted her. Why was she putting them both through this madness?

All it would take was one look. One cocked finger and a raised eyebrow to tell him she wanted him in her bed and he'd come running.

But then she feared what was between them would gutter out and die, like a candle she'd dunked in water. He wouldn't want her after she'd given him what he wanted.

Therein lay the issue. She couldn't afford to lose his attention or his regard, but she also feared what would happen if she didn't give in to him.

Another image of her dream flickered through her mind. What would happen if she touched him like that? Would he groan like he had in her dream?

She felt her entire body flame with a blush. Of course, he would groan like that. He was comfortable with his body. He'd even let her explore him if that's what she wanted, and he wouldn't raise a finger to interrupt her. That's who he was, and damn it, that made her want him even more.

A flush of lust burned through her, and she knew it was dangerous to feel. But she was so overwhelmed with other emotions and the thought of him without his shirt, those pants riding low to reveal the dimples above his hip bones, and all that lovely, velvet skin just waiting for her to touch him.

Someone knocked on her door. A quiet three raps, as though they didn't want to interrupt anything that was going on in the room.

Blushing, Selene pressed the backs of her cool hands against her cheeks. "Thank you, I'm all right for now! Please come back in an hour. I'd like to rest!"

The knock repeated itself, insistent.

Was she supposed to entertain Greed more today? Was she expected to get ready for yet more embarrassing events?

With that, though, came reality barreling in right behind it. Lust. She was in Lust's bedroom and he'd slept with her the night before, so why hadn't he last night?

Frantic, she looked around the room to make sure he wasn't here. And thank goodness he wasn't, or she would have died from embarrassment. There was only the open balcony with wind blowing through the thin curtains. She sighed in relief and pressed a hand to her thundering heart. Or maybe the thundering was the damned knocking that continued as though that would make her come open the door quicker.

"Of all the ridiculous ways to wake someone," she muttered, swinging her leg over the side of the bed and standing. "Yes, yes, I understand you need me to come to the door right now. Why can't this just—"

She swung the door open and stopped, slack jawed, staring at the demon on the other side.

Lust had one palm braced on the top of her door, his arm raised over his head in a way that put all his muscles on display. He hadn't buttoned his shirt, and it left far too much space for her to stare at the wall of muscles in front of her.

Selene slammed the walls down in her head, shoving everything underneath the surface of the glacial lake until she almost felt the frigid bite in her body. He couldn't know. Couldn't guess. She was nothing but a calm piece of ice that stood before him with no emotions, no thoughts, nothing but cold.

Slowly, she looked up into his eyes to see they had flashed to a deep, glowing purple.

"Can I help you?" she asked. Did her voice sound breathless? Would he guess what she'd been thinking about just moments before he came here? He couldn't guess. She'd always kept things under wraps and this was no different from that.

But then he captured a wayward curl with his free hand, coiling it around his finger and giving it a gentle tug. "What were you doing?"

"I was sleeping," she said with a frown. "You woke me."

"Ah. That is good to know that, of all people, I was the one who woke you." He tugged on the lock of hair, forcing her to lean closer to him. His voice dropped low and gravely. "Your lust was the sweetest thing I've ever tasted, Selene. Better than mead, or wine, or honey. Sweet, just as I believe you will taste."

She hissed out a low breath, pulling away from him while ignoring the sharp spike of pain from her scalp as she nearly ripped her own hair out. "I don't know what you're talking about."

"You can't hide it from me."

"We both know very well that I do not feel lust!" she snapped. Selene needed to get control over this situation. She needed him to back away from the door so she could think and not stare at those washboard abs that were quite distracting.

He chuckled, and her entire body clenched at the sound. "Oh, Selene, of all things you could lie to me about, this is not one of them. I can taste it, you know. It is the emotion I feed off of, and every person has a flavor. Yours is my new favorite."

"And one you will never taste again, I promise you that." Was it hot in the room? She felt like her entire body was on fire and she needed to... well, she didn't know how to help herself. Back home, she would have walked outside into the snowy wonderland. But here, near the castle, they were too far away from those peaks to get snow.

He smiled down at her, far too amused. She wanted to slap the expression off his face, but the other half of her wanted to kiss him again. This time under her own terms, knowing that she controlled the kiss and that he was just as affected as her.

His eyes rolled back as he inhaled, deep and long and flexing those muscles as he did so. "Ah, even now I can taste you. What was it that set you off, little moon? I want to know so I can do it again."

"Absolutely nothing you did," she snarled, and then slammed the door in his face.

Pressing her back against the wood, she tried to calm her breathing. How did he know? She had everything under control, didn't she? She had tucked it all away and there was no way that he'd sensed her again. No. He couldn't have. Not again.

It wasn't possible. She was chosen for this role because he couldn't control her with his power. She knew how to control herself and her emotions, even in the wake of his power. Her unique power was born with her, given to her by the gods so that she would be able to take on this role and change the realm.

Right?

She didn't even have the space to consider all these thoughts because he was knocking on the damn door again.

"What?" she shouted, the word harsh even to her own ears.

But he just laughed. Chuckled as though he thought her aggression was adorable. "Have you ever been on a hunt?"

"No." Where was he going with this? "I have no interest in chasing down wild animals just to take their lives."

"Ah, so you have never met a bloodhound, then. They're remarkable creatures. If you give them the scent of any beast, they will take it and run. They will track the scent throughout the entire seven kingdoms if they must, but they always find their prey." A soft thud on the side of the door suggested he leaned against it as well. "You've given me a taste, Selene. Now I know what you taste like and I will not forget it. You cannot hide any longer from me, although I do wish to know how you hid yourself for so long."

She swallowed hard. "I will not be another one of your puppets, Demon."

"Haven't we been working so hard to prove that you are not? Trust, Selene. That's what you said I needed to work on and I have proven myself trustworthy to you time and time again. Perhaps you need to work on trusting someone other than that family of yours."

Her breath shuddered in her lungs, and she heard him walk away from her. As though he hadn't dumped a flaming pile of shit in her lap and told her to figure out what to do with it.

He could sense her now? Even if she shoved all those emotions away until she had to deal with them later? What was she supposed to do now?

But before she could sink into her panic, she heard him walk back again. He knocked on the door again, and she snarled.

"What is it now?" Selene might have sounded hysterical.

"I don't think I can control you," he added. "I did already try to send lust through the door, and I'm not sure you even felt it. Just thought you should know, in case you were worried that changed as well."

She hadn't felt it, but maybe that was because she was so panicked that she'd gone a little numb. "Two can play at that game," she replied. And then she chipped a hole in the lake in her mind. Just a tiny bit, no more than a tablespoon if it had been real.

The amount of lust and desire and passion that flooded through her was overwhelming. She slid down the door to sit on the floor, her hands in fists at her sides so she didn't take care of her problem herself. Her fingers itched to circle her clit, which appeared to have a heartbeat all of its own, to fill the aching hollowness between her legs.

An answering groan echoed behind the door and he slammed his fist into the wood. "Cruel woman."

"Go away then, Lust."

"And let you suffer on your own?"

"I will be managing this on my own, whether you stand outside that door or you leave. You aren't coming in." Maybe she should do just that. It would serve him right for being such a prick.

Another groan echoed down the hall. "And I wonder if you make any sounds when you take care of it yourself."

"Go away, Lust."

"Fine, but this conversation is not over."

She hadn't ever thought it was.

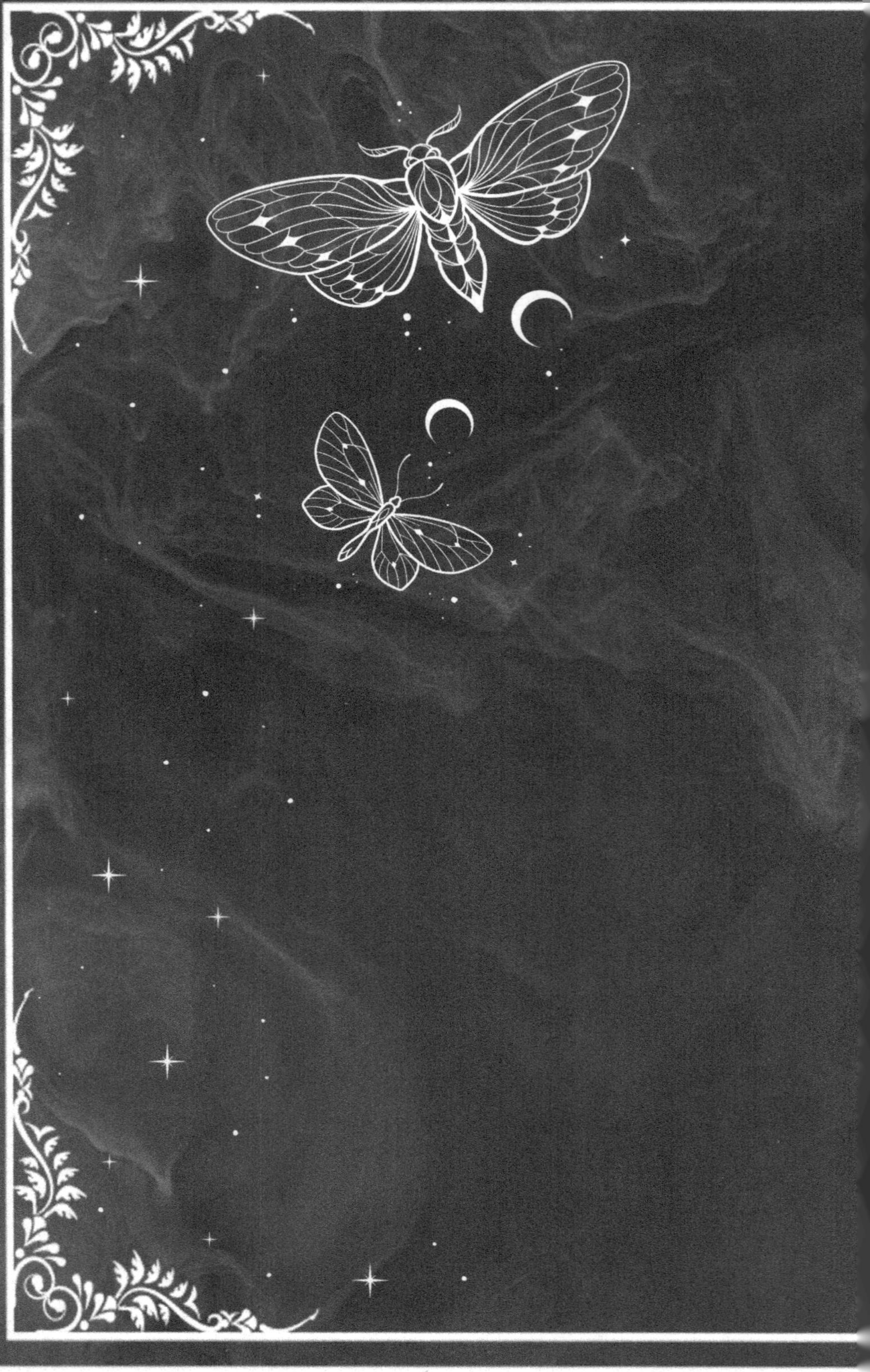

Chapter 23

He leaned against his bedroom door, grinning from ear to ear.

Lust had known it. He had been certain she wasn't cold to him and now he had the proof. How was she hiding it? He had no idea. Nor did he care. He was so elated that she felt the same all-consuming desire that he did. Who cared how she was hiding herself or even resisting him or his brother?

Jabbing the air with his fist in celebration, he tucked his hands into his pockets and meandered down the hall. He had a brother to entertain today, after all.

Perhaps he'd inform Greed that the situation had resolved itself. Greed thought that Lust was lesser for not convincing this woman to fall into his bed, and Lust wouldn't let that stand.

He didn't need to convince her to want him. He didn't need to do anything, apparently, other than be himself.

The new information was rather surprising. Women wanted things from him. They wanted an evening between his sheets. Perhaps they wanted permission to be uninhibited from someone who wouldn't judge them for their needs or wants. He was all too willing to be that person for them.

Selene wanted none of that. And the thought made him trip in the hall.

When had he forgotten why she was here? He'd gotten so lost in the idea of seducing her and making her admit that she wanted him, that he'd forgotten she did want something from him. She wanted her mother and her sisters in this castle with their fingers in everything he'd worked so hard to build.

Ah, that made everything a little murkier.

He had gotten lost in the taste of her for a bit and forgotten that she wasn't just some woman who had disregarded his power. She wasn't just an enigma he'd found on the streets somewhere and brought back here. For all that their story might align with that, it wasn't their story at all. She was still the daughter of the High Sorceress and a dangerous woman in her own right. Even if she wanted to pretend that she wasn't.

Sighing, he ground his teeth together until he heard a creak. Why couldn't all of this have been easier? Why couldn't he forget where she'd come from and then he could focus instead on seducing her even further? He'd join her in bed again, stroke his hands down her sides and wait for her hand to wrap around his wrist the same way she'd done before.

He could still feel her grip on him. How she'd hesitated because she wanted to draw his hand down farther. Closer to where he desperately wanted to touch, if only to see how she would quiver beneath him.

Damn it. He had to stop thinking about her like this or he'd forget she wasn't a normal woman again. She was more than that. Selene had layers to her, more than he liked, and that turned this entire endeavor upside down and inside out.

Huffing out a breath, he stalked into the great hall, where he knew his brother waited for him. His mood had gone from elated to downright horrid in the matter of a few seconds.

And his brother's people made that mood even worse, as they were all hungover and draped about on his floor. A few of them clutched their heads or some foul smelling drink in their hands, others were apparently pretending they weren't alive. Quite a few of them had pillows over their eyes, as though the sun hurt them.

Good. They should all question why they felt the need to come to his kingdom, drink all his alcohol, and then fuck his people into the wee hours of the morning. They could do that in their own land and not bother him with the nuisance.

Though most of the people in the great hall were clearly in pain, his brother was not. Greed sat on the same throne where Lust had left him, although this time he was alone. No women at his knees. None of his own people at his sides. Not even the giant twins who had glared at everyone who looked at Greed.

Lust stalked up to his own throne, sitting down on it as he waited for breakfast to arrive. His servants would have known to wait until he was ready, although they might hesitate at the missing woman who usually came down with Lust.

None of them seemed to know how to act around her. Was she a favored of Lust's bedmates? Should they wait on her hand and foot? He had never clarified why she was here.

Should he? Perhaps he'd been remiss in not taking the time to sit them all down and tell them exactly who she was, rather than rely on rumors to do the speaking for him.

And then he realized Greed had said nothing since he'd sat down. His brother, the man who never seemed to shut up, hadn't said a word.

That did not bode well for him. Frowning, Lust glanced over to see Greed was pulling on his bottom lip and staring off into space. It seemed like his brother hadn't even noticed he'd sat down, which was wrong all on its own as well.

Sighing, Lust hooked a leg over the arm of his throne and cleared his throat. Loudly.

Greed flinched and then glared at him. "What was that for?"

"You're here to visit me, are you not?"

"I am allowed to keep quiet thoughts to myself."

"If you want to do that, then go back to your own kingdom." Lust nodded at a servant, who looked at him with a questioning glance. They could bring breakfast out. He'd return to Selene later with a plate of food and a bottle of maple syrup. Maybe she'd let him play now that they both knew how she felt.

His thoughts turned wicked. He needed to distract himself before he joined his brother, staring off into the distance, wondering what it would be like to lick syrup from between those beautiful breasts of hers. He'd only touched a small amount of her, and now his hands itched for more.

Greed's voice interrupted those thoughts, and he found it almost impossible to think of licking Selene's velvet skin when his brother was rambling.

"What if she's more than a sorceress?" Greed asked.

"There are only sorceresses in my kingdom. Are you suggesting she's a witch? They're the same thing." He waved a hand when another servant held out a jug of wine. As if he needed more of that. "She already showed you her power, brother. It's not much, but it's enough to label her as one of them."

"I'm suggesting that she has more than one power."

Impossible. The thought made Lust snort. "Sorceresses have been the same for centuries. They are not all that interesting, Greed. They have one power they are born with. Their parents toss them to the Tower because magic is frowned upon even these days, and then the girls grow up there. They can do paltry tricks and spells that take ages to cast, that's all."

"What if she has two powers?" Greed looked at him then, those golden eyes slicing through every ounce of certainty Lust felt.

"I have not seen such a thing before."

"There's a first time for everything. We've felt the warning signs. Even Pride has admitted there's a change in the air."

Lust rolled his eyes. "I'll believe it when Wrath agrees."

"He has."

Silence stretched between them. If Wrath admitted something had changed, that the world felt different, then they all had to believe it. Their brother in the depths lived with the ancients who had shaped this world. He would know more than any of them.

Uncomfortable now, he ran a thumb along his lower lip. "What would you propose, then?"

"I have no interest in knowing what you do with the girl. I only see that you are growing weaker while she seems to be growing stronger. Perhaps she is like us. Perhaps more spirits have taken mortal form."

He snorted again. "Oh, it's not that."

"What would you suggest it is, then?"

"I wouldn't be surprised to find out she has another power. But she's let me taste her now, and I will not let that go so easily."

Greed's eyebrows rose and reached for a plate a servant held near his elbow. "Well, that explains why you're so energetic this morning."

"Ah, not in the way you're thinking." Another servant appeared beside him, and Lust took the offered plate that was full of bread, cheese, and fruit. "She let something slip. I could feel her lust this morning, taste it in the air like a wave. Like she'd been bottling it up somehow."

"I dislike the unknown," Greed muttered.

"Yes, you are as greedy with information as you are with everything else. You don't need to remind me."

But his brother had brought up a good point. He knew nothing of Selene's history. Who she was. Where she came from. What if she was something else entirely? Not a sorceress or a witch, but a creature they had yet to discover?

The thought lingered a little too long, and suddenly he had to know the answer.

Standing, he balanced the plate in one hand while grabbing another.

"Where are you going?" Greed asked.

"To seek the truth."

"Ah, a word of advice, brother. If I may."

Lust had no interest in the advice from someone like Greed. But he had to endure this visit, so he paused. He eyed Greed, who looked a little too pleased with himself.

Greed's tail flicked side to side, the tuft at the end a little ragged this morning. "Fuck her, brother. And quickly. We do not know if she is using your powers herself, or what she is doing to you. But you are weak. I can feel it. My people can feel it. You are not as you once were, and you need to remedy that."

A flare of anger burned in his chest. "I will do with her as I wish, in my own time."

"You may not have as much time as you think." Greed's brows furrowed with worry before his eyes flared brightly again. "But if you die, I will fight to absorb your kingdom. I suppose that would be a good consolation prize for you not listening to me."

Seven kingdoms, he hated his brother sometimes.

Teeth bared in a snarl, Lust turned away with both plates in his hands. Let his brother play the bastard. He didn't care. There was a woman waiting for him, and she was starving. In more ways than one.

His heart skipped a beat, and every muscle in his body clenched at the thought. He needed to get answers from her, not do as his brother wished for him to do, but... Maybe he could do both.

Lust planned out their meeting on his way to their room. It would take a bit to convince her, but he was certain that he could have a repeat of the night before. Only this time, he'd convince her to touch him when she answered questions. Surely she wanted to touch him. He could feel the lust rolling off of her the moment she'd seen him.

He knocked again, not waiting for her to respond to him before opening the door.

"I brought you breakfast," he said, trying to sound happy and not so fucking horny that he couldn't think. "I assumed after last night with Greed you wouldn't want to eat with…"

He forgot how to speak.

A bronze tub was now in the middle of his bedroom. His servants had likely carried it up for her, or perhaps it had been in her room. He didn't know. All he saw was the condensation running down the sides from the hot water inside. Selene sat within, bubbles covering the top of the water, but not quite enough so he couldn't see the rise and fall of her breasts as she stared at him.

Her dark hair was slicked back from her face, though a bead of water slid down her temple, catching on her jaw that was slightly open in shock. One leg was still gracefully lifted out of the water, hooked over the side of the tub as though she was too hot.

And oh, she looked so lovely he wasn't even certain he was breathing.

"Lust," she murmured.

He'd give her anything if she spoke to him in that tone again. Did she want the kingdom? Certainly. He'd hand it to her on a silver platter if she'd say another word in that throaty voice.

"Yes?"

"You're going to drop those plates. Maybe you should set them down."

Right. He had food in his hands and if he wasn't careful, he'd dump that food onto the floor like an idiot. But still, he couldn't remember feeling like this in a very long time. She captivated him. Him. He'd been so bored for years on end because everyone was like the rest and this woman somehow had broken that mold.

It was unsettling.

He set the two plates down on the nightstand before walking over to the bath.

Her eyes grew rounder with every step. "What are you doing?"

"Joining you."

"You're absolutely not getting in this bath with me."

He'd already started unbuttoning his shirt, but paused at her tone. "Why not?"

"Because I don't want you to."

Lust finished his movements, letting the shirt fall open. And there it was. The same lovely taste that flooded through his mouth, a tempting mixture of honey, whiskey, and peppermint. "You're lying."

"I'm not lying."

"I can taste that you want me." He tilted his head to the side, frowning down at her. "But you're still fighting it. Why?"

She sank lower in the tub until the bubbles touched her chin. "You don't need to know the answer to everything, Lust. You're not getting in the bath with me. Thank you for breakfast. You may leave now."

Oh, he would not do that, but he was very curious about what was going on. She acted like this was a horrific thing to happen. Him finding her in the bath. And here he was, straining to touch her, his cock so hard in his pants that he worried it might burst.

But she was troubled. She was fighting against this thing between them when she shouldn't. He already knew that she felt lust, so why…

Sighing, he knelt beside the tub and rested an arm against the warm metal. "Where did you come from?"

She blinked at him. "The Tower."

"Yes, yes. The White Tower of Silver Thread. Home to the Eternal Sisters, Wives of the Night Sky." He crossed his eyes for good measure. "That isn't where you came from, it's where you were placed. So, what is your real story?"

Amusement softened her features. Perhaps she enjoyed his foolishness, because at least she sat up a little more in the tub. Though she did gather some of the bubbles closer to her chest. "I'm told I was from Harpswell."

"Is that so? It's a very pretty area." He had fond memories of the place, though it was rare to find families who had any magical abilities whatsoever. "And your family gave you to Minerva?"

"They didn't want me." She shrugged, but he felt all that lust disappear in an instant. "They left me out in the snow to die. Minerva found me, and it was by her grace that I live. She could have ignored me. Such a death is not pleasant but not, perhaps, the worst."

His heart broke to hear her say those words. "I'm sure your family wanted you. It is tradition to leave magical children with the Tower."

Her smile didn't quite reach her eyes, and then she shook her head. "No. Minerva was very specific. They didn't want me."

Something in his chest cracked open at the words. A feeling he'd never felt suddenly swam to the surface. He didn't have a name for it, but it made him move.

Slowly, so he didn't startle her, Lust smoothed the backs of his fingers down her cheek. "I can't imagine anyone not wanting you."

He met her gaze without hesitation. There was no motive to his words, just the truth. As furrows appeared on her brow, she stared into his eyes as though searching for the lie. The joke at the end of all this.

There was no joke. He continued to stare back at her until she let out a little breath.

"I don't know that anyone but you believes that."

Lust's hand tightened at the back of her neck. "Then they are the fools, Selene, and I am all the better for it. I would hoard you to myself if I could. If you would let me."

He felt her swallow against his hand, even as she gave him a nod. "I believe you."

And then he remembered that she was very wet and very slick and entirely blushed from head to toe. It took every ounce of control to not look down as the bubbles floated away from her body just enough for a tempting glimpse.

But he was here for a reason, and though his plan had been for her to touch him, perhaps he could still use this moment.

Leaning closer, he pressed his forehead to hers and closed his eyes. Drawing deeply into his lungs the scent of peppermint and whiskey. "My brother believes you have two powers. One to conjure light, and another that lets you deflect our powers. Is that true?"

"I cannot tell you."

"Oh, you should not tell me. But you will. Trust, remember? We are trusting each other in this and damn what the Tower says about me. What do you believe, Selene? Do you believe I am worthy of your trust?"

He pulled back, staring down into those big dark eyes that watched him. He saw the universe in her gaze and a thousand lifetimes of happiness or pain.

She chewed on her lip. At some point she'd crossed her arms over her chest, though she likely had no idea she was pressing those lovely breasts together as though offering them to him.

But then she hissed out an angry breath and admitted, "I have two powers. It's not that I'm deflecting yours, it's that I'm absorbing them and burying them very deep. I cannot feel them. And apparently neither can you. Or Greed."

Ah, the flood of pleasure he got from her trusting him. It made him feel like a man. Not a spirit or a demon or even a king. Just the man she trusted, as she trusted no one else.

He dragged her forward to press his lips to her forehead. "Thank you for telling me."

"Please don't make me regret doing so."

"Ah, I can promise little, but that one I can make." And because he couldn't help himself, he tilted her head back with his hand and kissed her.

He took his time, enjoying the way her lips molded to his. How she remained stiff for all but a few heartbeats before she melted into his touch. He delved into her mouth, tasting her on his tongue so he could leave with something other than the faint promise of pleasure.

And when she was breathless, he let her go.

"Enjoy your bath," he said, leaving the room before he lost his nerve and went back to her. "I'll see you tonight."

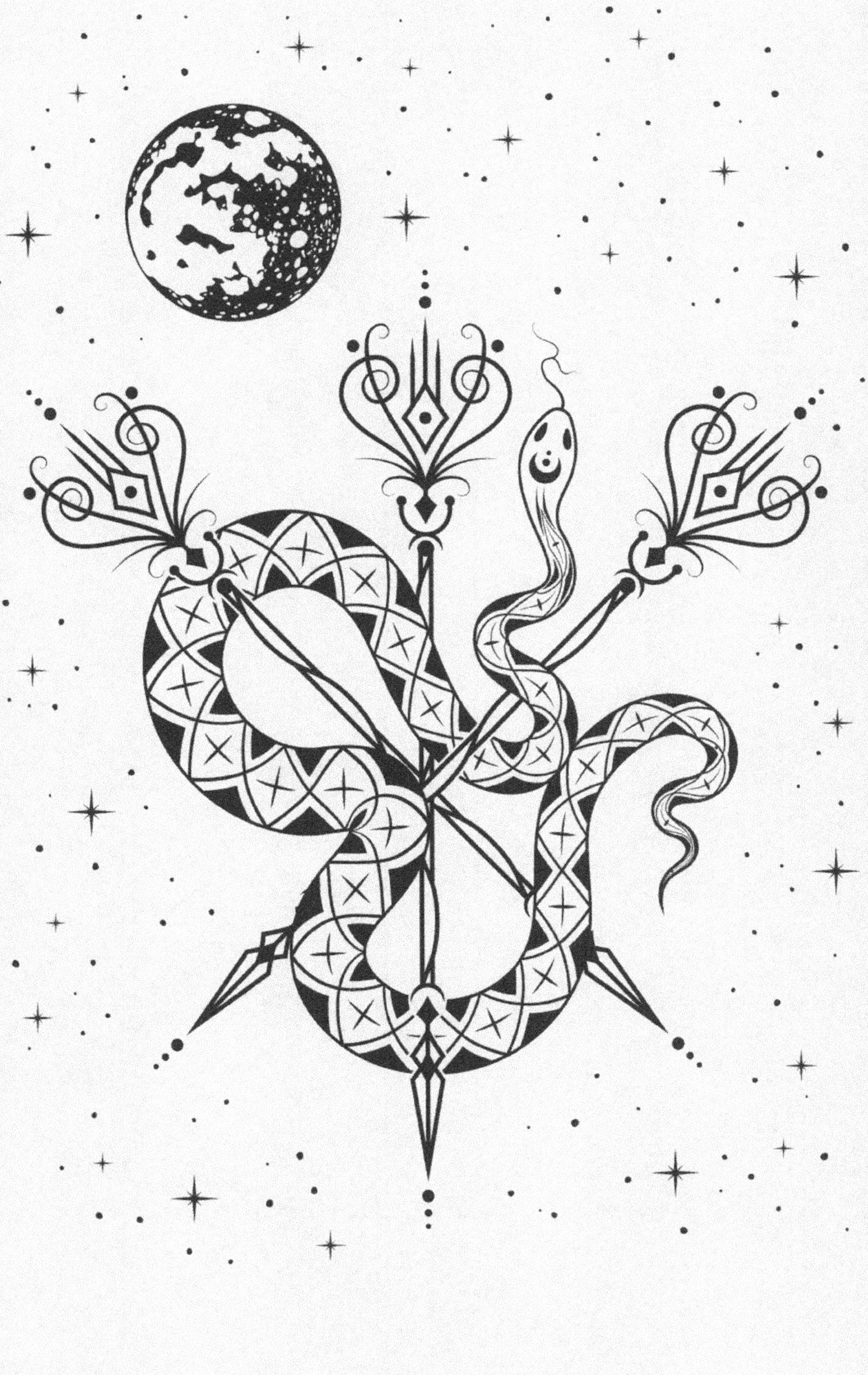

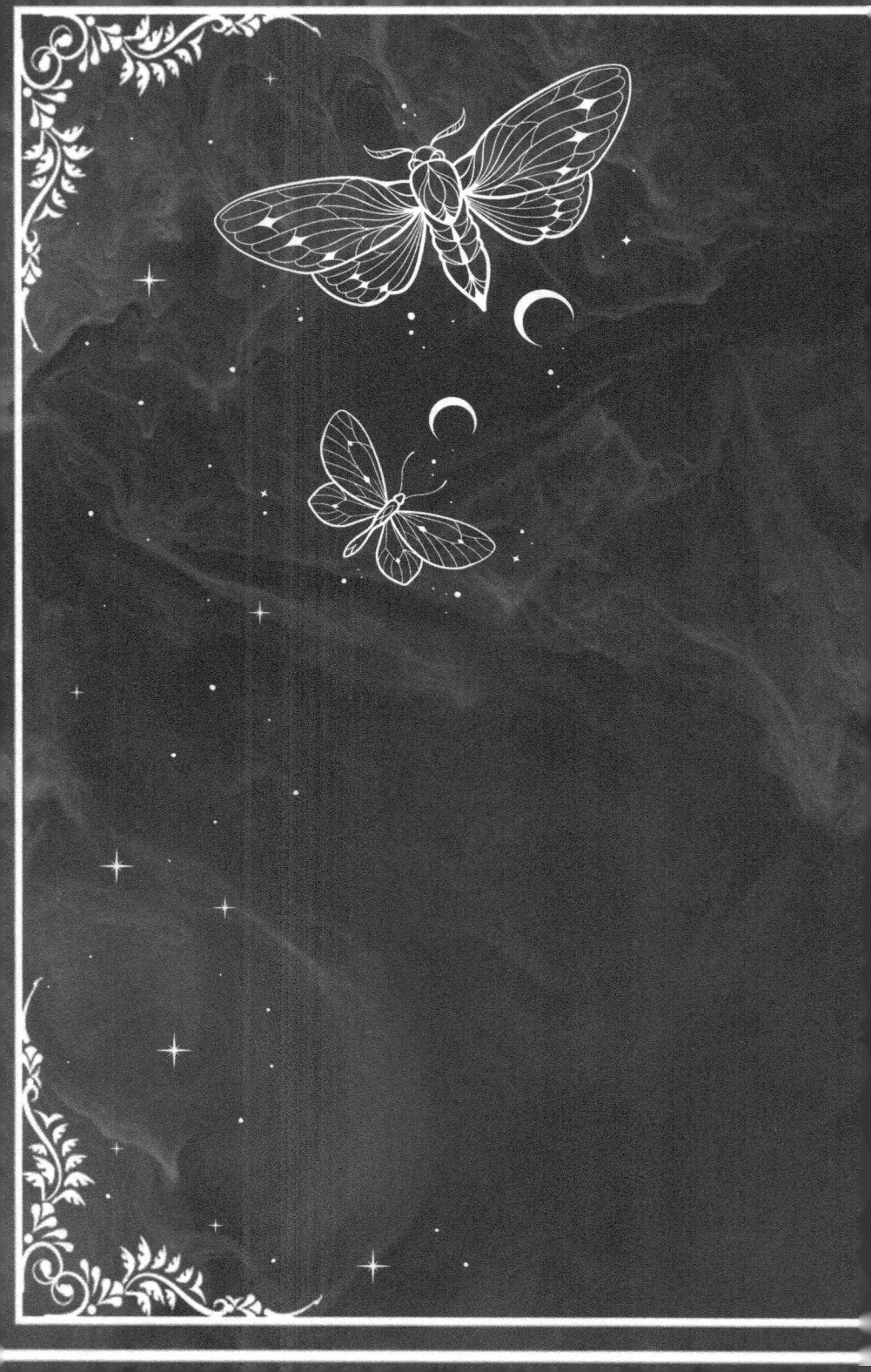

Chapter 24

No, no, no. This was all going so wrong. She had to get control over herself and the situation or she was... lost.

Selene laid on the floor of the balcony, staring up at the sky while trying to cajole herself back underneath the icy waves of her mind. But every time she tried to convince herself to shove those emotions back underneath the ice, it just hurt. Physically made her ache, like she was putting away something very important.

She was being stupid. Her mother and her sisters had sent her here for a reason. They'd left their mark on the back of her neck so she would never forget they were her real family. They were the ones protecting her.

He needed to be under her thumb, not the other way around.

Lust didn't know how much he affected her. Of course, he could sense her desire now, and he used that to his advantage. But if he really knew how fond she was of him, how he'd wiggled his way into her heart, then he would exploit that. She knew he would. He had to. He was a demon, after all. He'd want to know that he had somehow changed her for the worse.

"For the worse?" a melodic voice interrupted her thoughts.

"Affection, please don't read my mind. You know I don't like it when you do that."

"I didn't mean to this time! Your thoughts are so loud." The spirit gathered itself on her chest, coiling on her like a cat. "He's not going to hurt your feelings, you know."

"You have no way of knowing that for certain."

"I do. Because I can also look into his thoughts, and I know he's very enamored with you. You're the first person he's ever had to work for, you know?"

She had no idea what that meant. "Because he doesn't like me, but he wanted to understand what makes me tick? Of course. But now he knows the answer to his question and he can do whatever he wants now. He can send me back to the Tower. All I had over him was that I was a curiosity, and now he can make me leave with satisfaction that he figured it out."

She'd been so stupid! Why would she offer him up the truth that easily? Everything she'd worked so hard for, gone. In an instant.

Selene had no more cards to play. Nothing to hold over his head to get her mother and her sisters here so they could at least try to bind him. Nothing. Now she was just another woman who had come to the castle, and what use was she to him?

Affection leaned over her, sunlight playing through its form. It had... features, now. Sort of. A cute little button nose and bright red lips that sort of floated in the mass of color.

The spirit looked a bit like a puzzle missing pieces, but it was clearly trying to look more mortal.

"What happened to you?" she asked at the same time Affection spoke.

"He's not going to toss you aside."

They both stared at each other before again answering at the same time.

"Why wouldn't he toss me aside? He's figured out the question he wanted an answer to."

"Nothing has happened to me. I thought you would be more comfortable talking to me like this."

Selene took a deep breath and blew it out. "Can you listen to my answer before you talk?"

Affection nodded, although sullenly. "If you ask questions, then I'm going to answer them."

"Yes, I understand that." She sat up, letting the little spirit roll into her lap. "Why do you think he will not toss me aside? He has every reason to now. There are plenty of women in this castle who will warm his bed, and I'm sure some of them are even keeping secrets from him. There's no reason to keep me around."

"Other than for the reason I already said. He's never had to work for anyone to like him. All he had to do was snap his fingers and people threw themselves at him. Women. Men. Everything in between. He's been viewed like a god here for many years." Affection rolled over in her lap, staring up at her with wide eyes. "But now he knows what it's like to fight for someone. And he's very intrigued by it."

"I don't want to be intriguing." Or maybe she did. She could use that to her advantage, but her gut said she didn't want to be some new shiny toy for him. She wanted... wanted...

No, this was all wrong. He could think whatever he wanted as long as he wanted her happy. That she could use. Everything else didn't matter.

Which meant she needed to get him even more addicted to her. If he wanted her around after finding out her secret, then she needed to manipulate him even further. She needed to... give in.

He'd been begging for her body since the moment she walked through these doors. Since he bumped into her on the street and thought she was pretty. Would that be enough to keep him around? Would that be enough of a temptation to convince him that he did actually want to be with her for longer than a couple of days?

If that was the price she had to pay, then she'd pay it. Sure, it made the feeling of her desire a little duller. It made sex with him feel like a transaction. Her body for the right to be here and continue this game a little longer.

Suddenly, all this felt less about her and more about him. She could please him, even though all she knew about sex was much less than what he knew. Still. If he wanted a pleasing partner, he should have picked someone less confrontational.

It would do. She'd endure sex with him, telling herself she didn't have to enjoy it because it was all for her family. She'd keep that barrier around her heart intact and nothing would threaten that.

Affection shrank a bit in her lap, gathering itself tighter into a bright coil. "I don't think this is a good idea."

"Then get out of my head."

"Again, you're a very loud thinker, Selene! But Lust, he's not interested in you for your body. He doesn't want to only sleep with you. If you would just listen to me—"

She'd already dumped the spirit out of her lap and walked toward the wardrobe. She had made up her mind. Tonight, she would seduce Lust so that he would not let her go. He'd keep her here, and she could continue to interest him until she could either control him, or destroy him.

She wouldn't fail. Even if it felt like she had sold herself to a demon.

Wasn't that the point of this all? A flash of anger ran through her, and Affection latched onto the thought.

The spirit tumbled in front of her, getting itself kicked in the process. "You're right to be angry at them! You got sold. They wanted you to do this, knowing how it would make you uncomfortable. They don't care about you, Selene."

"Please stop."

"But you know I'm right! You know they don't care about you at all. They want you to believe you're only worth this. To sell your body for the Tower and then do their bidding again once it's all done. But you've found yourself here. With him. And I know you haven't made any friends other than that, but it has to count for something that you're happier here! You're free, Selene. Don't throw that all away by trying to deceive him again."

Softening, she bent and patted the top of Affection's head. "I have made friends here, little one. I've met you."

Affection sighed, turning into little more than a glimmering puddle on the floor. "But that's not the same and you know it."

"I have made no effort here. If that's what he wishes, then I will do so. I'll lick the boots of the nobility if he wants just to get my family here. Where we all belong." She threw the wardrobe door open and pawed through the layers and layers of silks.

She'd never chosen to wear the clothing he'd given her thus far.

Her clothes were just fine, and if she didn't have to put on the flimsy silk, then she would rather wear her own thick wools. No matter how warm it was. But tonight, she needed to seduce him. And that required her to look the part.

A flash of memory had her think of Lara. The woman had worn a white gown that was entirely see through just to clean the castle. How did Selene compete with that?

In the very back, she found the perfect nightgown. The silver fabric looked like moonlight in her fingers. It trickled through her touch, tiny sparkling bits whispering with the slightest movement. It was lovely and fine and barely a gown at all. It was perfect.

"Selene," Affection whispered one last time. "Please let me convince you this is wrong."

She shook her head. "I need to get ready, Affection. I don't think you'll want to be in the room for this."

The little spirit slunk out of the room underneath her door, and her chest burned with guilt. She hadn't meant to make the poor dear sad, but it shouldn't be in the room while she seduced its master. After all, it wouldn't take much to convince Lust to sleep with her.

Just the thought of Lust made her body clench. The hollow between her legs ached to be filled, and she knew denying these feelings would only prolong the inevitable.

He would not be a terrible man to have between her legs. She'd enjoy touching him, just like in her dream. And considering how many women he'd fucked in the last ten centuries, he would probably be an excellent partner in bed.

So why did this still feel wrong?

Sighing, she stepped into the pretty nightgown and resolved herself to wait. She spent the hours dry brushing her skin until it was so soft it felt like velvet. Then she took a comb to her hair and counted to one thousand until each strand was as liquid as the gown that covered her body.

Until she heard the door open and voices angrily hissing at each other on the other side.

"Enough, Greed," Lust snapped. "I'm going to bed."

"I'm telling you, there is more to this story."

The door slammed in Greed's face, all while Lust muttered about meddling family members. "The man has no boundaries and refuses to take no for an answer. I know why he wants to investigate the situation. All so he can hold it over my damn head and request that I pay him a price for something I already could figure out on my own."

He didn't even look at her. He just shed his clothing, layer by layer, muttering more about his brother as he stomped into the wardrobe.

"Do you have anything to say about it?" he shouted from within. His shirt hit the ground next to the vanity. "You didn't seem to be all that fond of him. I'll admit, I could use someone agreeing with me that he's an idiot."

"He's an idiot," she replied, amused. Selene stood, and the dress clung to her form, cold and unfeeling as the rest of her. "But you are no less of a fool if you do not use him to your advantage."

"Ah, right. You're from the Tower and all they teach you is court politics." A grunt followed his words. "Not everything has to be political. My brother can be both right and an idiot."

"Those two do not usually go hand in hand." She set his shirt on the back of the chair before calling out, "Lust?"

"Yes, yes. Having the servants move your clothes in here, as well as mine, made it all the more difficult. I know you don't like it when I wander around wearing little."

"I wouldn't mind it tonight."

She thought she heard him hit his head against something. "Excuse me?"

"Would you come out, please?"

Nerves had been rumbling in her stomach, but they settled the moment she remembered he was rather awkward around her. And that made little sense, but he wasn't entirely himself if Selene was in the room.

Maybe Affection was right about a few things.

Lust stepped out of the wardrobe, shirtless in silk sleep pants, only to freeze when he saw her. And she knew what she looked like. She'd checked a million times in the mirror before he got there. Her long hair nearly touched her waist, brushed so many times it looked like water falling down around her shoulders. The dress molded to her body, too tight and yet not showing entirely everything. She wore a single diamond necklace around her neck, a gift from Minerva long ago. When Selene hadn't yet agreed to be the sacrificial lamb for the man in front of her.

His throat worked in a hard swallow. "What are... What are you doing, Selene?"

"I know that I've been avoiding you the entirety of my time here. I know that hasn't been easy on either of us." She stepped closer, then paused as her pulse went wild. "I think it's time we stop playing this game. Don't you?"

"I..." His hands flexed at his sides, as though he battled with himself not to touch her. "You have given me no reason to believe you were going to give in any time soon."

"I changed my mind. You can feel my desire, Lust. Surely you know I'm not lying."

And she did desire him. The broad expanse of his chest made her want to touch him. She thought about her dream, about how she'd wanted to slide her hands underneath that waistline just to feel what she'd seen so much, and he groaned.

"Selene."

She didn't want to listen to that voice. She had to stay in control.

So she stepped forward and threatened him with the only thing she had. "I won't offer again, Lust."

He narrowed his eyes on her, and for a moment, she thought he would refuse. And she didn't know what she would do if he decided to wait. She needed to let off some steam, and she needed to know for certain that he wouldn't throw her away. If this was the only way to convince him to keep her, then she couldn't afford for him to make another choice.

Why this meant so much to her, she didn't understand. Familial ties had never made her this crazy, but she… she couldn't let this go.

She took another step closer and watched his pupils dilate. His nostrils flared as if breathing her in, as she stopped directly in front of him.

So much muscle. So much warm skin just begging for her to touch it. And as she watched, his chest rippled as though anticipating her touch.

"I've wondered what you feel like," she whispered. "I don't know why I've held back for so long."

She lifted her hands, and he let out a low groan that echoed through her body. Before she could touch him, he'd caught her wrists in his grip and backed her toward the bed.

No, not the bed. The mirror.

The cold glass hit her spine, making her arch into him with a hiss of surprise. And then her breasts were pressed against his chest, cushioned by all that hard plane of muscle, and it made her mind scramble.

He leaned down, and she closed her eyes, ready for the kiss that would sear her very soul. Except he didn't kiss her. He whispered against her mouth, "Why now?"

"Does it matter?"

"More than you think."

Because she had no choice. Because she wanted to fuck him, and she didn't at the same time. Because she was ready and not and if she didn't do this, then she feared what else would happen, so why was he overthinking this?

Selene couldn't say any of that. Instead, she looked up into his eyes and she cracked that icy lake inside her mind wide open.

Weeks of lust, desire, passion, and need flooded out through her body. It filled the room, and she funneled it all toward him.

The cords of his neck suddenly stood out in stark relief. He stiffened against her, then let out another groan that echoed in the bed chamber. Lust leaned into her then, his lips against her neck as he rolled his hips against hers.

She felt him rub against her core and the sizzle of heat that spiked through her body promised an orgasm that would change her life. Breathing heavily, she couldn't think of anything other than the size of that cock and what he was going to do to her.

One last thing. One last attempt to make sure he wouldn't say no.

Selene grabbed the back of his neck, tugging him so he had to look her in the eye while he drowned in weeks of her lust all at once. She dragged her mouth against his, nipped his bottom lip, and whispered, "I want you."

The look in his eyes when he pulled back was... soft. Like she'd said something that no one else ever had before.

"You really do, don't you?" he murmured, before drawing her back to his lips.

She sighed into him and felt herself crack open yet again. For all that she'd prepared to build a wall between them, she had forgotten how he'd already wiggled into her heart.

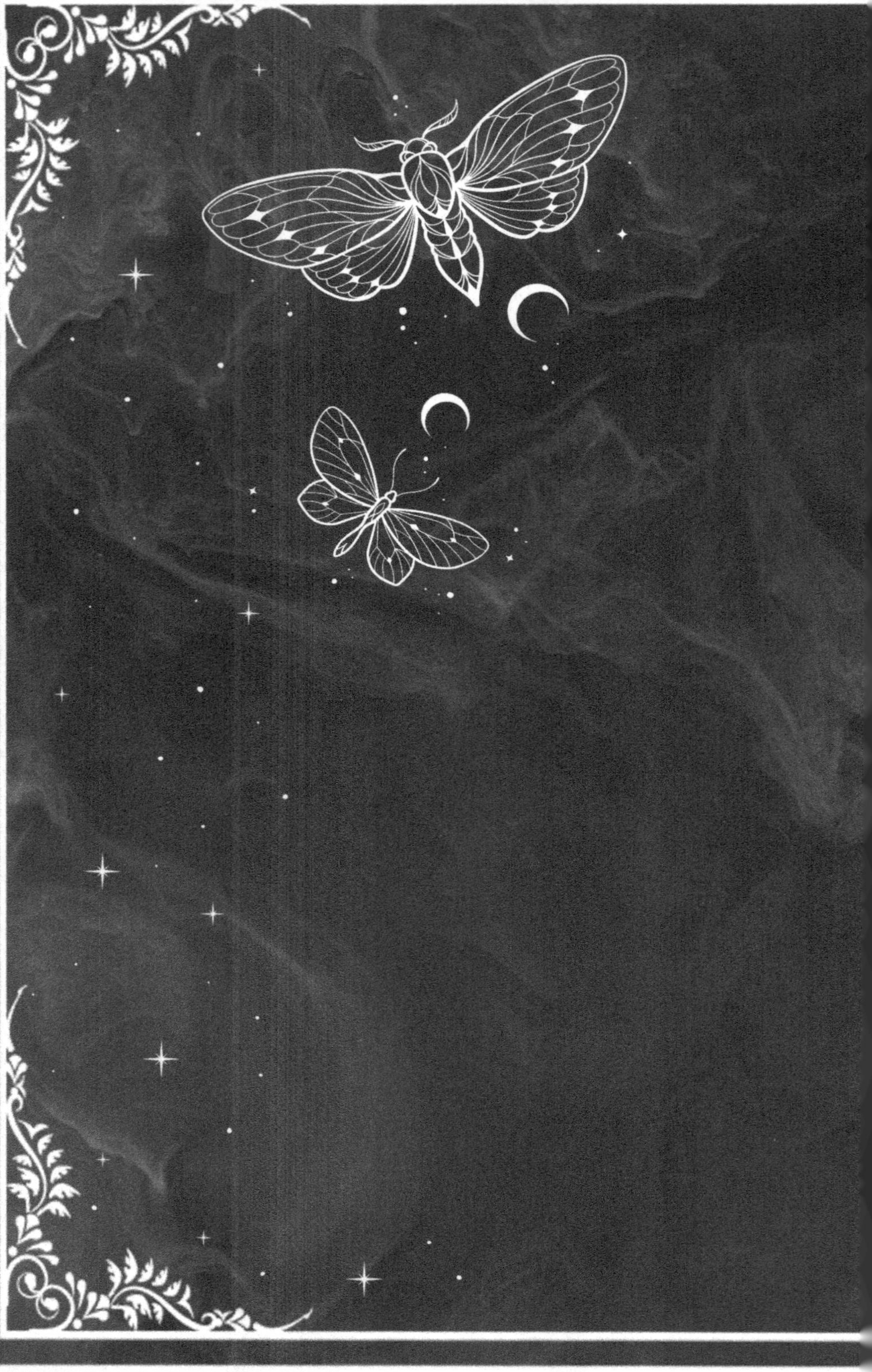

Chapter 25

He had a very hard time believing she wanted this. Selene had argued from the moment she'd stepped through his doors that she had no intent on sleeping with him. Or even looking at him, really. Or anything else that even remotely seemed close to this.

But she kissed like she wanted him. He could taste it, feel it swirling all around them and sinking into his skin until he could think of nothing else. She kissed like she'd been denying herself for too long and all those walls had crumbled.

He groaned into her mouth. How long had it been since someone set him on fire just from a kiss? Sex had become rather clinical in the last few centuries. He knew every spot of a woman to touch, every nerve ending to stroke, every soft place to grab that made them all squirm in his arms. But with her, it didn't matter how much he knew.

Lust wanted to know what made her make those little sighs. Maybe it was the same spot or touch as countless women, but he'd never heard her make those noises.

And then her hand touched his chest. Her delicate fingers stroked his skin, and he nearly came apart. She'd never touched him like this before. Never even suggested she wanted to.

He should have known this the evening she'd helped him out of his clothing and she'd followed the red welt down his back. That moment had been... sublime. For both of them.

She dug her nails into his chest and drew them down. Hard. Hard enough that he leaned back with a hiss, at the same time, a flare of desire shot up from the base of his spine.

He hardened, painfully, staring down at those half-lidded eyes that lazily looked back. "You said you liked a little pain," she whispered. "I'd rather give these to you than that stupid corset."

"It's not stupid," he growled, cupping the back of her neck and bending her spine until she was trapped between his body and the mirror. "Some people think it's fashionable."

"Then I think they're stupid, too."

He put his hand over hers, keeping their gazes locked together as he dragged her nails down his chest. "Do it again."

The low hum in the depths of her throat made his cock jerk in his pants and he realized he was dangerously close to coming already. How did she do that? It took him hours to find his release these days, and she'd turned him into a newly changed spirit who had never had a woman touch him. She was nothing special, he told himself, even as he licked his way up her throat. Nothing special, but she turned him inside out.

Perhaps it was the waves of lust that rolled between them. Lust that she swore she didn't feel for him, and yet now he couldn't think through the haze of her desire. It flavored his tongue, but he didn't want to taste her lust. He wanted to taste her.

Lust leaned down to kiss her, clinging to her lips with his, before he wrenched them away with a snarl. "If we do this, there is no going back."

"I know."

"I will not let you go, Selene. You will be bound to me. I don't care what your mother or the sorceresses claimed you could do. I will never let you go."

The soft smile on her face almost made him pause. He thought about pausing and asking what that expression was, but then she traced a finger over his lips and he was lost again.

"I know you think that," she whispered. "You believe that you will want me all the more after this is done."

"That won't change, Selene. I want you. Since the first moment we brushed against each other and you denied having any reaction to me. You were the question I needed an answer to, and I've found that answer with you here."

Her hands smoothed down his chest and her fingers dipped below the waistband of his pants. Those delicate fingers were dangerously close to where he wanted her to touch, where he knew she would find him hard and wanting. "Stop talking, Lust. You can put your mouth to better use."

And oh, he certainly could.

In an instant, he had her pressed back against the mirror. He hovered his lips close to hers, not quite touching, a promise but never fulfilling it. Her skin felt like velvet underneath his fingertips as he trailed them down her shoulders, biceps, to her hands, where he curled her fingers around the edge of the mirror.

With everything in him, he promised her an evening she would never forget. An evening that he'd prepared for with centuries of practice so he could bring this woman to an earth shattering orgasm that made his ears ring for days afterward.

He sank onto his knees before her. Slowly moving his hands down her body. The silk fabric of her lovely nightgown was like a second skin. It was cold against his palms, against her pebbled nipples, down the flat plane of her belly.

Her chest rose and fell with the ragged sound of her breath. She watched him with those dark eyes, daring him to continue and yet never once hesitating. Perhaps she wanted this. Perhaps she was giving in to what they both had desired for so long.

The hem of her dress pooled at her feet, and it took so little to drag it up her lovely calves, the thickness of her strong thighs, to her waist.

Completely hairless. The woman always surprised him.

With a wry grin, he looked up at her with a lifted brow. Her cheeks were already flushed, the lazy tendrils of lust curling off her in little wisps. Lust leaned forward and breathed her in first, slow and divine, as the earthy scent of her filled his lungs. The first flick of his tongue wrenched a groan out of her lips. That sound... Oh, he couldn't wait to hear it again.

He learned her as if she were someone entirely new, skating around the little nub where she needed him to touch. Working her until she was dripping and ready.

Her hands sank into his hair, grabbing onto his horns with a force that surprised him. Only then did he drag his hands up her inner thighs, spreading her wider, lifting a long leg over his shoulder so he could sink a finger deep inside her.

He looked up, watching as she tilted her head back. And, by all the seven kingdoms, she was glorious in this moment. Her hands held onto his horns. Her neck arched back and her muscles cast shadows in the hollows of her neck and collarbone as her jaw clenched.

"You are lovely," he said, giving her another long, slow lick. "Absolutely divine."

"Stop talking." Her voice was ragged.

"Or what, little moon? You'll punish me?" He added a second finger, a chuckle echoing deep in his throat as her knees shook. "I'm the one doing the punishing here."

And finally, because he knew she needed it, he paid attention to her clit. He licked long and slow, then sucked hard as she let out a little mewl of pleasure. Circling his tongue round it, he twisted his fingers, working them in and out of her as his cock longed to do. He was relentless. He gave her no chance to even catch her breath until he felt the hard clench of her pussy around him and the cry that echoed out of her throat that was everything he'd hoped for.

Music. A symphony of pleasure.

"Good girl," he growled as he pulled back from her, catching her in his arms as she fell.

She fit perfectly against his chest. And how naturally she wrapped her legs around his waist, knowing without question that he would carry her, as if she trusted him. As if she didn't think for a moment that she was in the arms of a man she'd called a demon more times than he could count.

Selene twined her arms around his neck, her hands delving into his hair as she drew him close for a kiss that seared him to the very bone. He'd expected her to be hesitant, not this.

He didn't even look as he stumbled toward the bed, nearly falling on top of her as he laid her out across the covers.

The dress was still up by her hips. Her dark hair splayed around her, the curls so lovely he wanted to wrap them up in his fist and hold her there. For hours. Days. Until he finally got his fill of this woman who tempted him in unnatural ways.

He leaned back, running the back of his hand over his mouth as he stared down at her.

"Why are you stopping?" she asked, breathless.

"I'm not." He let his eyes dance over every part of her, then reached for her dress. "I've been dreaming of this moment for so long. I just want to make sure I remember every detail."

Her lips parted in a soft gasp, some emotion flickering that he didn't like. So he kissed her again. Devoured her. Bringing her attention to him and only him because there was no room for second guessing or anything else. This moment was for them alone. He would invite no one else in, even if only in her mind.

She met him with passion, her back arching so more of her could touch him. Chuckling, he palmed her ribs, smoothing his hands up her sides until he cupped her breast in one hand. And, ah, but she was perfect. His thumb flicked over her nipple and her gasp made his cock twitch.

"Lovely," he murmured against her mouth. "So lovely."

And he couldn't stop himself from bending. He sucked the hardened tip of her breast into his mouth and worried it with his teeth, because how could he not? When she made those little sounds in the back of her throat, wriggling underneath him as though a temptress rather than a sorceress.

Oh, he could make her body do all sorts of surprising things. She'd scream for him all night long. He'd wake her up every hour to plunge inside her, even though he had no idea what her warm, wet heat would feel like gripping him. Not yet, anyway.

Groaning, he let her wet nipple pop out of his mouth before hissing against her, "I need you."

"Then take me."

Ah, if only it were that easy. He was no small man and she...

His thoughts scattered as she reached for him, dragging him up her body and holding his hand in hers. "I want you," she whispered, her eyes locked with his as she pulled his hand between her legs. "You can feel it, Lust."

He could. Even through her own fingers, her wetness seeped between them, coating both of their fingers with what he knew tasted so perfect on his tongue. He couldn't take his eyes off her. Not when she stroked herself using her fingers and his, their hands twined together. She dipped their fingers inside herself, together, their fingers twined together as they stretched her.

She felt the pleasure deeply. He could feel it rolling off her, feeding into his power like no other had done before. But even through the haze of his own desire, he could feel it was slightly tainted. Not quite what it should be.

"Selene..." he asked, the word a question more than the moan he wished it was.

"I want to see you," she whispered. The shadows in her eyes briefly disappeared.

Enough for him to wonder if she was nervous. There was a question he should ask her, but he scrambled off the bed and his thoughts obliterated as she moaned again.

Lust didn't think he'd ever undressed so quickly. His pants hit the floor and then he was crawling over her. Her gaze locked onto his cock, and he knew what she was thinking.

He was larger than most men, the perks of a spirit taking mortal form. Still, he knew how intimidating it must be for a woman who'd been locked up in a tower her entire life.

A sudden fear spiked through him.

He cupped the back of her head, drawing her attention back to him as he licked her lips and tangled his tongue with hers. And when she was well and truly breathless once more, he whispered, "Have you done this before?"

She snorted. "Do you think I'd be so forward if I hadn't?"

"And when would you have had time?" He leaned back a little, then wanted to see even more of her. Lust straightened until he was on his knees, legs spread around her hips. "Little moon, you are ever surprising."

"Do you want to hear about another man while we're doing this?"

He grinned and fisted his cock, roughly giving it a quick pump before watching her gaze focus on where he gripped himself. "I don't care. You'll forget all about him when I'm done with you."

Her cheeks flamed bright red, and there it was again. Those damned shadows that made him wonder if she wanted this. If she was only doing this for some strange reason that he hadn't figured out yet, because he couldn't quite understand what went on in her head.

If she wanted to wait, he would. Tasting her fucking perfect pussy had been more than enough. He'd feast on her for the rest of the night, because he'd certainly come enough in his lifetime to last a few nights without.

He dragged his hands up her legs, fingers already dipping into that honey with his mind made up. "Selene, we don't have to..."

She sat up so quickly that he almost didn't track the movement. Blinking in surprise, he hissed out a breath as she wrapped one arm around his shoulder and grabbed his cock with her free hand.

"I want you to put this inside me," she whispered against his neck, pressing kisses between the words. "I want to feel you come, to know what it is like to be taken by a man who has destroyed women before. I want you to destroy me, Lust. Make it so I cannot think for one night."

Oh, if only he could.

Those were not the words he wanted to hear because it meant she was battling her thoughts back. She didn't want to think tonight because of those shadows, and he refused to fuck her unless there were no shadows between them.

Instead, he reached between them and held her hand fisted around him. Slowly, he settled them both onto the bed. He squeezed her fingers harder, showing her how to grip him and how slowly to move. She gasped at the feel of him, her eyes heating with the moment like she thought she'd won.

In a way, he supposed she had.

Lust braced himself above her, his free hand sliding down to slip between her legs again. "You feel so good," he groaned against her throat. "You are everything I dream of, do you know that? No one... has ever..."

Ah, the words wouldn't come. Not when she was whimpering in his ear as he pressed his thumb against her clit and her little hand moved so delicately against him. It was everything, not enough. Fuck he needed her to come, or he'd beat her to it.

Snarling in her ear, he ground his teeth and used all his vast knowledge to bring her right to the edge. She was panting, writhing underneath him as he sank his middle and ring finger into her while the palm of his hand ground against her clit. He'd never fucked anyone without using his powers to manipulate them. And hearing her noises, knowing that every reaction from her was because of him and only him?

Fuck, she'd ruined him.

"Come for me," he growled. "I want to hear you."

"I can't," she whimpered.

"You can, and you will. Fucking come for me, Selene."

She arched into him, her hands stilling as her thighs squeezed his hand between them. And, oh, that sound. That keening cry of her release seemed to startle her with its force.

Lust couldn't wait any longer. He pulled his fingers from her and used her wetness to coat his cock as he squeezed her fist with his own. Normally he'd be ashamed at how quickly he came, but how could he feel anything but pleasure when she tilted her head away from the danger of his horns, her long neck exposed to his lips as he spurted onto her stomach?

No, there was no shame in this moment. It was perfect.

She was perfect. Warm and soft and so comfortable beneath him.

Fuck, he had to keep her, Lust thought as he collapsed beside her. No matter what, now she was his.

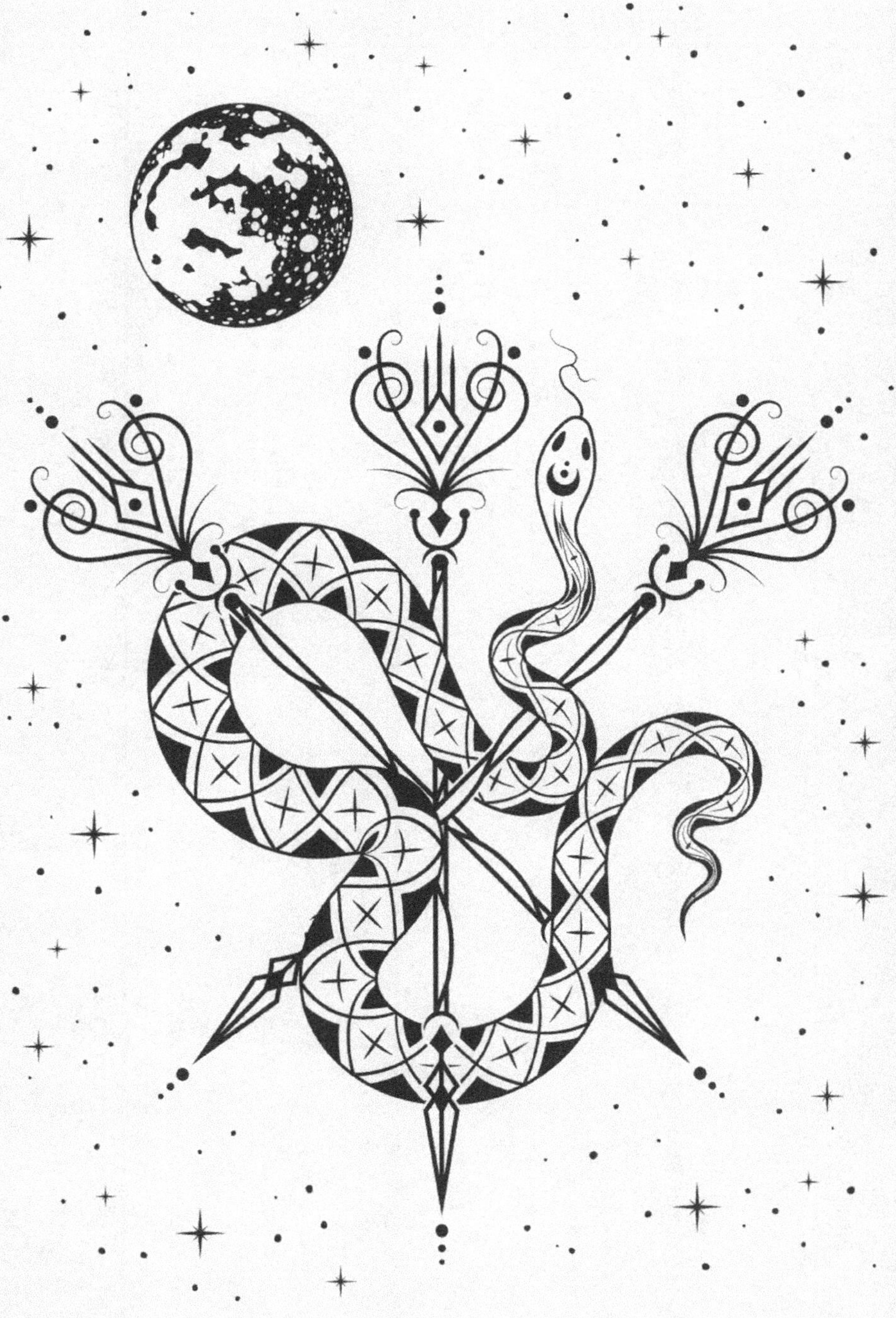

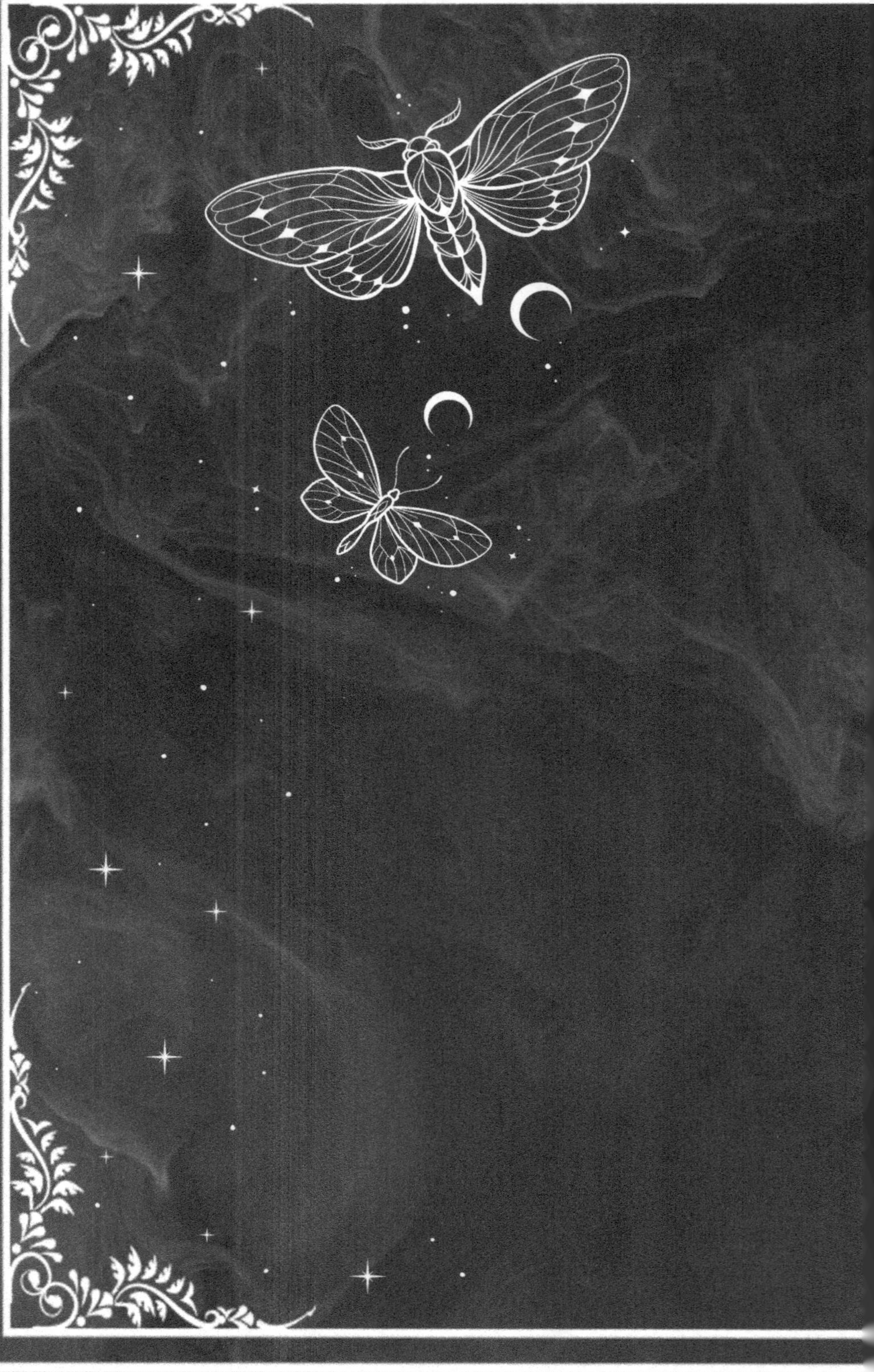

Chapter 26

Selene hadn't thought this through. She'd assumed sleeping with him would tie them together in the only way she had left. It was a last ditch effort to solidify their relationship, but she'd forgotten how tied up in him she'd become.

These were the thoughts she woke up with. Literally. Like her mind had turned off after multiple earth shattering orgasms, only to turn back on as she woke.

She shouldn't have done this. She shouldn't have let him touch her like that because now all she wanted was for him to do it again. Her stomach clenched and her mind already whispered that she could roll on top of him and it would take no time at all to take him inside her. He'd wake before he knew what was happening and then he'd groan, rolling her over onto her stomach as he took control.

Those deep, guttural sounds would echo in her ears again and... and...

"It's too early for you to be so awake," he grumbled, rolling and throwing an arm over her chest. "Give me a minute, little moon."

"I'm not asking for anything," she whispered.

And yet, he smacked his lips as though he'd tasted something divine. "You cannot hide from me anymore, remember?"

Ah. Right. He could taste her lust, and now that he'd gotten the taste of it she'd never be able to hide it from him anymore.

Damn it. That complicated things.

Everything about this made their situation more complicated. She'd thought this would remind her that her position here was sacrificial. Her family had raised her to be this, and if she didn't sacrifice herself, then she had no idea what her family would do to her.

Allowing a demon to be inside her, to see him looming over her in the darkness with those horns silhouetted in shadow, it was meant to remind her of her place. Instead, he'd touched her with soft hands. He'd whispered words in her ears that made her feel like the only person in his kingdom who mattered.

She'd never been the only person to matter. Selene had never even met someone who would have put her before themselves. And now she didn't know how to feel because she would have to betray him at some point. He knew this. She knew it. They were together on borrowed time.

Lust sighed and moved a little closer, settling his chin on her shoulder while his breath puffed against her neck. "You're overthinking already, aren't you?"

"I am not."

"You're letting that mind run away with what the future brings, when you should be enjoying the morning."

"How am I meant to do that?" She wanted to list all the problems she had running through her mind, as a way to scold him for such foolish thoughts.

But then he opened his eyes and that wonderful softness was still in his gaze. He let his eyes flicker over her features, lingering on all his favorites, and she knew which ones he liked best because he had to tear his gaze away from her lips, her nose, and her neck.

Finally, he sighed and shook his head. "Let me help."

Help? How was he going to…

He dipped low and captured her lips. He took his time with this kiss, languid, slow and sweet. There was no heat, no intent on making her lose her mind with desire.

This kiss was a good morning. And how are you doing and I hope you're well, and if you aren't, let me make it better for you.

She sighed into him, her hand lifting to cup his jaw and hold him against her. He had no idea what he did to her. Surely he didn't, because if he knew then he would have rolled on top of her and had his way with her.

He chuckled into her lips, pressing once, twice, a third time for good measure before he pulled away. "As much as I would love to spend the day in bed with you, I have to entertain my brother."

"He's still here?" She blinked owlishly up at him. "I thought he'd left."

"Why would you think that?"

"Well, I just…"

"You don't like him." He grinned down at her, dimples appearing on his cheeks. "I thought I'd save you the suffering of entertaining him alone. He never says how long he's going to stay, though I would like him to see you a little more now."

That sounded a little ominous. "Why now?"

He danced the backs of his fingers down her cheek, curving around to her neck, which he followed with the barest hint of a touch. "Because he'll know you're really mine."

As if his brother would be able to tell what they'd done. She snorted and then rolled her eyes for good measure. "No one can read me that well. Unless you intend on telling him yourself."

"Oh, it would take a blind man to not see how enamored you are with me." He pressed one last fierce kiss to her lips before he rolled out of bed. "You watch me with a hunger in your eyes, now, sorceress. One might think you actually like me."

She had the perfect retort ready on her tongue, but then lost all sense as she stared at his perfect ass. He stood from the bed, the silk sheets falling away from his hips as though even they didn't want to stop touching him. He stretched his arms up over his head, the muscles in his back flexing with every movement. Long lines curved up his form, the golden texture of his skin appearing even more like polished metal in the morning sunlight. The breeze from his open balcony played across him, leaving goosebumps to rise in its wake.

And she wanted to touch him again. Just like that. Her fingers actually itched to do so.

He chuckled and glanced at her over his shoulder. "Oh, come on now. We have a busy day."

"You have a busy day. I have no expectations here." She sat up, clutching the sheets to her chest as she watched him walk to his closet. Even his thighs flexed in a way that made her eyes almost cross.

She had to admit he was lovely. Every part of him was so attractive it made her body clench with need. And she supposed it was freeing now that she no longer had to hide her reaction.

"I think I'd like to change that," he said, throwing open the doors to the closet and pausing for her to take one last look at his naked form.

She licked her lips. "Change what?"

His grin widened even further. "Pay attention, Selene. I'd like you to get more involved with the kingdom. You've been here long enough to at least try."

And before she could argue, he turned toward her fully, letting her eyes widen at the sight of his erect cock before he disappeared into the closet.

He knew what he was doing, she decided. He knew she was tempted by him and that the sight of him like that would make her entirely miserable while she sat here trying to figure out what had happened last night.

And without him in the room as a distraction, she worried about everything that had happened. She feared she'd changed something between them, and not in the way she'd hoped. He was no more under her thumb than he'd been before all of this had happened, but she was completely and utterly in love with him.

No.

She clenched the sheets a little harder to her chest and shook her head in denial. She was not in love with him. Lust was only a demon she had to betray for the sake of the kingdom. He was not a kind man who had cared about her last night, and even this morning.

He was the person who had taken her as a sacrifice. That was all. He'd seen what she offered, and he took it because he was selfish enough to do so.

Except... He hadn't. He hadn't even fully had sex with her. Almost as though he could see into her head and knew that she was second guessing whether this was what she wanted or what her mother wanted. He'd known and instead, he'd given her orgasm after orgasm and still used her own wetness to bring himself to completion, but he hadn't...

He hadn't had sex with her. Even though she'd agreed to it.

Frowning, she drew the covers up over her shoulders and head to think.

That was where he found her. Buried upright in a mound of blankets while she tried to understand what had happened between the two of them.

She heard his deep chuckle first before she realized that the door to the closet had opened again. She peered at him through the blankets, hating how handsome and awake he looked this early in the morning. The open neck of his shirt revealed those planes of muscles that she'd touched last night but hadn't been able to run her tongue over like she wanted. His pants clung to powerful thighs that had flexed against her while he used her hand to make himself come, groaning with that deep, deep voice.

Her thoughts were interrupted by his head peering through her blankets. "Selene?" he asked. "I really have work to do today, so you're going to need to stop it with those thoughts."

"What thoughts?" She blinked at him innocently.

"Whatever thoughts are making you taste like that, darling. And I believe you need to get out of bed as well. If you're interested in coming to court with me today, that is."

"Not really." She needed to think over last night. Then maybe she could show her face to others without turning a dark crimson.

"I think you should at least try." He sat on the edge of the bed and gently drew a blanket away from her head. He pulled the second down as well, until her face was at least partially visible. "You're overthinking again, little moon. Want to tell me why?"

No.

Yes.

Maybe she should tell him at least a little of what was going on in her head, but she hardly knew what it was herself.

So she settled on letting out a long, defeated sigh. "You know why I'm here, Lust. So why did you let me…"

"Ah." He sighed as well, but then brushed his fingers through her hair in a delicate touch. "I am not afraid of your mother or her people, Selene. This is not the first time a sorceress has tried to kill me, tame me, or force me to rule the way they wished. I've had a long life, and frankly, these attempts bore me at this point in my life. I've seen it all. This isn't even the first time a sorceress has tried to fuck me." He tucked a strand of her hair behind her ear. "But this is the first time someone like you has walked into my life. I'm not going to waste that because your mother has other plans for you. I trust you to do what is right for you."

"What if what is right for me is the same plan as my mother?" She knew her eyes were wide and perhaps a little shiny. "What if I ruin all this? What if I break you and bring this kingdom to its knees?"

He leaned forward and pressed their foreheads together. Lust inhaled, taking a deep, long breath that was as measured as it was sad. "Then such will be the way I fall. It's you, Selene. Only you are making this decision."

She squeezed her eyes shut as her heart felt like it was breaking. "That feels like a lot of pressure."

"I've lived a thousand years, Selene. Ten of your lifetimes, if you're lucky, twenty lifetimes of the unlucky. I have seen humans live and die and kingdoms change and people grow. It has been a long life. A good life." He pressed his lips to her forehead and smiled against her skin. "And now I have met you. I can safely say that these last few weeks have been the most entertaining of all my years. Do with me as you will, sorceress. And I will be at your feet, thanking you for whatever you decide."

He drew away from her even as she wanted him to hold her against his chest. It didn't feel fair that he'd been able to withdraw from her arms when she wanted him... here. In bed. She wanted him to scoop her back up and hold her against his heartbeat for a little while longer.

Maybe then she could sort through these feelings. These strange emotions wouldn't let go of her heart.

As she stared at him, golden in the morning sunlight, she knew she didn't want to hurt him. She didn't want to do anything that would take that smile off his face.

Swallowing hard, she looked down into her lap. "You didn't... Last night... I mean, I thought you would—"

Selene had no idea how to ask why he hadn't fucked her. She'd been begging for it. She'd even grabbed his cock and asked him to put it inside her. She didn't know any other way to make it more clear that she wanted to have sex with him. He'd been the one to deny her, and that shocked Selene to her very core.

"You weren't entirely ready," he replied. Then shrugged. "I didn't want there to be any regret this morning. Any more than I knew would be there regardless, that is."

"Why?"

She looked up at him when he didn't immediately reply. Lust's eyes had wandered, staring over her shoulder as though lost in his thoughts. Perhaps he didn't even know the answer.

She'd never heard anyone claim that Lust had much control. If it was offered, he took. He even took when there was the smallest hint that someone wanted something. The next morning be damned.

Lust was fleeting, wasn't it? The emotion itself heralded a short, enjoyable time and then the two people, or more, would move on. That's why so many in the kingdom loved it here and loved his festivals. They were enjoyable for a time, and then they went about their normal lives.

So why had he stopped? Why had he held himself back?

Finally, he murmured, "It is a strange feeling, you know."

"What feeling?" Her heart stuttered in her chest.

"Restraint." He smiled at her, and those dimples flashed. As though he were utterly pleased with himself. "I'm not interested in rushing this, Selene. For the first time in my life, I'm enjoying that there is no hurry. I will give you all that you desire in time." And then he winked before heading to the door. "But I will make you beg for it."

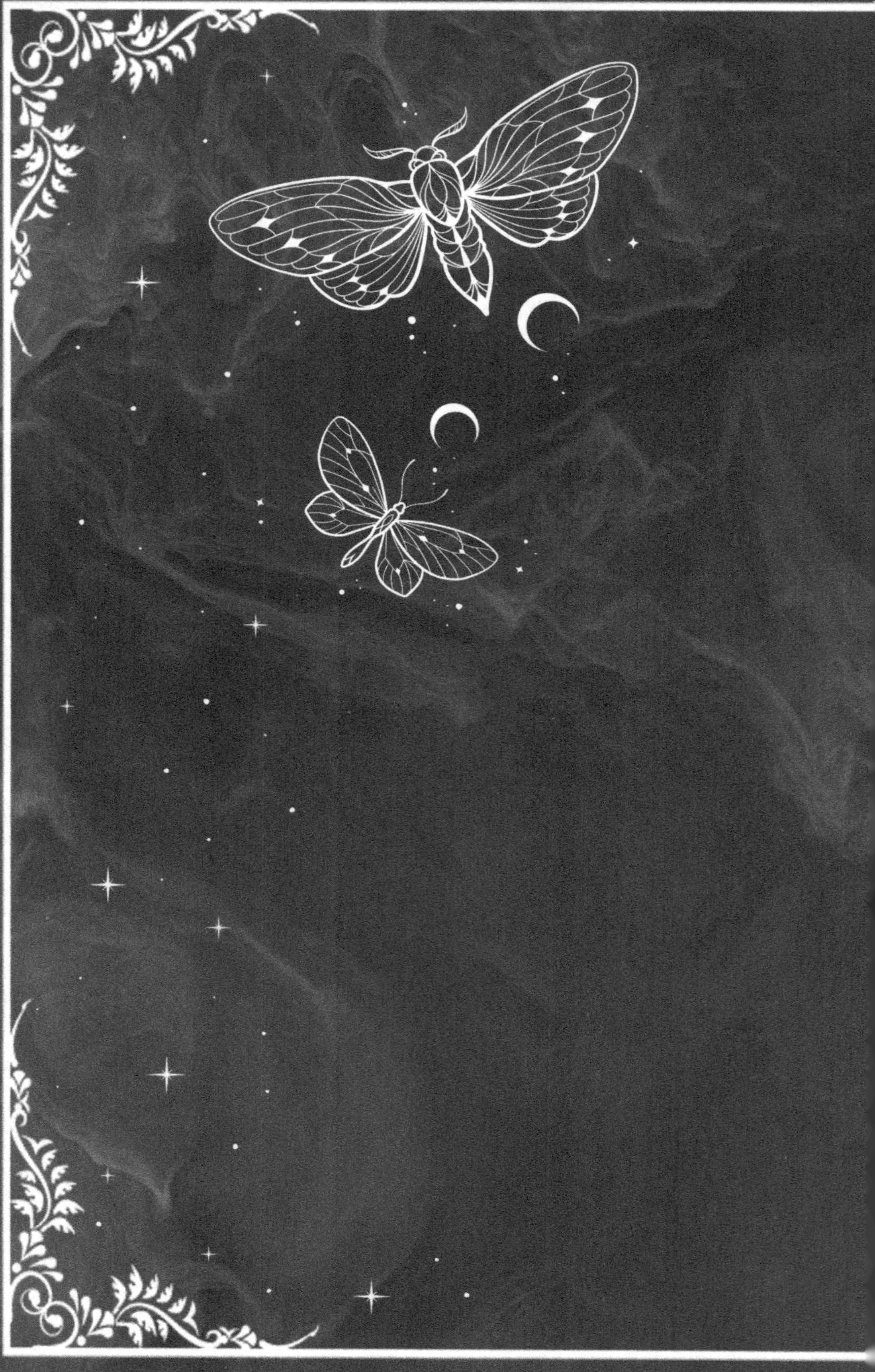

Chapter 27

Lust practically waltzed to meet with his brother. He found it strange how light he felt after spending the night with her, but he also realized there was no other way he could have felt.

Something new, after all these years.

He'd been so caught up in the repetition of life. He would go to the villages, find a lovely young woman, continue the myth that he was grand and adventurous and more than any other could possibly be. He stayed to himself in the castle with those who knew him well, so he didn't really need to live.

All of those had been done to keep himself safe. And he was. Safe, that is. Living life in a bubble of his own creation without ever looking outside of it.

Now? She was there. On the outside of the bubble, daring him to look through the glass orb and see her for what she was.

A woman unlike any other he'd ever met.

No, that wasn't right. He sidestepped a servant who walked past him with a shocked expression on her face. Selene wasn't any different from any of the others, and maybe that was what made her so unique. He'd met a hundred women who looked just like her. At least fifty of them had smelled like peppermint or had eyes the color of caramel when they got angry. He'd probably made someone so angry that they couldn't think straight on many occasions.

But none of those people had been her. And therein lay the strangeness to the entire situation.

It didn't matter that she wasn't entirely unique or a unicorn who had crawled out of the mist to bring him good luck. She was a woman with real wants and needs and desires, and he was obsessed with her. Entirely. Utterly.

Just thinking about the sounds she'd made when he had licked between her legs was enough to make him turn right around and join her in bed again. Was she still there?

He made to turn before forcing himself to stop. No, there was time. Like he'd said. He wanted to take his time with her, to learn what she liked, what she didn't like. He wanted to hear every sound she made, even if those sounds were in frustration.

Whistling a tune he hadn't heard in years, he walked into his study where Greed was waiting for him this morning.

His brother stood by the windows, hands clasped behind his back and tail angrily flicking behind him. "Finally. You should know there is no security in your castle to speak of. I'm disappointed, brother. You should at least have guards at the castle gate."

"There is no need for guards while I am in the castle." Nor did he care to argue about that this morning. He poured himself a cup of coffee from the tray one of his servants had left out and sipped at it. "Are you enjoying your visit?"

"Not in the slightest. I came here to talk some sense into you, and instead I find you wrapped up in a woman who couldn't care less about your existence."

Lust waited until Greed turned around and then grinned.

His brother rolled his eyes, but let out a long, exhausted sigh. "Ah, well nevermind then. She's finally given in?"

"I wouldn't call it given in as much as finally accepting what she needs." He took another long sip of his coffee. "It's different with her. I don't know how to describe it. She's…"

Greed's eyes narrowed. "She's…"

"Different."

"Yes, you already said that. I don't understand why you think saying it twice will explain it any better."

A mist pooled underneath the door and then rolled toward them. Affection gathered itself up, almost to his knee in height now, shockingly. The spirit hadn't grown in ages and yet here it was, larger than it had been since the first time he met it.

Lust looked down as his jaw dropped open. "What are you doing here?"

"Of course, this is different!" The spirit almost shouted. "This is the first time he's had to work at getting a woman to like him."

The loud snort that echoed from Greed broke the silence that followed those words. His brother shook his head, clearly trying to hide a smile. "Well, you would be right about that one. Women fall at Lust's feet when he wants them to. Literally."

"And I tried with this one many times, but she had no interest in falling at my feet." And considering the evening he had, and the morning reception he'd gotten, he added with a grumble, "I still don't think she has any plans to do so."

Greed and Affection made eye contact before they both burst into laughter. His brother pointed at the spirit while saying, "I like this one. Where did you get it?"

"I didn't get it anywhere. Affection has been with me since the beginning."

"Affection, is it? Curious little spirit." Greed bent down to look at it, his golden eyes glowing with desire. "Perhaps I should take this one back with me."

"Absolutely not."

Affection puffed itself up. "You'd find I'm very hard to contain. Besides, we're not talking about me. We're talking about Selene and how Lust is going to keep her."

He set his coffee cup down a little harder than he'd planned. "There's nothing to talk about. Of course I'm keeping her."

"Just because you slept with her doesn't mean she's going to stay."

"I didn't exactly…" Lust heaved a sigh and stared up at the ceiling. "We didn't exactly sleep together."

Again, silence. From both the spirit and his brother.

Greed straightened, the creaking leather of his clothing the only warning before he said, "What do you mean you didn't exactly sleep with her? Did you fuck her or not?"

"Not. I mean, kind of. We certainly did enough of other things. I don't—" Lust shook his head and frowned at his brother. "Why am I telling you any of this? You don't need to know what happens behind our closed doors."

Greed stared at him for a few moments before tilting his head back and barking out the most awful laugh. Loud and like a thunderclap, the sound carried throughout the entire room before he got a hold of himself. "You know what fucking is, Lust! Does that sound like fucking to you?"

"There are layers to it, and please stop being so crude. It wasn't fucking."

"What was it then?" his brother asked, amusement glittering in his golden eyes. "Making love?"

"Both of you get out."

"You're visiting me."

"You're in my castle!" Lust threw his arms out in disgust before pointing at his brother. "You have no say in how I feel about this. If I say we fucked, then we fucked."

"I suppose having your fingers or mouth in her is one thing, but I've never seen you so upset. Fucking is getting your dick wet, brother. You didn't manage to do that."

His dick was soaked by the time they were over, but he didn't need to tell his brother the finer details. Grumbling, he shook his head before looking back at Affection. Though the conversation was not one he wanted to have, it felt important to ask, "What did you mean we have to figure out how to keep her?"

The spirit drew itself up, and he noticed for the first time that it had eyes. And a mouth. And what looked like a nose it was trying to conjure up, but it was very much in the wrong place. "There are nuances to keeping someone in your life, and you've never done that before. Just like you've never had to work to get someone in your bed—no, don't argue, we all know that's the truth—you've also never had to convince someone to stay with you."

"Isn't it enough that I am the king of this entire floating island and that she is lucky to have me around?" He shook his head. "I will fulfill every fantasy she has and provide her with startling new ones. There is nothing that will stop me from pleasuring her until she is uncertain which direction is up. Is that not enough to keep a woman around?"

Even Greed gave him a look that said he was an idiot.

As one, both the spirit and his brother said, "No."

Lust sank into one of the plush leather chairs in his study and held his head with both hands. "What do you mean, no? I will give her everything she's ever wanted."

"Do you even know what she wants?" Affection asked. "She's told you stories about her childhood, and she's invited you to enjoy in her body, but how much do you know about her?"

"As well as anyone else."

"Precisely." Affection rolled its eyes when he nodded like that was a good thing. "Women don't want to be fucked all the time. They want to know that you care, that's how you keep her around. By caring."

"And how do I show her that?"

Greed made eye contact with him and then shrugged. His brother sank into the opposite chair, leaning forward on his forearms so he could better pay attention. Apparently, they both needed to learn this lesson.

The spirit was all too happy to oblige. It rolled in front of them and gathered itself up again. "Flowers. Affection. Kisses! Romance her to show her that she means something to you."

"Romance?"

"Yes."

"What is that?" he asked, an uneasy feeling settling in his stomach.

"What do you mean, what is that?" Affection shouted, the wispy edges of its form rioting with the question. "Are you an idiot? Romance is romance! It's about love and feelings and telling someone else your feelings. It's about caring how they feel and learning what they like and listening when they talk. How do you not know what that is?"

He glanced over at Greed, who, again, shrugged. "We are the embodiment of what we are. Just as you are the embodiment of affection. Lust and romance do not... Not necessarily mix."

"Then it's time for you to learn. Or she'll leave this place and go back to the Tower with all those dreary white walls and women who hate her." Affection sniffed. "You'll lose her, Lust. If you only want her for her body and all you do is reaffirm that you're only interested in her for sex, she'll walk out of these doors and you'll never see her again. Mark my words."

And with that, the spirit rolled out of the room with a huff. The edges of its mist vibrated with anger.

The two brothers sat in silence for a little while. Lust leaned back in his chair, gently tugging on his bottom lip as he thought about what Affection had to say. Would Selene leave? No. She enjoyed being here far too much for that. And last night had certainly solidified that she would want to stay. Who would ever pull themselves away from such incredible sex? And it would be incredible sex. Maybe tonight, if she was a little less shy.

Pulling himself out of his thoughts, he saw Greed staring at the ceiling. His jaw ticked, so he could only guess whatever his brother was thinking wasn't all that pleasant either.

"What do you think?" Lust asked.

"I think this is still dangerous. My gut says there's something about to happen that we cannot change, but I can't figure out why." He looked down, catching Lust's gaze and holding it. "I want to tell you to be careful. Danger's afoot. But I also want to tell you to run headlong into this because it feels right for you. It's a strange feeling."

His brother's feelings were usually right. Greed didn't know how to see the future, but he had some sixth sense to him that Lust had always trusted.

"Two very different kinds of advice," he murmured.

"Indeed." Greed slapped a hand to his thigh. "And yet, I think right now you should go find her."

"Find her?"

"If Affection is right, then she's already planning to make her great escape. Change her mind, Lust. Whether she's dangerous or the woman that will alter everything, we need to keep her around." Those golden eyes flashed with humor. "For some reason, I don't think you'll allow me to be the one forcing her to stay."

The words made him imagine Greed's arms around Selene. She'd hate it, but in his mind's eyes he saw her lips curve into a polite smile. He saw that long neck tilt to the side as Greed pressed his damned mouth against her neck and he refused to indulge his imagination any further.

Lunging to his feet, Lust stalked out of the room without another word.

Instead, he went to find her.

First, he searched their bedroom. She might still be getting ready, but he couldn't find her there. Not even the faint hint of her scent remained. Curious now, he walked through the halls where he usually found her frequenting. But again, Selene was nowhere to be found.

He even asked a few servants if they'd seen her, but they only gave him blank expressions and asked who Selene was.

Right, because he hadn't been parading her about the castle as someone that was important to him. Sure, there had been the rumors of a queen. But even those were getting a little less frequent the longer they didn't see her. Only the servants who worked at the feasts knew what she even looked like.

Damn it, so where was she?

A feeling in his belly whispered that perhaps she'd gone out to the gardens. He tried to still himself, wondering what that feeling even was. Lust had never been one for premonitions like Greed. He'd never even had much of a power other than electrifying people with their deepest desires.

As he stilled in the hallway, closing his eyes and focusing on that feeling, he realized there was a warmth in his chest that was new. A warmth that at first seemed like the cold bite of winter but inside, the warmth of a cottage with a hearty fire, good food, and a warm bed filled with long limbs and dark hair.

It was her, he realized. A connection between the two of them that had bubbled up since last night. He'd tasted her lust, yes, but it had also fueled him in a way no other had before. This new power came entirely from feasting upon what only she could give him.

She was in the gardens, he knew without question. And she wasn't alone.

Lust took his time now, wandering through the halls to the second level, where he could peer down into the flower beds. And there she was. Her dark gown trailed behind her like the shroud of a woman in mourning. She wore the dress that covered her up the most today, the dress he hated more than any other. The dark embroidery glistened in the sunlight as she meandered through the rows. And beside her? A little glowing spirit who had already shouted at him today.

Affection. He should have guessed it would meddle.

Lust leaned on the railing and stared down at the two of them. As he watched, a strange softness bloomed in his chest.

Where he had been in such a rush to go to her, to prove that he wanted her to stay, now he just wanted to look at her. So he did.

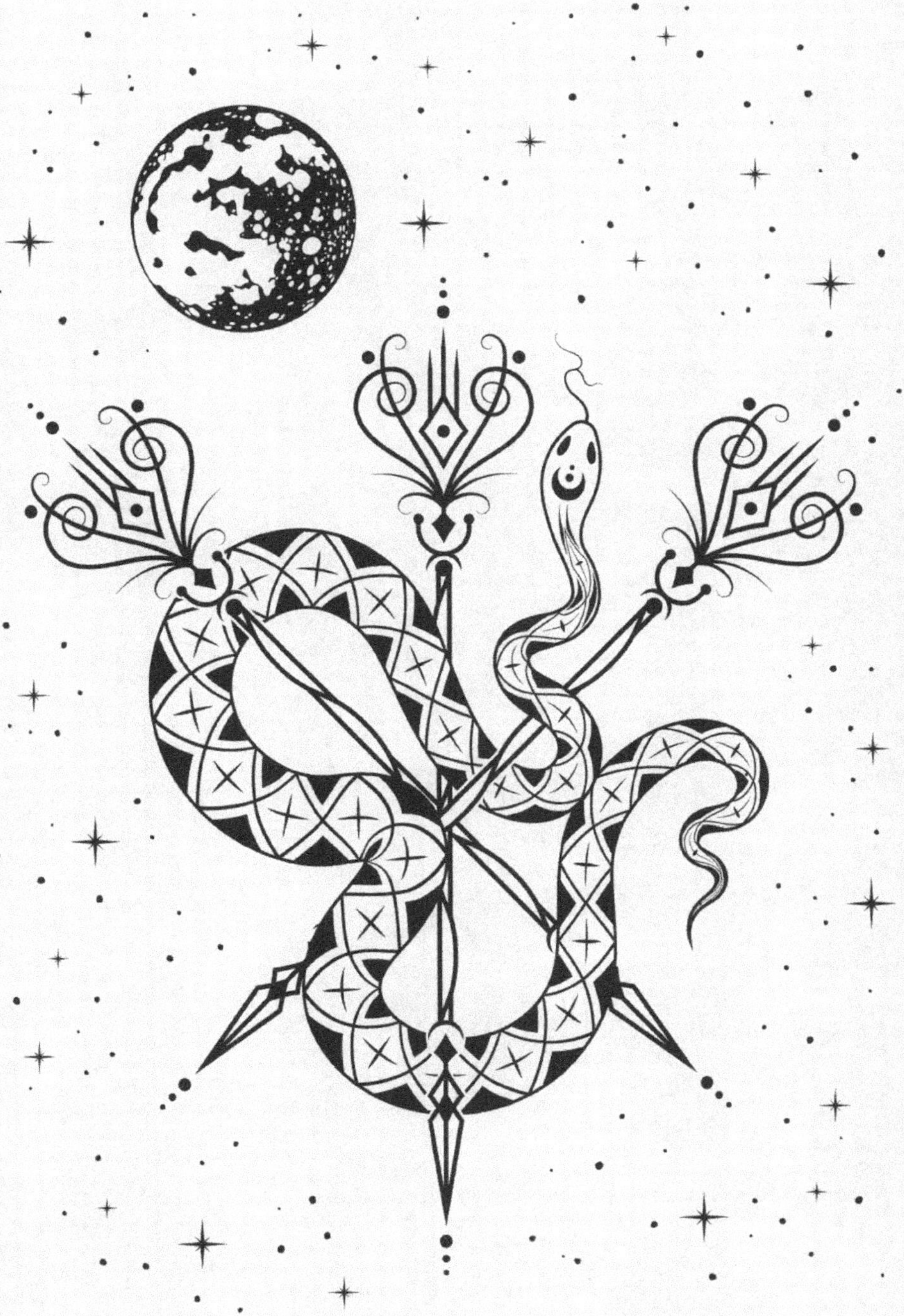

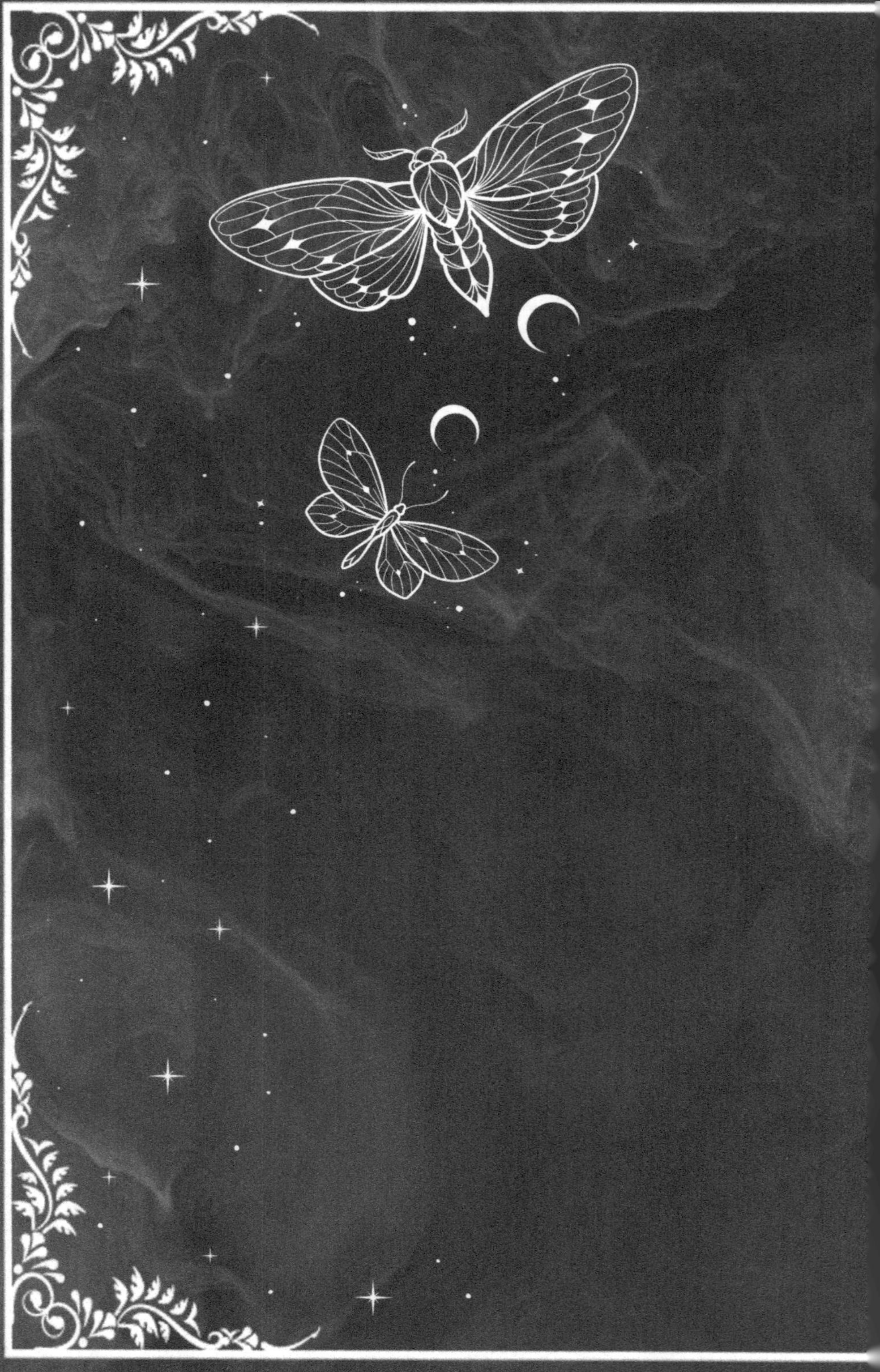

Chapter 28

Selene hated how twisted her heart was now. She wanted to let go and allow him to... what? To enjoy her body the way she wished him to? That was silly. She didn't have it in her to give in to a man she had assumed was a demon her entire life.

And there was the added layer of her family to add to this mix. They thought him demonic as well, as they had sent her here to betray him.

Surely she couldn't ignore all that? Years and years of living with them, owing them her life, knowing that her sisters and her mother were the only people there for her. Even the townsfolk wanted nothing to do with sorceresses. That was why they left their children on the front steps year after year.

Just like Minerva said. Sorceresses were the forgotten, the

unwanted, and the powerful. Their parents had good reason to leave them on the steps of the Tower. They were too dangerous to be with the others, no matter how small their magic was. And the people would never accept them for who they were.

If Selene had stayed with her parents, she likely wouldn't even be alive.

She paused by a dahlia and traced her finger over the many petals. She'd lived her entire life knowing that her own parents feared her. That the minor act of conjuring light was enough for them to think she was too dangerous to raise on their own.

That guilt had walked beside her for her entire life. And Minerva had never let her forget it. Her sisters hadn't either. They all lived with the knowledge that they were unwanted, impossible to love, and that all they had was each other.

But what if all that was wrong? Lust had made it seem like he wanted her last night. He'd touched her like a man who desired a woman, and the look in his eyes had been more than just physical desire.

He'd made her feel wanted, and that was the cruelest part of all this. What if he really did want her? What if he wanted to know more about her, and to have her trust him because he was interested in her and no one else?

She'd give him anything if that was true. Even her soul.

The thought terrified her. She didn't know how to act around someone who could take so much from her with only a simple request. If she wasn't careful, she'd end up like all the others. Nothing more than a slave at his feet, begging for attention that he couldn't deign to give her.

"You're awfully quiet," Affection's voice interrupted her thoughts.

Selene glanced up with a bright smile. "I haven't visited the gardens yet. There aren't any in the Tower. We get our food from the villages, so I never got to see plants like this unless we were traveling."

"And I take it you don't travel very often."

The little spirit was larger yet again, but this time, she didn't mention it. Instead, she crouched down and met its gaze eye to eye. "No, we did not travel very often."

"Lust would travel with you if you'd like. He enjoys going throughout the kingdom to all the villages."

A small spark of jealousy churned in her belly. Oh, she knew how much he enjoyed going out into the kingdom. He'd become a legend year after year for indulging himself in every pretty woman or man that the town threw at him. In fact, she was quite certain that he'd done exactly that even after they met.

Selene had no right to be jealous. He was a god to many of the people who lived here, and their king. If he wanted to go out and find whatever pleasure he wanted in the bodies of countless women, then there was nothing she could say to stop him. Nor should she. It wasn't her place.

A nasty voice whispered in her mind, "You aren't his queen."

Because she wasn't. He'd never intended to make her so and honestly, she'd never thought he would either. Lust had a kingdom all of his own, and no reason to add a queen to that. Not in the slightest.

Sighing, she trailed her fingers through her hair and tried to not pull the locks out by the root. She turned and started down the nearest garden row. Perhaps the repetitive motion of her feet would help the strange emotions that threatened to swell over her head. Or maybe the feeling of the plants trailing along her sides would distract her. Unfortunately, it was rather hard to find that distraction when a certain spirit didn't want to let it go.

"Why did that make you sad?"

"I thought you were affection only? Shouldn't you be more attuned to that emotion rather than sadness?"

"I still know what you're feeling," the spirit grumbled. "Traveling is something you love. You have a lot of fond memories about travel and how many people you'd met during those adventures. So why does the thought of going with Lust make you sad?"

She had no intention of answering that question. She opened her mouth to say just that before they were both interrupted by a voice overhead. "Yes, Selene. Why does the thought of traveling with me turn your stomach?"

She looked up and found Lust leaning much too far over a railing above her head. The light glittered through his hair and turned his lovely features into melted gold. Even his horns were sparkling this morning and she didn't remember him putting glitter on them.

Sighing, she waved a hand in the air. "What are you doing up there?"

"Spying."

"Why?"

He lifted a shoulder. "I thought you might pour out your heart to your dear friend Affection and I might overhear how you feel about me."

"Obviously, my feelings are complicated."

He flashed her a bright grin. "I'll take complicated."

And just like that, he vaulted over the railing. She pressed her hands to her mouth, quite certain she'd soon hear the terrible cracking of his legs as he struck the ground hard. But instead, he merely stood up as though he hadn't just fallen from two stories high.

"What—" she whispered, incapable of saying more.

The proud grin on his face made him look even cockier than normal. "Didn't know I could do that, did you?"

"No."

"So you believe I'm a demon, but you aren't willing to believe that I can jump off a tiny overhang like that?" He arched a brow as he prowled toward her. "You really don't think much of me, Selene."

"I don't think of you much at all—" Her words scattered as he wrapped his arm around her waist and tugged her against his chest.

She let out a little oof, her palms coming to his chest to plant against hard muscles and... oh. She remembered how these flexed against her last night. How sturdy he'd felt when she tried to hold on to him so she didn't feel like she was flying off into the sunset without him.

He'd been a rock then and was now. Even though he'd yanked her around like some kind of behemoth.

"What are you doing?" she whispered, staring up at him through her lashes.

"I was reminded that it's important to share how important you are to me, and that I'm not just interested in you for sex." That handsome face nodded at Affection. "You might want to disappear now."

"I think I'll stay."

He bared his teeth in a snarl at the little spirit, who let out a tiny eep and then disappeared.

"Why did you scare Affection away?" But she had a feeling she already knew.

"Because I want this moment to be private." His hand slid down her back and squeezed a handful of her ass. Or tried to, at least. Her dress got in the way and he mostly grabbed fabric. "And because once you are certain that I'm interested in you for you, I plan to spread you out on these flowers and tunnel my way under this ugly dress."

"It's not an ugly dress."

"We can disagree on some things." He tilted his head to the side and looked at her with no small amount of disdain. "Not on this, though."

She sighed, rolling her eyes up to the clouds in the sky. If this was his way of reassuring her, then she had no idea what the opposite would look like. "Lust, I don't want you listening in on conversations between myself and Affection. Everything is fine. And whatever advice a spirit gave you regarding us, I'm uncertain you should waste your time listening to them. Affection is not mortal. You are not mortal, and I'm aware that means you both will look at the world through a different lens."

Lust tunneled his hand through her hair and forced her to look back at him. "Why did you hesitate after Affection mentioned traveling with me?"

She didn't want to tell him. Admitting that she was jealous of his past felt... wrong. She had no right to be jealous, even if he had another woman with him now. He was Lust. He could do whatever and whoever he wanted and she would have to endure.

The only control she had in this situation was whether or not she gave him the ability to affect her happiness with his philandering. And Selene decided right then and there that she would never give him that.

Except he was so gentle as he tilted her head up to look at him. Softly brushing his fingertips over her lips, up her nose, and smoothing the furrow between her brow. "I don't need to read minds to know I don't like what you're thinking, little moon."

"There's no good reason for my reaction to what Affection said. I apologize for upsetting your spirit." She looked away from him again. "It's not a mistake I will make again."

"Ah, the ice queen is back, I see." Lust pinched her chin between his fingers and forced her to stay still as he pressed his lips to her forehead. "Do you want to know what I think?"

"No."

He kissed her temples, one after the other. "I think you're afraid of what this is between us." His lips moved over her eyes, forcing her to shut them as he ghosted feather light touches over each one. "And I think you're jealous about the idea of traveling with me. Although I cannot guess why. I'm a very good travel partner, quiet, humble, easy to get along with. So I suppose what I would rather know is why you think traveling with me would be such a chore."

Selene snorted, but then gasped in a breath as his lips ghosted over the tip of her nose, then pressed to each corner of her mouth. "I... I know what traveling with you entails. I'm not interested, Lust."

"What? Long boring evenings in the carriage while we travel from place to place? Having to eat the terrible food in taverns? I believe you've already done that." He pressed the softest, sweetest kiss to her mouth. Not indulging himself in anything other than a single press of their lips. "Or is it something more than that?"

If she wasn't careful, she'd get drunk on him. She wanted more of these kisses. More quiet moments in the sun with him as his hands came up to frame her face.

But her mind wasn't so certain. The fear of what life would be like with him ran away with her tongue. "I know that you go to those villages only for the sacrifices they lay out before you. You indulge in their pleasures just as much as they use you for an excuse to behave however they wish. I do not want to be there while you are... are..."

He pulled back to grin down at her, his thumbs stroking over her cheekbones. "My, my, sorceress. It sounds as though you might be jealous."

"I'm not... I'm not jealous." But she was. Oh, she really was. Just the idea of those women touching him, stroking their hands up the chest she was touching... It drove her mad. She was jealous, yes, but she also knew they might be more skilled than her. Less complicated. It would be easier for him to be with them, and the tantalizing nature of that ease was surely something that would summon him.

But he wasn't leaving now. In fact, he was watching her with a rather odd expression on his face. A softening of those sharp features that were both handsome but also something far more than she'd expected.

He ghosted his thumbs over her cheekbones again. "Little moon, let me tell you something very important and I need to know you are listening to me right now. Do we have a deal?"

She nodded.

"When we first met, you said you were something new. You claimed you were capable of changing my world and standing out among all the rest. Those words called to me. They pulled my soul out of that dark place I've been resting in for so long and I know without a doubt that you were right. I fought against it. I didn't want you to be new or different or surprising. But I'd be lying if I didn't admit that you are all those things and more." He kissed her again, his hands running down the length of her throat and then down her back. Lust pressed her against him, shoulder to thigh. "I am so very pleased you are here, Selene. It feels so good to be surprised again."

Oh, well. That was rather nice. She let her cheek rest against his chest, feeling the rise and fall of his breath even as he smoothed his hands down her back. And this was... nice.

"That doesn't mean I want to travel with you," she grumbled. "I know what they're all expecting from you."

"Trust, remember?" he chuckled. "I have no interest in any other woman than you, Selene. You are more than enough questions for one man to answer."

She wasn't questions. She was a woman with needs and desires and thoughts of her own. He had no right to put her in any other category. But... She supposed it was nice to know that he wasn't looking at anyone else. That he was focused entirely on her and whatever was happening between the two of them.

And though he hadn't said it in so many words, she had a feeling he was as affected by all this as she was.

"I didn't know Lust cared about what anyone else feels," she whispered.

"Ah, of course I do. I want everyone to enjoy every moment. Pleasure is pleasure, whether inside another or not." He laughed, his chest bouncing with the sound. "But I will admit, I have not laughed so much in a very long time."

"Laughter is rather frowned upon in the bedroom, I suppose."

He drew back enough to see her face before he solemnly added, "I believe if it was your laughter, I would endure."

Shaking her head, she rolled her eyes up to the sky. Perhaps an afternoon with him wouldn't be so bad, even if he was a fool.

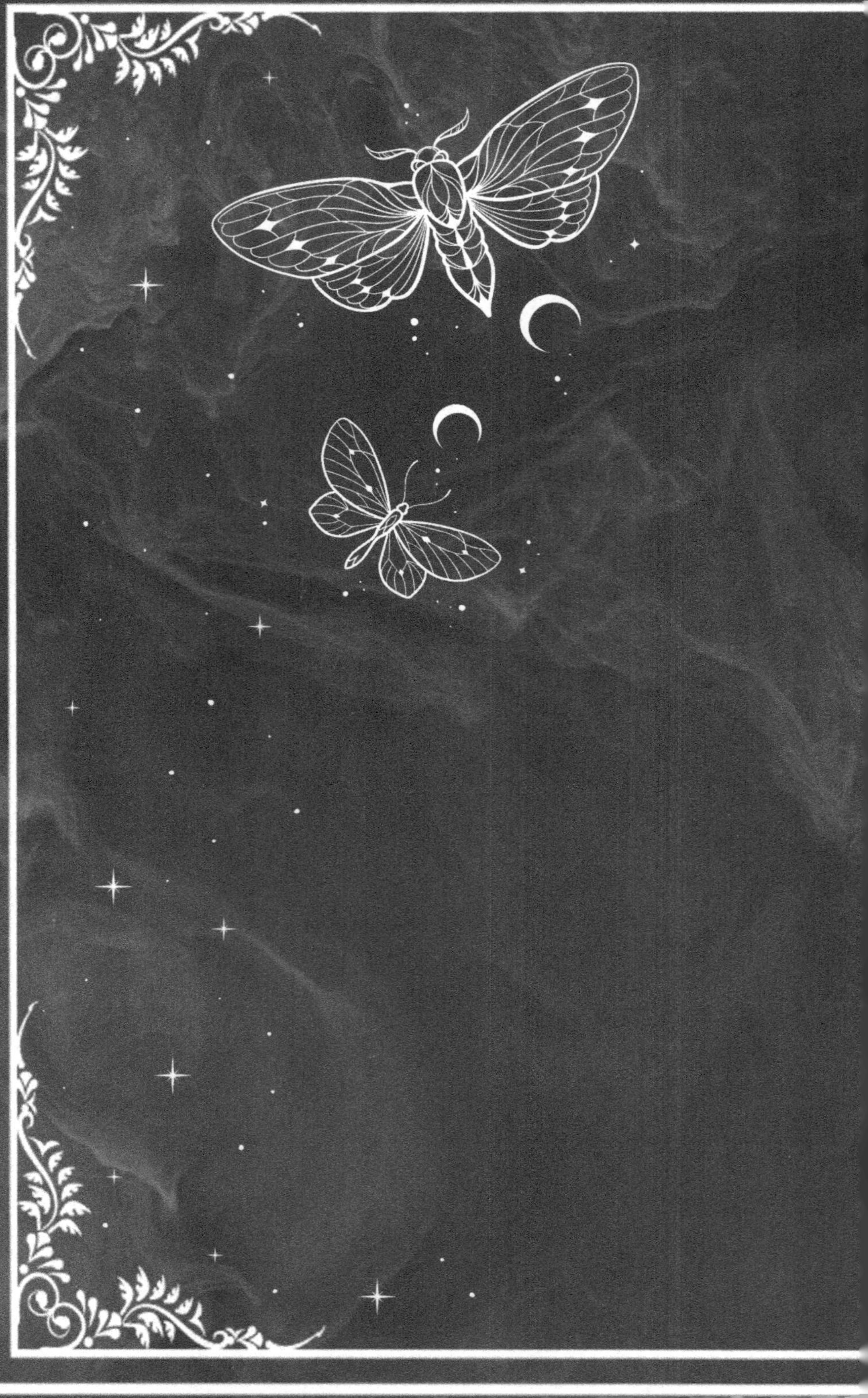

Chapter 29

He'd long since decided she would come with him today. He needed her to be at court and for others to see her. Why? He couldn't quite put his finger on it.

Lust knew that it had bothered him when half the servants hadn't realized who he was talking about when he asked where she was. They all knew that he had his own little pet in his room. Some of them even talked about how he'd been so fascinated with this new pet that he'd not even left the room.

And then, when he'd had his butler ask around, he discovered there were others spreading darker rumors. Rumors about how horrible she was. How he hid her because she was ugly, and that he wouldn't touch her even though the sorceresses wanted him to.

The moment he found out who had spread that particular nasty rumor, he would make sure they spent a few nights in the dungeon.

A dungeon he did not have. Considering they'd already turned it into a dark, damp place where many of his followers enjoyed the torture. But he would figure out that punishment once it came to it.

For now, he wanted her to come with him. To present herself before all his people as the queen they needed. And he refused for that first outing to be anywhere in the castle.

The castle inhabitants were aware of her. The nobles had seen her a few times now, and that impression was a sour one that wouldn't be easy to fix. He didn't want to throw her to the wolves. They'd tear her apart for judging their chosen antics.

Not that he could blame them. She'd behaved poorly when she walked in on their usual affairs of state, but that would come in time. Eventually, she would realize that his life was led very differently than regular people in his kingdom. She'd learn how to love his ways, he was certain of it.

Waltzing into their room, he had a brand new cloak over each arm to prepare them both for travel. "I hope you're comfortable riding. I don't want to bring the carriage with us today. It's far too nice out to be stuck inside those stuffy walls."

Really, he just wanted to watch her ride a horse. Those strong thighs would grip down on the saddle, and made him want to bite his knuckles just at the mere thought. Watching her ride would be a torment that he was so incredibly ready for.

Except, when he laid the cloaks out on the bed, he turned to see her ready for their journey and was greeted by a vision in black.

Black. Was she allergic to color?

The woman was never in anything but dark and dreary fabric. He refused to bring her around his people while they wondered if she was mourning the loss of someone important. She wasn't. He was the most important person in her life and he was very much still here.

Tsking, he looked her up and down with obvious disdain. "Now, what are you wearing? I don't think I've ever seen this particular monstrosity."

Selene frowned at him, then joined him staring at her gown. It was perhaps a little less stuffy than the others. Though this dress still had a neckline that almost reached her chin, it at least parted in the middle and reached her collarbone, exposing lovely pale flesh. The sleeves were a little thinner than the others, and he watched the fabric stretch as she moved to reveal a hint of skin underneath. But the entire dress was still black as night, without a single embroidered decoration.

"This is my best gown," she said, staring back at him with anger in those dark eyes. "You said we were going to be walking through the town around the castle. You said to dress like a queen."

"You're dressed like you're going to a funeral."

"I'm dressed formally!"

He stared up at the ceiling as though there was something up there that could help him. "I thought I'd made it very clear by now that the Tower's idea of dressing is drab, sad, and covers far too much of your body."

"It's appropriate to cover your body when you are going to a political event." She threw her hands up at her sides. "Do you want me to parade around in front of your people completely naked? How serious would they take me?"

Lust tilted his head to the side. "Well, very. I've seen you naked now and I can attest that you are quite beautiful and they would be lucky to see you without a stitch of clothing."

"And that doesn't make you jealous?"

"Why should it?" A burn bloomed in his chest, eating its way up his throat and nearly pouring out of the feral grin that spread across his face. "They all know not to touch what is mine. If even one of them laid a hand on that lovely, lily white skin, I would pull their skeleton out of their body while they were still alive."

A small smile sparked on her face, but she shook her head and pretended to be disappointed with him. "That's not possible to do. You'll need to be much more creative in your threats if you want to actually scare them."

"Oh?" He stalked over to her, hands flexing at his sides. He didn't want to startle her, but he also wanted his hands on her. "And what do you know of what is possible and what is not?"

"I'd like to think I know a lot about that."

"You didn't know I could jump down a mere two stories. It wasn't that far, and yet I remember you pressing your hands to your mouth in shock."

"Anyone would have done that."

"No one questions me but you." He couldn't stop himself. Lust palmed each side of her hips and drew her against him. "I wonder why that is."

"Oh, probably because no one would dare argue with you. They think all the things I say. I am but the fool who gives the thoughts flight." Selene rolled her eyes, but then laid her hands flat on his chest.

He marked all the first moments in their relationship. And this one? She touched him willingly. Not while in the throes of passion, but just to touch him. He'd never felt more powerful or more like a god than he did in this moment with her tiny fingers pressed against him.

"What would you prefer me to wear?" she asked. "I imagine naked is not your first choice, either."

It was. He'd love to see her ride through town in nothing but her skin, with that long hair parted over her chest and pooling in her lap. He wanted to ride behind her. He'd thread his arm around her tiny waist, pull her against his hard cock and let the rocking of their ride do most of the work.

Of course, they would not do that. It would be rude to the poor horse.

Sighing, he released her to disappear inside his sizable closet. "Did a servant not help you?"

"She said I could wear whatever I wanted, so I chose what I wanted."

There were plenty of gowns in here that were far more suitable for a queen. And while she would not be announced as that yet, he wanted people to see her as his... consort.

He settled on the term at the same time he found the perfect dress.

"Your mother wanted you to be my queen," he said while walking out. A crimson gown draped over his forearm. "I do not believe that you have earned that title yet, nor do I trust you to choose me over your family."

Her mouth dropped open, cheeks reddening with an argument he could already hear.

Lust held up his hand for silence. "You have come a long way from that little puppet that I met all that time ago, Selene. But that does not mean I trust you with an entire kingdom. I will call you my consort to anyone who asks, and you will do the same. Do you understand me?"

Her jaw snapped shut, and she gave him a firm little nod.

Ah, but he'd angered her. He couldn't imagine why. Being a consort was a true title in this kingdom, and one that many women had fought each other for. He couldn't count how many of his bedmates had shown up with missing handfuls of their hair while a bruise formed on their cheeks. But they had won their little battle, and he always took the winner to bed.

Now, he couldn't imagine Selene fighting for him. Ever, really. If she did, then she would win. If she didn't and wore the mark of another woman, he was uncertain what he would do. Some ugly feeling bubbled up in his chest and he was ashamed to admit he would protect her, no matter the cost.

He needed to distract himself from these thoughts. They were unlike him and thoroughly terrible for him to even consider.

Lust laid the dress out on the bed and turned toward her. "If you would be so kind."

She arched a brow. "And do what?"

He twirled a finger in the air, indicating she should turn around.

"I know if I let you undress me, we will be late."

"I told you I was practicing restraint," he replied with a chuckle. "Trust me, little moon. I'm all too happy to see you undressed, but I'm also quite excited to see my people. It's been a long time since I've left the castle."

"But you're always wandering about." Confusion wrinkled between her brows. "I haven't kept you in the castle all that long. Have I? I'll admit, all the days have blurred together."

If she would not turn, then he would have to move around her. Lust stared down at the back of her dress and frowned down at the hundred buttons all down her spine. "Ah, Selene. They've locked you in a prison."

"Every gown should have finer details that prove its value."

"Spoken like Minerva's daughter." He pressed a kiss to her shoulder before he attacked the buttons with as much gusto as he could. It took a while for him to unbutton them all, and even then there were more layers underneath.

There was another dress underneath this outer layer. At least six crinkly skirts that made his hands itch after he touched them, and then there was another pale layer of underclothes that he wouldn't recognize if someone held a sword to his throat. Each layer was more frustrating than the last.

"If you wanted to bundle yourself back up in sheets, why did you not just do that?" he grumbled as he yanked the last ribbon free from her underclothes.

"I am dressed the way I was raised to dress," she replied with a laugh. "Are you quite finished yet? I think we're actually going to be late."

"Because you insist on dressing like an onion!"

"An onion?" She whirled on him, holding the last layer to her chest before it fell to the ground. "Are you telling me I smell?"

He leaned in close and inhaled deeply. Peppermint. She always smelled like peppermint. "No, you smell fine. But the amount of layers on your body is absolutely disgusting. Now let me dress you."

They were going to be late if he wasn't careful. So Lust did not stare at the luscious swells of her breasts or the way she banded an arm around them while a lovely blush dusted them pink. He absolutely did not let his eyes linger on the curves of her hips or the rounded bottom that made him want to bite it.

Or perhaps he did. At least a little.

Lust efficiently set her into the red gown that wasn't so revealing that she'd be uncomfortable, but also made sure that she wouldn't stand out as someone other than who they expected. The red fabric was painted like a leaf, wrapping once around her throat before it created arching shoulders that then twisted around her torso, weaving back and forth to her hips where it fell like a wave to her feet. The fabric was very sheer, nearly see through, but thick enough in all the places that would make her blush. No one could see the outline of her nipples or the shadows between her legs, but they certainly would see the long lines of her legs and that tempting valley between the top of her bottom and her spine.

"This is indecent," she said when he finished, staring at herself in the mirror.

"You look lovely." And if his voice was a little deeper than before, he tried to hide it with a press of his lips against her bare shoulder. "Now sit down. We can't have you going out with your hair down like this."

"I thought you liked my hair down."

"I do." He wanted to see how far she'd let him go, so he wrapped the length of it around his fist, once, twice, three times. Then, gently pulling, he forced her head back to look at him. "But you hide behind it when it's down, and I want them to see your pretty face."

The breath caught in her throat. She stared up at him with bright eyes, and then he noticed the taste of whiskey and peppermint on his tongue.

So she liked it when he used her hair like reins. How interesting.

His cock grew painfully hard, and it took every ounce of his control not to say fuck everyone who waited for them. He could bring her back to that bed and lay her out like the offering she was.

But he couldn't do that, so he let her hair go, and she meandered over to the vanity where she sat down. "You can call for the servants, but it takes a while for them to come up."

"For what?" He leaned around her and picked up the brush. "We have no need of them."

"I thought you wanted my hair to be done?"

"I do." And he wanted that honor himself.

Lust let her fall silent and watch his reflection as he ran the brush through her hair. He'd watched her brush these dark locks so many times, and now he got to do it himself. The soft waves felt like silk in between his fingers and he had to bite his lip so he didn't groan at the feeling. He wanted these spread across his chest. He wanted to feel the weight of her draped over him after he'd thoroughly exhausted her.

There was no time. He had responsibilities, and those weren't to bury his face between her thighs. As entertaining a job as that might be.

Weaving the first strands away from her head, he started in on the intricate braids he had envisioned. "My people will be glad to see you. And I will be glad that everyone knows you are mine."

"I never took you as someone who thought running this kingdom was worthwhile or serious."

"I'm sure that's what Minerva would like everyone to think." He started on the other side, leaving thinner braids loose so he could use them later to tie it all together. "There is time for fun and there is time for work. There's a reason this kingdom runs better than any of the others. And a reason why my people are happier."

She let out a low hum that ran straight down his spine. Damned women knew what she was doing and yet she still moaned like that. "My mother would have everyone think otherwise. I grew up hearing that this kingdom was worse off than all the others. Spinning wildly into the cosmos with a lack of leadership."

"If that were the truth, don't you think the monstrous beings who live in the darkness below us would have swallowed up this island already?" He tugged hard on one of her braids before returning to his work.

"Are they real?"

"Of course they're real. Everything terrifying is." One of her braids had loosened a bit, but he decided to use it. The looser it was, the better he would weave them all together at the back of her head. He'd leave the bottom half of her hair loose, he thought. He just wanted the strands away from her face, so she couldn't hide like she usually did.

"Lust?" she asked a few moments later, and he realized he'd been lost in his work.

"What is it, little moon?"

"Why do you think you run this kingdom better than the others?"

He met her gaze in the mirror and flashed her a cocky grin. "Because I'm the prettiest brother, and people love me the most."

She tilted her head back and burst into laughter. The sound pealed through the room like the ringing of bells, and something settled in his chest that he'd never felt before. A quiet sensation of such utter happiness and bliss, but it was not startling or overwhelming. It was merely quiet and calm.

Lust rubbed at the feeling in his chest. He couldn't quite get rid of it, no matter how hard he tried.

When she finished laughing, her grin still turned her face somehow more beautiful than before. "What is it? What is that look?"

"I've never heard you laugh like that before," he said, returning his attention to her braids. He needed something to distract him. Something that would keep his hands busy so he didn't grab onto her like she was the only rock in the middle of a storm at sea.

"Why should that matter?" she asked, her voice quiet.

"It made you beautiful," he replied. "More than ever before."

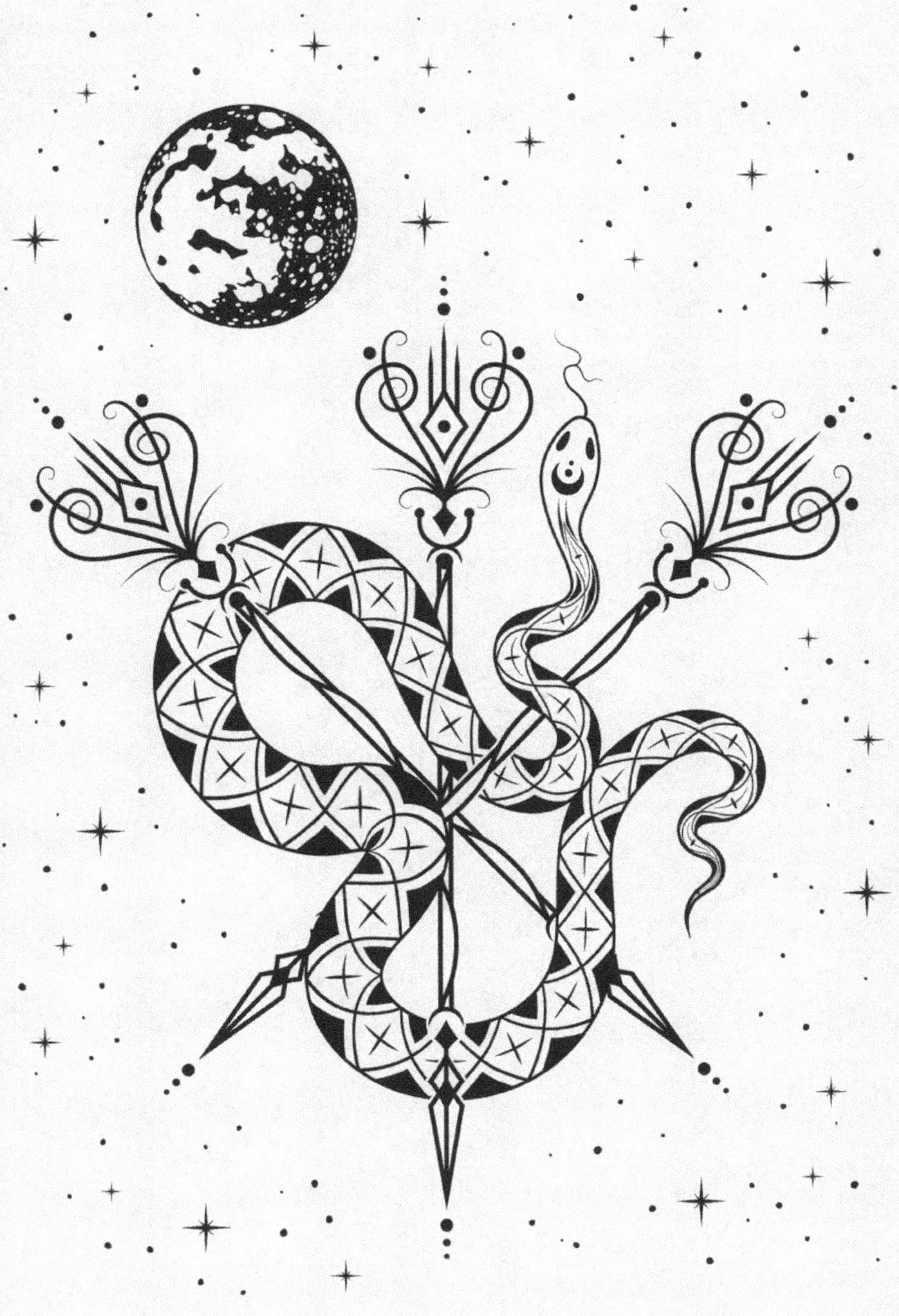

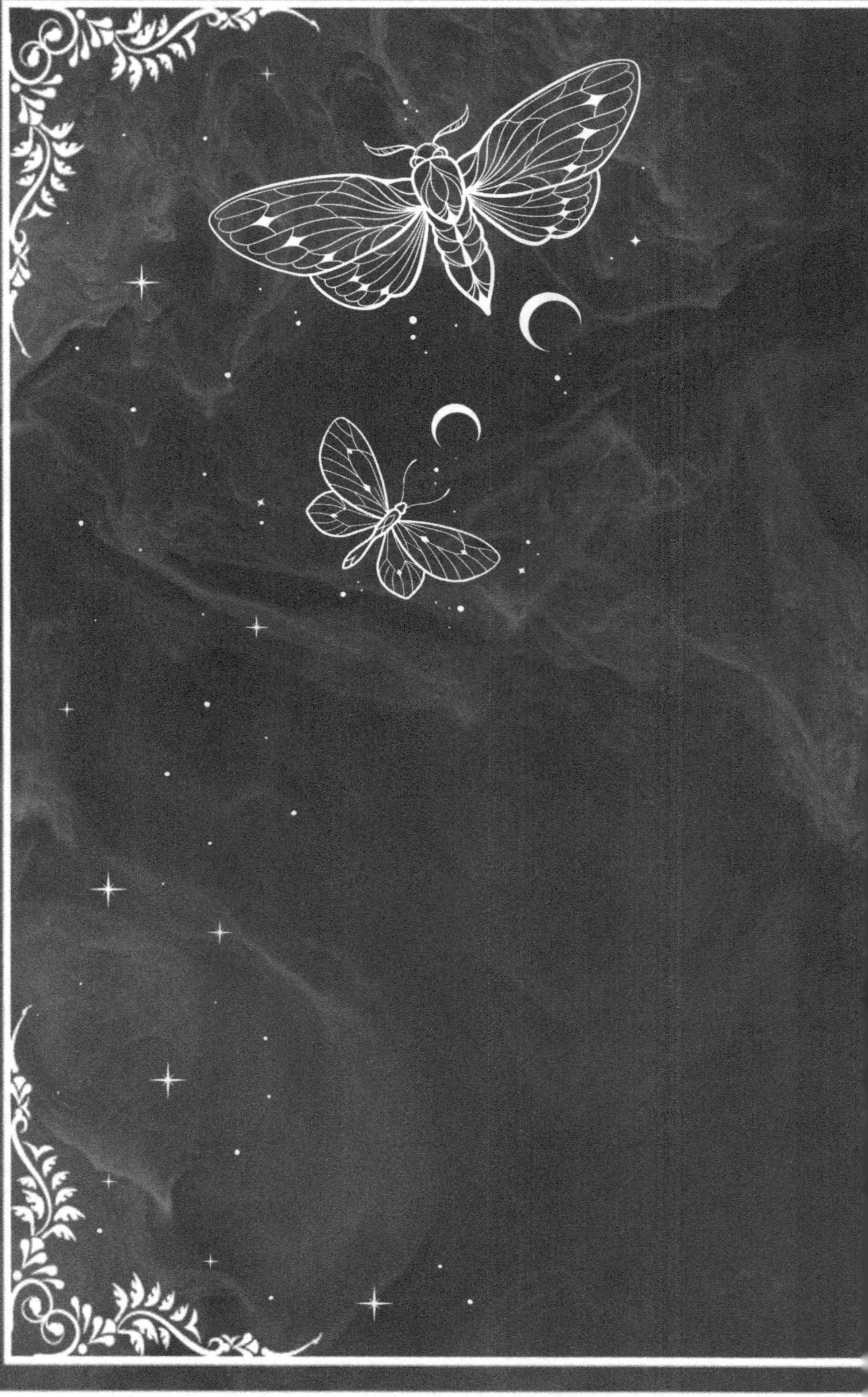

Chapter 30

Though she had thought this would be uncomfortable, Selene quickly realized two things.

First, his people weren't monsters. They didn't want to make her uncomfortable, they just didn't know what to do with her. When she walked around in her thick, dark gowns, they thought something was wrong with her. How did she know this? A few of them asked if she was feeling better, and when she told them she'd been fine since she got here, Lust gave her a look of utter satisfaction. Clearly, he had known they were worried about her.

Second, Lust looked all too good on top of a horse. His thighs gripped it with practiced ease. He took his time making sure that everything was situated on his mount before he swung up with all the grace of a dancer.

Selene hadn't lied when she said she'd ridden before. Minerva loved horses, and there were quite a few afternoons where she'd joined her mother on rides around the Tower.

But she'd always had a riding dress on. Particularly the one that he'd taken off of her. Now, she knew that if she wanted to get on this horse, she would leave her thighs bare. Everyone would be able to see quite literally all of her leg, and she didn't know how to be comfortable with that.

Gritting her teeth, she looked at the bay roan horse in front of her, eyeing the lovely dark legs and the pretty dark mane that someone had braided. It was a beautiful beast who likely rode like a dream. But she didn't want everyone to see her bare like that.

"Lust," she muttered, so the servants wouldn't overhear her complaint. "How am I supposed to ride this horse?"

"Like you always do, I imagine."

"This dress—"

He interrupted her before she could say anything. He kicked his horse closer, coming at her in a rush that should have spooked her mount, but instead the beast remained docile and quiet. Lust leaned down and captured her chin in his hand. "There is not a single person who would deny how beautiful you are, little moon. Be proud of that beauty. I want them to see you exist, but I also want to show you off. You are mine. And I want them to know it."

His touch seared her chin. Her face flamed bright red, angry that he'd suggest such a thing but also because... Well. She didn't know what he wanted.

One moment he was forcing her to strip in front of him, even though she did not want to do that. And the next, he was telling her how beautiful she was and that he wanted his entire kingdom to know it.

How was a woman supposed to survive this kind of attention?

Fanning her face, she glared at him while she decided it wasn't worth the argument. If he wanted to make her show off her legs to everyone, then she would force herself to be all right with it.

Swinging up onto the back of her mount, she settled into the saddle with a grimace. Leather didn't feel as good between her legs as she had hoped.

"Fine," she muttered. "I will endure."

"You'll do more than that." His eyes raked over her body before he bit his lower lip. "You look good on that horse, Selene. It's too bad we're busy."

"Or what?"

The command in her voice must have done something to him. His hands creaked as he gripped his reins and he let out a long breath that sounded like a tortured laugh. "Oh, I won't let you in on my thoughts that easily."

She could see his thoughts. The way his entire body clenched at her question let her know just how much power she had over him. He didn't want her to know that she could make him think of sex with just a throaty tone in her voice, because it let her know how much she controlled him.

And yet... Maybe this could work to her advantage.

Selene gave her horse its head since the creature wanted to follow the other. It figured that he'd given her the most docile horse in his stable, probably because he didn't want to see how far she could get if he let her run.

They didn't have far to go, at least. The town surrounding the castle was unlike any other she'd seen before, and she'd only seen glimpses of it when she arrived here. Clean streets, gleaming cobblestones, ridiculously full shops that were brimming with vegetables, art, fabric, and more. All of those had been a snippet of what she had seen.

But now? She was given so much more to look at from the back of this horse. And maybe that was his intent the entire time.

Selene's eyes ate up the beauty that surrounded them. Every building was built out of white marble with gold accents. There were balconies dotted here and there, with people who leaned out to smile down at Lust and call out his name. Everyone wore good clothing. Nothing threadbare or moth-eaten.

She wished she could say her mother's ramblings about him at least were true near the Tower. That there were towns hidden from the public eye where poverty plagued the people. And sure, there were some towns who weren't nearly as wealthy as this. But none of them were abused, hungry, or angry. Not that she'd seen, and she was coming to realize that maybe there wasn't a town like that in this kingdom.

A group of children ran out in front of their horses, not so close as to be worrisome, but enough that Selene stopped her horse.

Lust did the same, watching them with amusement as they jostled each other. Finally, one of the tallest boys was shoved forward, and he squared his shoulders. The boy stared up at Lust with no fear in his eyes, only confidence.

"My lord," he said, then swallowed hard. "We've got a question for you."

Lust leaned an elbow on the pommel of his saddle, looking down at the boys as though he were considering their request very thoroughly. "Proceed."

The tall boy then pointed at her. "We want to know who that is."

Selene blushed. It was a ridiculous reaction to daring little boys. It wasn't as if they were nobles who had asked or if it even mattered for children to know that she existed. But she had been quite happy with her position in the shadows. If Lust had let her, she would have stayed in those shadows for good.

He looked her over, his eyes lingering on the smooth planes of her legs and the way her dress nearly hung off her shoulders. Then he responded, "My new consort. Perhaps you can help us in letting everyone know that she's here."

"A consort?" The boy's face scrunched up. "What's that mean?"

"The closest thing you'll ever get to a queen."

The boys let out a little whoop and raced off in different directions. Selene couldn't tear her eyes away from Lust, though. He stared at her with a hungry look, as though saying those words had reminded him how much he wanted her. How terribly it burned inside him that he couldn't have her right now.

And an answering bloom unfurled in her own chest. She wanted him.

She knew this wasn't the right place for it. Nor should she even be thinking about how he'd sank to his knees in front of her and worshiped her body as if she meant something to him. It shouldn't matter that his tongue was talented when there were so many eyes on her, but once she thought about the memory, it was not so easy to dash aside.

He let out a little groan and shook his head. "Don't you start now."

"I'm not doing anything."

"You are." He pointed at her with a wry grin. "You're the one who wanted to come to town. Now behave."

Her jaw dropped open as he urged his horse forward. She was the one who had wanted to come? He'd quite literally dragged her to the horse while she told him maybe there was a better time for them to meet everyone. How was he blaming this on her?

Just to get back at him, she let her thoughts run wild.

As they meandered through the town, speaking to anyone who reached for Lust's leg, she thought about all the countless things that drove her wild. She let her mind linger on the memories of his tongue and how he'd lashed at her clit before sucking it all too perfectly. She thought about his hands moving up her thighs, those big strong fingers squeezing her flesh.

And then she thought about that ridiculously thick cock that had slid so easily between her fingers as her own wetness coated it. How would that feel between her legs? Sliding through her folds and then sinking deep, deep inside her until she couldn't even choke out a sound?

He flinched when she thought about that one. Lust had been leaning down so a young man in a bright green cap could talk to him in a slightly more private setting. And though he still listened to that young man speak, he stared at her. His burning eyes promised retribution when they got back to the castle.

She hoped he would. Maybe he'd tie her to the bed and make her endure the entirety of his lust. Would he last longer than most? Last night it seemed as though he was the same as a regular man, finished when he was done and that was the end of it. But what if he could go more rounds than that? Clearly, he wasn't human. He'd vaulted off a two story building!

She was so lost in her thoughts that Selene didn't notice that he'd urged his horse closer to hers. Lust grabbed her mount's reins, forcing her to stay in place while he leaned in. Brushing his lips over her cheek, he whispered in her ear, "Stop these games, or I will bend you over whatever surface I can find."

A shiver rocked her shoulders. "We're in public, Lust. I thought you respected your people too much to make them wait even longer?"

This was her "gotcha" moment. The time when she broke him and proved he was what her mother had said. A man so focused on lust and desire that he didn't know how to run a kingdom.

Instead, he grabbed her by the hair and tilted her head back. Just enough so that she was frozen in place with all eyes on her. "You are a temptress as well as a sorceress, I know. But the flaw in this plan is that no one here would mind if I simply let my power loose. You think we'd be the only people fucking, Selene? Oh, no. I would make them all join us and they would like it. They'd listen to you scream my name and it would make them all come at the same time. Have you ever shared a moment like that with a hundred people? All of you coming as the energy in the room becomes electric?"

She couldn't breathe. Couldn't think. Could he do that? Really?

Did she want him to?

His hand gentled, smoothing through her long locks and giving her neck back to her. "We're busy, Selene. As tempting as you are, I find I wish to keep you to myself. At least for a little while longer, and then we'll play with whatever fantasies you might have."

But he couldn't end it there. Apparently, he didn't care that so many eyes were on them, because he still cupped the back of her head and kissed her like a drowning man. Like a starving creature who knew he only had a few days left, so fuck the rules and fuck everyone who had made them.

Lust groaned into her mouth, the sound obscene and inappropriate, but… she liked it.

A cheer rose around them. It startled her out of the haze of lust that clouded her mind and Selene realized they were very much in public and he was kissing her in a way that should only be done in private.

Wrenching away from him, she felt her cheeks turn an even darker shade of red. If she could crawl back inside the dark robes that she usually wore, that would have been better. But he still had the cloak that he'd brought for her, because apparently it wasn't cold enough for him to let her have it.

She wanted to hide. Wanted to get away from all these people and their eyes and their judgements.

Lust cupped his hand under her chin and turned her to look at him. His eyes locked on hers, and suddenly she couldn't look anywhere else. "You are meant to be here. Right here. Nowhere else that mind of yours has you running. They are happy you are with me, Selene. You are a beautiful, strong woman who has suffered more than the eyes of a few people watching you kiss the man who holds your attention for now."

She nodded, his words filtering through the cloud of her mind. And yet... What would her mother think?

"You are not in the Tower any longer." He pressed one more kiss to her lips, grinning against her as another cheer erupted. "There is no one to make rules for you any longer, little moon. Make your own. With me, preferably."

And then he wheeled his horse away and continued to meet with his people. She mulled over what he said as she trailed along behind him.

What if she made her own rules? What if she didn't care what the Tower had taught her and allowed herself to live here? It didn't seem so bad. She'd have to endure him kissing her in public, but people seemed happy that he'd done so.

So many people in the crowd grinned at her now. A few of the women looked on with a little jealousy, but even they smiled at her with happiness. They all seemed to be pleased that Lust had settled down with someone specific. Which made little sense to her. Their king was known for never taking a woman twice, or at least that's what the Tower had claimed.

But maybe she'd been wrong about a lot of this. And maybe this was the final straw before she let herself believe that.

Lust paused again to speak with someone else, and a soft hand touched her foot.

Selene glanced down to see an elderly woman holding onto her. The woman's wrinkled face showed a life of happiness, with so many smile lines and crow's feet around her eyes that she appeared permanently wrinkled, even when not smiling.

And the woman held out a rose for her to take.

"Thank you," Selene whispered.

"We've been waiting for him to take a queen for a very long time," the woman said, her voice warbling with her age. "It's good to see him so happy."

"Oh, I'm not his queen." Nor did she think he would ever make her one. Lust knew his limits, and that was one of them. Why would he make a sorceress a queen, anyway?

The old woman smiled at her and rolled her eyes. "Dearie, anyone can see the way he looks at you. That boy has fallen head over heels, even if he won't admit it yet."

Selene felt her stomach churn. Was he? No. He couldn't be interested in her like that. Lust didn't have the ability to do so if he was a spirit like Affection. She'd learned what she could about them. No spirit could change, no matter how much she'd like to believe he could.

But then he looked over his shoulder at her and a smile as bright as the sun radiated across his face. And for a moment, she let herself believe he wouldn't always be a spirit of lust. That he could feel more than his desire for her.

It felt good to dream of a future with him. Even if it was only for a moment.

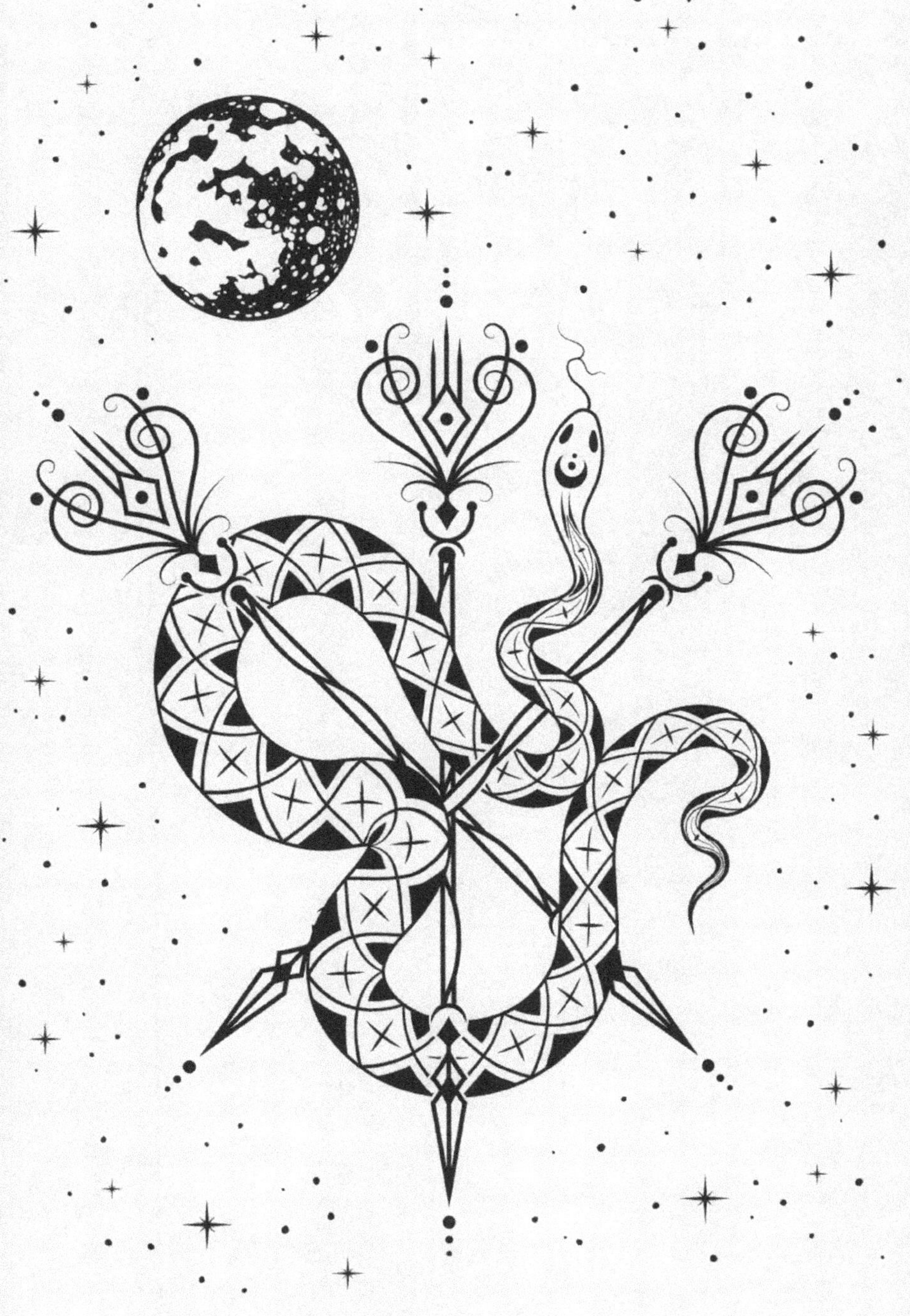

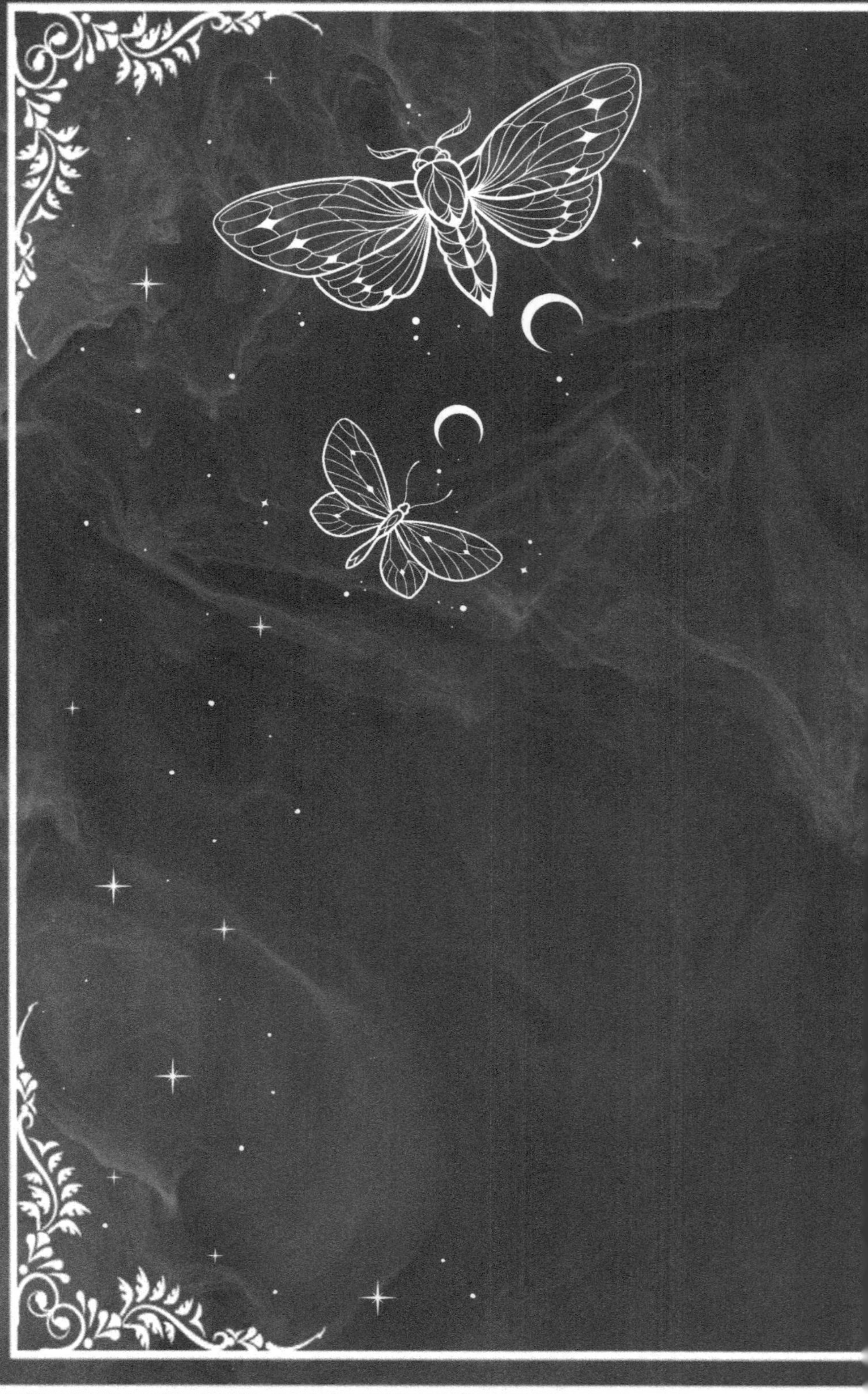

Chapter 31

Oh, this was all getting confusing and Lust knew very well that he couldn't afford for it to be confusing. He stood in his great hall, taking off the layers of clothing he'd had to throw on as the night fell. Winter would be here soon, it seemed, and he looked forward to the colder months.

After all, what was a better time to tuck underneath the covers with a certain beautiful woman?

But then he remembered how his attention must be split between his people and her. No one had ever commanded his attention like this sorceress. Selene was a strange mixture of confidence in the settings that she was familiar with, and shyness as soon as she was taken out of her comfort zone.

He could almost see what was pressed into her mind by that fool of a mother. Minerva liked to keep her girls under her thumb in more ways than one. Selene believed that she was not worth showing off. That their people shouldn't care to see her at all. A sorceress's place was in the shadows and by them looking at her, she was certain they would judge her for whatever he'd asked her to do. As though they didn't live their lives in the exact same way he did.

He enjoyed pulling her out of the shadows. He enjoyed watching her face as she let go of those preconceived notions that she wasn't good enough. Selene feared she wasn't the person that others wanted her to be, and he proved that thought wrong. It was thrilling to help someone's confidence grow.

And yet, he'd had to let her return to the castle without him or he wouldn't have gotten a single thing done.

Dangerous thoughts. He'd never let a woman run through his mind this much. He'd never been distracted by a pretty face or brown eyes or the lovely way her dark hair curled over her shoulder. It was so wrong and it was so right at the same time.

Sighing, he handed his cloak off to the closest servant and started for the stairs. He wanted to see her. And he knew she'd tucked herself away in their bedroom because that had already been more than enough time with people for his little Selene. She'd have to get used to being seen that much, he thought with a grin that he couldn't stop from spreading over his face. He wanted to show her off a lot more than that.

"My lord!" A voice called out.

He paused and looked down the railing to see Lara standing in the middle of the great hall. The long tendrils of her skirts played in the pool behind her, and the pale fabric draped off her shoulders, nearly exposing her breasts to his eyes.

When he didn't respond, she asked, "Do you have need of company tonight?"

"No," he replied, then flashed her a bright grin. "I've already got company."

A disappointed expression marred her pretty face, but he couldn't find it in himself to feel guilty. He had another partner for the evening. One who was beautiful and thoughtful and all together too curious for him not to indulge.

Ah, maybe he should feel bad about making Lara feel left out. She'd been by his side for years now, and he should acknowledge that there was fear layered into her reaction. It wasn't that she cared for him all that much. Of course, she cared for him in some way, mostly knowing that her family was safe if he was pleased with her. But she didn't live her life for him. She lived it for her daughter.

Maybe he needed to take some time to settle her nerves. Lara needed some extra money or perhaps an extra job to make herself feel better. And that was something he could do.

But the idea of her in his bed again? It was not one he could entertain while Selene lived under his roof. Not when there was no comparison between the two.

Taking the stairs two at a time, he rushed down the hall toward their bedroom.

Their bedroom.

He'd always enjoyed his privacy and rarely did he take a lover in that room. The bedroom was a safe haven for him to hide away from prying eyes and expectations. Now? He was so pleased to know she waited for him behind that door.

Straightening his shoulders, he ran a hand down his chest and wondered if she'd help him remove the corset again. She'd liked that the first time, and he wondered if she'd been hiding her lust at that moment as well. He'd been so angry that he couldn't taste her, but now he wondered if she was very good at hiding it.

How long had she been attracted to him? How long had she desired for him to be between her thighs?

Lust needed to ask her. He had to know the answer to these burning questions, or he feared he might explode.

Entering the room without knocking, he started talking the moment he stepped over the threshold. "Little moon, have you always found me attractive, or did it take time? I'll admit, I like the idea of you bumping into me in that little town and then hiding away with those pretty fingers between your legs, but it doesn't sound like you."

The room was dark and quiet. He frowned, his furrowed brows certainly making him look less attractive as he surveyed the room. She had to be here. Where else would she be?

But there were no candles lit. No fire in the fireplace. No warmth in the room at all.

Strange. He swore he could sense her. Lust could feel her somewhere close by. If he tilted his head slightly and closed his eyes, he could sense the way the low simmer of lust echoed out of her body, as though she knew he was here and wondered what he would do to her.

Was she hiding? No, it didn't feel like that.

Then a breeze toyed with the sheer curtain that led out onto his balcony and he knew where she was. His little sorceress apparently enjoyed her day outside, at least, and hadn't been willing to let go of it just yet.

Sighing with pleasure, he brushed aside the curtain and found her.

She stood as though it wasn't cold outside, her hands wrapped around the stone railing. The long, graceful line of her back was bared to his sight, until her dark violet gown obscured the rest of her. This dress was not meant to seduce, nor was it meant to be anything other than be serviceable. But the loose tangles of her hair, a riot of different shaped curls after she had unbraided them, blew in the breeze around her face. A full moon rose on the horizon, its silver light toying with the outline of her body. Warm, sparkling lights glowed from the town below them and then disappeared into darkness at the very edge of their kingdom. Lost into the nothingness beyond.

All the thoughts in his mind of throwing her onto the bed and devouring her suddenly disappeared. Not just lingering as they usually did, but they were entirely gone. He didn't want to fuck her. He wanted to hold her. Snuggle her against his chest and feel her breath rise and fall as they both looked out over a kingdom they loved.

"Oh," she startled, glancing over at him. "I didn't hear you come in. I'm sorry."

"No, don't apologize." He wouldn't hear it. Not when he wanted to hear other words coming out of her mouth.

And though he'd thought tonight would be the night when he fed himself into her, inch by thick inch, now he wondered if he wanted to spend his time breathless for other reasons. He could tug her into his arms and ask her a million questions. All the ones that he desperately wanted an answer to.

He remembered when he first brought her here. How he'd forced her to stand in this room and take her clothes off. How he'd brought Lara into this room, thinking that maybe she would enjoy the touch of a woman first. And then how she stood in front of his people today, all icy exterior with kind eyes whenever someone talked with her.

Lust knew other people had layers like this. There were plenty of women who were the same as her. Women with lives and dedications to others, women who were made to be nobles and who had spent their entire lives learning how to be the best political weapon they could be.

But he'd never noticed them. This woman had wrapped her hand around his throat and demanded that he look at her. See her. Understand that she wasn't like the others, even though he swore she was.

He joined her at the railing, leaning his arms against it and staring out at the twinkling lights. "You know, when I first made this kingdom, I thought that seeing lights at night would never be possible."

"Is that so?"

He nodded. "There weren't enough people to gather the lights bright enough. We all started with so few subjects. There weren't many humans left, you see."

The faint rustle of fabric came before she shifted a little closer to him. "That's not what we were taught. The kingdoms of mortals were known throughout the realms, all better and larger than the last. Then the seven demons arrived, each one manipulating the kingdom into the worst forms of themselves. People who could not live without fighting. Mortals who couldn't deny their bodies base desires. Others who stole and raped and pillaged because they knew no other way."

"Is that why you were so cold to my brother?" He snorted. "Greed's kingdom is not the same as ours, certainly, but the nomadic tribes enjoy going to war with each other. He's more or less tamed them, although it's taken hundreds of years to figure out the best way to do that."

"Tamed them?" Selene looked at him as though he'd suggested her entire history was wrong. Which, he supposed, he had. "What do you mean, tamed them?"

"The wilds of man." He gestured with an arm to all around them. Then pointed far off into the distance, where there was the faintest outline of color. "That's Gluttony, in case you were ever wondering." He pointed in the opposite direction. "Greed's kingdom is there. We arrived in our mortal forms with a singular purpose. Humanity was going to kill itself. Wipe itself out of this realm and then what would spirits be?"

"Spirits? The same as they always were, I suppose."

He was going to tell her a secret that the others would be furious at him for admitting. "Spirits feed off mortals. We can not feel your emotions. We cannot generate them or develop new emotions. We live because you are alive, not the other way around. Without you all feeling, we would wither away into nothing. And many of them did. Many, many spirits died in those days."

The stony expression never faltered from her face, but he thought there was a softening in her at his words. Almost as though she felt pity for the spirits he had lost.

A quiet silence stretched between them. And he could only hope that she realized how important the information he'd given her was. She could tell no one the truth about the kings, and in some way, he trusted her not to.

Sighing, she shifted closer to him, so close he could have tilted his hand and linked their fingers. He'd never wanted to hold a woman's hand before. He'd wanted a lot of other things, but never something so innocent as that. Yet, now he thought the slightest brush of her fingers would be a blessing.

She licked her lips. "So you're like parasites then?"

Lust reared back, all those happy thoughts disappearing in the insult's wake. "Parasites?"

"You feed off us." She nodded, staring off into the distance with determination on her face now. "I understand it. If we weren't around, then you wouldn't have a natural food source. Of course, that requires you to have a regular meal, and that makes all of you a bit like parasites. Or symbiotes, if you wish to think of yourself in kinder terms."

He had no words. Not a single word to respond to her insulting his entire species like that.

He opened his mouth, ready to spout whatever he could to tell her how utterly wrong she was, only to see her lips twitch.

Just the side opposite of him first, and then she slanted her gaze to his. Those glittering dark orbs were filled with so much mirth, he thought she was going to burst with it. Then she did. Selene tilted her head back and a rush of laughter bubbled out, the sound tumbling from her lips and easing all the wounds she'd delivered.

"Parasites," he snarled one last time, giving her shoulder a shove with his. "Do you really think that?"

"No." She shook her head, still chuckling at her apparently very enjoyable joke. "You feed off something we have in abundance. And I'll admit, even after you claimed to have tasted my lust, it did not dull the sensation that I felt."

"It doesn't," he grumbled. "We're not taking your emotions away from you, foolish woman."

"Ah, don't call me that because you're upset with me."

"I'm not."

"You are." She giggled again, shaking her head. "But that's all right. I deserve it for such a comment."

He grinned. She looked so pleased with herself, so happy that she'd made him smile. How could he not? And it was the first time she'd joked with him. The conversation between them was so easy. So simple that it was hard to not grin at her, knowing how precious these quiet moments were.

They both returned their attention to the glittering lights of the city below them before she blew out a long breath.

"What is it?" he asked, eyes still trained on the horizon.

"You don't touch me like you used to."

He scoffed. "Do you want me to?"

"I'm saying that you used to force me to touch you. There were all these lingering touches, gazes. You were constantly pushing me with your body, as though you had something to prove." She cleared her throat. "You don't do that anymore."

"I do not," he whispered.

"Why?"

Lust had to swallow the sudden lump in his throat. But she deserved the truth, so he told her. "You didn't like it."

The quiet stretched between them, so thick that he almost didn't hear her say, "Well, maybe I would like it now."

He straightened. His damn chest puffed out like she'd told him he was her god, and he stared at her in shock. She didn't look back at him, though the peaks of her cheekbones turned bright red.

Was she really letting go? Was she asking him to touch her because she wanted it?

Hesitantly, he reached for her. Selene let him guide her against his chest, sighing against his skin as he settled her in his arms. He didn't know what to do with them, so he wrapped her up in his grip and hoped he was doing this right. He'd never snuggled with anyone before, never had to. But right now, this felt good. Right. Exactly the way it should.

He set his chin on the top of her head and asked the question that sat on the tip of his tongue. "Things have changed between us, then?"

"I suppose so. I'm no more happy about it than you are."

But he was blissful. So pleased with this that he could stay out here in the cold air with her in his arms for hours. Still, he licked his lips and tried his best to convey how he felt. "I'm not unhappy about it, Selene. Not at all."

Her breath fanned over his collarbone. She didn't respond, and he supposed she didn't have to.

Right now, all he wanted to do was hold her in his arms and watch the stars blink to life.

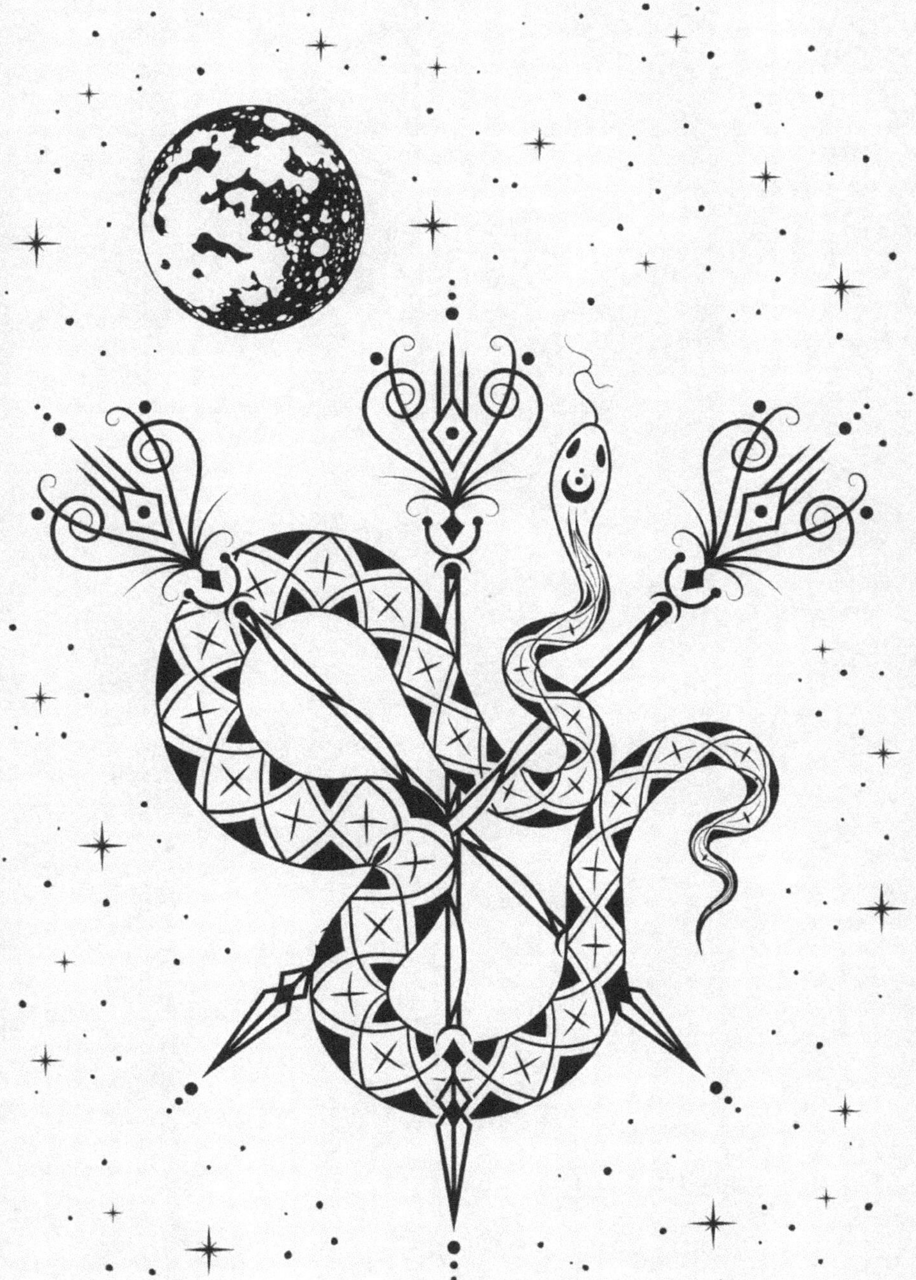

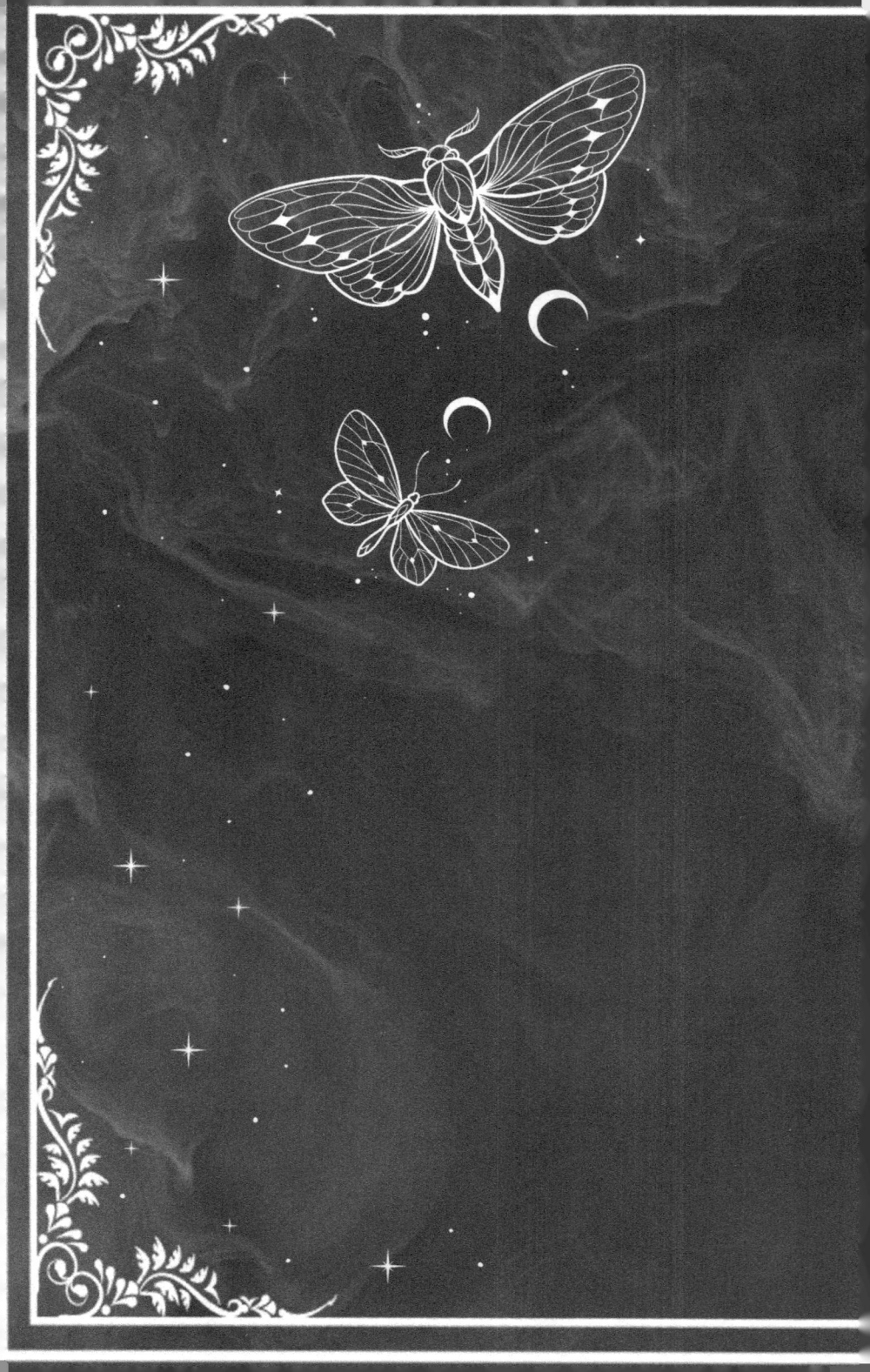

Chapter 32

She'd fallen asleep in his arms again. Not because he'd wrung out another orgasm that rocked her world, but because he'd been sweet and comforting and she'd sought him out. What a change in such a short amount of time.

Selene had gone to him when he reached for her. She'd allowed him to undress her, his hands gentle as he ran his hands down her sides and soothed any knotted muscles. But, just when she thought he'd want to take things to the next level—and hopefully actually finish the job this time—he hadn't. He'd braided her hair and then pulled her toward the bed.

He'd cuddled with her. Lust. The demon king she'd been raised to fear more than anyone else in any of the seven kingdoms had wrapped her in his arms and cradled her until she fell asleep.

And she'd liked it.

She thought about all this as she stared up at the ceiling, knowing he wasn't yet awake. She was in too deep. Her family had sent her here for a reason and warned her against all the things that she'd done. They told her he'd try to get into her head. They'd warned her that he would resort to trickery.

Selene knew all this and more. She'd researched him her entire life and now she knew more about him than any other person, and yet, she had still fallen for this. He'd lulled her into a false sense of security.

If she didn't get herself back, then she feared what would happen.

Lust shifted with a sigh on his lips as he turned toward her. Even in groggy sleep, he was careful with his horns, so they didn't catch her face when he moved. His muscular arm wrapped around her waist, tugging her closer into him until he was wrapped around her side.

Was he still asleep? Did he seek her out even while he was dreaming?

Her heart squeezed in her chest. She couldn't handle this. She couldn't betray him when she was already so wild for him. What would she do if she had to disappoint him the way her mother wanted her to? Selene's entire being rebelled against harming him. She couldn't take away what he loved and cherished.

She couldn't. And if she continued on this path, she would bend to whatever whims he whispered into her ear.

"Good morning," he said, his voice rough with sleep. "You're up early."

"Couldn't sleep."

"Mm," he tightened his hold on her. "Perhaps I can help with that."

But as his hand slid down over her belly, fingers leaving goosebumps in their wake, she grabbed onto his wrist. Every muscle in her body screamed, why? If he wanted to explore, if he wanted to take care of this persistent problem that made her head spin, then let him. He was good at it. Lust could make her come within minutes of his fingers being where she desperately wanted him, so why would she try to stop him?

She knew why. Her mind knew that if she let him do this, then she would only fall deeper into his web and the longer she stayed in it, the harder it would be to get out.

"You don't need to," she whispered, still holding him still.

"I'd like to."

"You must have a very busy day."

He nuzzled her neck, his tongue flicking out to touch her skin. "Ah, but my day would start so much better if I had the sound of your moans ringing in my ears."

No, she couldn't do this. She couldn't keep encouraging this sweet man or otherwise she'd spend the entire day in bed with him and then how would she ever leave?

Selene bolted. She wasn't proud of how she flung his hand off and how she rolled out of bed like it was on fire.

He watched her with an amused expression. "What are you doing?"

She couldn't breathe, therefore, she needed space between them. She stood at the foot of the bed and paced back and forth. Selene fanned her face, trying to make it feel less hot, but she couldn't get that figured out. She couldn't stop the heat from burning through her cheeks or the feeling that the air itself was pulling out of her lungs. She couldn't... do this. Not this. Not now. And not with him.

Shaking her head, she pointed at him. "I don't know what all of this is, but I don't want to deal with it anymore."

"What are you referring to?"

Selene gestured wildly between them. "Whatever scheme you have going on, with this, with us, it has to stop. Now. I won't let this go any further than it already has."

"Isn't that the exact opposite of what you've been telling me since you got here?" He sat up and the sheets fell away to reveal that beautiful chest. "You've been arguing until you were blue that you wanted me to trust you. To develop something real between us. Why the sudden change?"

By the look in his eyes and the curious smile on his face, Selene saw he knew what was going on in her head. He knew she was running because she was frightened by her own feelings for him.

Shit.

Shit, shit, shit.

What was she supposed to do now? She had to put space between them.

She had to do what her mother wanted, though. Space would only slow down what she had been sent here to do. And the longer she took, the more likely the others in the Tower would get involved. Them getting involved would complicate things even further.

But if she stayed true to what she was supposed to do, then she would lose her heart and mind in this castle that made her want things she'd never wanted in her life.

Oh, if her thoughts kept going round and round like this, then she was going to vomit. She might anyway, just to see his expression when she puked all over his expensive sheets.

"Selene?" he asked, a half smile on his lips. "What do you want? Not your mother, not me, not even that voice in your head. What do you want?"

She had to pull herself back together. He was controlling this situation and she couldn't let him. No. She was better than this. She was a sorceress of the Tower and she'd trained her entire life to manipulate and control this exact situation.

Selene drew herself up and shoved all her emotions away. Strangely, it was the first time that she'd ever felt remiss without them. Why did her entire body feel hollow?

She smoothed any emotion from her face and folded her hands at her waist. "I would like my own room again. I think I have sufficiently proven that I'm not going anywhere and that your brother has no great interest in me other than curiosity. I've earned my space."

He frowned. "You will stay here with me. I believe we both enjoy each other's company enough to remain as we are. Even if you are suddenly uncomfortable with the circumstances for some unknown reason."

"And I believe it is better to have space. We do not know each other well enough—"

Apparently, it was the wrong thing to say.

He surged out of the bed, all lean muscle and golden skin as he prowled toward her. She'd never seen his face so angry. Never seen his horns twist like that as they grew longer and stretched behind his head. "You think I do not know you?"

She'd rattled his cage. "I think you have an opinion of who I might be, but we have hardly given each other enough time to know each other."

The feral grin on his face was not one of kindness. He moved like a lion, tracking her until her spine hit the wall. Lust braced himself on a forearm above her head and stared down at her with those all-knowing eyes. "Are you running, Selene?"

"I'm not even moving, Lust."

"And yet, you think that having another bedroom will stop you from feeling what we're both suffering from. Do you think I wish to have a weakness in the form of a mortal woman? Do you think I have not noticed how affected you are as well?"

That is what she was afraid of. And knowing that he'd noticed only made all of this worse.

She felt as though a wave was waiting right in front of her, ready to swallow her if she didn't hold her breath and sink beneath it.

She shoved all of that anxiety and fear underneath the ice of her imagined lake. Eventually, she'd have to feel these. Eventually they might even overwhelm her because she had so many feelings buried deep. But hopefully, she would have enough time to be alone and suffer through it.

She tilted her chin up and told herself to be as icy as a snowstorm. "You think an awful lot of yourself if you truly believe I've told you anything important about myself."

"And you are more foolish than I thought if you don't believe I know you, little moon." He traced the backs of his fingers against her cheek. "You seem to think that knowing a person requires you to want them. I have told you that I want you, and you have said the same to me. You have told me more about yourself than you wish, and I respect that. But make no mistake, Selene. You and I are bound together now. You need me just as much as I need you."

She was afraid of that. But she tried not to show it in her gaze. Impassive. Cold. Smooth as glass, so he'd never know the riot of emotions she was steadily burying inside herself.

Finally, he sighed and shoved himself away from her and the wall.

"Fine. If you want another room, you may have it. But if you believe a few extra walls will stop what is happening between the two of us, then you're very wrong. This will only make you want me more."

She snorted. "I think a little privacy will show me just how far I wish to be away from you."

He grinned back at her. "Ah, little moon. Your innocence is refreshing. I am curious to see which one of us breaks first." Lust pointed at her. "I believe it will be you."

As if.

She was not a young woman anymore, nor had she been sequestered her entire life. Selene had read a thousand books on court politics and intrigue. She'd handled his people and his brother like a true queen. She would not break.

Sneering, she fumbled her hand on the wall as she searched for the door handle to leave this den of madness. "You know better than to challenge me, Lust."

"It's not a challenge. Only the truth."

Selene grabbed the doorknob behind her and twisted it. She backed into the hallway without another thought before she realized she was standing in the hall wearing only her sheer nightgown. Alone. With no clothing to change into.

Hissing out an angry breath, she spun and crossed her arms over her chest. She couldn't go back into his room. He'd laugh and assume that was her admitting her own fault, but that wasn't at all what she was doing.

She was...

She was....

"Can I help you?" Lara's voice cut through her thoughts, although the woman's voice was at least a little kinder this time.

When Selene glanced up, she almost flinched at the sympathy in Lara's eyes. "I'd like to find another room."

Her words apparently only solidified the theory that Lara had made for herself. The maid's sympathy grew even stronger as she set aside the broom in her hand and brushed her beautiful blonde hair off her shoulders. "Come on, then. No one touched your old room, and you're more than welcome to stay there again."

"I don't—" Selene didn't know what to say. She didn't want to correct the other woman. Selene hadn't fallen out of Lust's favor. She'd just... well. Hadn't she fallen out of his favor? She'd stepped in it this time and she didn't know how to fix it.

Sighing, she ducked her head and let the other woman lead her through the hall.

The last person she'd wanted to see was Lara. The maid was a favorite of Lust's, and it felt strange to speak to another woman who had shared his bed. But was it really all that strange? After all, everyone in this castle had likely been in his bed at one point or another. Lara was just another woman who had been there, and she'd handled it like Selene was handling it now.

The awkwardness only deepened when Lara stopped in front of Selene's old door and pulled out a small ring of keys. "He insisted we keep it locked. Some of your things are still in here, and he didn't want anyone else getting ideas. Even though the dresses you brought were ugly."

Selene had stiffened at the insult, but she was prepared to take it. Until Lara glanced over her shoulder and blushed.

"Sorry," Lara muttered. "Ugly isn't very nice. They aren't clothes anyone else wears, and certainly not in the castle."

The door swung open. The room beyond was clean and tidy, just as she'd left it. Strangely, Selene had been expecting dust even though she hadn't been gone that long.

Pursing her lips, she shook her head and started into the room. "I'm going to have to get used to your style sooner rather than later, I suppose. I think I've been fighting against it."

"You have."

Of course she had. The castle and its inhabitants went against everything she believed in. She'd wanted nothing to do with any of them! And now their damned king had made it so that she couldn't even think straight here.

"If I could be so bold?" Lara asked.

"What is it?"

"You've been here for months now. You know how to carry yourself like a noble, but there are many nobles here. You are strange because you can resist his powers, but there are plenty of strange people in the world." Lara shrugged. "If you want to keep him, then might I suggest trying something different?"

"And if I don't want to keep him?" Selene held the other woman's gaze. "If I have no interest in him other than a means to an end?"

"We both know that's a lie. I've seen the way you look at him. And the way he looks at you." The last bit seemed almost hard for Lara to admit. "He's different with you. I don't understand it, but I don't think it's for me to understand."

Some of her anger deflated at the admission. Sighing, she shook her head. "I don't know what's happening between us. But what would you suggest? If I wanted to keep him?"

The hardened expression on Lara's face softened. "Love him. I know many people who have spent hours in his bed, myself included. We all talk. But I don't think I've ever seen someone in his bed who wanted to be there just for him and not for what he could offer them. I don't know if anyone's ever loved him, to be honest. I'm not sure it's even possible."

It was. And she was so afraid it had already happened to her.

Selene swallowed hard. "That will be all."

"Think about it."

"I said that will be all, Lara."

The maid bowed and closed the door behind her. Selene had no idea what to do now. Her heart twisted to know that he'd suffered, without even realizing why he was suffering. All he wanted was the same thing she wanted.

Someone to love him. To care for him and him alone. He wanted to matter to someone. Anyone. And here she was, running from being that person for him.

With those complicated thoughts on her mind, Selene turned and found a single white letter with a red ribbon waiting on her bed. The glittering silver wax seal was stamped with the shape of a single pale tower.

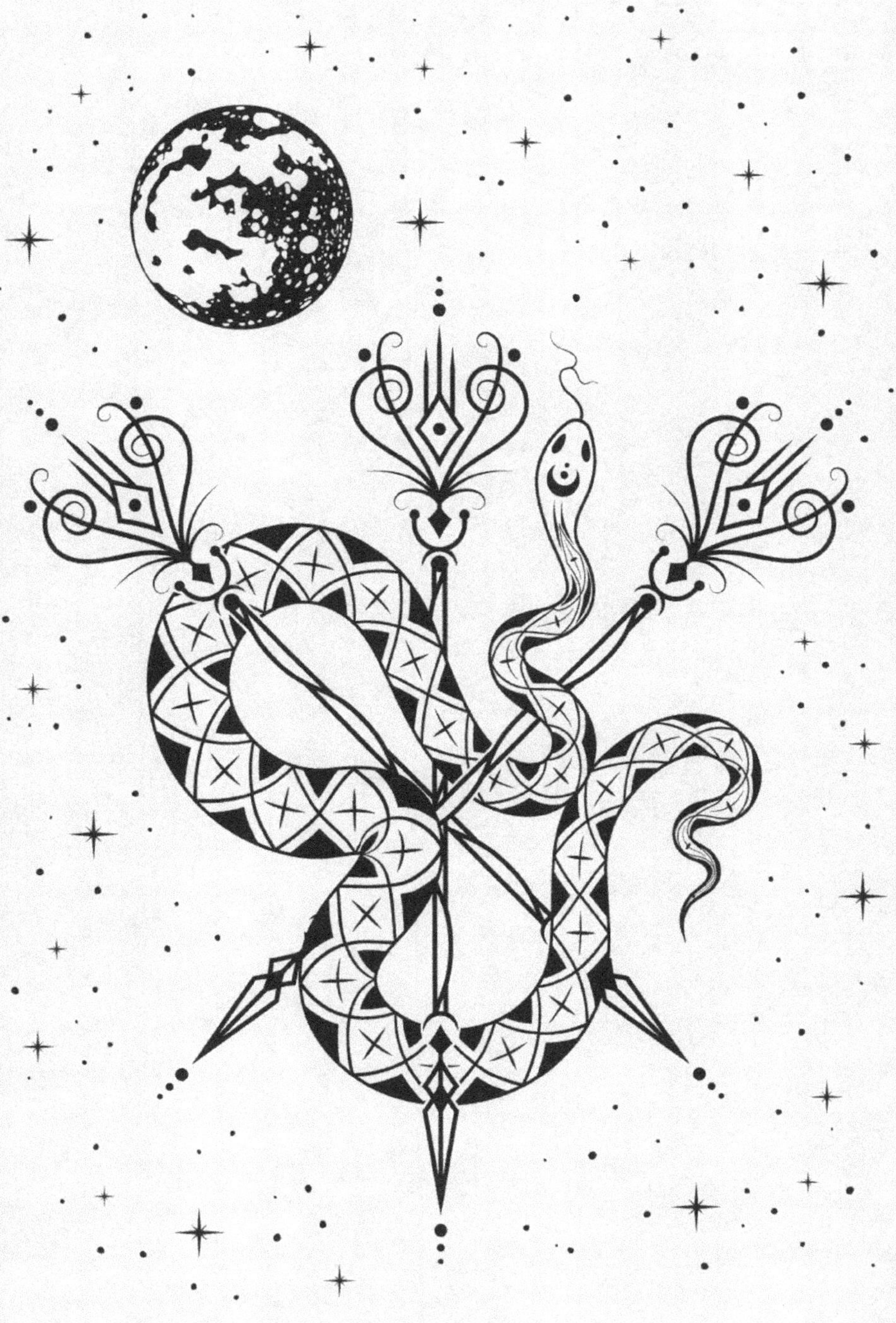

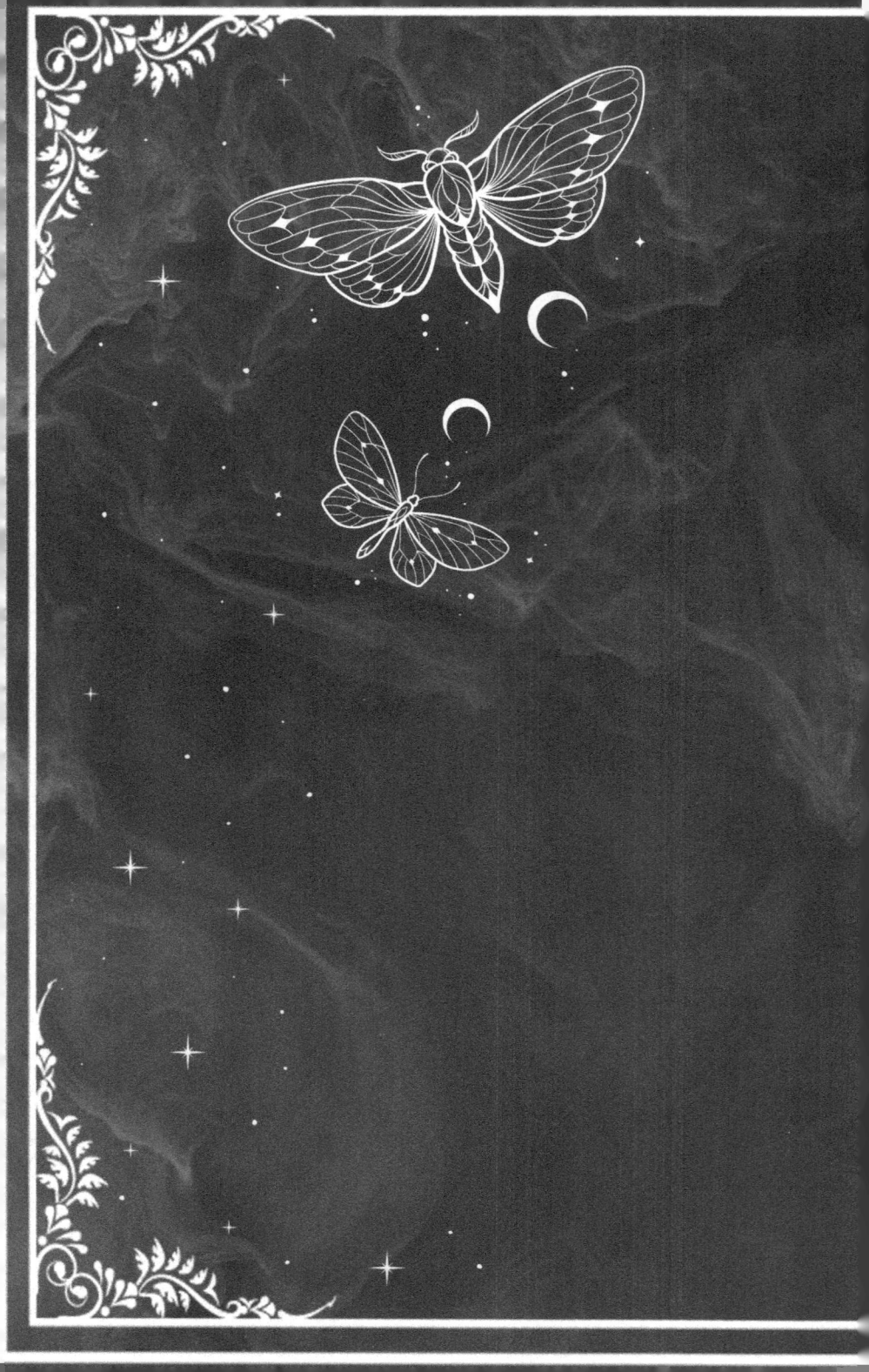

Chapter 33

"You aren't concerned in the slightest that she's no longer in your bed?" Greed asked, a goblet dangling from his fingers as he stared at Lust.

They'd spent the better part of the day drinking. Lust had dumped all his issues in Greed's lap, and his brother had done the same to him. Apparently, his kingdom wasn't doing as well as he'd hoped, surprise, and Lust was having issues with relationships.

How had the world turned on its axis?

"Of course I am," he replied. "She's supposed to be in my bed with me. What woman in her right mind leaves the bed of a god?"

"We aren't gods."

"We might as well be to them!" Lust gestured to the windows, as though just by doing so he was pointing at all the people in his kingdom. "We're thousands of years old. We're stronger than they could ever hope to be. We have power that they'll never be able to emulate."

"Some of the sorceresses can." Greed tried to drink out of his cup, only to find it empty. Frowning down into the depths, he added, "Although I'll admit even they seem to struggle with the powers we naturally control."

"Exactly." Lust didn't know what his point was. He'd lost it. "She should be in my bed without me having to ask, is what I'm saying. She should want to be in my bed and see it for the honor that it is."

"Other people do."

He nodded. "They do. They do. There are countless women in this castle that would crawl to my bed on their knees if I asked them to. Some of them have."

The gold in Greed's eyes flashed brightly before his brother said, "Then why don't you ask one of them and leave the little sorceress in the past?"

A flare of anger, dark and powerful, burned in his chest. The mere thought of another woman in his sheets, tarnishing the scent of her, made him want to wring necks. He squeezed the metal goblet so hard that it bent in his hands. He tried to get control of that emotion. But he'd drank enough alcohol to make his anger take center stage, no matter how hard he tried to push it away.

"No woman would dare," he snarled. "No other deserves to be in her place, her rightfully earned place. She is the only person who will have that honor."

Though Greed had instigated dark emotions, his brother looked very smug. "Then there's your answer. You seem to think that you can let her go as easily as she seems to have let you go. But you can't. She has you wrapped right around those pretty fingers, and if you aren't careful, you'll go mad without her."

"Indeed."

"And yet, here you are. Sitting with me." Greed waved the goblet again. "When you could spend some time groveling?"

He could.

Why was he drinking with his brother when he could beg her to return to his room? Where he could get down onto his knees and whisper sweet nothings against her skin. Maybe he'd press his lips to her belly, listening for that soft sigh she gave so he knew to continue. He'd lick his way up her inner thigh—

"Ugh," Greed groaned and threw the goblet at his head. "Just get out!"

Right. He was still in public.

Lust stood and staggered from the room. The alcohol in his blood wasn't helping, but he had to find her. To convince her that she was more than just a woman, more than just a bedmate to entertain him. There was something different about her, like she'd claimed, but maybe not for any reason that she'd thought of before.

He... wanted her. No, needed her. That was the right word. He needed her in his life and he wouldn't suffer another minute without her in his arms.

That was a perfect plan.

Except when he got to their room, there was no one in it. How he continually lost her in this castle was beyond him.

"She's not here," Lara said from behind him.

He startled, flinching at the sound of her voice before blowing out a long breath. "Don't do that."

"Are you drunk?"

"Only a little." Enough to make foolish decisions, because apparently he was running after a mortal woman like the castle was on fire. "Where is she?"

Lara blinked at him before crossing her arms over her chest. "I thought you knew."

"Obviously not."

"She got a letter from the Tower requesting her presence urgently. Considering the way she was ordering everyone around, I assumed you had given her permission to go."

"Go?" Why would she leave? Was she that upset about all that had happened between them?

No, he wouldn't stand for it. She would not return to that tower on her own where they had made her feel like less than a person. He remembered how she'd spoken of them, and it didn't take much to read between the lines. They were not her real family. They'd made her feel like nothing when they should have been helping her. Guiding her. Pushing her toward what she wanted in life, rather than puppeteering her around like they had.

She'd gotten so close to something like friends here. With him and Affection. She had more here than what the Tower could offer her.

Grinding his teeth, he shook his head. "Where is she now? They couldn't have gotten far yet."

"I'm not sure they've left, but all her things have been packed. You can't go with her, Lust. You'd have no clothes, no food, nothing to prepare you for waiting outside the Tower—"

He interrupted her. "Send a second carriage with all those items for me. I'm going with her."

"Why?" Lara asked as he swept past her. "What is it about this one that matters so much?"

He didn't have the answer to that, and it scared him. But being scared wasn't that bad. Not as bad as it could be, at least.

Lust didn't respond. Instead, he raced through the halls, blasting past servants who shouted while asking if something was wrong. Nothing was wrong. Not yet, at least. He had to find her in the courtyard before she left. He was certain he would, and then everything would be fine.

Lust was breathing hard by the time he slammed the doors to the castle against the walls and rushed down the main steps. Of course the carriage was moving already, but the driver quickly reined the horses the moment he saw Lust.

It gave him all the opportunity he needed. Clattering down the steps, certain that Lara would do what he asked even though she might not wish to, he opened the door to the carriage and slid inside.

Selene had pressed herself back against the seat, a hand against her heart and eyes held wide as she stared at him. She was breathing hard, too. Had she been rushing to get out of here before he could find her?

Unlikely. She wasn't that sneaky.

He gave her what he hoped was a disarming grin and said, "Miss me?"

She blinked at him a few times, almost as though she didn't know how to reply. That was surprising in itself. The woman always had some kind of response for him, no matter what ridiculous thing came out of his mouth.

When she didn't reply, he took the time to get control over his breathing. Lust slammed his fist onto the top of the carriage, and off they went. They rolled quietly down the cobblestone streets of the castle toward the city beyond.

"What are you doing?" she finally asked.

"Coming with you. The Tower is no place to go alone. I think we both know that." And making sure she wasn't running, of course. He didn't want her to run without at least giving this a chance.

Because... What if they were both avoiding something amazing?

She didn't look like she wanted something amazing to happen. She glared at him, plotting his murder, perhaps. But then she said, "You weren't invited."

"No, I don't suppose I would be. No one at the Tower is very fond of me, in case you hadn't noticed." He leaned back, spreading his legs wide to get comfortable. She was forced to place her legs between his, and the way her eyes narrowed upon him only made him preen. "But I didn't want you traveling alone. That's rather dangerous, don't you think?"

"Isn't this kingdom the safest in all the seven kingdoms?"

"Indeed." His chest puffed a bit with pride. "Even safer than Wrath's, and that's saying something."

Selene leaned forward and sniffed. "Are you drunk?"

"Why does everyone keep asking me that?" He held up his fingers, pinching them just slightly. "Only a little. Anyway, why are you going to the Tower?"

"Because I was summoned."

"And why were you summoned?"

"Minerva did not deign to give me a reason why." She shifted uncomfortably in her seat. "I assume it has something to do with you."

"Ah, of course." Why hadn't he thought of that? Probably because he was already way too drunk for this conversation. Lust crossed his arms over his chest and nodded. "Right. Well, I'm going to sleep this off so I don't have to talk to Minerva while I'm already far too drunk to give two shits about her. Wake me when we get there, will you?"

He didn't need to open his eyes to see the outrage on her face. He already knew it was there.

Lust drifted off into sleep rather quickly, but it was not restful. His dreams were filled with what his impaired mind hadn't thought about.

Minerva trapping Selene in the Tower. Him waiting outside those white, terrifying walls only to realize that he would never get her back. Listening to her screams as they tortured her for information about him. The sounds of Selene's begging as she cried out that they were supposed to be her family. Why were they doing this to her?

It was more than he could suffer. So when he woke, sober and far too scared, he found himself rocking gently in the carriage. She stared out the window, her chin on her fist as she watched the landscape turn from bright green to a pale gray, and then nothing but white as far as the eyes could see.

His heart squeezed in his chest. She was worth so much more than what they saw in her. So much more than anything they give her.

Because she was his. His and his alone and he would be damned if they somehow convinced her that she was less than wonderful.

Lust didn't even realize he was moving until he felt the hard floor of the carriage pressing against his knees. Selene turned her attention away from the view and frowned down at him. "What are you doing now? I thought you were asleep."

"I was," he murmured. Lust framed her face with his hands, drawing her lips to his. "Now, I am awake."

It felt like those words meant a lot more than just that his eyes were open.

He kissed her, trying to press into her the thoughts that flooded his mind. He found her beautiful, stunning, heartbreakingly perfect for him. She terrified him every waking moment, but he wouldn't change a thing. He kissed her like a drowning man who only wanted a single drop of water that was her attention.

And though he thought she would fight, Selene wilted against him. Her hands laid against his chest, then shifted up to his shoulders so her arms could hold on to him. Her breath caught in her throat and suddenly she kissed him back.

But her kiss wasn't sweet or soft or sensitive. She nipped and bit at him, tugging on his bottom lip with a sharpness that made him hiss. Lust didn't want this to be rough. He wanted it to be tender. He wanted to show her his fears in a way that wouldn't let her entirely into his head.

He could do this, though. If she wanted to prove they were both alive and together in a rough manner, then so be it.

He fisted her hair, ripping her away from his mouth so he could attack her throat. He wasn't gentle in the way he left red blotches on her neck, marks for her mother and all others to see. Dragging his teeth down the sensitive column, Lust groaned as he heard her whimper.

This wasn't any time for luxury or lingering kisses. He pushed her skirts up, tunneling his hand through all that damned fabric until he palmed between her legs. His two middle fingers slid along her slit, finding her already wet and soaking for him.

"Were you thinking about me?" he asked, breathing in the scent of her lust and already tasting her on his tongue. "You didn't get this wet just from a kiss."

"Only the kiss," she hissed, arching against his hand.

"Little liar." He tugged at the neckline of her dress with his free hand, forcing the buttons to open without ripping them apart. He wanted to. Oh, he wanted to rip this dress to shreds so everyone would see what they had been doing on the journey.

The fabric sagged on either side of her body. He wasted no time, leaning down to suck a pink nipple into his mouth, biting down with his teeth before licking away the sting. Selene hissed again, shifting her legs to give him easier access.

And, oh, he planned on taking whatever she gave him.

Lust sucked harder as he plunged his fingers inside her. Working her to a fever pitch, each draw of his mouth mimicked by a deep plunge of his fingers. Deeper, harder, and faster until she was writhing beneath him.

Freeing her nipple with a pop, he slid down her body and lifted her skirts over his head.

"What are you doing?" she asked, breathless with desire.

"What I've been wanting to do ever since the first time I tasted you," he growled.

Lust never stopped the onslaught of his fingers as he added his tongue into the fray. He worked her little clit with long, languid strokes. His fingers were too slow for her to do anything but suffer in his arms. As she arched, trying to get closer and create the friction she desired, he banded his free arm around her waist and held her still. A feat in itself while he was underneath her skirts.

But this was not something he'd rush. Not when he was surrounded by her in the darkness, the scent of her overwhelming as he tongued her into oblivion.

Finally, he took pity on the woman who was putty in his arms. He stiffened his tongue, drawing tight, tiny circles around her clit as he worked his fingers harder. Twisting them inside her so he scraped that perfect point that soon made her stiffen... arch...

Her throaty cry was nearly his own undoing. He wanted her. Now. Needed her like he had realized only such a short amount of time ago.

Hissing out a breath, he tossed her skirts away from himself and loomed up. Lust ground his cock against her center, and she let out another guttural cry as a second orgasm burst through her at just that mere touch. Grinning, he grabbed her chin and pressed a hard kiss to her lips.

"I'm going to fuck you now," he breathed into her. "It's not the place I wanted, but if I'm not inside you in the next few seconds, I will stop breathing."

"Yes," she groaned, her hand reaching between them to stroke him. "Please, Lust, I—"

The carriage rolled to a harsh stop. Lust had to catch himself against the back wall, braced over her as he was. And though he felt a bit like he'd been caught with his cock in hand, not quite but close enough, he realized he couldn't fuck her in the courtyard of the Tower while her entire family listened.

"Fuck," he hissed before slamming himself into his own side of the carriage.

She stared at him with wide eyes, pink cheeks, and an "I just came" expression that almost made him launch back onto her side. Minerva be damned, he needed her now.

Common sense reminded him that she'd never forgive him for it, even if she enjoyed the sex while it was happening.

Running a hand over his face, he grumbled, "We're home, darling."

"This isn't home," she replied. It sounded as though she'd even surprised herself.

Lust gave her a wry grin. "You're right. It isn't. And yet, we're still here. Go greet your family, little moon. Let me get a hold of myself before I join you."

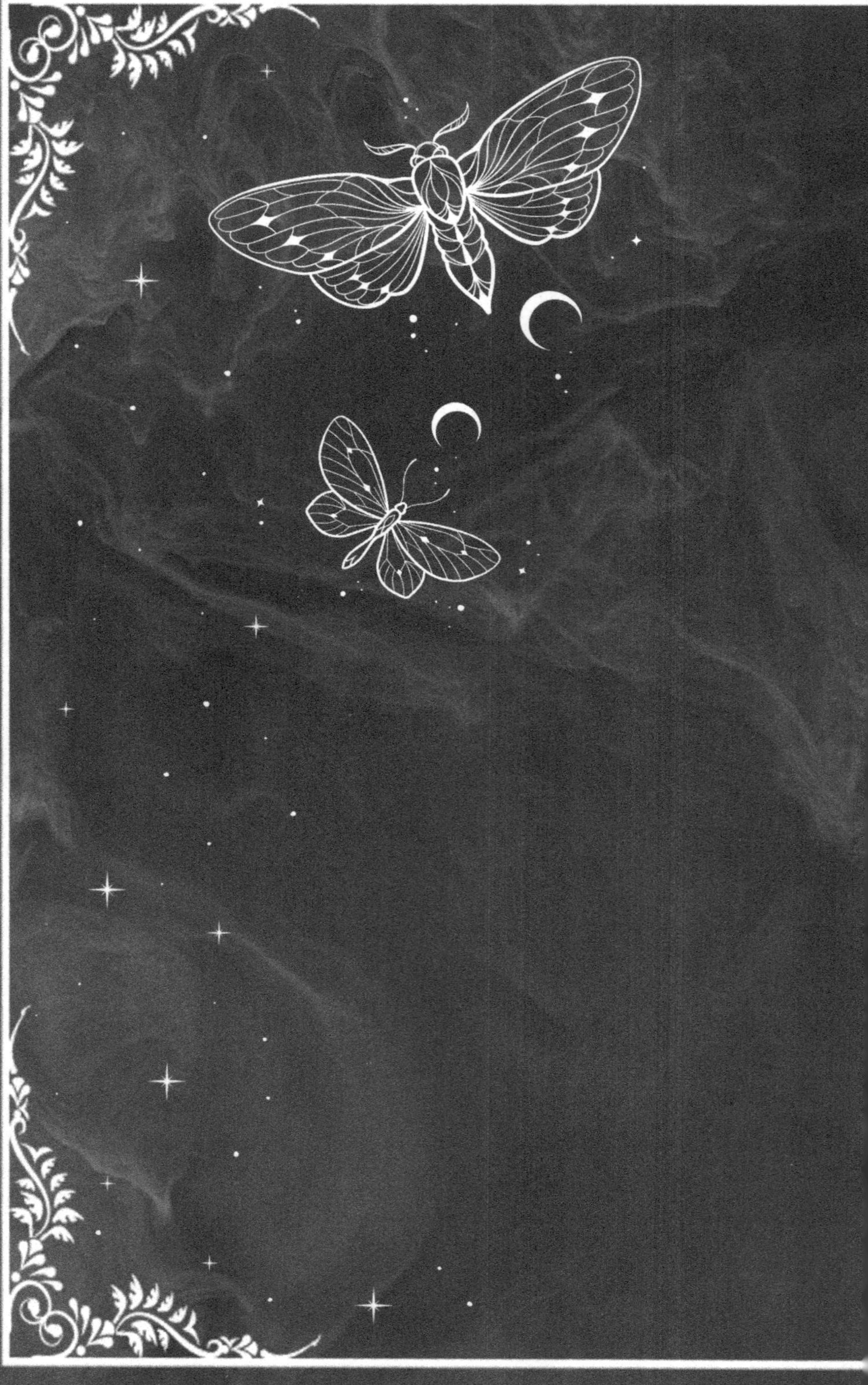

Chapter 34

They denied him access to the Tower. Selene had known they wouldn't let him in, of course. Since when had any of her siblings allowed a man to be in their home without repercussions?

What she hadn't expected was to miss him. She'd thought she would walk into her old home, the same young woman she'd been before. Selene truly believed nothing had changed.

She would see her mother and her sisters, and they would all rejoice that she'd survived thus far. She thought they would smile at her and tell her they were pleased to have her back. They'd eat good food, the kind she'd missed since leaving. She wouldn't be the person dressed in odd clothing with odd ideals.

Of course, Minerva would pull her aside to hear her story about what had been happening in her absence. Her mother would want to know every detail and Selene would spare nothing.

Except... She wondered what Lust would say about the portraits on the walls. She wondered if he'd like the food, or if he would laugh at how simple it all tasted. He'd want more spice. More colors on the paintings. More everything.

And now, strangely enough, so did she.

Minerva pulled her aside quickly, before she could even sink back into the comfort of familiarity.

"You are to stay here for a few weeks," she hissed. "I don't care what that demon thinks. You will remain with us while you acclimate back to your own home."

"I have no wish to force him to linger. If you want me to control him, Mother—"

"I think you have forgotten your task." Minerva drew herself up to that great height, looking down at Selene with so much disappointment it made her chest ache. "You have been in that castle for too long. Don't think I have forgotten the temptations that lie there. Remaining here will remind you why you are doing this. Do you not agree?"

She didn't.

She wanted to go back to the castle where there were colors and laughter. Where people didn't look at her with calculating expressions, nor did they want her to betray another person without remorse.

Everything was so jumbled in her head. She was supposed to manipulate Lust, and if she failed in doing that, then she was supposed to gather as much information about him as possible. Which she had done.

Minerva stopped her in front of the great white door that led into the dining hall. "You will tell me everything you have learned."

She opened her mouth to do just that, but... couldn't.

There were secrets in that castle that were now hers. Entrances and exits that only servants knew about. The truth was that Lust wasn't a demon at all. He was a spirit. There were other spirits as well, and she'd met them. Some in physical form like his brother and some like Affection who existed outside of their realm. She also thought that Lust might be changing, and that terrified her more than anything else that she'd learned.

Because now she had a gut feeling that spirits could change. And she didn't know what that meant.

All of that, and more, pressed against her tongue and she felt her throat working around them. But nothing came out. Not a single secret, because she didn't know what her admission would do to those people she had come to care about.

Minerva tsked. "Do you see why you need to come home? You need to stay here, little girl. With us. And if you are incapable of remembering your own people, then who are you? Just a sad child left out in the storm. Remember that's who you are without us, Selene."

At Minerva's harsh gesture, the doors to the dining hall opened more and Ursula stepped out. She kept her eyes on the floor as she said, "I'll take you to your room, Selene," she whispered.

"I thought we were having dinner?"

Minerva shook her head. "Dinner is for family. You, my dear, are a guest in this house until you remember who you are."

The sting of her words burned like a slap across Selene's face. It was fine. It would all be fine. She didn't have to be the person who everyone wanted her to be, not unless she desired to be so.

And yet... She still found herself becoming that little girl again. The one who wanted to be like the others and was never allowed to be. She wasn't given to the Tower. She was left here. A foundling with no family to her name, other than this one who didn't want her.

Sighing, she nodded and dropped into a low curtsey. "I will not let you down, Mother."

"See to it that you do not."

Minerva disappeared into the only warm room in the Tower. Selene turned toward her sister and nodded. "Let's go."

"It's the same room," Ursula said, as though that somehow made it better. "No one touched anything. I made sure it was clean, just in case you... for when you came back."

In case she failed, her sister meant. When Selene did not respond, neither did Ursula. They both walked up the countless stairs, all the way to her door that had been her haven for years. Except now, it was to be her prison.

Sighing, she planted her hand against the door and held Ursula's gaze. "Do you think she'll ever consider me part of the family?"

Ursula hesitated, then blew out a long breath. "I don't know."

It was enough of an answer.

Selene swung the door open and stepped into her old bedroom. The same room she'd been in since she was a child. There used to be paintings on the wall, drawings that she'd done of the Tower and her family. She'd wanted to paint the walls, but Minerva had told her it was too childish to do so.

Instead, the white walls were more gray than she remembered. Her wardrobe to the right had a fine layer of dust on the top, and her blankets on the bed were still mostly composed of fine white skins because she always got cold here. It was so cold. All the time.

She hated it. She hated feeling cold when she'd been shown what warmth felt like. And suddenly that thought blossomed into something else. Something that whispered warmth wasn't just physical, and everything here lacked what she now knew she wanted.

Her heart thundered in her chest. There was a cloak in the closet that she'd left. It had a few tears from countless years of use and would have made a poor impression. But it was her warmest cloak. If she put that on, she might be able to sneak past the others and then she could find him.

Him. Lust. The only person she really cared about seeing right now.

"Well, well, well. You look like Minerva grabbed you by the tail and yanked. Can't say I'm all that surprised."

Gasping, Selene whirled to find him leaning against the wall to her left. How had he—

She supposed she shouldn't even think the question. He'd gotten in somehow, and she knew it wasn't through the window. She had a room with only a small slot for a window, where it might have been used to shoot arrows at enemies. Selene could barely fit an arm through, let alone a full grown man.

"How did you…" She let the question trail off into nothing.

Lust grinned, his eyes sparkling with some emotion she couldn't quite name. "Don't ask questions of demons, little moon. Don't you know answers come with a price?"

Anything. She'd pay anything for him to remind her of a time when she hadn't felt so cold. And then something clicked in her mind. She didn't have to feel cold if she didn't want to. He was the only one who knew how to warm her.

Selene darted toward him before her mind could warn her that this was a terrible idea. There were better places to seduce a man like him. Less taboo places than her childhood bedroom with a gaggle of sorceresses below, all of whom wanted him dead.

But the moment her arms wrapped around his neck and her body plastered against his, she was lost. Selene devoured his lips, consuming them with her own. Nipping and biting until he hissed out an angry sound because she'd almost broken skin. She didn't care. He had a duty right now, and that was to make her forget.

His arms snapped around her in a vise. He wouldn't let her go now, not even if she begged for it. Selene had walked right into the arms of a demon king, and her body was the sacrifice he'd claim.

Groaning into his lips, she writhed against him. He was already rock hard against her belly, likely from their fun in the carriage. Had he ever taken care of himself, or had he been like this since they parted?

She liked the idea of him suffering. Waiting for her to touch him.

He drew his lips from hers, leaving a wet streak across her cheek as he moved to her throat. "I'm not complaining, but why—"

She palmed his cock, drawing her fingers from the base up to the head that she could feel almost escaping his pants. "Stop talking."

"Understood."

Lust flipped them around, shoving her back until her spine hit the wall beside the door. Flushed and breathless, she watched him as his eyes hungrily trailed from the bottom of her skirts to her neck.

"I'm going to ruin this dress," he growled. "You're going to have to burn it when I'm done with you."

"I want to."

He lunged forward and grabbed either side of her bodice. With one harsh rip, he tore it in half, the buttons pinging all over the walls and floor as they scattered. It didn't matter, she didn't care where they went.

All she cared about was his lips that crashed down onto hers as his hands palmed her breasts. Those talented fingers flicking over her nipples, tiny circles sending her deeper and deeper into madness.

"You don't know what you do to me," he groaned, ripping his mouth from hers to circle his tongue around her nipple. "You consume me, Selene. Body, mind, soul, all of it is yours."

"You don't have a soul." She arched her back. "You're already a spirit."

"I am a soul who took flesh." He gave her one more lick before dropping to his knees before her. "But if I do not have one, it is because you own it. Crushed between your delicate hands."

She looked at him on his knees, ready to service her yet again as though she were a goddess. And she nearly came undone then.

He looked up at her with a wicked grin, then licked his lips. "You're in charge, little moon. What do you want?"

She should stop. She should tell him that her mother and her sisters would hear them downstairs. That this room was special to her and they couldn't do this here, of all places.

And yet, the only thing she was capable of doing was hiking up her skirts and wrapping a leg over his shoulders. Biting her lip, she grabbed onto his horn with one hand and braced herself against the wall with the other.

"My pleasure," he growled. "But I want to hear you scream."

Oh, she would. She had every time he'd done this and yet he'd never complained once that she hadn't done it back to him. That she hadn't slid his cock between her lips and sucked hard enough to make him moan like she wanted to hear.

Like the way he moaned at the first long lick he gave her pussy.

Selene let out a hiss, her head thudding against the wall. How was she meant to stay standing for this? His tongue circled her clit, too gently, not hard enough, but then he suddenly sucked. Hard. Two of his fingers sank inside her at the same time and she swore she saw stars.

A curse tumbled from her lips. She rolled her hips against him, chasing his tongue so he'd just put it where she wanted him to be. But no. He licked and sucked and avoided all those tantalizing places because he wanted to torment her.

He wanted this to last a long time.

Selene wanted the exact opposite. She wanted a swift, blinding orgasm that would make her forget everything that had transpired. She didn't want to be in this room, and he could transport her away from it.

With a snarl, she grabbed onto his horns with both hands and held him in place where she wanted him. He met her gaze, those bright blue eyes seeing far too much and she almost came right there.

He licked, tormenting her until she couldn't take it anymore. "Make me come, Lust. Then I want you to throw me onto that bed and fuck me into the furs."

His eyes suddenly glowed violet with whatever power he had that she hadn't seen before. Only then did he finally start to devour her.

Selene let her head thud back against the wall, hissing out a "Yes," and he ate her. Consumed her. Devoured her until all the stars in the night sky seemed to get closer, just within reach.

Until someone pounded on her door right next to her head.

Selene flinched, dropping her leg from his shoulder immediately and trying to get away from him. Lust palmed her hips with both his hands, a silent warning that he wasn't letting her go. Not until she came on his tongue, just like he wanted.

But she couldn't. Not with someone standing a foot away from her. Giving him a warning glare, she called out, "Who is it?"

"Selene! Enough of us begged Mother to have you come to dinner with us!" It was Bathilda. The last sibling she wanted to hear from. Bathilda wouldn't leave until Selene came out. "She said you could join us all. Are you ready?"

"I'm changing!"

The doorknob started to turn.

Eyes wide, desperate to hide him, Selene stumbled past Lust and tore herself out of his grip. He let out a low, frustrated growl, but reluctantly stood when she gestured for him to get up.

"What—" he stared, before she slammed his back against the wall and slapped her hand over his mouth. Using the other hand to hold her bodice closed, she watched as Bathilda opened the door to her room.

Her sister couldn't see him. All she'd see was Selene leaning in the doorway, one hand holding her dress shut with perhaps too much of a wild expression on her face.

"What's going on?" Bathilda asked, her eyes narrowed in suspicion.

"I couldn't get the dress off myself, and I'll admit, I got a little frustrated." Selene hoped that explained why her cheeks were so red. "I'll be down in a moment."

"Are you sure you don't need help? I can tie your dress."

"No!" Selene almost shouted the word before blushing an even deeper scarlet. "I can manage just fine. I have a dress that would be perfect for dinner. I just... just..."

Lust curled his tongue around one of her fingers. He gripped her wrist, forcing her to lower her hand as he slowly sucked her finger into his mouth. The sensation of his tongue doing that to such a sensitive digit scrambled her mind.

Her sister's frown deepened. "Are you sure you're all right?"

"I'm fine!" Selene squeaked. "Just a little distracted right now, is all. Can you give us—me— a few moments?"

"Of course. Take all the time you need and I'll bring you to the others."

Because she didn't know how to get back to the dining hall without someone watching her, obviously. "Thanks," Selene breathlessly whispered before tugging the door shut. Her sister likely got an eyeful of breasts but...

"For fuck's sake!" she hissed, yanking her hand out of his grip. "What are you doing?"

"Exactly what you asked." He prowled toward her until her hips hit the mattress. "I'm licking you until you come and then ruining those furs as I finally feed my cock into your wet pussy."

She trembled. By the seven kingdoms, how was she supposed to do that with her sister right there? Or not do it and suffer through a dinner knowing that he was waiting for her?

"I have to go," she whispered. "I have to or they'll know."

The grin on his face never budged. He merely shifted to the side and let her fly past him to the wardrobe, where she pulled out a simple dress. He didn't say a word, but she heard the creak of the bed as he laid down on it. Would he wait for her? What was he planning on doing? What man was all right with her leaving in the middle of all this?

She dressed quickly, turned around, and gasped.

A naked demon waited for her in her bed. The soft furs caressed all that golden skin. He fisted his cock in one hand, a slow drag from the head to the base captivating her. She licked her lips without even realizing what she was doing.

"Hurry back," he said, his voice a deep rumble. "I'll take the edge off, but then I expect to need you all night, little moon."

She could barely rip her eyes from the glistening drop dribbling down the head of his cock before whirling and rushing out the door.

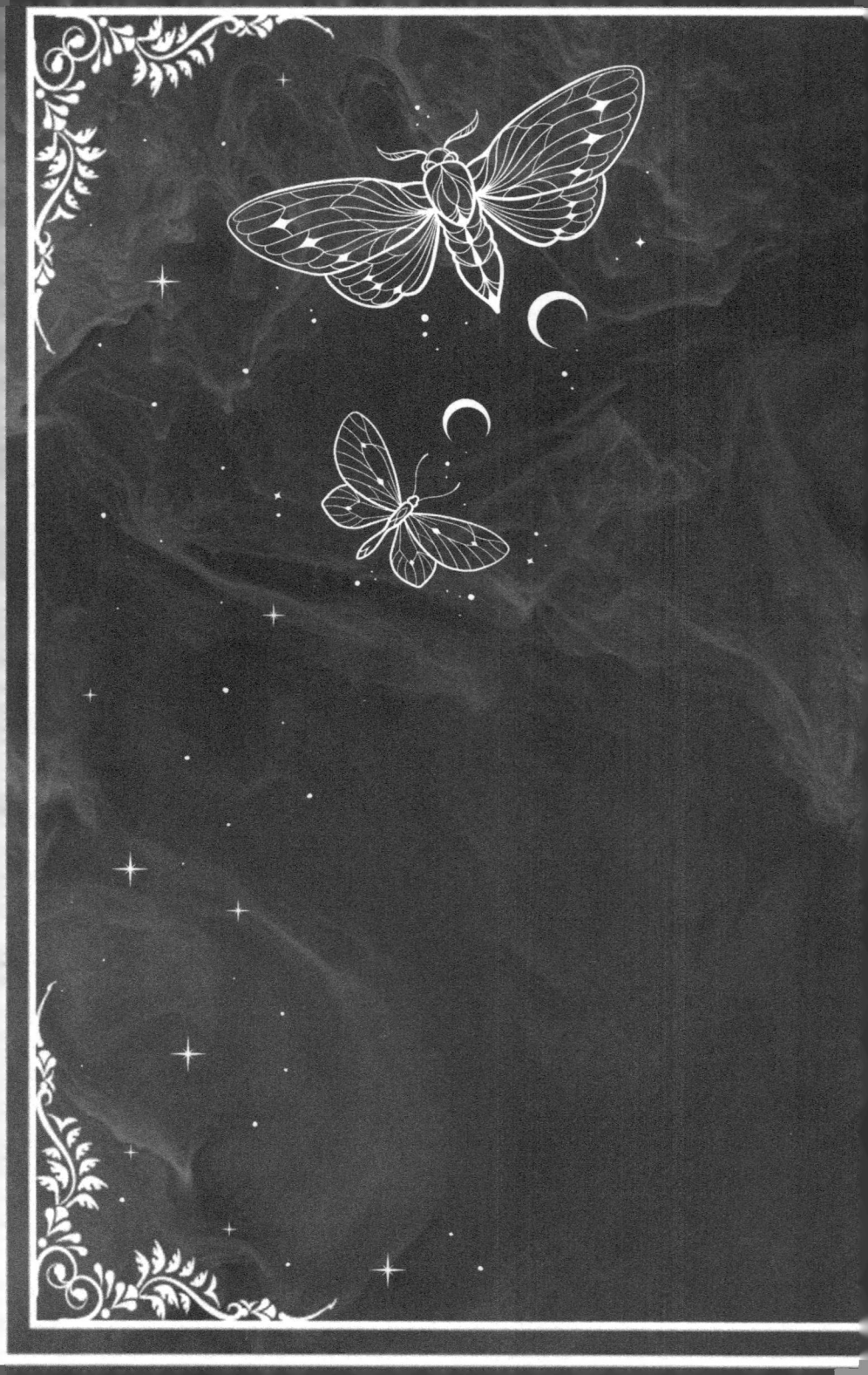

Chapter 35

Bathilda talked her ear off the whole time they walked down to the dining hall. And Selene had no idea what she said. Not a single word.

Her mind was back in her old bedroom. Where a long-limbed man waited for her, white furs caressing his skin as he stroked that massive cock. His words haunted her every step, trying to drag her back to that room.

"Hurry back. I'll take the edge off, but then I expect to need you all night, little moon."

All night? Was that even possible?

Selene had been with a few men before, but the memories were so foggy now that she'd survived Lust's touch. He'd branded himself into her, wiping away any and all men who had touched her before. And now, she couldn't remember what sex was like.

Only that it had been something to endure. The men had tried. She remembered that. They had touched her thighs just like Lust. But none of them had lingered so long with their tongue in her pussy. None of them had eaten her like she was the elixir of life and they were a dying man. And none of them, none, had looked at her like he had.

She sank onto her old chair, staring down at the dining table like it was a foreign scene. Her mother sat at the head of the table, all of her would be sisters grinning at her like they'd won something. And maybe they had. Maybe they'd argued on her behalf for such a long time that her mother had finally gone blue in the face.

That must have been it. She could feel the tension in the air but no longer cared that it existed.

"Welcome back," Minerva said. "Would you like to fill your sisters in on what you have encountered in Lust's castle?"

She took a plate offered by Ursula and met Minerva's gaze. "It was warm."

The silence ringing after her statement was enough to make her smile. Selene demurely ate her food, her thoughts still on the man upstairs. Had he affected them all? Maybe she was feeling his power through the floor, and that was why she couldn't focus on what was happening in front of her.

But no. None of her sisters were wiggling in their seats like she was. And she couldn't imagine they could stay still if their thighs were as slick as hers.

Why was she here?

Minerva frowned. "Anything else? Anything more interesting

than that?"

"Not really."

"You were sent there for a reason. Did you forget that purpose?"

"I did not. I was sent there to get the demon king under my thumb, and if I could not do that, then I should gather as much information about him as possible so that we can all take the castle. You claim it is our rightful place in this kingdom." She popped a cherry tomato into her mouth. "I did not forget."

"Then have you failed?" Minerva's face turned bright red. "You were always a worthless little foundling. I trained you for years, preparing you for when you could save us all. And instead, you have forgotten your entire life's work for a man who has made the entire world fall to their knees before him. He has corrupted you."

Corrupted? Yes. That was the word for it. She felt him deep inside her, even though he'd never been there before. Did it matter, though? She didn't mind being corrupted, and he certainly enjoyed corrupting her.

Clearing her throat, she nodded. "Perhaps he has. But he also was kind enough to offer me a home in that castle. A place to rest my head in safety, with people who wanted me to be happy and welcome. It's more than I can say for my life here."

She could have cut through the shock with the butter knife next to her plate. Everyone stared at her as though she'd grown a second head, and maybe she had. A better one. A better mind that knew how to deny her mother from her cruelty and how to prepare herself for the life that she actually wanted.

She wanted a life with him.

A life with Lust that would be filled with color and warmth and sure, some things that made her nervous. Moments that would push what she thought was right or proper, but did that matter in the slightest? No. Not at all.

She didn't want to be here. She wanted to be with him.

"Mother," she breathed. "I want to have a relationship with you all here. I want to have you in my life and I want to know that you are happy. But I do not want to live here forever. What he has offered me is something I hope to someday offer all of you."

The color drained out of her sister's faces, but she never stopped meeting Minerva's gaze. She wouldn't back down this time.

Minerva put her fork down. "You will stay here for the two weeks we require of you. Clearly, you are not the daughter I sent away."

"I am not." Selene stood. All the weight she'd been carrying with her seemed to drip off her shoulders as she said the words that freed her from this place. "And I don't intend to stay. If you'll excuse me."

"I'm not done speaking with you."

"But I am done speaking with you." And with that, the chains around her shoulders released. She could almost hear them clang as they hit the floor, and she left them behind in that room. Her sister's jaws remained open as she swept out of the room she'd just entered.

Selene didn't care. For the first time in her life, Minerva's opinion of her didn't matter. And by all the seven kingdoms, that was freeing.

Her feet flew up the stairs to her old room. It wasn't the highest point in the Tower, but she was breathing hard by the time she stood outside her door. Her fingers itched, her hand raised to push open the door, but her stomach twisting in fear. Did she want to do this? Could she?

Before she could overthink everything that had just happened, she heard his voice. "Get in here, Selene."

She shivered at the dark promise in his voice. Breath catching in her throat, she stepped into the darkness of her bedroom. Night had fallen quickly, and there was no light other than the candles he'd lit next to her bed. A bed that was absent of the large man she expected to see.

Instead, all she saw was darkness and furs in glimmering golden light.

His dark voice whispered in her ear, "Are you sure you want to do this?"

"I am."

That dark voice deepened even further, the rasp of a demon in her ear. "I will consume you, Selene. There's no going back."

A bargain with a demon. Never to be unmade again.

Swallowing hard, she froze as his heat pressed against her back. "I know."

"Tell me you want this."

"I do."

"Tell me you want me." A warm breath fanned where her neck and shoulder met.

"I do." She shivered again, goosebumps raising all down her arms.

"I need to hear you say it, Selene."

"I want you," she whispered, feeling like she was falling apart. "I want you, and only you, Lust. I want to feel you inside me and I want to be consumed by you."

As though the words unlocked a chain around his throat, he lunged. He grabbed her by the waist, his fingers nearly touching as he spun her around. Lips crashing down on hers, he seized one of her thighs in a punishing grip. Hiking it up over his hip, he ground himself against her as he kissed every part of her he could. Her jaw, her neck, biting at the cord of muscle there before he grabbed her hair and tilted her back. Spine bending, she dangled in his arms as he devoured her.

Kisses rained down from her throat to her chest. He snarled against her skin, little more than the demon she'd always thought him to be.

Hissing, he dragged her toward the bed. And all the while, his teeth bit down on her shoulder, leaving bite marks on her neck while he rocked against her.

Soft furs hit her back. She gasped at the sensation of warmth and heat as he crawled over her.

The light illuminated him. His eyes burned bright violet, and his horns had grown. She was certain of it. But as she reached up to trace them, trying to prove to herself that they were indeed larger, he tilted his head back. That grin, that dangerous, terrifying grin was back.

"Just how much do you want me?" he asked.

"More than you know."

"Good." His warm body poured over hers, and she felt the fabric rip. "Then I'm going to tear you out of this dress and make you scream."

That should terrify her. But all she wanted was him inside her, and it didn't matter what he said at this point.

She arched up, helping him pull all those fucking layers of fabric off her until he finally pressed himself bare to her. Her chest molded against the hard plank of his, his thigh wedged between her legs, and she rubbed her wetness against him.

He groaned at that. "So wet. All for me."

The kiss he gave her was searing, but not nearly enough. She needed him to touch her.

No, she needed to touch him.

Even as he palmed her breasts, stroking his thumbs over her aching nipples, she knew she'd never get tired of this. She ran her hands down the muscles of his back, but she wanted more. It was like he wasn't close enough, even though she could feel him all around her.

Bucking beneath him, she ripped her mouth from his to whisper in his ear, "I want to taste you."

His hand trailed between them, bumping between her breasts and down her tense stomach. She knew what he was doing before he reached his goal, but she still felt her breath wheeze from her lungs as he cupped between her legs. His fingers stroked between her folds, gathering up the wetness there before holding his fingers up for her to see. "I think I'd like to taste you first, little moon."

No, she couldn't survive it. He'd already made her come more times than she wanted to admit without ever taking anything for himself, and right now, she wanted to take care of him.

Gritting her teeth, she locked her legs around him and rolled them both. Any other time, she might not have been able to. But he was so surprised that he went with it.

And then the sight of him beneath her? She could see the heat flushing his cheeks and how affected he was. Selene brushed her hair back, astride him for the first time, and feeling ever so powerful.

Now she could look at him. She could run her fingers over his beautiful chest. She could count the freckles that dotted down his body, and the long lines that brought her to that beautiful, massive cock.

Her mouth watered. She'd never wanted to taste a man, but this one? She refused to wait.

Sliding down his body, she looked up at him as he fisted the furs at his side. "Selene, you don't—"

His voice choked as she licked him from base to tip. His head slammed back into the furs, the cords of his neck standing out in stark relief as she slowly tongued him. And if this didn't make her feel even more like a goddess. Here was a demon king in the palm of her hand, literally, and she had never felt more in control over anything in her life.

He was too thick to swallow, but she tried her best. She tongued his head until that pearlescent liquid glittered at the tip. Salty and musky, just like him, she licked it up before sucking him deep into her mouth. Over and over, she worked him until his breath was little more than a hiss from his lungs.

And then suddenly, she was flipped again. He splayed her out on the bed, breathing hard and glaring down at her like she'd done something wrong.

But his hands were gentle as he stretched her arms over her head. Arching up, she presented herself like some kind of offering for a dark god.

"You're fucking perfect," he snarled, his voice at odds with his words. "And you drive me mad."

The broad head of him settled against her entrance. Too big. She knew he would fill her to near pain and for some reason, the thought had a rush of adrenaline running right to her head. "No more than you drive me mad."

One of his hands released hers, sliding between them as he dragged his cock against her slick folds. "Are you thinking about those other men right now?"

She shook her head, biting her lip. "Only you."

"Why's that?" That flare of jealous violet grew even brighter.

"There are none worth remembering."

"Good." He pressed against her, not enough for the head to enter her, but enough so she could feel a slight burn. "You'll never remember anyone but me after this."

She spasmed, only to feel him press further into her. Stretching, aching, pulsing with so much heat, he speared through her.

A choked sound erupted from between her lips as he slid inside her with a groan that she could feel deep in his chest. Deeper, continuing, could he go any deeper? Surely not. Surely there wasn't more of him that she had to take?

Selene didn't know if she was even breathing. He drew back, and she sucked in air, only to feel it all rush out of her again as he pulsed forward, more of him pressing inside her until she felt his hips brush against hers. Seated. Fully. Stretched beyond what she'd thought she could take and so. Damned. Full.

"Beautiful," he whispered, his arm banding beneath her shoulder blades and tilting her back, sinking deeper with even that slight movement. "Absolutely beautiful."

He sucked her nipple into his mouth and started moving. Stroking inside her, slow at first and mimicking each long flick of his tongue.

Was she supposed to move? She couldn't remember. All she could do was let him hold her as he fell into a rhythm that felt so good she could already see stars. Her core spasmed around him, and he groaned again.

"Yes, baby." Lust nipped at her, the sting of pain quickly soothed with the long stroke of his tongue. "Let me feel you come."

Like lightning had struck, that was all it took. She exploded around him, clenching so hard he had to stop moving as she whimpered in his arms. She'd never felt like this before, as if the stars were close enough to touch.

As she spiraled down, he snarled in her ear. "I said to scream my name, Selene. We won't stop until you do."

And then he slammed into her. Hard. Enough for the pleasure to get brighter, and that wasn't possible. She'd come. She'd already gotten so close to the stars and every hard stroke of him seemed to prolong it. To thrust her closer to that bright pinprick of light with every movement until she was shaking her head. "What are you doing?"

"What I'm good at."

"Lust." No, it was too close to pain now. Too close to pleasure that bit and ached and shattered.

He didn't listen to her. Every hard stroke was merciless to her whimpering pleas, and he slid a hand between their bellies to press his thumb hard against her clit.

It was too much. Belatedly, she realized she could feel his power. The air was thick with it, pouring out of him in waves that wrapped around her senses until she could almost feel his own pleasure. The way he slid into her so easily and the grip of her pussy around him, how she held onto him with every retreat as though she didn't want to let him go.

She refused to endure this on her own. This was them, together, and it always would be.

Wrapping her hand around the back of his neck, she pulled him back to her lips. Snarling into his mouth, she said, "You are mine, just as I am yours. Come with me, Demon."

He bared his teeth that suddenly looked filed and sharp. And Selene opened the floodgates in her mind. All her buried lust. Years of it. Drowned out with so many emotions that came barreling out at the same time.

Though they were locked in a stare, she saw his eyes roll back in his head. His fingers flexed against her, pressing harder and circling around her clit until it was too much. The perfect feeling as those talented fingers brought her closer and closer.

He nipped at her neck. "I want to feel you come around my cock, little moon. Come for me."

Every inch of her body did. She seized around him, squeezing so hard that she could feel his own orgasm rip through him. She felt the pulse come up from the base of him as a heat spread through her. He groaned, long and low as she tilted her head back and screamed his name.

Breathing hard, she gathered up the stars in her arms and tossed them down to him. All that light and energy and brightness she would bring back to his underworld. For if he was the demon king, then she would be his willing slave for all eternity.

Arms wrapped around him, she held onto his shoulders as if he were a lifeline. Lust pressed his forehead against her shoulder, trying to catch his own breath.

And then he pulled out of her and rolled her onto her belly.

Limp, pleased beyond delight, she happily sighed. "What are you doing?"

Her eyes snapped open as he slid into her again, seemingly harder than he'd been before. "I told you, little moon." He gave her another sharp, hard thrust that left her gasping. "I'm not done with you until the sun rises."

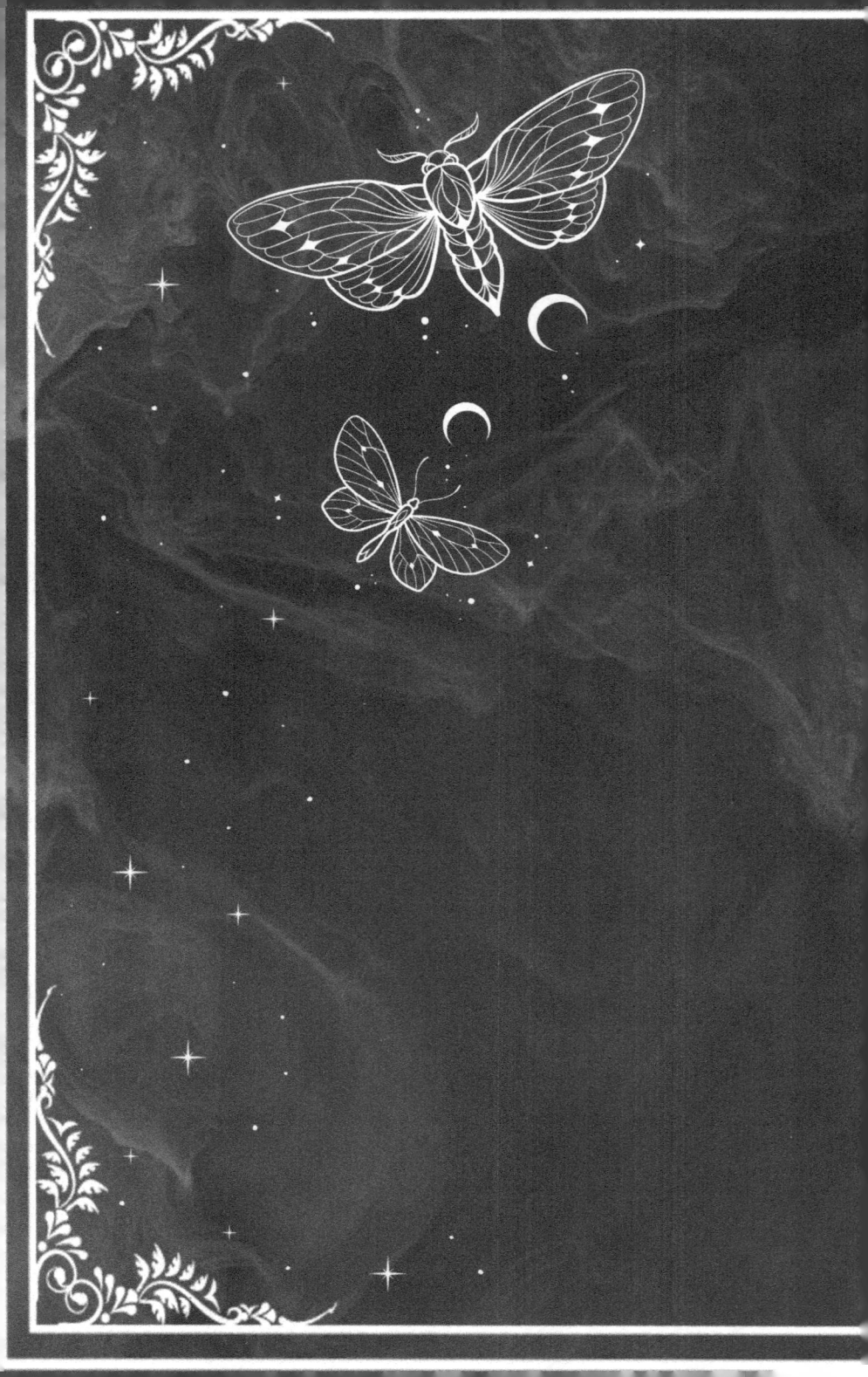

Chapter 36

He watched as the rays of the sun filtered through the thin slit of her window. Lust needed very little sleep, especially compared to his little human curled up on his chest. She was exhausted, far more than he'd thought she would be.

Perhaps he'd pushed her too far. She shifted slightly, and he smoothed a hand down her back, smiling as she settled against him. She'd started doing that in the first rest he'd given her. Only an hour or so before, he couldn't help himself. But every time she'd almost woken, all he had to do was touch her before she settled again.

It was different with her.

Oh, the slow slide into her pussy was familiar. The feeling of complete euphoria, though? He'd never been so close to the heavens until this moment. Only Pride could live there, and yet this woman brought him to the very stars.

Why? What was so different about this one? When all others had only scratched an itch or entertained him for a night or so?

The evening they'd spent together had become a feast for his senses. Even now, he felt glutted on power such as he'd never had before. He had always been a powerful spirit, and he'd gathered enough of his chosen emotion to take on physical form. Few spirits were ever so gifted. And still, somehow, there was more power for him to gather from this little mortal who had split him open from heart to soul.

Sighing, he buried his fingers in the soft locks of her hair. Lust had taken his time while she slept, gently pulling apart all the tangles he'd created. He liked the way the silky strands fell through his hands and how lovely they were laid out on her pale back.

He could stay like this for hours. Days. Centuries, if he was being honest with himself.

He'd let the world burn around them and remain in his bed with her. It was the first place where his soul finally felt complete. A soul she was so certain he didn't have.

She'd breathed new life into him, and now he didn't know what to do. Because, in a strange way, it felt like this new power wasn't his at all. It was hers.

Sighing, he tried not to think of what he had to do today. He'd promised she could see her family, and that was partly why he'd let her go. But Lust had seen the writing on the wall.

Minerva wouldn't let her pet go easily. She wanted Selene in her pocket, and Lust had changed that reality for her. Which meant Minerva would do whatever she could to get Selene back.

He wasn't sure what she'd do. But he'd seen what sorceresses could do, let alone the High Sorceress herself. There were a great many terrible things that could happen to the woman in his arms, and he'd destroy them all if that would make her safe.

The thoughts frightened him. He'd only been protective of his brothers. They were the few who he connected with, and they felt the same about him. They'd torn the world apart together to rebuild it better than it had been before. This little woman had nothing to do with that promise to the very world itself.

And yet... he would give it all up for her.

Frowning, he shook his head to clear it of those thoughts. He had to focus on the task at hand.

Minerva needed to understand that her daughter was no longer hers. The little foundling that she'd sent to sabotage him would have to be released into the wild. And he'd play dirty, if that's what she wanted.

Selene had family. Real family. He could find them in one of the villages, bring them together in the way only a god could. And if that meant he had to pay her family off to lie to her that they'd wanted her, then so be it. He would survive that lie. Selene would be happier with him than she would in this horrible, cold place.

And putting off meeting with Minerva was only him stalling the inevitable.

She moaned as he moved out from underneath her, though she didn't wake. He must have been too rough with her last night.

Lust smoothed his hand down her back, his fingers slipping between her legs just to feel her again. The mess he'd made still lingered, and he'd take care of that when he got back.

A flare of heat sizzled from the base of his spine. But first, he'd bury himself inside her one last time. Just because he couldn't resist her, even in this state.

He'd let her rest, though. She needed to sleep so he could bring her back to his castle. So he could fuck her on the ride back, then in his garden, then in their bedroom, on the balcony... Oh, there were so many opportunities.

She had much to learn about pleasure, and he wanted to show her all of it.

Dragging the blanket over her shoulders, he made sure she wouldn't be cold before he left. And then he quickly dressed, so he didn't do something foolish. Like barricade the door and roll her onto her back.

Lust tried his best not to look over his shoulder at the sleeping beauty, who would never even know he was gone. At least, if he got this over with soon.

Minerva didn't like to wait. She'd set up this meeting with a letter after he'd returned to town, apparently an attempt at being civil after their rather explosive conversation. If she wanted to play that game, he wouldn't complain. He didn't need her permission to stay the night with Selene, after all. And now she would expect to find him outside of her Tower for their meeting. He would relish the look of surprise on her face when she saw him.

Her expectations were that she'd condemned him to an uncomfortable night in his carriage. That he'd arrive, half asleep, in no state to talk with her about dangerous things like deals and who would have the castle when all of this was done.

Instead, she'd get an even more powerful version of him.

He slipped through the halls, sneaking past any of the sorceresses who were blinking through the early morning exhaustion. They were stumbling to the dining hall for coffee, most likely. A delicacy that he provided them because no one else could afford it.

Sighing, he slipped out into the courtyard and walked toward the front door. There was only one entrance here. And only one exit.

Minerva stood with her back to him, the icy wind of the mountains blasting her hair back from her face. She was beautiful. Even he could admit that. But she wasn't nearly as beautiful as his own sorceress.

Tucking his hands into his pockets, he ignored the cold. The power that he'd siphoned off Selene last night would keep him warm enough for days to come.

"You wanted to speak with me," he said, letting the wind carry his voice to her. "And yet here you are. Waiting for me like you weren't aware that I was comfortably under your roof all night."

The sorceress whirled. Her hands raised and eddies of snow gathered at her feet. The wind altered its course to cling to her form, and he knew those icy daggers that hovered in the air were sharp. Minerva liked people to think she'd gotten her position as High Sorceress because she was intelligent. And she was. But she was just as dangerous with her power as she was with that sharp wit.

"Demon," she snarled. "You are not supposed to be inside."

"No, I am not." He held his hands lax at his sides, drawing them up in a shrug. "Yet, here I am."

"True to your cursed nature."

"Now, now. That's not very pleasant to say about your new son-in-law." He tilted his head to the side and grinned. "That was the plan, after all. Wasn't it? You gave me your daughter so that you would wriggle your way back into the castle. Such a shame that she's bent to my side rather than yours."

He had the distinct pleasure of watching Minerva's face turn red with anger. She was usually such a beautiful woman, but right now?

She was ugly with rage, and that was the most rewarding thing he'd seen in ages.

"I banish you from this Tower, Demon," Minerva snarled. "If I see you within its walls, I will cut you down."

"You couldn't even if you tried."

"That has always been your greatest fault. For centuries you have underestimated those with power in your kingdom and I will be the first to watch the horror on your features when you realize just how capable we are."

He shook his head, hands turning to fists in his pockets. "Oh, you are so very wrong. Many have tried to do what you are attempting, Minerva. You are not the first person to think that you can capture me. Neither are you the first to think you could sway me, or find out secrets about who or what I am. Just be happy that you've named me demon and surrounded yourself with others who believe the same tale."

"You know I will not. Asking me to do such a thing is asking us all to deny our purpose."

"Which is?" He watched the swirl of a small storm gather around her. It made her appear as though standing in the center of a whirlpool with glittering snow and ice floating around her in wide circles. "You think your purpose is to destroy me?"

"My purpose is to rule this kingdom with the other sorceresses. This place was meant to be a Tower dedicated to the people. Our power will bring the kingdom out of a period of debauchery and lust."

He nodded slowly. "Yes, of course. That is what you would think. But you are all so incessant about that last fact, aren't you? Lust is evil. My people are feeding their baser instincts when they should be piously begging the world to forgive them for ever having such needs. The people use me as an excuse to do what their hearts desire. Is that what you think, Minerva? You call me demon because you do not want to see it in yourself."

Her mouth gaped open before shards of ice flew at his face. But she had expected him to be weak when he was not.

Lust didn't want to play all his cards just yet. He didn't want Minerva to know that while she had elemental power, he had them all. He and his brothers were more than mortal. They were spirits taken flesh, and that gave them more magic than she or any of the other sorceresses could beg to have.

So he threw up his cloak and let the ice strike it. All the while, he whispered spells beneath it so they melted on impact. She'd think someone had given him an enchanted cloak, likely another sorceress who he had seduced to perform spells in his own castle. Hubris had always been her weakness.

When the sorceress had exhausted herself, he let the cloak fall back down and straightened. "I do not have any interest in whatever madness you wish to spout, Minerva. I am merely here to tell you that the girl is mine. Not yours."

"Selene will never be yours," she hissed. "She is my daughter. I raised her for this purpose and she will never back away from it."

"She already has."

"Then she will remain here and learn again what it means to be a foundling," Minerva spat. "The old ways run deep in that girl's heart. You will never be able to trust her, Demon."

Ah, and there was the rub. Perhaps he never would be able to trust her, but damn if he wouldn't enjoy chasing her for the rest of eternity.

"Perhaps not," he agreed. "But even a week here, two, a year or more, would not turn her gaze away from me. You underestimate just how connected we are now, Minerva. Your plan has failed. So leave the girl alone and look for another to enact whatever plan you think will work next time. I don't want to destroy the Tower, but I will do it if I must."

A slow smile spread across her face, and for the first time in his life, Lust felt fear. Oil slick and ill omened, it slithered down his spine as though a snake had wrapped around him and squeezed.

"I would advise you to not get too comfortable with your new pet," she said. "She is mine, Lust. If I cannot have her, then no one can."

He did not enjoy fear. He thought it would be interesting to experience a new emotion, but no. It was terrible.

Lust stepped out of her way and gestured for her to return to the Tower. "I will give you a few days with her. That's all. Then I will come back for what is mine. I do this to prove she was never yours, Minerva. She was just waiting for me."

That sly grin never shifted from Minerva's face. "We shall see, Demon."

And he hated that he watched her go. He hated how his stomach twisted and his heart thundered in his chest, irregular and worried.

Minerva was intelligent. She had more to this plan that he'd expected and even though he knew there were countless experiences for him to draw upon, he couldn't let go of the thought that he'd missed something. And if he had? Then he was the fool, after all.

Stepping back into the snow, he started away from the Tower toward where he'd told his man to wait in the carriage. They'd return to the nearest town, at least to get out of the cold and fill their bellies before he returned for Selene. Then he would never let her go again.

"Demon!" the hissed whisper came when he was but a few steps from the Tower.

Turning, he looked back to see a woman with long hair, white as snow, and skin that glistened like a black pearl. She waited for him to make eye contact with her before she rushed forward and pressed a letter into his hand. "Don't tell anyone that you saw me."

And then she rushed back into the Tower and slammed the door in his face.

Strange.

But when had sorceresses ever made sense?

Bemused, he continued his journey. Perhaps Selene had heard that he was being sent away again and wanted to give him her goodbye. Though he doubted it, the soft thought made his heart twist in his chest. It was stupid to miss her when he'd just gotten out of her bed. But he did.

The letter unfurled in his hand, the wind wrinkling its edges as his eyes scanned the unfamiliar handwriting.

MOTHER NEVER WANTED TO LET SELENE GO. YOU HAVE RUINED THAT PLAN AND SHE WILL STOP AT NOTHING TO GET HER BACK. IF SELENE DOES NOT PLAY BY HER RULES, THERE IS A TATTOO ON THE BACK OF HER NECK. IT WAS PLACED THERE TO ENSURE NOTHING CHANGED AND THAT MOTHER'S WILL WOULD ALWAYS COME TO LIFE.

IT'S A SPELL, DEMON. A NASTY SPELL THAT WILL KILL HER.

PLEASE LET HER STAY HERE. LET HER COME BACK INTO THE FOLD. WE WILL FIND ANOTHER WAY FOR HER TO BECOME A SORCERESS, LIKE THE REST OF US. I PROMISE. I WILL DO ANYTHING I HAVE TO TO KEEP HER ALIVE.

DON'T LET HER DIE BECAUSE YOU HAD TO DEFY OUR MOTHER. IT'S HER DEATH OR YOUR LUST.

Anger surged through him. And suddenly he realized why Wrath claimed that he was the most powerful of all their brothers.

In this moment, he could have torn apart the entire kingdom. Bit by bit. Lust would rip it to shreds and listen to all the screams as the people who had denied them both peace to be with each other. He would wrap his claws around that bitch of a High Sorceress's throat so he could hear her screams. He wanted to destroy her.

Lust wanted Minerva to know what it felt like for this fear to run through her body. Would she not be able to think or breathe, either? He wanted her to know that if she laid a single finger on the woman, he... he...

The thought drew him up short. And though his fingers had turned into claws, ready to tear into whoever dared stand in front of him, he had no idea what to do with these thoughts.

He was lust. That was all he felt.

Until now. Now he felt so much more, and the raw edges of that reality nearly sent him to his knees.

Overwhelmed and bitter, he veered away from the carriage and made his way to the snowy edge of the kingdom. And he stared into the darkness below his feet until night came. This time, he swore there were knowing eyes staring back at him.

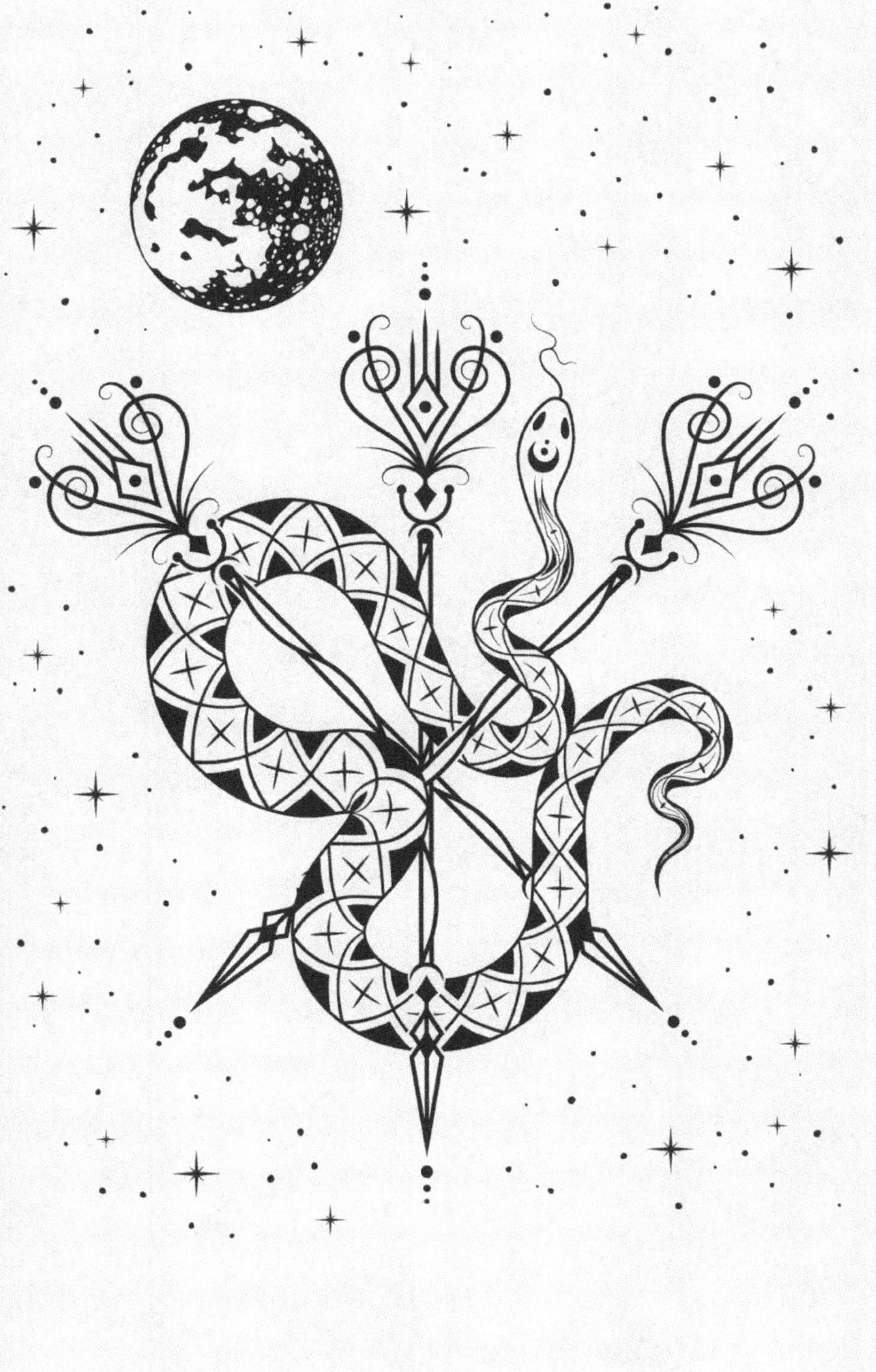

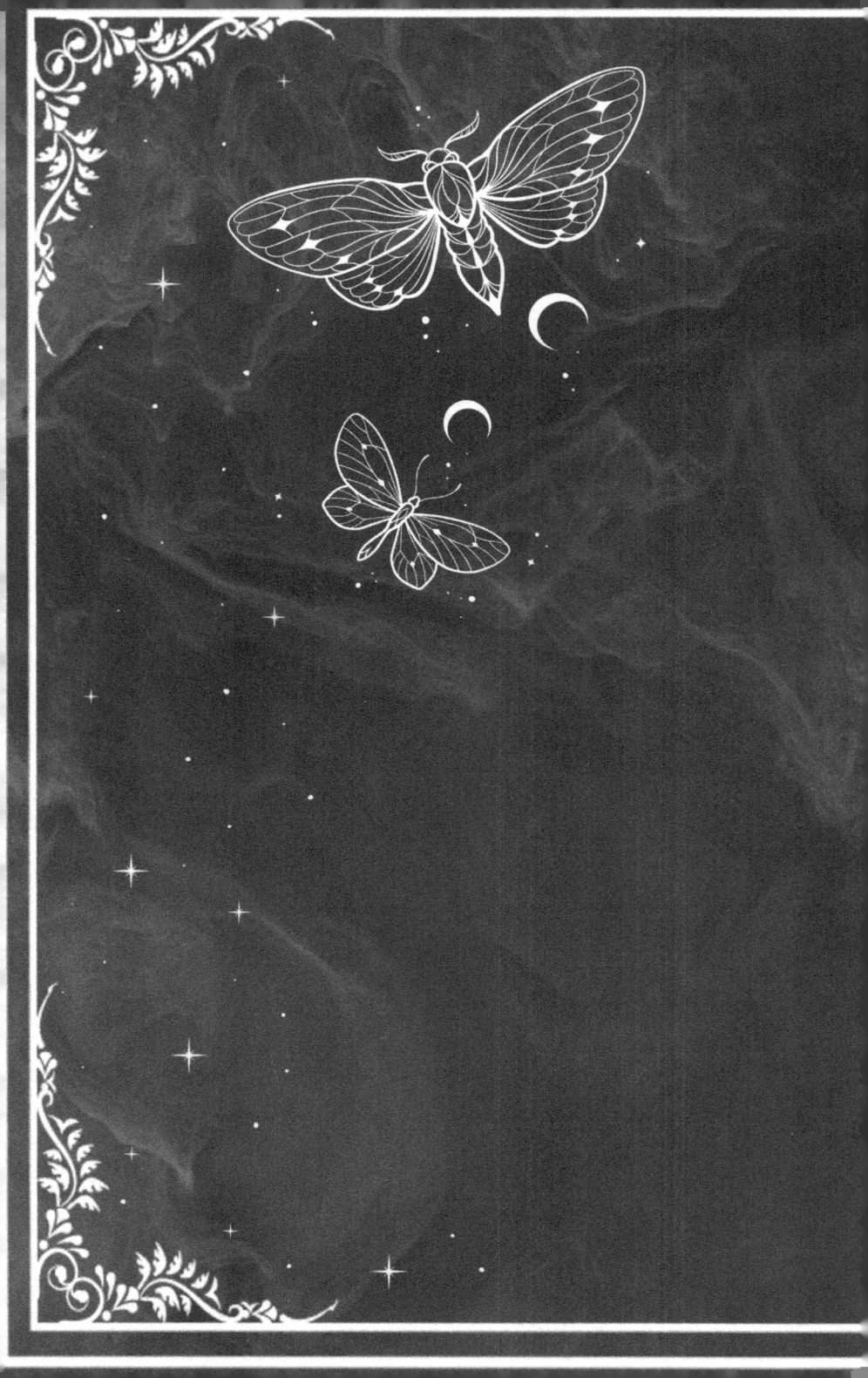

Chapter 37

Selene floated through the next few days. He'd gone back to the castle, according to Minerva, and he hadn't said goodbye to her. But she still had the faintest memory of a hazy morning wrapped in his warmth. How he'd stroked her hair like she was made of glass and how his heart beat underneath her cheek.

It was enough for a while. But by the second day, a few stray thoughts of doubt plagued her. She didn't want to think about why he had disappeared. She didn't want to think about anything other than how he'd completely changed the way she would ever view sex.

He was… magnificent. That was the only thought in her mind. She'd never truly had sex until him and now all she could think about was being in bed with him, him in her mouth, his fingers between her thighs.

She couldn't stop having those lustful thoughts, and she swore everyone else could sense it in her. Even her sisters gave her a wide berth when they walked around her.

Other than Ursula, of course. Her dearest sister who had been suspiciously absent since Selene had returned.

"Don't you have something else to do?" Selene asked as they meandered toward the dining hall. "I know how busy everyone is. It's strange to not be one of the busy ones."

Her sister laughed, and the chiming sound was like bells ringing through the halls. "I'm happy to spend time with you, Selene. Any chores can wait."

Except they couldn't. Which meant that Minerva had told Ursula to keep an eye on her. Selene wasn't foolish. She knew she wasn't welcome back in the Tower, but what she couldn't figure out was why. Beyond what she was supposed to do, beyond the meaning of her life as Minerva would say, why did her entire family seem to not want her?

Frowning, she peered into the dining room where all her other sisters waited before glancing over at Ursula with a sly expression. "Do you want to go to our hiding place again? You can tell me what's really going on in this castle."

Ursula's face paled. "Um... We shouldn't. Mother has been very strict about what we're allowed to do. You're supposed to go back to studying with the others..."

Minerva had thought putting Selene back in the same life she'd had before would somehow convince her that this was the better way to live. Or something like that. Maybe her plan was to remind Selene how nostalgic it was to be here, as though she were a child again.

"Oh, come on." She grabbed Ursula's hands and held them close to her heart. "I'll tell you all about the castle. There are so many stories to tell you about the people there, the way they live, the clothing. I haven't gotten any time with you at all since I've been home. Not really."

The words were manipulative and even she could admit that. But she couldn't go back to that cold room with the others when all she wanted was to splash the entire space with a little color. Maybe bright red, just to make them all come alive again.

"Selene..." Ursula's face paled even more and then she grabbed onto her. Ursula pulled her to the side, away from the doorway and into a small alcove that was likely intended to be a reading space. "There's something I need to tell you. You have to put all your effort into being like us again. You've changed and Mother doesn't like that."

"I know she doesn't like it." But Selene liked it. For the first time in her life, she felt as though she was doing something right. "People change, Ursula. Going to the castle, living the way they do, it would be impossible to stay the same. Did she really believe that I wouldn't change?"

"Yes," Ursula hissed. "And if you don't go back to yourself, she's going to—"

They both fell silent at the sound of rapid footsteps. The clacking of heels had them stumbling out of the alcove and standing straight. Waiting for their mother to walk past them.

"You little witch," Minerva hissed. She stalked toward Selene with no attempt at slowing. Her mother barreled into her, catching a hold of Selene's face and slamming her back to the wall. "You told him to come here, didn't you? Two weeks, Selene. That's all I asked him for."

"I didn't—" Selene tried to jerk her head out of her mother's grasp. A faint burning at the back of her neck sent panic skittering down her spine. "I don't know what you're talking about."

"The demon is here. Two weeks early," Minerva said, slamming Selene's head back against the wall even harder. "I thought I made myself very clear, Selene. No one was to summon the demon here until you were back to yourself. He has affected you in ways that none of us could ever have guessed. You are no longer my daughter, and I want her back."

A burst of anger seared through her soul. Selene shoved at her mother, catching the other woman by surprise because no other sorceress would dare touch the High Sorceress like that.

But the shove made her feel better. So, as her mother's grip loosened on her face, Selene shoved her again.

Minerva stumbled back, shock on her features as she stared at Selene as though she'd lost her mind. And maybe she had. Or maybe she was finally experiencing what it felt like to be herself.

"I'm not going to be that little girl you raised any more," she said, her voice strong and sure. "I don't want to be. This is the first time that I've gone out on my own, and the changes that may or may not happen to me are natural, Mother. You can't keep me locked up forever."

And there was her mistake.

Selene had always thought that Minerva looked at her and all the other young women like daughters. She called them all by the name. She'd taken them in. Given them a roof over their head and trained them to use their magic. No one else had done that for all the lost girls of this kingdom.

But Minerva was not the woman that Selene had been raised to believe she was.

Minerva's expression hardened. "You ungrateful little brat. I gave you everything, and this is how you repay me?"

"By becoming my own woman, yes."

"By going against everything you promised me you would do. By falling in love with a demon and selling your soul to him. You want me to believe you are more than a foundling? Then prove it. Give me something to use against him, Selene. Or you will never return to this place as my daughter."

The words stung. But not as much as they might have months ago.

Selene tilted her chin up and met her mother's triumphant gaze. "Then I will not return."

Silence stretched between them. Stunning and dark, as magic crackled between them.

"Selene," Ursula whispered. "You don't mean that."

"I will renounce this family if I must. You were not a good mother. You are not a good High Sorceress either. Everything you've done has been for yourself and I see that now. I see right through the lies and the torture and the torment. Nothing that you made me endure turned me into a better person." Selene clenched her hands into fists. "That took a demon to show me. And I'm ashamed to admit that I wouldn't have seen it on my own."

The air popped. Minerva's magic gathered at her fingertips and Selene knew that she only had a few moments to run. She'd seen what Minerva could do to those she had no use for. She knew exactly how much it would hurt, too. It was hard to forget the sizzle of lightning as it rocked through her body.

The spell that fell from Minerva's lips was not that, however. It was much darker.

Selene didn't quite recognize the words, but she heard Ursula's gasp as her sister threw herself at their mother. It was like time slowed. Ursula's frantic movement couldn't stop Minerva from whispering whatever curse flew from her lips.

Selene felt it strike her. The words opened up some darkness that they'd placed inside her. It spread inside her like wide wings, burning at the base of her neck as she realized why Minerva had painted the mark.

"What have you done?" she whispered before the doors to the Tower blasted open.

She thought she'd felt dark magic in that moment when her mother unleashed her curse? She'd been very wrong.

Evil walked into the Tower. It simmered below her feet and stretched up in dark tendrils of shadows that left dark stains in their wake. And then evil was given a voice that rumbled the very stones that held up the Tower.

"Selene." The voice called for her, and she felt it in her bones. "Where are you?"

Minerva glared at her, then gestured with an arm for her to go. "He calls for you, foundling. Your demon awaits."

And that was when it hurt. She'd given up her family, her people, all for him. For the beast who stood at the door and couldn't even give her time to make amends for what she'd done.

Panic swelled as the realization of what she'd done really settled in. Maybe she should try to fix things with her mother. At the very least, she should say goodbye to Ursula. Maybe Bathilda as well. She needed a few more days to make amends with the little girl in her chest that didn't want to leave.

Selene had a right to all that. She needed to take that time for herself and yet he was stealing that by being here too early. He hadn't given her time to heal.

Then another traitorous part of her felt vindicated. Because she'd missed him.

And even if her mother didn't want her, nor her sisters who had largely ignored her since she'd gotten back, it didn't matter. None of it mattered because he was here. For her.

Minerva read those thoughts in her mind as though she'd said them out loud. Her mother leaned closer and hissed, "You're nothing more than property to him. He's here to take back what is his, but that doesn't mean he cares for you. He's a demon, Selene. Don't forget that he has no ability to feel anything other than lust."

"Maybe that's all I need," she whispered. Then turned to make her way to the front of the Tower. She couldn't deny his order any more than her body could deny the flare of heat and the rush of wetness between her thighs as a low growl filled the tower.

"There you are," he growled. "Selene, I can taste you."

Her cheeks burned bright red, but she held her head high. She stepped around the center staircase and there he was.

Lust stood in all his glory, just as he had all those months ago. The corset around his chest was too tight, and his eyes blazed with heat. The horns on his head were larger. She had no question about that, and somehow he seemed even bigger. Which wasn't possible. Was it?

"Lust," she whispered, and his eyes locked on her. There was something in his gaze that unsettled her.

As though he were frantic to see her. As though part of him didn't think he'd ever see her again.

Why?

Ursula raced up behind her and grabbed onto her arm. "Wait, Selene, you can't go with him."

"I don't want to be here." She held onto Ursula's hand, and then gently pushed it away. "I don't want to stay where I am not wanted. Can't you see that? He wants me to be with him and I want to be with him as well. This is a good thing, Ursula. I'm sorry we have to say goodbye, though. We might be able to figure out another way to see each other."

Maybe she would get all her sisters out from under her mother's thumb. Maybe that was how she fixed this. By taking over the Tower herself, or building another one entirely. Lust would support her. He'd probably build it right next to this one just to spite Minerva.

"No, Selene, you don't understand."

Minerva stalked into the room and shoved Ursula away from her. "She is no longer your sister, Ursula. Get back with the others."

That was when she noticed all the rest of her sisters standing at the railings. One on every level. They stared down at her with cold, vacant eyes.

And Selene realized she would never convince any of them to come with her. She'd lost them the moment she defied Minerva's wishes.

"Selene," Lust snarled. "Come here."

But her eyes stayed on Minerva's, and her voice rang. "This was my home. The only one that I was ever given. I trusted you to not take it away like everyone else. I see I misplaced my trust in a woman who has no idea what that means."

She hoped her words would sink through whatever haze her sisters were stuck in. Perhaps they could see the light for a brief moment and understand that if Minerva could do this to Selene, then she could do it to any of them.

Until Minerva spoke again. "Then you should have earned that trust." Her mother's face twisted into an ugly snarl. "You should have deserved this family's love."

Oh, and if that didn't make her heart ache.

She thought she had deserved their love. She'd always thought that she had given enough to this family for them to at least love her

the demon court

back. Was it so much to ask for someone to love her? For someone to care that she existed?

Hands shaking, she clutched her heavy skirts so no one would see. Instead, she squared her shoulders and walked toward her demon king.

He eyed her with those glowing purple eyes, and they lingered on every part of her. As though he could see right through her fear, right through her skin, and he needed to make sure not a single part of her was harmed. When he met her gaze, she knew the moment he saw her heart breaking. He bared his teeth in a terrible snarl, and she swore she saw his skin ripple.

With those sharp teeth bared, he turned that icy gaze to her mother. "You will pay for this, Minerva."

"I will pay for nothing." Minerva's eyes glazed over Selene, and she couldn't help but wonder what the two of them knew that neither of them had shared. "You, Demon, will be the one to pay. I cannot say I am shocked that this happened. But I will admit, I couldn't have planned it better if I tried."

The snarl that ripped out of him was nothing short of beast-like. "She is mine, Sorceress. And I will tear this world apart if you touch so much as a hair on her head."

Why would her mother ever hurt her?

But then Selene looked back and saw the determination in Minerva's gaze. Her entire body went ice cold, and Selene gently touched a finger to the mark on her neck.

She wouldn't. Would she?

Lust slipped a clawed hand behind her back and turned her toward the doors. Selene let him guide her from the Tower without ever looking back.

She was afraid of what she'd see if she did.

Chapter 38

She'd thought she would be prepared for this. Selene had known that there was a good chance her family wouldn't want her there. Denying her mother of the one thing she wanted, control, was another good reason for them all to leave her behind.

But she'd still thought that at least someone would stand up for her. Someone would care enough to at least say goodbye, even if Minerva didn't want them to.

None of them had.

She'd walked out of the Tower with Lust's hand on her back. He practically vibrated with anger, a hulking monster who stood behind her while he fought to control his own rage. It was terrifying and fearsome, and she had no idea what to do with him.

He had cared about her enough to come back. But he'd also been the one who caused this issue. If it weren't for him, she could have stayed. She'd never have become this person who wanted to see more of the world. She'd never have wanted to become someone else.

And that... hurt.

Everything hurt. Her heart. Her mind. Her soul.

The carriage ride back to the castle—only a few days after they'd departed—was much different. This journey was quiet. She kept her tongue laced within her mouth for fear of crying. And every time she looked at him, it was as if the demon king was barely holding himself together.

Again and again her mind went back to that moment when he and her mother had looked at each other and some dark knowledge had passed between them. They shared some dangerous information. Information about Selene that neither of them had told her.

Her heart twisted every time she thought of it. Selene just wanted one person to trust in this world. How had she been so foolish as to fall back into that desire? She'd learned a long time ago women like her didn't get to hope for someone to be a white knight or an armored prince coming to save the day.

She had to save herself. Because no one else would do it for her.

In too short of a time, the carriage rolled up to the castle. She gathered up the shredded pieces of her dignity and folded them around her body like a shield. No one would know she was upset. No one in this castle would think anything beyond wondering why her expression had hardened into a mask.

A crew of people stood at the ready, waiting for the order from their king. Selene was thrown back to the moment she'd arrived, when they were all shocked to see him leave the carriage with a woman.

And yet, this time, they actually looked at her. Not with curiosity or surprise, but concern the moment they realized she was not quite herself.

These people barely knew her. And they were more concerned for her wellbeing than her own family.

Looking around, Selene realized they'd always been more concerned for her. They'd always wanted to welcome her into their home with warm arms. She'd been the one to deny them that, and eventually, even the kindest person would give up.

This was all her fault.

All of it.

Swallowing hard, she shoved all those emotions down until she felt nothing. She was nothing. Just an empty vessel without a soul.

It was suddenly overwhelming to have so many eyes on her. Even if they were concerned or caring, none of those eyes were what she wanted. She didn't want anyone to realize that she was struggling or to know that her entire world had flipped upside down and she felt like a broken doll tossed aside by a child who no longer needed it.

Her eyes locked on Greed as he sauntered down the steps. His handsome face had curved into a devious smile, and his tail flicked behind him with obvious aggression.

"You're home early," he called out. "Did you finally see reason and realize those sorceresses are nothing more than puppeteers?"

"Greed," Lust snarled behind her, and a wall of heat pressed against her back. "Now is not the time."

"Not the time for the truth? There's always time for that."

"You're thoughtless with your words," Lust snarled. "Neither of us are entertained by your blind idiocy."

A small wrinkle appeared between Greed's eyes, and it was the first time she'd ever seen him frown. "You're testy today. Why? What happened?"

Lust didn't let anyone else question her. He used his body to physically move her up the steps, forcing her beyond the others and through the great hall. The pools of water rippled as they hurried past. And then she was in his arms.

He'd scooped her up, turning her face to his chest and holding her legs around his waist with one arm underneath her bottom. He hurried up the stairs, ignoring the startled gasps and whispered rumors that had already started.

She wasn't even sure how he'd carried her with all the folds of fabric between them, but he did. And the warmth of his body soaked into hers. Trembles started, and she shoved those emotions down too. Over and over again until they were in their bedroom and she didn't know how they'd gotten there.

His heavy boots struck the floor in a harsh staccato as he strode toward their bed, spun around, and then sat on the edge with her in his lap. He banded his arms around her, too tight, squeezing the air out of her lungs as though he needed the comfort as well.

With a soft sigh, Lust buried his face in the side of her neck and pressed a single kiss to her throat. "Are you all right?"

"I'm fine." Even her voice sounded wrong.

"You're fine?" he snarled, lifting his head to glare into her eyes. "You aren't fine, Selene. I can see it in your face."

No, he couldn't. She had no expression at all, and she knew it. The numbness was spreading down to her fingers, and she had the dull thought that maybe she was hurting herself. Maybe she was using her power too much.

What if she couldn't ever feel again? Would that really be so bad?

His gaze searched hers, and then hardened. Apparently, he'd seen something he didn't like. "You're doing it again, aren't you?"

"Doing what?"

He cupped the back of her neck, forcing her to not hide from him. "Feel it, Selene. You have to feel it."

"I don't know what you're talking about."

The tips of his fingers turned into claws, pressed against the sensitive sides of her neck. "You know exactly what I'm talking about. They didn't want you, Selene, and that's bound to hurt. Avoiding it will only make it worse later. You are not cold and you are not empty. You are not whatever they made you believe that you are."

Though she still couldn't feel the emotions, a single tear tracked down her cheek. Warm and wrong and oh so weak. "I don't want to feel any of that."

"But you have to." He smoothed the tear away with his thumb. "You have to feel it, little moon, so you don't forget it. They were wrong for what they did. You didn't ask them to give you up. You didn't ask for them to make you feel unwanted."

The ice in her heart cracked. It hurt. Zings of emotions rolled through her as more tears tracked down her cheeks. "I'm afraid they were right. No one has ever wanted me, and I'm so afraid that no one ever will."

His hands spasmed against her back, and his jaw tightened. She watched something flip over inside him, like she'd stuck a knife in his very heart.

"You think I don't want you?" he asked, his hand shifting down her back. Pops of fabric followed his movement as her bodice slowly gave to the sharp claws growing larger on his hands. "I'm not a man of words, little moon, but I will show you just how needed you are."

Her heart stuttered in her chest. An answering rush flooded between her legs because yes, she needed this, she needed to forget for a little while. And he could help her forget.

Selene wrapped her arms around his neck and kissed him. She poured all her emotions into him and he took them without complaint. He gathered her up in his arms, standing as her dress fell away from her.

"I won't be gentle," he said against her lips. "I'm not making love to you."

A pang of pain rocked through her. "I know."

He never would. She knew that. They both knew he could feel nothing beyond lust, and that was all right. She'd take what she could get.

He turned her in his arms, standing her in front of the full-length mirror. She was entirely naked in the arms of a demon, and he looked like one. The curved horns on top of his head jutted toward the ceiling. The sharp features of his face were cast with shadows across hard angles. Every part of him seemed larger, more immense, making her appear even smaller in his arms.

Lust trailed his hand between her breasts, flattening his palm on her stomach as he cupped her jaw with the other hand. He forced her to look into her own eyes in the mirror.

"I need you," he growled, his voice low and echoing in her ear. "Your biting wit. Your insults. Your laughter. I need your heart that beats for the people of this kingdom. I do not want you, Selene. I need you. And I will stop at nothing to have you."

He bit down on her neck. His hands roved over her body, squeezing her breasts, delving between her legs. His groan echoed as he found her wet was nearly enough to send her to her knees.

"You want a distraction, Selene, and I will give you one. You trust me, and now we're going to test that trust."

And though the words made her throat feel like it was closing, she nodded.

Lust moved past her and pulled out a bundle of ropes from one of his drawers. They looked similar to the ones he'd used to create the dress for her, but now she had a feeling it would be for a very different purpose.

He unraveled them, taking his time as he explained what he was going to do.

"We'll start easy. No need to scare you. But you'll put your entire trust in me, in the ropes, that neither of us will drop you. Do you understand?"

Again, she nodded. It felt impossible to speak.

Lust rounded behind her and looped the ropes over one of her shoulders, twisting them between her breasts before he flung it over her other shoulder. As he wound them underneath her breasts, safely around her ribs until she was presented to him with rope twisting around each globe, he whispered compliments against her skin.

"You're so good," he breathed against her neck as he finished tying around her chest. "You're so beautiful like this."

Heart racing, she said nothing as he bent in front of her and started winding another rope around her thigh. Twin circles that bit into her flesh as he tightened them a little too tight.

He stared up her body, holding onto the ends of that rope with both hands. "You once asked me why I wore the corsets, and I said it's because I enjoyed the pain. There will be some pain with this, but not enough to scare you. Not my little moon."

"How bad?"

"Only enough to leave a few marks. The same as a corset."

Lust flicked his gaze to the ceiling. Selene glanced in that direction and noticed hooks that she'd never seen before. And as she watched, he threw the ropes over each one. Secure, safe, held in his hands.

But then he pulled on the rope attached to her thigh and lifted her leg. "Look at you," he whispered against her neck, securing the rope to the bed frame and then circling behind her. "So pretty and wet. Perfect for me."

Selene didn't recognize herself in the mirror. The red flush on her cheeks had spread down her neck and chest. Her breath rattled as she waited for him to do whatever he wanted to her. This wasn't the Selene she knew and maybe, just maybe, that was all right.

"You're going to take me like the good girl you are," he said gruffly. "And you're going to forget everything. I can give you that."

She leaned her weight against his chest, hearing his belt hit the floor and then feeling the hard flesh of him, warm and overheated, pressing against her entrance.

He hadn't lied. This wouldn't be a long, slow seduction. Not like the first time.

He pushed inside her, only wedging himself in halfway before he withdrew. With each movement, he rocked himself deeper. Easing further and further until she was too full, too sensitive, too much.

With her head against his shoulder, she watched the way his jaw clenched as he maintained control over himself. He stared at them, at their reflection, as though he'd never seen anything more perfect.

The other rope was still in his hand, and slowly he tugged it. Her foot dangled above the ground, just on tiptoe if she wanted to hold onto that control. But she didn't. She trusted him.

Lust grabbed her throat, tilting her head so she could look nowhere else but their reflection. At the way his hand ringed her neck, her knee hooked over his elbow, the slow glide of his cock slipping into her pussy. Back and forth, in and out, it was almost too much. More than she could take in this moment when she felt so breakable.

The ropes bite into her thigh as she struggled to free herself for a moment before letting him take control again. She wanted to do something other than hang here, completely at his mercy. She needed…

Him.

That's all she needed.

"Look at me, Selene." He moved his hand from her throat, and she couldn't stop herself from watching it glide down her body.

Fingers touched her sensitive clit, and she hissed out a long breath as he started slow, deliberate circles. A low groan ripped out of her throat.

"That's it," he said. "I want to hear you."

She tilted her hips, and he hit a spot inside her that she hadn't known existed. Selene threw her head back, mouth open on a string of moans that grew louder with each long, languid stroke. His fingers… she needed to tell him to… Yes, that. Harder, more intent, deliberate.

He played her body like an instrument he'd mastered. The orgasm hit her hard, rocking through her body as she saw stars.

"Good girl," he growled in her ear. "Now we can start."

Start? Hadn't they already?

He slammed into her so hard her orgasm didn't have a chance to stop. He prolonged it with his movements, pounding into her as he stretched her legs even wider. Suddenly she was tighter, clamping down on him as another orgasm chased the first.

The ropes dug deeper into her skin, never hurting or tearing but enough to remind her that she was suspended from the ceiling. They bit around her breasts. Their rough texture turned her thigh red around them.

Hot breath played down her neck to her sensitive breasts. She wanted to touch them, but the only thing she could do was hold on to him as he lifted her weight in his arms. She had nothing to hold but him, and her world shifted on its axis.

A third orgasm chased the others, impossible to consider that she'd come so many times in such a short amount of time, but she had underestimated a spirit of lust.

If he wanted her to come, she would come.

Letting out a keening cry, she arched into him the exact moment he shoved into her as deep as he could go. His teeth clamped down on her neck and they both groaned into each other.

She could feel his cock pulsing, and his seed already dripping down her legs. She was overheated, and somehow still not close enough to him.

He unraveled the ropes from her body slowly. Taking his time with her so she could see the red marks left there, the welts that looked exactly like ones the corset had left on him.

They didn't hurt, so much as heighten the feeling of her being completely and utterly owned. She felt blood rushing to the areas the ropes had restricted. She felt the clench of her aching pussy and how much she wanted him back inside her. The rush of sensation and emotions was exquisite.

Pressing another kiss to her neck, he cleared his throat and whispered against her skin, "I have spent my entire life in service to others. Giving them what they want so that I could experience their pleasure. I have wanted for nothing. I have been given a kingdom, a castle, servants, and countless partners throughout the centuries. And I have never wanted anything more than I want you. You make me whole, Selene."

And that was all it took.

The final layer of ice inside her shattered like a broken mirror. The shards embedded themselves throughout her body, but this time, Selene did not run from them. She didn't run from him.

She turned in his arms as the tears fell and he gathered her up against his heart. Carefully. So gently. Like he knew how breakable she was.

Lust lifted her and carried them both to the bed. He got underneath the covers with her, holding her as close as he possibly could as she cried for the family she should have had. The family she could have been given. And for all the opportunities she'd missed to make a better one herself.

It took a long time for her to feel everything again, as he'd told her to do. But once she had emptied herself of all that emotion, she felt better.

Selene realized he traced his fingers over the red marks on her thighs. Lust dragged his touch up her sides to the ones just underneath her breasts, gently trailing along them like she had done to him.

As she slid into sleep, draped across his chest, she whispered, "I need you too, Lust."

"I know."

"Not because I want you, or for anything you give me." She pressed a kiss over his heart. "I lo... I like you for who you are, Lust. I think you're a good person underneath all that flash and ridiculous glitter."

Seven kingdoms, she'd almost admitted how strong her feelings for him had become. She hoped he didn't notice the almost slip of her tongue. But then again... Maybe that wouldn't be so bad.

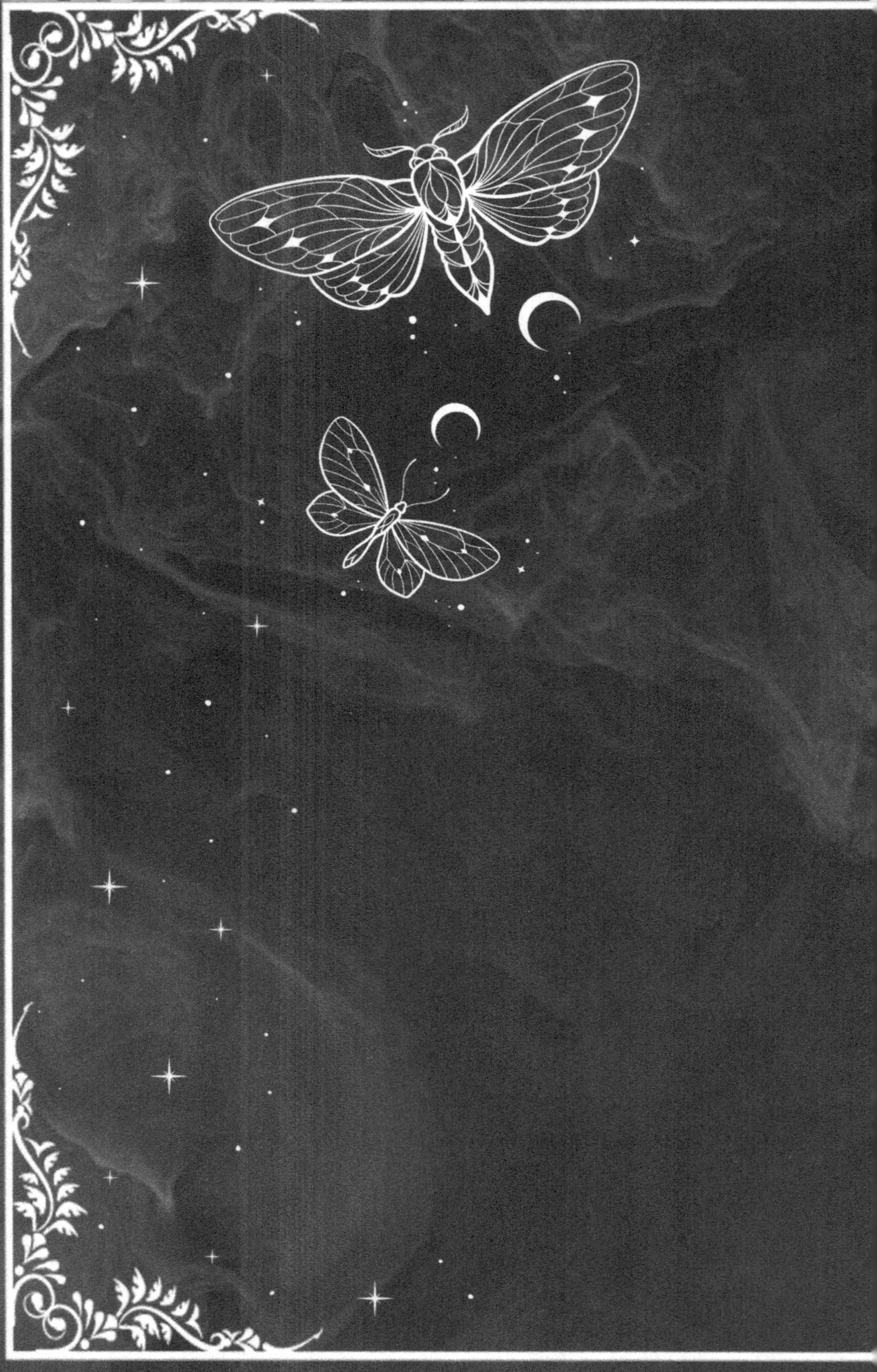

Chapter 39

His heart shattered the moment hers did. It broke him to hold her as she cried, and he knew there was nothing he could do to fix this. Her family didn't want her. She'd grown up with the fear that no one would ever want her. She'd been abandoned, forgotten, and then told she had no value other than her use to her family. And she'd no longer been useful.

If he could take the pain, he would. He would rip Minerva to shreds and feed Selene her still beating heart if it would make his little sorceress feel better. And yet, he knew it wouldn't.

This was a wound she needed to heal for herself, and all he could do was wait.

Time wasn't on their side. He let her rest in their room for a few days while he scoured their library for whatever answer he could get. Minerva would try to kill her. The mark on her neck was the key source of that, and he'd already sketched it while she was asleep.

There had to be some explanation in his library. Some book to help him understand what spell Minerva had used and what might help him prevent that spell from ever taking life.

Except there wasn't. Lust spent hours every day trying to figure it out, and when he couldn't, he tore pages out of books and shattered windows in his rage.

He had to save her. He had to do something other than just sit here and wait for the others to attack her. And some part of him knew that if he didn't do something, then he was waiting for her to die.

A small mist fluttered out from underneath the door and then stood. Affection. The little spirit had grown yet again. It straightened its spine and stood as tall as his waist, though it didn't look like a child. It appeared to be a smaller sized... person.

With a mop of hair on top of its head, lips and nose all in the right places, Affection looked very much like one of his court nobility. Although, it wasn't male or female. Apparently, it hadn't chosen yet.

"What are you doing in here?" Affection asked, its voice soft.

"She's dying." He slumped in his chair, legs spread wide and chest still heaving. Pages floated in the air around him, still fluttering down onto the floor with the quiet hush of the earth anticipating a storm. "And there's nothing I can do to stop it."

Affection's eyes wandered over him and the mounds of paper nearby. "So, you are destroying the library?"

"I am destroying every book that doesn't have the answer I seek."

"What if it contains an answer for later?" Affection stepped over one pile, and the movement of its body was unnerving. "Books have lots of answers, and not all of them are for the present."

"I don't need your philosophical scolding right now."

"I'm not scolding you. I'm telling you that you need to talk with her." Affection sighed, and then grumbled something under its breath that sounded like, "For two people who are so fond of each other, you both ignore the other a lot."

"Excuse me?" He stood up, pacing from one side of the library to the other. "I don't think you understand what I'm doing here. It's my job to fix this. I was the one that took her in from the sorceresses. If I hadn't done that, then she wouldn't be cursed. I could have saved her if I wasn't so selfish."

"But then you never would have known her."

"At least she would have been safe. She'd be alive, and that's all that matters, isn't it? I wouldn't have to be afraid that she was going to die at any second, and she would be back with her family, who likely would love her more than I can."

And there it was.

His greatest fear.

By the seven kingdoms. A hole opened up in his chest and he suddenly felt like he could fall into it at any second. She deserved someone to love her, more than someone who just needed or wanted her. She deserved a man who would feel the entire island shake every time she looked at him.

He didn't know how to love. He didn't know how to feel much of anything other than lust, and that wasn't fair to her. It wasn't fair for him to keep her.

A small hand slipped into his, and he looked down at Affection with surprise. "You are putting a lot of responsibility on your own shoulders, Lust. You need to talk to her. To tell her how you feel and what you know. Together, you can fix this."

"I broke her," he whispered. "What right do I have to beg her to put herself back together after what I have done?"

"It is not your fault. It is not hers either. Bad things happen in this world, and all you can do is rely on each other." Affection squeezed his hand before the sensation faded and it returned to a being made only of light. "You have given me much strength, Lust. That is a beautiful thing."

"Are you going to take mortal form, then?" No other spirit had in a very long time, but he wouldn't mind having another like himself. A new spirit who would experience new things might liven the place up.

"I don't think that is my destiny," Affection replied with a soft smile. "I think I'm needed more like this."

"You will always be welcome here, my friend." He patted his hand through the bright mist. "Now where is she?"

"The gardens, last I checked." Affection shrugged. "But I think it's likely she's near the edge. She's been finding herself there more and more lately."

A spike of fear shattered through his chest. "Why?" Was she thinking about throwing herself off it? He wouldn't allow that. He'd plunge into that darkness with her and he didn't care if the beast underneath their kingdoms devoured them both. At least they would be together.

Again, Affection shrugged. "She said it makes her feel small. And I don't know why she'd want to feel like that, but I think it makes her feel better."

Of course. She didn't want to feel like herself. All she wanted was a distraction from the emotions she'd hidden for years. At least she was feeling them, though. And at least he could help distract her when she needed it.

He left the library and the glowing spirit behind. Instead, he turned his attention to the gardens and to the spot he'd brought her when they first decided to trust each other. That memory felt so far away now that he thought of it.

He remembered how feisty she was. Selene hadn't wanted to trust him in the slightest, and she'd fought him tooth and nail the entire time they worked toward that trust. But he had gotten through to her, just as she had gotten through to him.

Lust wasn't alone anymore. If he needed her, Selene would come running, because that was what she was good at. In knowing that she was there for him, even through the hardest part of her own life, he had become stronger. So much stronger.

Though it took him a while to find her, Lust paused when he finally did. Selene stood on the edge of the cliff, the wind whipping in her hair and the jagged thorns of roses surrounding her. The sky beyond disappeared into the darkness below her feet. Dark hair tangling around her shoulders, she wore a dress from his own closet. Ropes twisted around her shoulders and hips, holding the pale lavender fabric against her skin, though it revealed every inch of her lovely curves.

So many words were left unsaid between them. He knew he had to tell her everything that he knew, and yet he wanted to taste her again. He wanted to lay her out on the barren ground that prepared for winter and pepper her frozen skin with kisses until she glowed with heat.

This woman meant more to him than he'd ever imagined. And he didn't know how or when that had happened.

"Selene," he said, his voice quiet and whipped away by the wind. "Come away from the edge."

Her toes curled over the stone as her eyes stared down into the nothing beyond. "I'm not going to jump."

"Good, because I would follow you." And he didn't like the thought of it. He took a few more steps closer and then wrapped his arm around her waist. "I don't believe Wrath would enjoy the company."

"Is he really down there?" she asked. "I thought the islands floated around each other. Like planets around stars."

"Some of them do." He rested his chin on her shoulder, holding her back to his chest so he could feel her heart beating. Even that wasn't close enough. "Pride is above us all. His kingdom is the clouds, while Wrath's is in the underworld."

"Neither of those sound pleasant," she whispered. "I don't think I'd want to be in either kingdom. I want to be here, with my feet firmly grounded."

That was enough flirting with certain death. He dragged her away from the edge, keeping her pressed against him because he was so afraid that his words would be the end of this. Of them.

"We have a lot to figure out," he said, allowing her to turn in his arms. "Your mother provided me with a complicated problem and I have discovered I do not know how to fix it on my own."

Selene looked up at him with those night sky eyes and he almost lost all his breath.

She knew.

Her entire body simmered with sadness and he knew without a doubt that she already knew the words that were about to come out of his mouth. His little moon was so intelligent, he shouldn't be surprised that she'd figured it out on her own.

"She cursed me," Selene said quietly. "I don't know the words or the spell, though. So I don't think there's much we can do."

He shook his head in denial. "There is something. We will figure it out. One of your sisters gave me a letter that claimed the symbol on the back of your neck is the marker for the curse."

And because he couldn't not touch her, Lust tunneled his hand underneath her hair and traced the dark mark. He knew exactly where it was. The damned mark was one he'd looked at many times. He'd even imagined tracing his tongue over it, wondering if that would give her pleasure.

Now he hated it.

"How long have you known?"

Oh, and he hated that expression on her face. The one where she disappeared from him. Dipping into the darkness of her own mind as she struggled to get away from these emotions. "Not long. Otherwise, I would have figured out how to break the curse."

"It's not your job to do so."

"It is." He surprised himself with the ferocity in his voice. "It's my job to keep you safe. You are mine, Selene. And I would do anything to keep you."

"You might not be able to." She seemed so resigned. As though the words were all she had been waiting for before her soul could let go of all the pain. "Minerva wants me dead because I disappointed her. We should make good use of the time we have left."

The snarl that erupted from his chest wasn't human. Not at all. "You will fight this, Selene. You will battle and rage and tear at the world until this curse is broken. Do you hear me?"

Her features smoothed, the vacant expression he hated so much like a mask of ice over her face. "I'm tired of fighting, Lust. I'm tired of all this."

Panic turned his heart into a drum. He framed her face with his hands, smoothing his thumbs over the high peaks of her cheekbones as his thoughts scattered to the winds. "No, no, that's not you. You're the sorceress who stood in the wake of a demon king and bent him to your whims. You're far too brave to give up that easily, Selene."

He expected some kind of reaction. Tears. Anger. A fight in her that should be there even through all this. But there was nothing left at all. She'd hidden herself from him again.

And it made him angry.

After all he'd done, all he'd proven to her, she thought she could recede into her mind? No, he wouldn't let her. He'd drag her kicking and screaming into this world if he had to, but at least she would be here.

"You're not dead yet," he snarled. "I know Minerva wants you to think that she has everything planned out, but all she did was give us another obstacle."

"Some are too big to crawl over."

"This is one we can beat together. You're a sorceress. You grew up in her home! Selene, you have to know more than I do." Had his voice become frantic? He couldn't focus on what he was saying in his desperation to reel her back in. "Get mad at me. Hit me if you wish, because I brought you here. I showed you what this world could be and broke through that ice in your heart. I made you want to change. So take it out on me."

"I don't want to be mad at you, Lust." Finally, something in that gaze softened, but it wasn't the way he wanted. She didn't look like she was coming back to him. If anything, this felt like goodbye. "You showed me what I really wanted, Lust. You made me feel like a person again."

"You aren't this," he whispered, drawing her forward so he could press their foreheads together. "Where did you go, little moon?"

"Somewhere you cannot follow."

"There is no such place. I will shatter this realm if I lose you."

"Don't put that on me." Selene shook her head, slowly rotating back and forth against him. "Don't make me the reason this kingdom falls."

"It's already at your feet." Didn't she understand? How did he tell her what she wanted to hear? How did he use words to explain to her that she was his heart, and it only just begun to beat?

After a thousand years of life, he had finally started to live. He couldn't lose that. Not now.

She took a deep, shuddering breath. "I do not know of a way to fix this. There is no spell that can remove the mark on my neck, just as there is no way we can convince Minerva to spare me."

"I will give them the castle."

"You will do no such thing." Her voice deepened, snapping with anger as he'd hoped. Selene ripped herself away from him.

His arms feel empty at his sides as she glared at him, the wind thrashing her hair against her cheeks like the lashing of whips. Her eyes sparked like an avenging goddess and he'd never thought her more beautiful than in this moment.

"Your kingdom comes first," she said. "Your kingdom over a single subject. Your court above one person. You cannot, and will not, give up everything that you have fought so hard to build."

"I would lay it at your feet if it will keep you alive."

"Then you are a fool," she hissed. Selene wrapped her arms around her waist like she needed someone to hold her. His fingers itched to do just that. "Let me die, Lust, if that is what it takes to keep them away from your castle and your throne."

He shook his head. "Tell them everything about me, then. Give away all my secrets and let me shoulder the pain."

"You do not know what they would do to you."

"After a thousand years, I don't care." He took another step closer and touched her again. He slid his fingers along her strong jaw and deep into her hair. "I can finally feel more than just lust. I can feel you, Selene. No sorceress will change that. No pain could end that. We're connected, you and I. I know you feel the same."

Her breath shuddered in her chest. Selene stood on her tiptoes and pressed their lips together, a soft kiss that seared him to the bone. "I have always known who you are, Lust. And I have accepted that you can feel nothing more than what you were made to feel. You don't have to lie to me just because I'm dying."

She slipped out of his arms and disappeared back into the castle, leaving him standing on the edge of the world. The tattered edges of his heart ripped open in the wake of her words.

He hadn't realized how afraid he was that she might be right.

the demon court

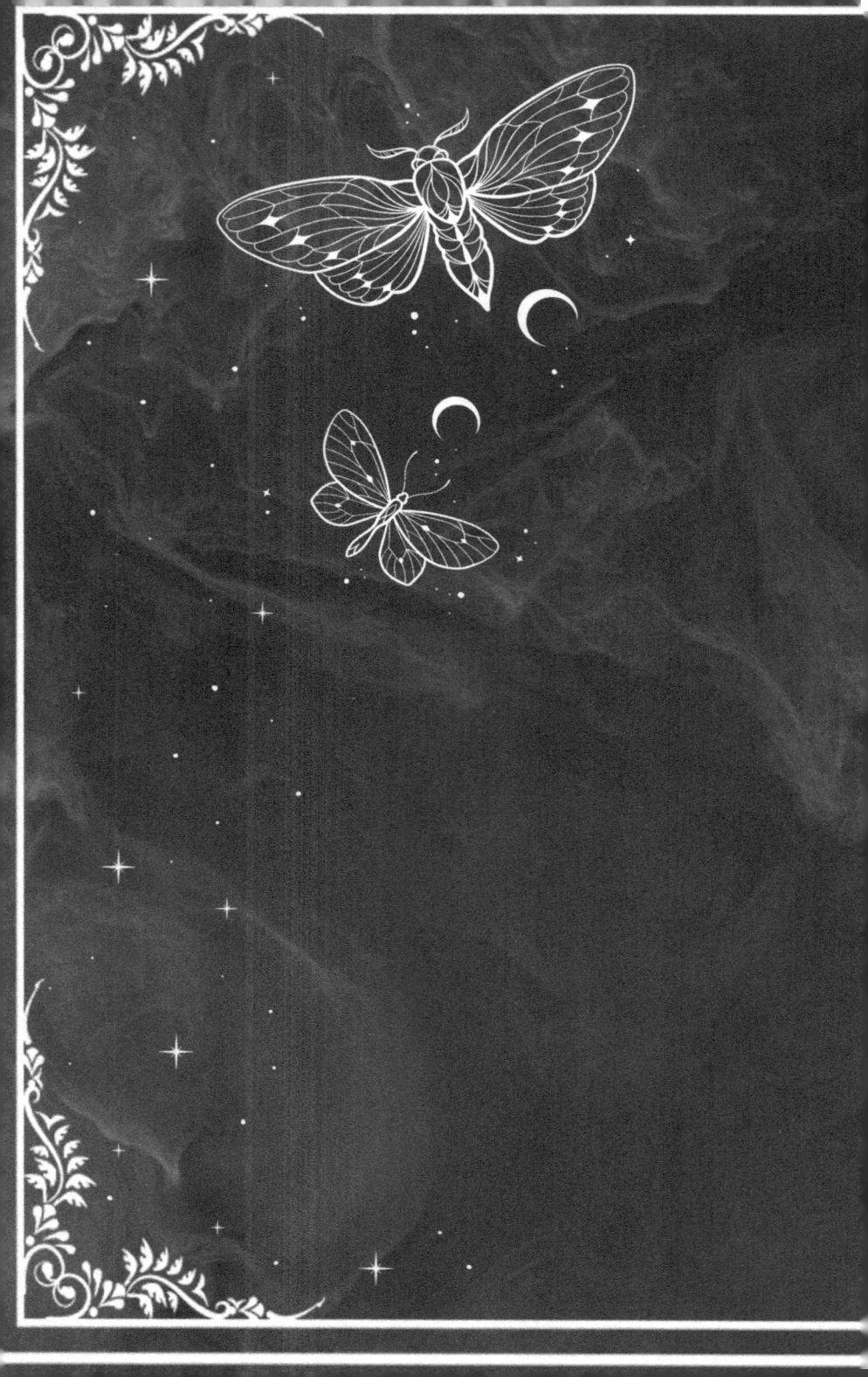

Chapter 40

She hated to lie. Especially when that lie was for him.

Selene knew there was only so much time she had left. The curse Minerva had struck her with was an unfamiliar one, and that meant there was very little she could do to prevent it from growing stronger.

Already she could feel it underneath her skin. It slithered like snakes, thick and rolling inside her, so they made it hard to sleep. All she could think about was the vile nature of them, consuming her as they moved slowly throughout her body. Spreading until they would all strike as one, and then she would know what it felt like to die.

It was not a comfortable death. Nor a quick one. The same death that Minerva had promised her enemies time and time again.

Hadn't Selene listened to her rants more than any other sorceress?

She'd been Minerva's closest daughter. Her mother had trained her from the very first moment that she remembered, and likely before that. As Lust had said when he first saw her, Selene was her puppet.

And once those strings were cut, Minerva had no more use for her.

The only way to live and get out of this situation once and for all wasn't to waste time trying to figure out how to break a curse that could not be broken. It was time to go home. To beg her mother's forgiveness and to prostrate herself on the cold stone floors of the Tower.

It took a bit of finagling to figure it out. Lara had been particularly helpful. She'd originally thought the other woman would only give her the servant's map of the castle to get rid of her. Without Selene, Lara could slip back into his favored position.

Now she suspected a second explanation. Lara didn't love him, and she didn't want Lust in her life any more than she wanted any other. But her daughter needed looking after, and she had more family back home that required payments from her every month, so they didn't die. And Lara was the only one working. Being in the favor of the king certainly helped with all those matters.

Selene didn't blame her for trying her best to survive. Wasn't that what they were all doing?

Map in hand, then she only had to distract Lust so she could slip away. Lara had offered her a warm cloak, and Selene didn't think there was much else she'd bring. It was all too easy.

Selene barricaded their door for a night, though keeping him out proved to be very difficult.

They argued through the door for hours. Lust grew more and more angry before all of that emotion seemed to seep out of him.

"I don't know how many more nights you have," he whispered

through the door. The sound of his voice was wrong. Broken. "I won't waste a single one of them."

Perhaps he gave up at that moment. He said nothing else after that. But she could only imagine the thoughts running through his head. She fed his fears while keeping him away from her. Selene didn't need or want him anymore, and wasn't that what she had said to him so many times?

Except she did.

She needed him more than she wanted to admit, and it hurt to her very core to do what she had to do. Tears burned her eyes until she couldn't take it anymore. She wanted to throw all those emotions back underneath the magic she'd always used as a crutch and never think about them again.

But then she remembered him. She remembered how Lust had begged her to feel those emotions and she couldn't do it. She couldn't tuck them away when he would want her to feel.

And so she felt them throughout the entire night and into the early morning. Until the silence on the other side of the door finally let her know he had gotten up and left her alone.

Now was her moment. She had to sneak out through the servant's quarters and through the hidden corridors in the walls.

Selene opened the door with a creak, peeking outside her room to make sure Lust wasn't leaning against the wall like he'd done all those months ago.

He wasn't. No one waited for her. Perhaps he'd gone to get her breakfast, or hidden himself back in the library where he thought he might find a secret about her malady.

Her fingers trailed over the door as she stepped outside, and they sank into deep grooves in the wood. She let her fingers linger in the marks left by his horns where he had slid down the door, and then twin indents where he'd likely pressed them so hard that they'd left two perfect holes. Exactly where his head must have been as he leaned there, hoping she'd let him in.

"Oh, Lust," she whispered sadly. "I'm so sorry."

And then she fled. Like the coward she was, she ran through the hall to the painting that shifted easily under her hand. She moved through the servant's hidden passages, all as clean and glistening as the rest of the castle.

She didn't notice any of the details. Tears burned in her eyes and turned her vision blurry. Her mind scattered with the thoughts of what he would do and feel when he realized she was missing, not just ignoring him.

He'd come for her. She knew he would. But Minerva had made it very clear that she would disappear if their home was ever compromised. There were secrets in this kingdom that even Lust didn't know. Caverns and caves and merchant paths to other kingdoms. They would flee somewhere he'd never find them.

Swallowing hard, she slipped out of the last room and into the gardens. She pulled her hood up over her head so she'd appear to be another servant moving about their day. Perhaps one who had been here all night and now struggled back to their home to sleep.

But as she stepped out of the shadows and into the light, a hand wrapped around her shoulder and jerked her back into the darkness.

Not back into the castle, as she'd have expected. Instead, she was dragged around the edge of it until she stood dangerously close to open air. The man who had her in his grip slammed her back against the stone walls, his forearm braced over her neck.

Wheezing, she stared up into the golden gaze of Greed.

He glared down at her, and she realized that though she had perhaps seen him annoyed, until this point she had never seen him angry. With his brows furrowed, his arm pressing against her windpipe as though he couldn't quite stop himself from causing pain, she realized he was far more dangerous than his brother.

"Where do you think you're going?" he snarled.

"Leaving," she ground out through a sharp exhale.

"And does my brother know? Or are you sneaking away before he can tell you otherwise?" The arm pressed even harder, threatening to break something important. "Don't answer that. I think I already know. Now, I'm going to bring you back inside that castle, throw you at his feet, and you are going to beg for his forgiveness. Sound good?"

He started to move away from her, but Selene could not let him ruin this. She stepped to the side, jabbed him hard in the throat, and then stepped closer to the edge.

Greed froze, eyeing her with perhaps a new found respect. He seemed to understand that she would throw herself off the cliff if he moved too close, and that she wouldn't hesitate to do so.

"I'm dying," she said, her voice raspy from his attack.

"I know. He told me." Greed rolled his shoulders. "It was hard to miss. He had torn the library apart."

Stones skittered from behind her heel. She froze at the same moment Greed flinched forward. His hand floated between them, just close enough that she could grab onto him if she needed to. But she got her balance and straightened.

Breathing hard, she shook her head. "I can't stay here."

"He's determined to fix you. And whether you want to stay here or not, I don't care. You have done something to him, something that I don't think can be fixed. You have no choice now. You have to stay."

Greed's eyes flashed like coins in sunlight. "Even if I want to keep you for myself."

"Ew," she hissed. "And if you think I've made some impact on his life, let me clarify something. Would he be better off thinking I'm alive and dealing with the loss of me, than watching me die in front of him and knowing he'll never get me back?"

A flicker of reality played behind Greed's eyes. He seemed to understand what she meant, and the difficult choice she had to make.

But Selene needed to know he understood. Completely. "If I could stay, I would. This curse is not going away. I cannot break it and neither can he. The best option I have of surviving this is to return to the White Tower and pray that my mother sees fit to cast some pity upon me. He will not let me return, because he knows if I go back, they will not let me go." Her voice choked with emotion and she had to shake her head to clear it. "Don't make him watch me die."

Greed swallowed hard, his throat working through some unnamed emotion that he shouldn't be able to feel. "I don't think you understand what you've done to him."

"Exactly what he's done to me," she whispered. "I know we carved each other apart and laid a piece of ourselves into those wounds. I know he thinks that we've changed each other. And maybe we have. But I will not let him sit there and watch me die knowing that he can do nothing. I can't feel the guilt for that while trying to save my own life."

Again he reached for her, shaking his hand as though he wanted her to take it. "You have underestimated your king. If anyone can fix you, it is him. Just give him enough time to do so."

"Don't make me choose between him and my life." Tears slid down her cheeks, the drops warm and burning against her skin. "Don't force me to make that decision, Greed."

"Because you would choose yourself?" He straightened and relief filtered across his face. "Perhaps this is not the situation I suspected it to be."

"Because I will die in his arms if I have to." Her voice sounded wrong. Thick and choked with emotion when she had never been an emotional person. "I am making this choice for both of us, don't you see? If I choose to leave, if I succeed in putting this castle and all that happened within it behind me, then I die alone. Or if I somehow don't die and the High Sorceress lets me live, then I will suffer with this choice for the rest of my life. He can move on. He can go back to normal and find some semblance of happiness while I..." She sniffed hard. "While I live with the guilt. I will shoulder the burden so he doesn't have to."

His shoulders rounded forward in defeat. "You feel something for him."

"I love him." Selene blurted the words even as more stones shattered beneath her heel and tumbled into the darkness below. She had thought letting those words flee from her lips would make all this worse. As if by giving them life, she was admitting to herself that she could choose to leave the man she loved. Like a monster.

But they didn't make her feel worse. They gave her life itself. She felt more powerful, more ready to take on this decision because it was what was best for him. She would never question that again.

Gulping, she met his shocked gaze and nodded again. "I love him. So much that it hurts sometimes because I know he'll never feel the same. And I don't love him like the rest of his subjects. I actually know him. We trust each other. I've seen him smile and laugh. I've seen him grow and change as I barged into his life and changed everything. And

I loved him before all that. I will love him in whatever form he takes, whatever changes he accepts, whatever monster he becomes. I will love him. Until the darkness beneath us devours this kingdom and all who are in it."

Her chest felt heavy with the words. She loved him. She could admit it now, and that hurt. Because she'd never say it to his face, but at least someone would know.

Greed grunted and took his hand away from her. "I should throw you over the edge. Maybe that would end this foolish mistake."

"Maybe." She braced for the shove. "We both know I'm going to die, anyway. If you want to end it sooner, I wouldn't blame you."

He snarled, baring sharp teeth and lunging for her. Selene let her eyes flutter closed because she didn't want to see the kingdom recede from her view. She wanted to remember it as glittering and glowing and beautiful.

But Greed's arm wrapped around her waist and yanked her against him. Her eyes flew open to see the small ledge she'd stood on crumble into the darkness. He'd... saved her?

Her back was pressed against his impressively large chest. Heaving breaths rocked her forward and back and a soft, furry something tickled her forearm. Looking down, she realized he'd even wrapped his tail around her waist as a last precaution. The tuft at the top was gently stroking her arm.

"Thanks," she whispered, her breath still hard to catch. "That would have been bad."

"I should have let you die."

"Probably. But at least now you won't have that on your head, as well as the knowledge that you let me go." She patted his thick forearm. "And you're going to let me go. Aren't you, Greed?"

His breath blew her hair like she'd turned her back on a raging bull. "Probably," he echoed her. "You're going to the Tower, you said?"

She didn't like him touching her. It felt like someone had thrown her into the arms of a giant. "That's my best shot. I think Minerva will receive me if Lust isn't there."

"What are your chances of her punishing you?"

"High." Selene shrugged. "But I'm already dying. She can't do anything more to me that the curse won't do. And I am her daughter. I'm hoping that after years of raising me, she'll have some ounce of humanity left inside her. My sisters will fight for me as well, I think."

"You think?"

"They wanted me to eat dinner with them?"

Greed growled. "That's not high praise."

"Not really, but it's something." Selene wiggled, trying to get free. "If you aren't going to stop me, I need to get going. Lust will realize that I'm gone, and he'll lock me up. I already explained myself well enough for you to understand why I'm doing this. So let me go, Greed. Or drag me back to his feet like you said you would."

Grumbling, he released his hold on her and then speared his hand through his hair. She stared at the red locks that spiked straight up from his head. What was he thinking? Was he going to let her go? If so, she needed to run. She needed to get out of here before she lost her nerve.

Baring his teeth, Greed pointed at her. "You are not going to the Tower by yourself. You'll die before you get there."

"I'm not that sick." But the snakes were crawling under her skin. She could feel them, even now. They would slow her and he had a point. She wouldn't get far on her own.

"You'll take one of my guards," he snarled. "They'll get you there safely and then return to me. I'm not keeping this a secret from my brother, sorceress. He will know where you went when my guard returns. But I will give you that much time to run."

It was more than she'd hoped for.

Selene nodded. "Then hurry. I have little time to wait."

Though she had thought the words were sobering, Greed flashed her a dark grin. "The jaws of death nip at your heels, sorceress. Outrun them."

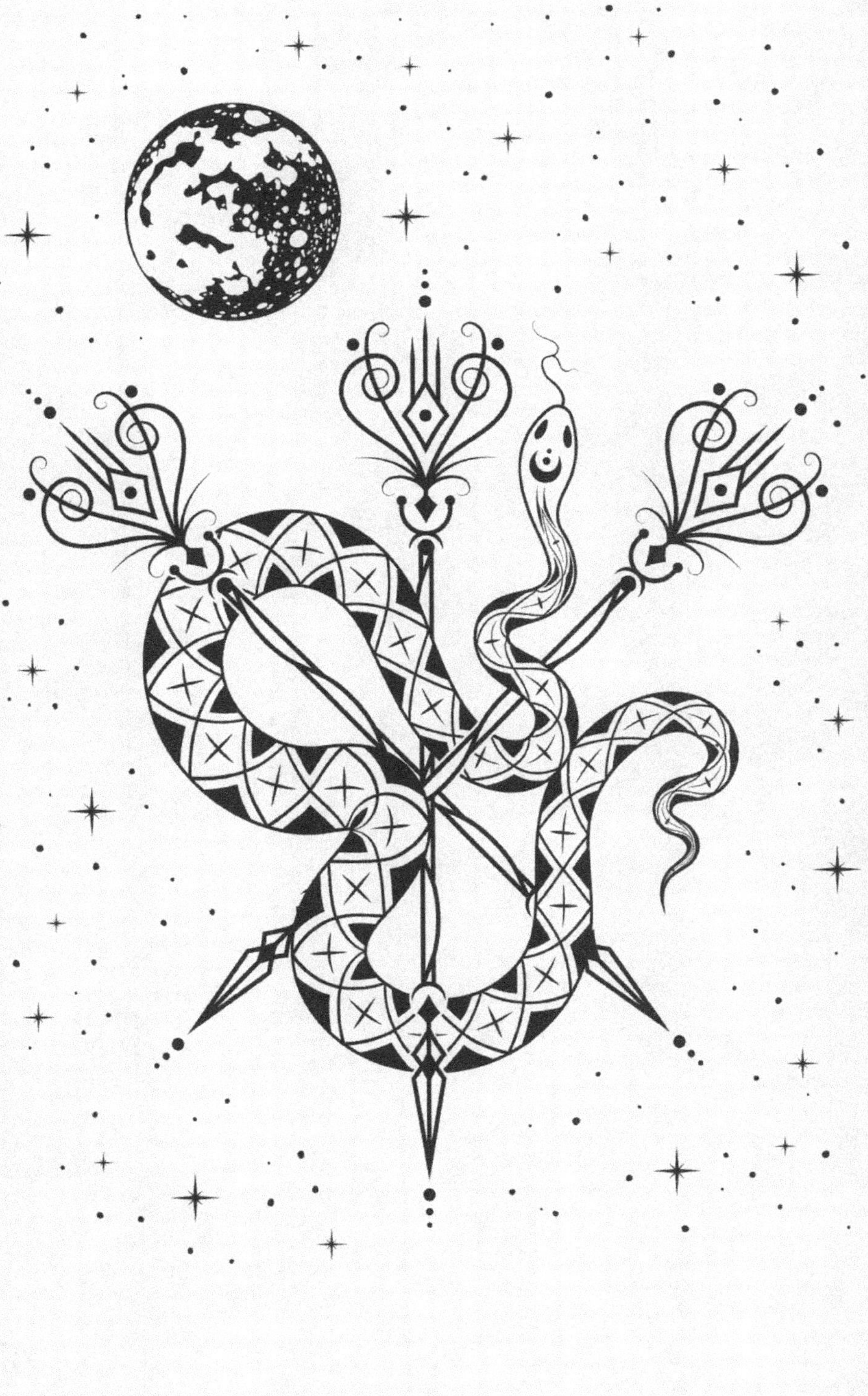

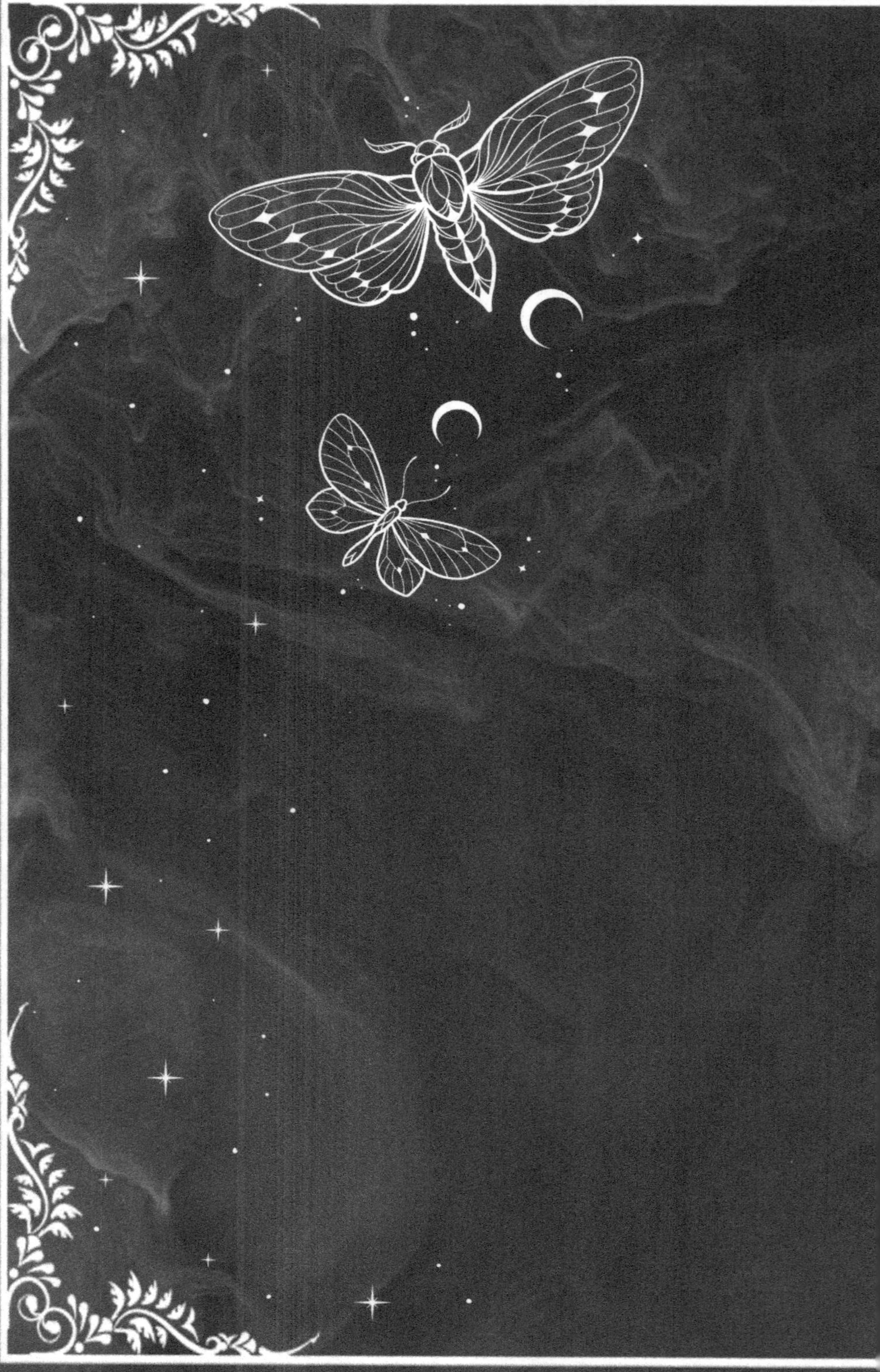

Chapter 41

He'd found it.

Since Selene wouldn't let him stay in their bedroom with her—a thorn in his side that he refused to think too much about—he'd dedicated too much time to his library. And as he was certain he would, he found the counter curse.

Or, in a sense, a way to get them both out of this predicament.

"Affection," he called out, his voice shaking with excitement. "Come here. I need you to tell me you see the same thing I see."

The spirit floated over the floor, even larger today than before. It was now almost up to his shoulder, although it had forgone the human visage. Today, it was merely a column of light. No features.

No face. Just light that glided over the floor toward him. "What is it?"

"I think..." He ran a hand down his face and then shook his head. "Just read it. Please."

The spirit hovered over his shoulder and read through the tome. It was in a very ancient language, one that only the spirits knew how to read at this point. Humans had long lost their old languages, and this was from a time when they remembered that spirits existed.

"You can pull the curse out of her?" Affection asked. "I didn't know we could do that."

"Spirits can reach into parts of this realm that humans cannot. Apparently sorceresses are known to live in between the realm of mortals and spirits. Their magic is from that realm, stolen from us." He thudded a hand to his chest, and stood up from his desk with the book splayed open in one hand. "If I can reach into that realm and grasp whatever curse remains in that area, which it should still be, then I can rip it out of her."

"Wouldn't that have the chance of hurting her?"

"Perhaps. But it is a survivable wound. At least, that's the thought." It didn't say much about what would happen if he tore a curse out of a mortal. But it had been done.

This journal was from another spirit who had taken mortal form. A spirit who had wandered the kingdoms so that it too could experience the world that only mortals had experienced. Though it had not wanted to become anyone other than a passing figure in their lives, it had seen much and grown stronger with each passing day.

"What kind of spirit was it?" Affection asked, its voice grave with the question. "Perhaps it is a spirit of deception and we should ignore the tome."

"It was a spirit of delight," he whispered. "All it wanted was to experience the mortal realm and to give them more of that emotion. It appears that it was in a traveling show. It created magic for the mortals to watch and it had come upon a man dying from a curse that had been laid on him by a simple hedge witch. It pulled the curse out of him and created a blackened spot on the land that would never grow."

"A black spot?" Affection's column of light shuddered. "I have seen none of those in this kingdom, Lust. It's too great a risk."

And yet, they had waited for too long already.

He hadn't seen her in two days, and he feared that was because she didn't want him to see her. The curse could already be wasting her flesh from her bones. She could be weak and in bed, just as Lara claimed she was.

The only person Selene would let in her room was Lara, and that was suspicious enough. The other woman had never been a friend to his sorceress, and he'd grown tired of waiting.

"It's a risk we have to take," he muttered. "If we don't do something, then we're just waiting for her to die. I have to tell her."

"Tell her what?" The doors to the library burst open and Greed strode in with one of his personal guards. The other big one was missing. "Are you talking about your little captive in your room?"

"She's not a captive." Lust waved the book at Greed. "I've found it."

"Found what?" His brother meandered through the library, seeking out the plate of food that had gone largely untouched all morning. He picked out a fluffy pastry and broke it apart in his hands. The flakes drifted down on top of the thick layer of pages that littered the floor.

"The way to break her curse. We can rip into the realm where that curse exists. If I pull it out of her and force it to exist here, in the mortal realm, then it will only affect whatever I place it on. Earth. Stone. Whatever can be destroyed other than her."

Greed popped a piece of the pastry in his mouth and loudly chewed. "The curse already exists in the mortal realm. You said she's dying."

"But that's energy that is being sucked out of her, not a malady that can be cured with potions or... bindings..." He growled. "Why am I explaining this to you? This will work. And now I'm wasting time."

Greed nodded at his remaining guard and she stood in front of the door with her arms crossed over her chest. As if that would stop him. As though she could force a demon king to remain in a room if he didn't want to remain there.

Lifting a brow, he eyed his brother. "What's this, then?"

"Are you sure you want to save her?"

"It's never been a question."

"I want to know why." Greed dropped half of the pastry back onto the tray and wiped his hands on his thighs. "She's a mortal. She's going to die anyway, maybe not now, but certainly in fifty years. A drop of rainwater in a giant lake of our lives. That's how long she's going to last. Why prolong the inevitable?"

The thought had crossed his mind, but he refused to think about it. She would die someday, and he would have to watch her die. But even then, he would fight for a few more days, a few more hours, a few more seconds just to stare into those night sky eyes.

"She's mine," he growled. "And I will not give her up."

"That's not a good enough answer."

"It is the only answer you will get from me!" Lust's voice rang throughout the library. "Now get out of my way, Greed. I don't want to kill your guard and I don't want to fight you because you remember as well as I what happened the last time we battled."

It was long and bloody, but Lust had won. Greed liked to think he had honed his body with centuries of battle, but Lust had one thing that his brother would never have.

Intelligence.

Greed tilted his head back and laughed. "Oh, brother, you think that five hundred years has not taught me a few tricks? No, I'm not going to fight you. But I am going to caution you against madness."

"It is not madness that compels me to save her, brother."

Greed's second guard joined the other. The dark look in his eyes caught on Greed's, before the man gave a soft nod.

What message was that? What game did his brother play? He would save her. Lust was going to piece her back together, and then she would stay in his arms until the very last moment of her breath. That was how this would end, no matter what Greed tried to do.

But then his brother snapped his fingers in Lust's face, drawing his attention back to Greed. "Can you not even give a name to what compels you?"

"It needs no name. She is mine, that is enough."

"That's not what she told me." Greed usually had a look of disgust on his face or one of desire for something that he could not have. But right now, that expression had softened into something that looked far too close to envy. "She begged me, you know. I never thought I'd see a woman like that so willing to get on her knees if that was what it took. All because she claims to love you."

Love? Anger had flared at the thought of her begging anyone but Lust for anything, but then he heard that word and it rocked through his chest.

She loved him?

No one loved him. They lusted for him. They thought he was handsome or beautiful and they wanted to put their mouth on him. Or they wanted him inside them or around them, just to know what it felt like. But no one loved him.

Until her.

Breath caught in his lungs. He reached for the back of a chair and braced himself on it because if he didn't, he was afraid he'd fall over. "She said what?"

"That she loves you. And that if she didn't run, then she would never leave. And you would be forced to watch her die rather than knowing she was alive and just not with you." Greed's mouth twisted in disappointment. "I'll admit, we both should have had more faith in you. I should have given you more time, but if you'd seen her, Lust, you would have done the same thing I did."

He couldn't quite keep up with his brother's words. "What are you saying?"

"I let her go." Greed met his gaze head on, and apology in his own. "She wanted to run, and she deserved to make that decision for herself. I sent my guard with her to make sure she got there safely. She said the High Sorceress would cast pity on her, and even if that meant she would be a slave for the rest of her life, at least you would not carry the guilt of her death on your shoulders. It was my mistake, but I do not regret making it."

The words barely registered. All he heard was that she was gone. His brother had let her go. She was no longer in his castle, under his protection, with a curse raging through her body that would destroy her from the inside out.

Selene hadn't trusted him to fix this. She'd gone back to her mother, the woman who had put them both in this mess. She had decided that Minerva was more likely to save her than him.

A blast of power surged out of him, thundering through the castle and sending every person in the room to their knees. It wasn't just lust that raged out of him. It was so much more than he'd ever had before.

The power he'd been siphoning off Selene felt different, but maybe it wasn't only the power that was different. It was him.

He felt his body warping and stretching and changing like he hadn't felt since they'd taken mortal form for the first time.

Memories flickered behind his eyes as another wave of power shoved everyone closer to the floor. Forgotten memories that none of them had remembered considering how embarrassing and heartrending they were.

They hadn't become kings because any mortal wanted them to be. No human wanted to see a spirit on the throne and even then, the mortals had feared the brothers that came to each kingdom. Their crusade had lost a soldier every time they devoured a floating isle as their own.

He remembered now.

He and his brothers were not mortal, then. They were monsters, and they had the power of the spirit world at their fingertips.

Fingers like his own. He lifted his hand and watched as it grew and curled into dark claws. His hands and forearms turned nearly black, so dark the purple sheen on them looked like an oil slick. It stretched up his arms, reaching for his shoulders, which were much larger than moments before.

A spike of pain raced through his skull as his horns grew larger, more massive, longer and more deadly than they had been in ages.

And suddenly he remembered where the name demon kings had

come from.

They were demons in that time. They were villains who devoured all who stood before them and fought. He remembered the blood coating his claws as he plunged his hand into the hearts of the wicked and those who would not bend.

He remembered the screams as they ran from him. His brothers at his side, all of them equally terrifying and monstrous and horrible. They had ravaged these floating isles, stomping them into the dirt beneath their feet as people screamed from inside their graves.

They had destroyed everything.

And then this battle form had receded, and they had fixed all that they had broken. Each of his brothers. All of them lingering in their kingdoms until there was but one left. Wrath. The beast had stood on his own to destroy a kingdom beneath their feet, who was the only one that kept the behemoth in the darkness at bay.

He stretched his hands, feeling those large claws clink as they touched the darkened plates that protected him from any attack. His brother looked so small now.

"You let her go," he snarled, his voice so deep that he barely recognized it. "Where?"

"The Tower." Greed bowed his head, showing his brother his neck as though Lust had turned into a wolf that desired prey. "She is safely there, and still alive."

"She will not be for long if Minerva has her way of it." His eyes found the guard who had taken her there, and he felt his lips peel away from his teeth in a snarl. "You will give that one to me."

"No," Greed replied.

"I will take his heart."

"You will not." Greed's voice was firm, though it shook slightly.

"We have not taken battle form in years, brother. What has this woman done to you?"

He opened his mouth to unleash all his rage upon his brother. Selene had done nothing to him, but the world had done so much to her. And now his own brother had sent her to her death. Alone. She would be alone when she died and that—

He felt a tendril in his chest snap. Staggering back, he pressed a clawed hand to his heart because he had no idea what it was.

Until the rush of nothing filled him.

That thread inside him, which had connected Selene and him together, had broken. Like someone had snipped it with scissors, she was gone.

And with that, every part of him that remained aware of who he was or what he was doing disappeared. He threw his head back in a roar that shook the castle's foundation, and then he was moving. Running. Racing faster than light itself to get to her because he could not feel her.

His heart thudded in his chest, the beat of it a lonely call. She couldn't be dead. Not yet.

Or he would bring that Tower to the ground, stone by bloody stone.

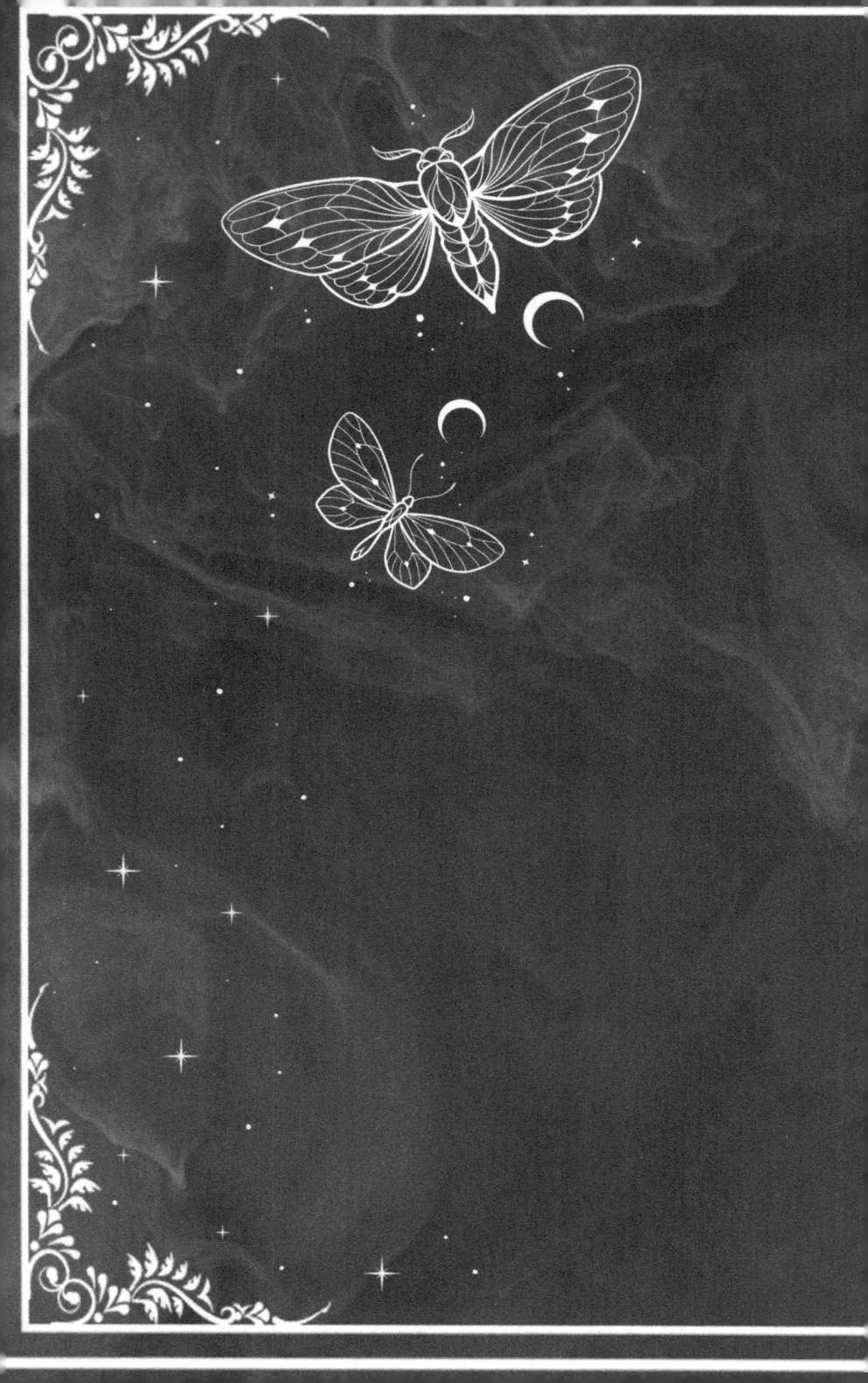

Chapter 42

The journey nearly turned her insides out. Greed's guard, a man who refused to share his name, set a pace that would have killed even the healthy. She pressed a hand to her chest and kept going, no matter how hard it became to breathe or how her lungs screamed.

Though she didn't like the pace, she could admit he was doing the right thing. With every step, she felt herself growing weaker and weaker.

It felt like they had been walking for days, though she knew they'd only stopped for one night. And every second of that night, she'd flinched at the barest sound near them.

Greed's guard had made fine work of setting up a quick shelter.

He'd only grunted when she thanked him and then pointed to the small mat of leaves and moss he'd made for her. She fell asleep fitfully, certain that every sound was Lust coming to get her. She feared he'd drag her out of the little lean-to and throw her back to his castle, where they would both have to suffer through this mess.

But every time she'd awoken, Greed's guard had been there. The man's eyes glowed with the firelight, and he never once looked back at her. Instead, he stared into the fields around them. The muscles in his shoulders were never relaxed, his body never once at ease. He always looked like he was ready to kill something.

That shouldn't have been as reassuring as it was.

The sun had barely lifted on the horizon before he woke her. A gentle, but firm, hand on her shoulder and a quick shake, so she knew there was no arguing.

Selene rolled back to standing and knew her time was even shorter than she'd imagined. Her face felt cold, and her hands were difficult to use. Her fingers were so stiff she could barely hold on to the walking stick the guard made her.

By the time the Tower came into view, the icy winds whipping at the cloaks around their shoulders, she saw worry in the guard's gaze for the very first time.

He looked her over, then looked at the Tower on the horizon. "Can you make it?"

"On my own? Absolutely." She tried to curl her fingers around the walking stick a little more firmly, but her fingers creaked with the movement. The bones snapped and popped as though even that little movement could break her. "You shouldn't get too close. They aren't very friendly toward men."

"I've heard." Though it was the first time she'd spoken with him,

Selene had expected the gruffness of his voice. The harsh tones made him seem a little less human. "I was tasked with seeing you there safely. Leaving you here alone is not completing it."

"Then stay here." She nodded toward the horizon. "You'll see my path. I'm the only dark thing in these fields. You'll know when I reach the Tower."

"And then?"

"Even if I fall, you leave me." He jerked at the harshness in her own voice, but Selene continued on as though she hadn't shocked a man bred for war. "It's not so surprising, is it? You knew you were bringing me here to die."

"Greed said they would save you."

She looked at the Tower and felt something inside her heart break. "No," she whispered. "I don't suspect they will."

And still, she soldiered on.

Selene didn't look back at the poor man who had thought he was saving her. She didn't look at the silhouette of the castle beyond him. The shadowy outline had always been there on the horizon, just out of her reach. How many times had she stared at it while she was here? How many times had she thought that maybe she'd visit Lust's sacred castle? As a child, it was a place out of reach but full of wondrous secrets.

Now she knew that it really did contain treasures. She could only wish that her sisters were so lucky as to see it someday.

The walking stick helped as she trudged through the snow. But the snakes underneath her skin grew angry the closer she got to the Tower. They rolled under her skin, coiling around her heart and squeezing until she felt it struggling to beat.

All they had to do was squeeze a little harder. Just a bit more. But all she had to do was keep her feet moving.

She recited spells under her breath, lessons from when she was a child. Each one grew more difficult than before. The elements. The kingdoms and who ruled them. The laws in each kingdom and why it was so important to know them. Etiquette. What was required to be a woman in a kingdom like this. Why she should hate Lust and why all of those rules were wrong.

And then she stood in front of the Tower once more.

Selene stared up at the monolith of white marble before her. It split the very sky, like a massive cloud in the middle of all that blue. So much blue.

Only then did she look behind her and see the guard still standing there. The wind whipped snow around him, trying to shove him back from his vigil, but he remained until the very last moment. And then he lifted his arm, a dark smudge against the horizon, and turned to leave.

She was on her own.

Again.

Sighing, she struggled to the door and lifted the knocker. Once, twice, three times, and then she fell to her knees before the door.

Selene had no idea how long it took them to open the door and see her there. Probably longer than she wanted to know. Whoever had opened it stood there for a long time, staring down at her crumpled form before they burst into action.

She was rolled onto her back, her listless eyes seeing the blue sky above. When had it become so difficult to keep them open?

"Selene?" Oh, that was Sibyl. Her dark red hair had been shorn so close to her skull that she was nearly bald. There was a black smudge underneath one eye as well. A bruise?

"Help," she whispered, the words hard to get past her thick tongue. "Please. Help me."

"Mother!" The scream echoed in her head, the pain arcing through her entire body until she couldn't think around it. The pain didn't stop at the scream.

Oh no, the snakes had felt her pain, and they congregated around it. They coiled through her, zeroing in on what had caused her pain and indulging themselves in the sensation. She endured the spike of that headache over and over again, countless times, until she wanted to scream through it.

And then a cold hand pressed against her forehead and it all magically disappeared. She shifted toward the touch, seeking the brief relief from her torment.

"My daughter," Minerva said, her touch as soothing as it was poisonous. "You've returned to us."

This was her chance. This was her moment to lie and claim she was sorry for all that she had done. That she could be the daughter her mother wanted her to be in every other situation, just not with him.

Though it was a struggle, Selene lifted her arm and grabbed onto Minerva's wrist. "Forgive me, Mother. I failed you, and I know it was wrong."

"I raised you to be a goddess," Minerva whispered, her fingers combing through Selene's hair. "You were supposed to be everything that you ever wanted to be. Powerful. Strong. Better than all the others because you would be the one to bring us to the castle."

Why did her words hurt so much when her touch was so gentle? Tears pricked Selene's eyes even as she knew Minerva would punish her. "And I am sorry to have failed you."

"Have you come to tell us all his weaknesses? To bring about the age when the sorceresses will sit upon that throne?"

The lie stuck in her throat. She wanted to tell her mother that yes, she was here to do just that. She'd do anything if Minerva would save her life. But Selene couldn't force herself to lie about him.

She opened her eyes again, though it felt as though they were full of sand. She met her mother's waiting gaze and slowly shook her head.

"No," she whispered. "I am here to beg for my life. As your daughter. As the child you found in the cold and now a woman who owes you her life."

Minerva gently lifted her head, cupping the back of it and holding her suspended above the snow. "You owed me your life when I sent you to destroy him, and you returned to me not only empty-handed but as a disappointment. What makes you think I'll save you now?"

"Hope," she whispered, and her gaze met Sibyl's behind Minerva's head. "I have never given up hope that you are not the monster I always feared, Mother."

"I'm not your mother. But you have given me a unique opportunity in coming here. I will fix you, Selene, and I will destroy him in the same breath."

Why did that sound so menacing?

Her mother stood and the cool touch disappeared. Selene tried to follow it. She tried to lift herself up, but her body betrayed her. She fell back into the snow with a wheeze of breath that didn't seem to reach her lungs.

Two pairs of hands reached underneath her and dragged her upright. The world spun. Trying to get control over her senses and her suddenly squeezing stomach, she blinked a few times to clear her vision.

Sibyl had helped her up, and Bathilda was on her other side. They held her with quiet strength as they strode into the Tower.

Minerva strode in front of them, her voice ringing through the Tower. "You have shown me that there are other ways to get what I want, Selene. If you could deviate from your plan, then so could I. The High Sorceresses before me were so certain of one thing. The demon must die for us to take the throne."

She had heard all this before. The death of Lust would bring about a new age. Selene couldn't have killed him on her own, but that was the intent. If they could not enslave him to her wiles, a very small chance at that, then they would destroy him with whatever secrets she'd learned. But there were no secrets. He wasn't even a man. He was a spirit.

Selene wouldn't be the one to tell her. She'd never let her mother know the truth, just to spite her.

"We don't need him dead." Minerva started up the stairs and her sisters forced her to climb. Together, they all made their way up the countless steps that led up the Tower. "We just need him out of our way."

Where were they taking her? Selene's neck spasmed and lolled forward. She couldn't keep it upright, no matter how hard she tried.

"Selene," Sibyl hissed in her ear. "Help us, please."

Her tongue was too thick to talk. She couldn't even lift her feet to help them anymore. They dragged her up the stairs with her boots clunking against each one. Her sisters were breathing hard, but then she wondered if they were really her sisters. If they were so willing to help Minerva in whatever madness this was, were they family?

Or was that guard who had been so reluctant to leave more family than they were? Or Greed who had listened to her every word until he decided that he'd let her go? He had helped her even though it would anger his own family.

Her head wasn't on right, that much she knew. And she wouldn't live that much longer if Minerva didn't do something.

Oh, Lust, she thought. I'm so sorry.

If she was going to die, then she should have stayed with him. She should have been in his arms right now, letting him wash the sweat off her forehead while he whispered how beautiful she was. How much she had changed his life.

"Here," Minerva said, and Selene couldn't guess how long it had been.

She'd hidden away in her mind the last bit of this journey. So when she blinked her eyes open and saw the vast landscape of the entire kingdom laid out before her, a gasp escaped her lips.

Selene had forgotten how beautiful it was here. The world looked so lovely while she stood so far above it.

"You will stay here," Minerva said, standing in front of her. "He will come to us and we will trap him. The Tower will become his tomb, even if he's still alive within it. We'll see how long it takes for him to crack open like an egg tossed off a counter. But for now, you will remain here as bait. And once he arrives, I will deal with you."

At her nod, her sisters released their hold on her arms. Selene crumpled onto the floor, but it was easier to breathe up here. Almost enough that she had a little energy.

The circle of magic, she remembered. This was where they had cast the spell, and perhaps this was where she could break it. Power still lingered in the air and it gave her strength.

Shoving herself up onto her forearms, she looked at her mother and croaked, "Are you leaving me here to die?"

"No. I will come back and I will change you into what you should have been long ago." Minerva lifted her arms and magic swirled at her fingertips. A storm built at her beckoning, raging toward them in a sky that gathered lightning. "With my power heightened by this place, you will become my right hand. The way you should have been years ago."

Selene felt it. The power that built around her as though it were all created here in the sky. Except it wasn't. Hadn't Minerva said this was the most powerful place in the kingdom? Perhaps years of sorcery in this tower had actually given power to this place. Enough to keep her alive.

"How do you know he'll even come for me?" she asked.

"Because he's already coming. I can feel him," Minerva sneered. "Now stay here and try to stay alive."

Her mother swept out of the peak of the Tower, beginning her long journey to the bottom. Bathilda started after her, but Sibyl hesitated.

Selene reached out a hand for her sister. "Please."

Sibyl shook her head, backing toward the door. "You shouldn't have come back here, Selene."

"What is she planning to do?" Selene tried to clear her mind enough to ask the question, but she couldn't say it properly. The garbled words were even hard for her to understand.

"Nothing any of us can stop." Sibyl's usually beautiful face twisted with sadness. "She never trained us to be more than servants, Selene. Look at us. You can conjure light. Bathilda sees the future. I can only conjure illusions. Even Ursula only summons the wind. We are nothing compared to her. We cannot stop this, we can only endure and hope she doesn't do to us what she—"

Her sister stopped talking, but Selene already knew what she was going to say.

Her sisters could only hope to avoid Selene's fate.

"Will she let me die?" she asked, the words quiet and contemplative.

Sibyl's expression cracked, and she pressed a fist to her mouth before shaking her head. "No. But I think you'll wish you had."

And so her sister fled, down the stairs and away from Selene, who rolled onto her back and stared up at the open sky above her. The top of the tower was surrounded by columns, but no roof. She could see the clouds as they rode the wind to pause above her. The great mist and blackened edges opened up.

She was glad to feel the rain. It was cold sliding down her cheeks, but the feeling was so much better than being numb.

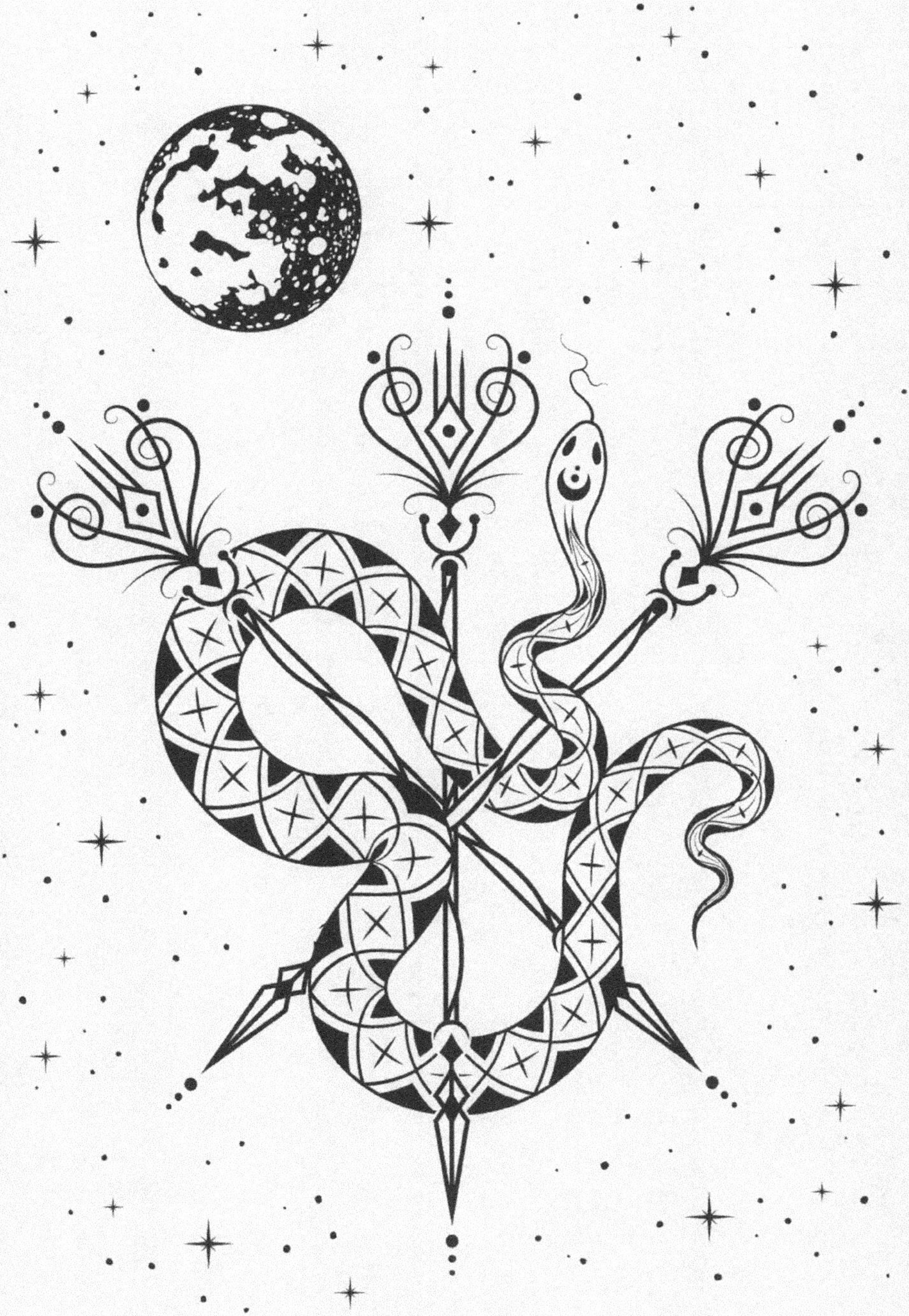

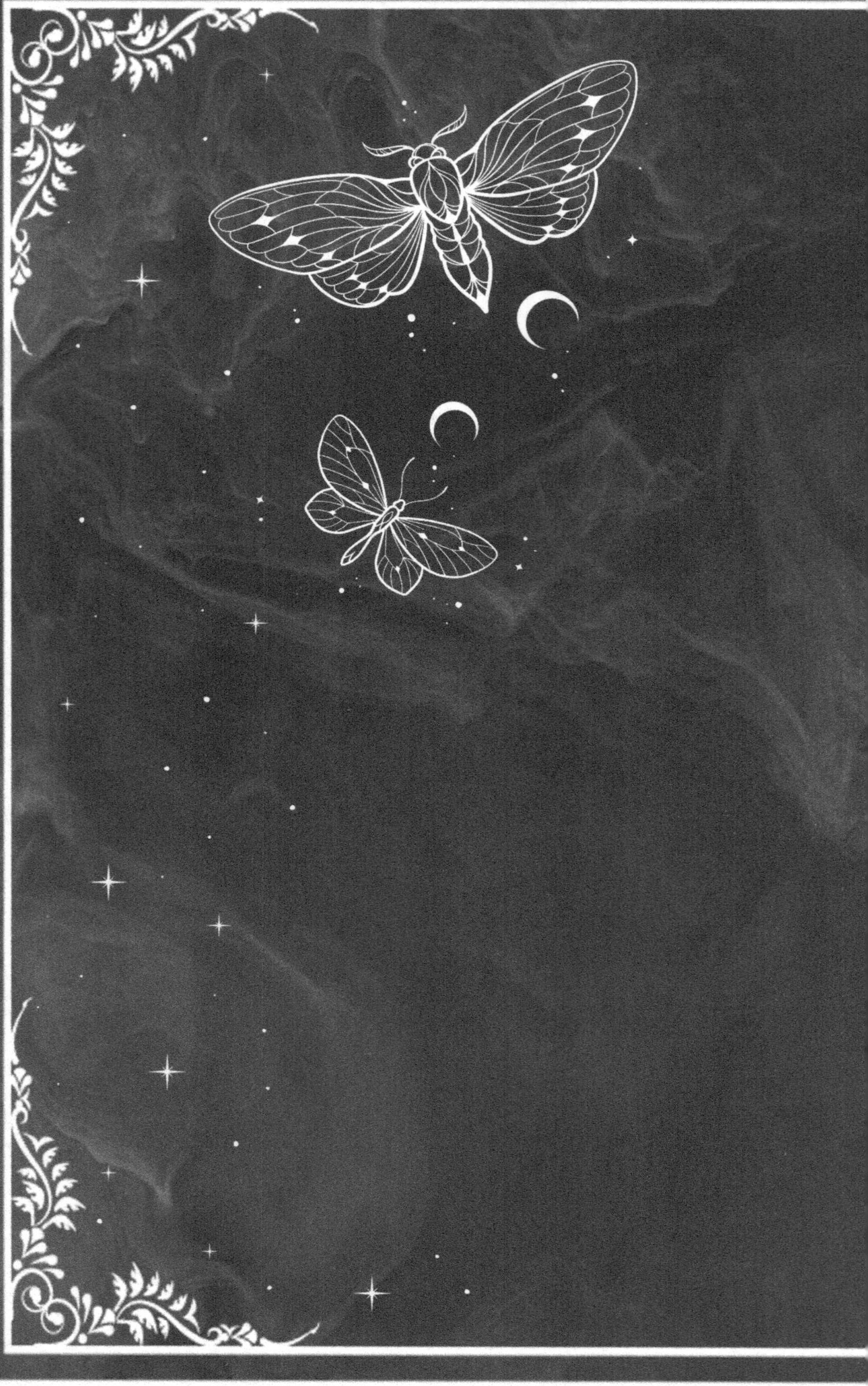

Chapter 43

He stood on the horizon beyond the Tower, his shoulders heaving with every angry breath he took. Lust had denied any help. His brother had offered a great army to ride at his side, but Lust knew what waited for him here.

Weak sorceresses who were afraid of their leader. A High Sorceress who thought she was far more powerful than she was and would stop at nothing to trap him. He'd seen this before. He'd endured worse.

Minerva thought she would hold Selene captive, and that she would trap him. She thought he would waste his time trying to save Selene first, and then ignore the rest of their people. But if she wanted a bloodbath, he would give it to her.

There were enough sorceresses in that Tower who deserved to die. He'd avoid the one with white hair, who had been kind to Selene and had thrown herself in front of Selene when Minerva had first enacted the curse. That one had earned his pity, and he would make sure she was rewarded for it.

The rest?

He ached to feel their skin parting beneath his sharp claws. Baring his teeth, his mind already screamed for their throats in his jaw.

He had become more than Lust, now. He had become the monstrous being behind the name demon king. If they wanted to see what he was capable of, then they had done the right thing. Minerva had finally provoked him enough to become the creature she so feared. Now he would show her why she should be afraid.

The snow parted for him, melting in the wake of the heat billowing off his body. He must have seemed a blur if any of the sorceresses were watching for him, and he knew they were.

Selene had come here to save herself. But her mother wanted her here for one reason. Him. Lust knew that Minerva would get desperate. Her plan hadn't worked, and her daughter had a mind of her own. The lack of control would drive Minerva mad. And mad people did desperate things.

There would be a trick waiting for him. Some attack or cage, or perhaps she thought she could use Selene as a shield. He had to anticipate every possible outcome.

The doors to the Tower were open for only a split second. Just long enough for him to see through and notice Minerva standing in the center of her domain. She lifted her arms higher, magic pouring out of her in so much energy that it made the world crackle.

Then the doors slammed shut, sealed with magic more powerful than he'd anticipated. As if that would ever keep him out.

He took a deep breath, inhaling the acidic scent of rain and lightning in the air. But there was also her scent, the faintest hint of peppermint that filled his lungs and calmed the worst of his anger.

He'd get her back. There was no other option.

"Demon!" Minerva called out from inside the Tower. "I have laced the walls with runes that will trap you forever. If you take one step inside this Tower, you will be forever entombed within it."

He doubted that.

"And you will be stuck with me, Minerva." Lust stalked the edges of the Tower, dragging his claws along the stone as the screeching noise burned in his ears. "Do you know how long I can keep you alive? Torture is too simple of a word for what I plan on doing to you. You took everything from me."

"I didn't take her from you, Demon. You took her from me."

How was she projecting her voice? He glanced up at the electricity crackling through the clouds and thought perhaps that was it. She used the storm to make her voice sound like it was coming from everywhere. As if that would confuse him. He knew where she was.

He could smell her.

"Runes will not trap me," he growled.

"Demonic energy can always be trapped."

Perhaps it could, but he was no demon. Obviously Selene had kept his secret, and his heart thudded hard in his chest at the knowledge. She hadn't come here to betray him, though it would have shocked him if she had. She'd come here to beg for her life, and her mother had little pity left to give even her dearest daughter.

Baring his teeth in a snarl, he flexed his own magic and sent it out into the walls. The runes were old, ancient even. She'd found the right ones, but she'd missed a single line in the center rune that was easily over a hundred markings.

That mistake would cost her.

"Where is she?" he called out. "I will leave you all alive if you tell me where she is."

"You are in no place to be making bargains, Demon. She came home because she doesn't want you. Because she knows you cannot give her what we can. She needed someone to save her life. You failed her, and that means she's mine."

Goading him? No, gloating, he thought. Minerva didn't think he'd come into the Tower and if he did, she was certain that she'd won.

"We both know this is a small chance you'll actually trap me. It's even smaller of a chance that I won't get her back."

"Perhaps I will kill her in front of you, just for the insolence of your belief that you are better than us."

"You wouldn't dare."

"I would dare much to keep my children alive."

And just like that, his anger snapped again. Lust drew back his fist and pounded it through the rune that she'd made a mistake on. Over and over again as the dust grew around him and the stone broke beneath the hard plating of his fist. A scream lifted and then more, until they were a symphony to every strike.

The sorceresses had scattered by the time he stepped through the rune and into the Tower. Power crackled around him, and his horns scraped the stones as he moved through them.

But Minerva? She stood in the center of all her chaos with fanatic jubilation on her face. "You are trapped."

He pointed to the destroyed rune. "You missed a line."

Her eyes only had a fraction of a second to widen before he was upon her. Demon he became, as his claws flashed and his teeth bared in frightening brilliance.

She fought. Her power lifted her into the air as though she were flying, only for him to catch her ankle and throw her onto the ground. Another sorceress screamed at him and he felt the strike of something hard on his back.

Glancing over his shoulder, he saw the pieces of a chair shattered on the ground. Snarling, he reached for the woman, who glared at him with anger and not fear. She would die, he decided. And so she did.

The spray of blood from her throat painted the white walls red. She spun away from him, her hands pressed against the wound as though that would save her. It would not.

Another sorceress launched at him, orbs floating in circles around her, each one filled with burning oil. A telekinetic, rare in these parts. He'd thought Minerva had trained them all out of strong powers.

Tilting his head to the side, he watched as she tossed one at him. Catching it in midair, he threw it back to the young woman, who went up like a candle. Her screams echoed through the walls and that's when he heard the others. So many more sorceresses than he thought lived here.

It was time to end this. Growling, he turned back to Minerva, ready to cut the head off this snake.

But she wasn't there.

She'd somehow scrambled up when he'd been certain he had hit her against the floor hard enough to knock her out. That damned wind magic, or whatever it was she called upon must have softened the blow. Baring his teeth, he spun toward the stairs and saw the dark outline of her body as she disappeared around a corner.

Did she think she could get away from him that easily?

He leapt, claws digging into the sides of the stairwell before he began to climb. The railings gave him handholds. He launched himself time and time again, climbing up the center of the Tower's circular stairs. He became their nightmare, a spider creeping up their walls to hunt them down.

A few sorceresses shrieked, and some tried to attack him. One held twin blades in her hands. He let her stab his shoulder before grabbing onto hers and tossing her into the open air. Her scream was cut short by a sickening crunch. Good enough. Another tried to throw fire in his eyes. An elemental? Where had Minerva been hiding these women?

The fire did little more than annoy him. He let her lob a few flame balls as he passed by before he leapt past to the next level.

Now, where was the bitch who controlled them all? He'd hunt her through the entire Tower and kill every last one of her daughters if he had to. But Minerva didn't care if they died, which meant she must have a place to hide.

On the seventh level, a sorceress with blood red hair started toward him with her hands raised. And somehow, Selene stood beside her.

He froze. Selene was so pale it frightened him. Her eyes were wide, her hands held out as though in prayer.

"Wait," she said, but it wasn't her voice. It was the woman's who stood next to her. "You have to stop."

He shook his head, trying to clear some of the bloodlust that raged through him. He needed to listen for a moment, but that new power consumed him. It was similar to his normal control over lust, but different enough to be hard to control. Oh, he lusted for flesh, but not in the same way any longer.

"Please," Selene said in that voice that was not her own. She took a step closer to him, and he saw blood leaking out from beneath her thick skirts. "You have to help me. Let them go, Lust. Help me instead."

This was... wrong. It wasn't her. It couldn't be her, and yet, she was standing right in front of him. Should he...

"I never wanted you," Selene whispered. "I only wanted to come home and you wouldn't let me go. What other choice did I have?"

He swallowed hard, his chest cracking open in fear. Had he trapped her? Had he forced her to stay with him when all she had wanted was her freedom? He'd never been that man before. His claws dug into the stone, and he shook his head again, like a beast trying to dislodge a thorn in its paw.

"Stop it," he snarled. "I don't know what you're doing, but this is not her."

"It's me. Of course it's me, demon."

She had stopped calling him that long ago. Lust's eyes narrowed upon the figure, and he noticed the details that his breaking heart hadn't let him see before. Her skirts weren't real. The very edges revealed the lines of the marble beneath her.

"Now!" the woman standing beside Selene screamed.

Another sorceress barreled out of the darkness. He didn't have time to brace himself before she struck him. Her arms wrapped around his waist, squeezing impossibly tight as they fell to the ground. Even this height would hurt him, and he prepared himself for the pain that would soon hit his back. But the woman? She was going to break his ribs.

Grunting, he spun them in the air so that she would hit the ground first. Her eyes widened in fear the moment before they landed. She hit harder than he'd expected, and her body made a noise he would remember for the rest of his life as it cushioned his fall.

Breathing hard, he glared back up at the stairs where Minerva was getting away.

Cursing out a breath, he stood and shook out his hands. Blood splattered on the ground, and he didn't need to look to know he was covered in it now.

"It's no use," a quiet voice whispered from the shadows beside him. "I've already seen it."

A fucking soothsayer. He should have known Minerva would have one of those. He moved nothing but his head to glare at her. "The future is malleable."

"She dies." The dark haired woman pointed above them. Her hand trembled. "She dies from the top of the Tower."

He looked up and flexed his hands. "Then I will climb faster."

"You can't get there from the inside. The peak is protected by our strongest sorceresses. If you think these women are powerful, you've seen nothing yet."

"They were not powerful."

Another woman joined the other, her hair white as snow, with sad eyes that met his. A wind whirled around her, and he wondered if, given the chance, she might have been as powerful as Minerva. "This was the plan the whole time. We fight you, so Minerva has a chance to get there first."

"She wanted to trap me."

The pale haired woman shrugged. "That plan failed. She had many plans, but this is the one I wanted to avoid."

"Why?" He was wasting time talking to them, but this felt important. He knew he had to listen to them now more than ever.

"Because she wants you to go outside. She wants you to see what she has hidden."

Every muscle in his body locked as he looked at the soothsayer beside the other. Both women nodded, but it was the one who had seen the future that he wanted to confirm.

"Good," he said. "She wanted me to go outside. Then I will climb instead."

He turned his attention to the top and let loose all the power he'd consumed from Selene.

All he had to do was walk this time. He strode up the stairs and sneered at the women on their knees or backs, their hands tunneled in between their thighs as they gasped at the sight of him. They had forgotten that he was a spirit of lust and he would use every ounce of his power to get her back. If that meant debasing them, or breaking his rule to never affect those who did not want it? Then he didn't care. They would all be on their knees before him, whether they wanted to be or not.

His stomach rolled as he passed the few women who felt violated by his actions. He'd deal with that guilt later, but first, he would save his woman.

This was better than their death, he told himself. Even as he made it to the top of the Tower.

He threw the door open and froze when he saw no one other than Minerva facing him. The High Sorceress stood with locked knees, battling against his magic as she stood over Selene's unmoving body.

"So," Minerva said. "We meet again."

"Let her go and I will let you live."

"You keep saying that as though life is better than death," Minerva spat. "You know what I want."

"And you know I will not give it to you."

"Then I will share with you a secret." Minerva twitched forward, as though her lust for something to fill her affected her more than she wanted him to see. "I realized I don't have to have a weapon to kill you."

"Is that so?" His eyes strayed to Selene, willing her to move. Even just a finger. "How do you think you're going to kill me without a weapon?"

Minerva hissed out a long breath. "You're the fool who fell in love with her. What a shame to find out you can feel something other than lust after all."

"I'm not in love with her." Just saying the words hurt. He wished he could. He wished he wasn't lust, that he was another spirit who...

"Then all I have to do is kill her, and you'll follow."

His heart seized in his chest and he lunged forward.

Not fast enough. For the first time in his life, he wasn't fast enough.

Minerva planted her foot on Selene's side and shoved her off the side of the Tower.

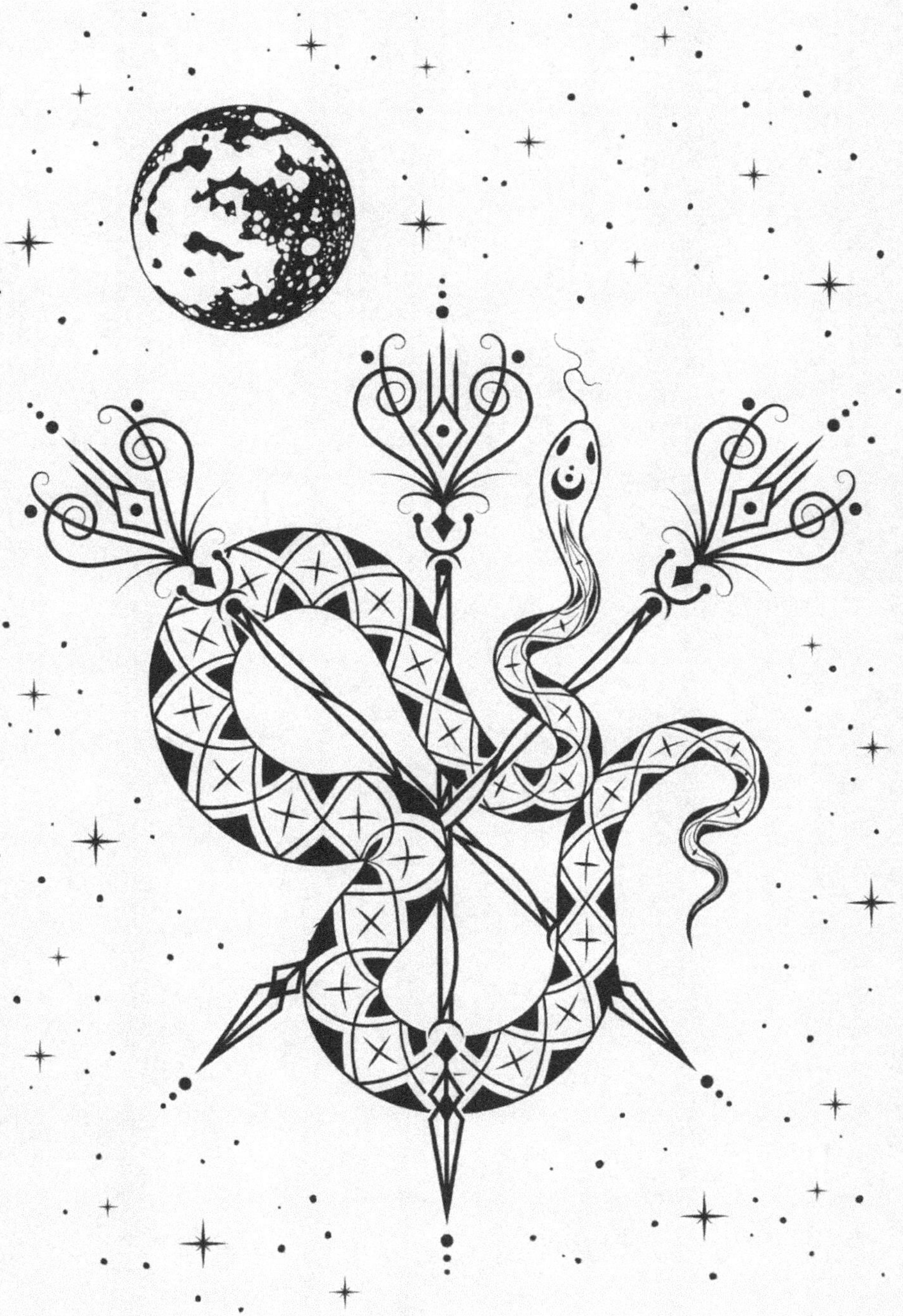

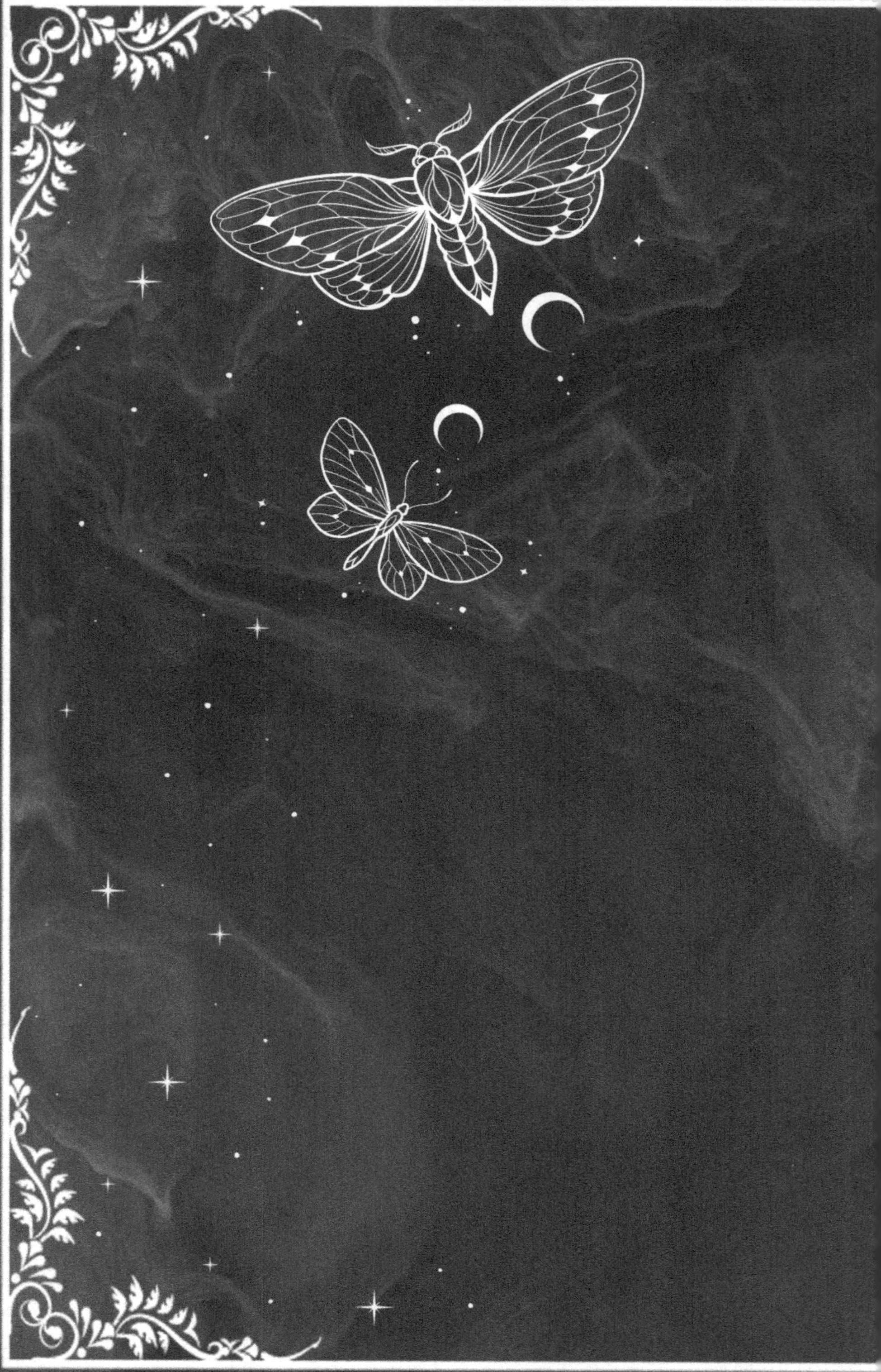

Chapter 44

The cool rain had turned to ice in her veins. She couldn't open her eyes. She had to focus on breathing or she would stop inhaling. Selene was alive, she was certain of that. And she was alone.

Nothing filtered through her mind as she felt the world passing her by. It was easy to think that no one wondered where she was. After all, she'd been here for centuries. Or maybe it was only a few moments.

She'd heard the screams. It was hard to avoid them as they ricocheted through the Tower and up to the highest peak. She heard them die, and she didn't feel an ounce of sadness for them.

They'd left her here. Her sisters, those women who were supposed to love her more than anyone else, had left her here to die, with only the wind and the rain to keep her company.

Her lips parted, and the rainwater gathered on her tongue. Soon she couldn't move in fear that she'd drown. It bubbled up around her lips, sliding down her cheeks and mingling with her tears. A cold, frozen way to die all on her own. Perhaps it was the right way to do it.

She'd been cold and frozen her entire life. Until him.

Selene thought she heard movement and then swore she could feel him. Lust's magic brushed against her like a warm embrace. A bubble of air escaped through the water in her mouth and she choked.

All she wanted was to say she loved him. She'd never gotten to tell him herself and suddenly it felt very important that he know. He deserved to know how much he meant to her, and how thankful she was that he'd helped her change.

But the cold didn't release its hold on her, no matter how hard she struggled.

And then her mind drifted through the good memories of her time with him. She dreamt of his first lingering touch that wasn't there because he wanted her body, but because he had found her interesting. She thought about laughing on a balcony while he looked surprised that he even could laugh. She remembered the way dimples appeared on his cheeks because he never really smiled unless he was with her.

All his warmth pooled in her chest around her heart, and she felt the ice crack just a little. Not enough for her to move or to whisper a single word, hoping that the wind would carry it to him. No. It was only enough for her to not feel so much pain.

Something moved against her. Not the snakes that had settled in her veins or the whispers in her ear that sounded like Minerva. It was a real touch, and she wasn't alone. She knew that now. She wasn't.

If only she could open her eyes. She'd know who was here with her in her last moments. Was it him? He couldn't come for her this quickly, but she wanted him to know where she was. She wanted him to find her.

Taking a deep breath, she struggled to the surface of her mind. She used the warmth he had gifted her to push back the curse enough to open her eyes.

Minerva planted her foot at her side and glared down at her. And then Selene felt herself shift, and she knew what was happening.

Her mother was kicking her off the Tower. Nothing below her would soften her blow, and she would die where she had been laid as a baby in the hopes that Minerva would save her. The beginning of her life and the end, meeting in one poetic moment.

But she wouldn't go out without a fight.

The last bit of her magic popped free from her body in twin orbs that flew up into the air as she fell. They both landed over Minerva's eyes and then burst into light, like the sun. Twin supernovas that burrowed into Minerva's skull and seared her eyes from her head.

The satisfaction of revenge didn't last long. Wind whistled through her ears and Selene felt weightless as she plummeted down the Tower. It seemed as though time slowed as the white walls flashed by her. She remembered how beautiful this world was. And how lovely it looked from so high up.

She tilted her head to the side and watched the kingdom she loved come up to meet her. That's what she told herself. The land she had loved so fiercely since the moment she was born had come alive. It wanted to hold her one last time and she would not deny it. There was nothing she could do other than enjoy the feeling of the wind in her hair and the rain on her cheeks.

She looked back up at the storm raging overhead and swore she saw him. He stood at the top of the Tower instead of Minerva and launched himself into the air after her. As though he could save her from this fate, even though it had been written since the moment she was born.

Selene had never been meant to kill him. She'd never wanted to hurt anyone, and she certainly wouldn't have given him up to these wicked women who wanted to harm him.

But right now, she would go back in time and do it all again. The deception. The lies. The secretive plots to end his life. If only she could hold him in her arms one last time.

And then the ground hit her.

The sickening crunch her body made was not nearly as bad as she thought. Perhaps one of her sisters had softened her blow, but she knew it wasn't normal to feel this numb. She could feel nothing at all, just the cold and how limp her body was against the snow.

"Selene!" A shriek echoed through the air, and she knew it was Ursula. "Please tell me I didn't... I caught her! I caught her, didn't I?"

She didn't know. She didn't think so. This wasn't right. Her body should have some sensation, not just... nothing. Like she wasn't there at all.

Another thud echoed beyond her, but she couldn't tilt her head to look. Tears slid out of her eyes because she couldn't stop them.

"Get back," a deep voice snarled as a monster leaned over her. Horns longer than her arms arched over his head. His face had changed into something angular and frightening, and black marks covered his hands and shoulders. It wasn't him, but it was.

He looked like he was in pain. His mouth twisted and his brows furrowed. Why? Who had hurt him?

Selene wanted to pick up her hand and cup his sharp jaw. She wanted to drag him forward and press their foreheads together so she could breathe him in. But she didn't want him to look at her like she was broken and he didn't know what he could touch.

"Selene," he whispered, his voice breaking on the word. "I don't... I don't know what to do."

Nothing. He could do nothing but be here, and he was here. She wasn't alone now. Didn't he know how wonderful that was? How much easier that made all this?

Lust snapped his head up, parting his lips on a snarl. "What did I say? Get back."

"She's hurt."

"Take one step closer, sorceress, and I will tear your spine from your body."

"I can help." That was a different voice. Was that Bathilda? No, Sibyl. It was Sibyl.

His voice rose into a roar. "I said get away from her!"

They needed to stop arguing. They were fighting over the same thing. They all wanted to help her. And she wanted them to know that it didn't matter. They couldn't help her, so would they all just gather round so she could see their faces one more time?

She forgave her sisters. She forgave them for what they had no choice in and what they had to do. They deserved to know that before she left them forever.

Lust looked back down at her, and she realized it wasn't rain tracking down his cheeks. Tears leaked out of his eyes as he hovered his hands over her body, never touching her with those dangerously sharp claws.

"Oh," he breathed, the sound shuddering and sharp. "What did they do to you? Selene, my moon."

His moon? She'd always been little moon, not his. Her thoughts were scattered.

"Why didn't you wait for me?" He slid his hands underneath her shoulders, carefully dragging her into his lap. "I figured it out. I figured out how to save you and if you had just waited just a few more minutes, I could have…"

He didn't have to be so careful with her. She couldn't feel anything, after all. Even the cold snow wasn't sinking through the pain of the snakes wriggling underneath her skin.

She stared up at him with love in her eyes and struggled through the pain. "I—"

"Shh, don't talk." He pressed his lips to her forehead and her head rolled as though he were cupping it with his hand. "This is going to hurt, my moon. I cannot change how much it hurts, and I do not wish to harm you more. But we are running out of time."

"Wa-it," she swallowed, trying to tell him those three words that meant everything. Because he couldn't save her. It wasn't possible, and he had to know.

"She's trying to say something," Ursula called out, the crunch of ice suggesting she took another step forward.

His eyes flashed as he glared at her. "Take another step, sorceress. Your blood will stain this snow."

"Let her speak. What if she doesn't want you to heal her?" Another crunch. "What if Minerva was right?"

Those words apparently got through to him. What had her mother said to make his eyes look so hollow?

"Is that the way of it then?" he asked, brushing the back of his fingers against her cheek. "Did you flee here to leave me? Was I so terrible that you found yourself trapped in my castle, and the only way to leave was this ruse of a curse? They want me to believe that, Selene. They want me to believe you did not want me."

Oh, her love.

He had nothing to fear. Channeling all of her energy into the words, she whispered slowly, enunciating every word so he would not mishear her.

"I-"

Lust leaned closer, pressing his ear to her lips.

"Love-"

He reared back, his eyes wild and something dangerous flickering in their depths.

"You."

He bared his teeth in a horrible snarl, but it was a victorious look. As though he had saved the world and somehow been handed her soul at the same time.

"That's what I thought," he said, and she felt his magic twist around her. It pulled at her heart, her soul, her very being, and a bubble of magic seared around them.

Like a shield, it grew, stretching in a wave of lavender light. Streaks of brighter patches glowed over her head and she had never seen anything so beautiful. She could hear her sisters pounding on the edges as though it were made of glass.

"They will not bother us now," he whispered.

Her head lolled again as he shifted her in his arms. He turned her face to him, so he was all that she could see. And Selene was glad for it. She'd never wanted to stare at someone more than him.

Some of that terrible visage bled away, leaving in its wake a different man. Or perhaps she simply didn't remember how softened his face could be.

Deeper laugh lines framed his face. Small crow's feet spread around his eyes that suggested he'd smiled too much recently and marred that usually beautiful face. And those eyes, ah, those soft eyes that stared at her with so much emotion it made her heart ache.

"You are everything," he whispered. "My beginning and my end. I thought I was living before I met you, and my darling, I was merely surviving. You walked into my life and set my entire world ablaze. How could I ever let you go?"

She had no idea. But she didn't want him to.

A wheeze of air filled her lungs, enough for her to say, "Death nips at my heels."

Another flash burned in his eyes, perhaps in recognition of the words. He pressed his lips to hers, gently, oh so gently. "Then it's time we run."

Something twisted at the back of her skull. And she could feel him moving now, his long claws reaching through her skin as her warm blood dripped onto the snow beneath them.

"There has to be a weak point," he muttered, his claws dragging along her body as his magic poured through her.

It hurt, she wanted to scream. He was hurting her, but she couldn't say a single word through it. The snakes, which had been so quiet, suddenly revolted. They wriggled and writhed and tore her body apart from the inside.

"A weak point," he said again, his eyes meeting hers. "Selene?"

The spell. She had to focus on the spell.

The snakes moved again, all of them suddenly focusing on turning her skull into a bonfire that would destroy her. She had to think fast.

When her mother had first laced the spell through her, she'd touched it with her finger. The back of her hand, wasn't it? A small hole in the web.

Selene struggled against the curse hardening her veins and then held up her hand.

Lust looked at her with pride and then grabbed onto her. A single claw speared through the weak point, and then she felt blood at the back of her neck.

She arched in his arms, her back bowing against the pain that seared through her body. But worse was that she could feel it inside her soul. It pulled and tugged as though he were trying to rip her out of her body and she couldn't... she couldn't...

He pulled something important out. She felt the dark tendrils hanging onto her, digging inside her skin and inside her skull, and the blinding pain wouldn't stop.

She opened her mouth in a scream that could not come out.

"I'm sorry," he whispered over and over again, his biceps bulging as he tried desperately to yank whatever it was out of her. "I'm almost done. I have it, Selene. Hold on for just a few more moments."

"You're killing her!" The scream came from outside the bubble at the same moment she felt a pop.

A rip, a tear, a sudden void of the lack of something, and then her world went dark.

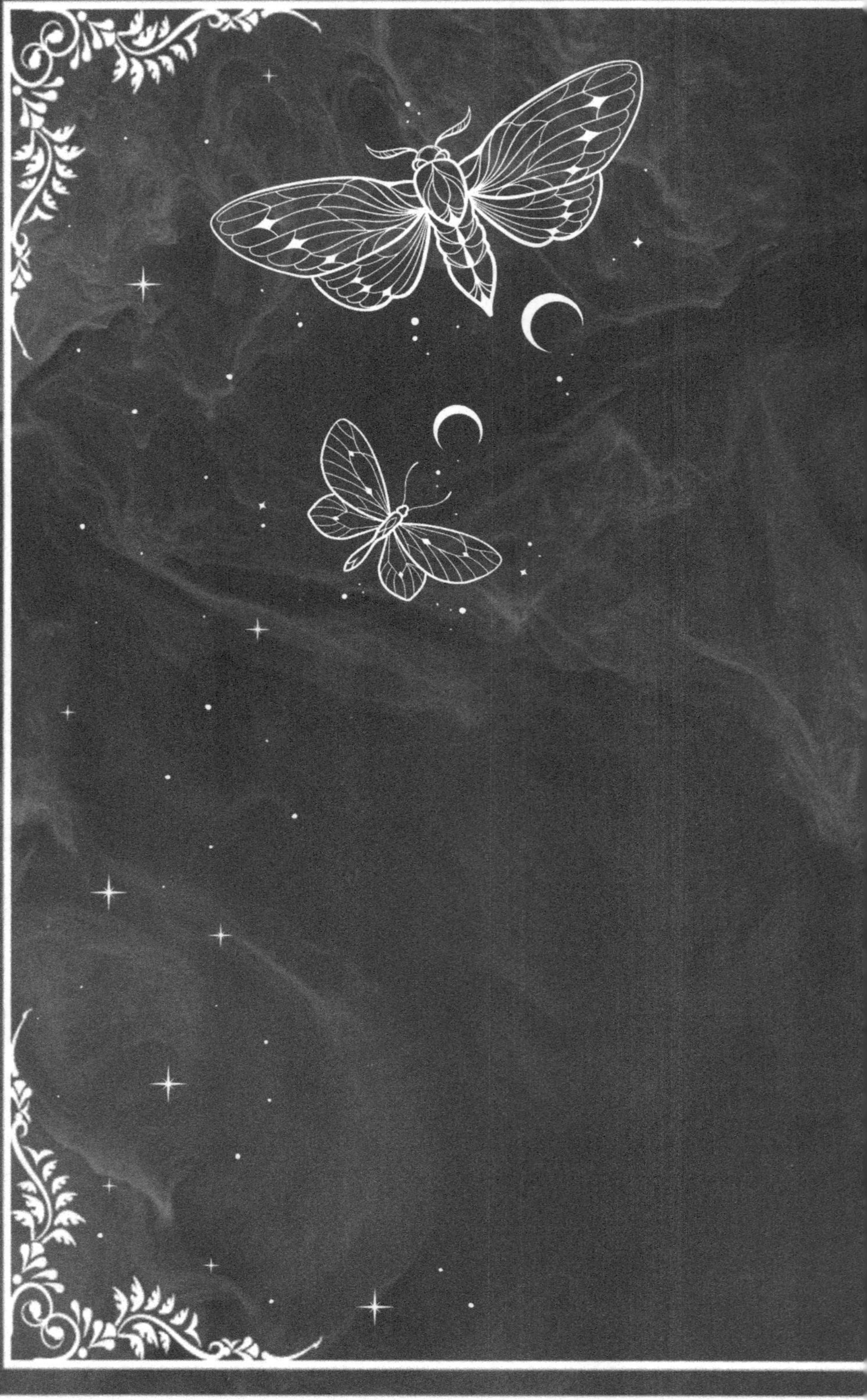

Chapter 45

Home.

It wasn't the same without her.

Lust stood in his office, his mind wandering through distant memories and better times. Hands behind his back, he stared out of the window and down into the grounds below.

The garden had already frosted over. Winter had arrived in the week since he'd returned from the Tower. Icy frost crawled over everything, spreading throughout his kingdom just like they did his heart. The entire castle could feel it. They were all lacking a certain snarky woman who usually had something to say in every circumstance.

Her absence spread like poison. Even his servants were testy.

They got in more arguments with each other than they ever had. He had to break them up time and time again as they bickered and claimed others were causing issues. Not to mention he was still aggravated by his brother's presence.

Greed tried to talk with him every single day. The ridiculous hovering was driving Lust mad. Yes, he was brooding. No, he wasn't all right. Yes, he would be all right. He just needed a little time to get his head on straight.

Because he was here and she wasn't, and that was unacceptable.

Sighing, he shifted his gaze from the cold outside and tried to feel something other than this strange cold that had spread throughout his entire body. The numbing quality was perhaps what she had claimed her power could do. If she had survived it, then he would as well.

The doors to his office burst open, the lock breaking under the immediate and far too powerful shove from a shoulder that could only belong to his brother.

"Get out," he snarled. "I have no interest in talking with anyone. Not yet."

"You've been talking with your servants and subjects for days and yet you have no time for your brother." Greed's snarl was no less intimidating than his own. "Would you at least look at me? I know everything happened so suddenly, but I would like to know you won't off yourself when I leave."

"I'm not going to."

"That's not enough. Telling me that you're fine through a closed door isn't the reassurance that I need." Greed paused, and then quieted his voice to a low murmur. "Pride has been asking about you."

Of course, their brother on high was getting involved. Any time someone even sneezed in the direction of their kingdom falling apart, he got involved. Pride made sure that all the kingdoms were doing exactly what they should, because his damned emotion wouldn't let him do anything else. All of their kingdoms had to flourish, or it looked bad on him.

"Tell Pride I am fine. My kingdom is fine. I will not let it fall because of a mortal woman that I... I..." He swallowed hard, the words thickening on his tongue until he couldn't even say them.

All the fire in him, that momentary rage, burned out. Lust turned around then, pinching his nose with his eyes squeezed shut. "How is she?"

The long pause before the response was enough of an answer, but he still forced himself to hear Greed say, "She hasn't woken yet. The healer is doing all she can, but her injuries..."

"Are extensive."

"Are fatal." Greed took another step closer until Lust stared down at the tips of his boots. "You may have to let her go, brother. I know you don't want to hear that, and I know it's not something any of us want. But it may be necessary to make the decision for her."

Never.

She could stay there in that bed like a princess, asleep until the day she struggled out of the darkness to find him again. And he knew she would. She'd battle through anything to get to his side because she'd said she loved him.

Wasn't that what love was? No matter what happened, no matter how hard it was, she would find him. That's how it worked.

His eyes burning—why were they doing that?—Lust finally looked at his brother and shrugged. "What am I supposed to do, Greed? I can't let her die."

Though his brother clearly intended to speak on that subject,

Greed's eyes widened in shock and his jaw fell open. "What... What happened to you?"

Lust ran a hand over his own scruffy jaw. "I haven't been sleeping well. Apparently these mortal bodies we took, although perfectly capable of rather impressive feats, don't do well with lack of sleep. It's been days since I could get my mind to stop racing with all the ways I could have saved her."

"No, it's... it's not that." Greed groped for the chair behind him and sank down into it. "You're... You're..."

Lust waited, but when nothing came out of his brother's gaping mouth he prodded, "I'm what? Tired? Sad? Worried? Yes, I'm all those things and I've never felt them before, so I'm rather frustrated with it all."

Again, Greed shook his head. "No, you're... not lust."

"I am the same person I was before." He took a deep, disappointed sigh and then sank into his own chair at his desk. "Albeit more tired and with more of a weight on my shoulders than I've felt in a long time."

"No, Lust. You're not... lust." Greed emphasized the last word. "Do you understand what I'm saying?"

He had no idea what his brother was getting at, but the headache already blooming behind his eyes was enough to make him throw the other man out. He needed time to heal from all that he'd seen and done. Even his body ached after that form change that shouldn't have been possible. He didn't remember it hurting the first time they'd all done this.

Another knock at his open door had his eyes rolling. "Who is it now?"

A glowing pillar of light glided into the room. Affection had grown to the same height as Selene, its form now lithe and shifting with a slight breeze whenever it moved.

"Your brother means that you are no longer a spirit of lust," it said, and the tone in its voice was full of pride. "You have changed because of her."

His fingers flexed on his thighs, feeling suddenly coming back to them as shock rocked through his body. "What did you say?"

"You're not who you were before her. Saving her life, it has altered the spirit inside you." Affection lifted a glowing hand and gestured over its heart. "You are no longer lust. That is what your brother is saying."

Greed stared at him like he'd grown a second head. "I didn't know it was possible."

"It's not," he snapped. "We are the way we are. We were created as such and we cannot change."

But they could.

He'd heard of it before, although it had been said to be impossible. Spirits had changed before if they were bent under circumstances that made even a spirit question their life's intent. A spirit of honor could be swayed throughout the tidings of war, and become a spirit of rage. A spirit of hope could be thrust into a world with none of that emotion until it was nothing more than a speck forced to become a spirit of woe. These were changes that only happened under dire pressure or desperation, and had never happened to one as powerful as him.

His lungs expanded in a huge gasp of air as he met his brother's gaze in both horror and hope. "I'm not," he whispered. "I'm not a spirit of lust."

"Then what are you?" Greed leaned forward, licking his lips and eyeing him with an emotion that Lust could not name. "What are you now, brother?"

He stretched his hands out in front of him and eyed them. There were faint lines there now, lines he'd seen in the mirror as well. Not necessarily bad changes, but a softening of his features, a warmth in his soul that he hadn't noticed before.

"Love," he replied, his voice little more than a croak. "I think I'm a spirit of love now."

Greed slammed his spine back against his chair, his eyes wide as he shook his head. "It shouldn't be possible. We've been in mortal form for a thousand years. We can't change."

"Apparently we can."

Under duress, his magic, the spirit that had given him life, gave up its desire. And instead, it had planted a deep and soul binding love for a single woman who had changed his life for the better.

What would he do without her now?

Groaning, he palmed his head in his hands and leaned over his knees. "I can't lose her now."

His heart stuttered in his chest, squeezing even at the thought of losing her when she had changed him so much. She was the reason for the breath in his lungs, but he also knew that he would continue on without her. He'd bring her as part of his soul, changing the way he ruled this kingdom and likely for the better.

She'd shown him there was more to the chase than a quick fuck, or a long term understanding. He no longer wished to provide someone a life if only they shared their body but never their thoughts.

He wanted a connection, now. He wanted to know what someone was thinking and feeling and he wanted to know the names of their children.

How long had he spent inside Lara's body and yet he didn't even know the name of her child? Or how old her daughter was? He'd never cared once, and now he cared.

More than just about Selene, but about every person in his kingdom who deserved more than just his fleeting attention. They deserved his love just as they had so willingly given their own.

Fuck, this made life a lot more difficult, didn't it?

Greed shook his head in disbelief one more time, but then leaned forward to match Lust's position. "This changes things."

"No, really? I thought life would continue forward as usual."

"Don't be a dick. Listen, you were going to have to deal with this, eventually. She's still out, and very mortal. If you're going to drag out her death, then maybe it's better to let her go now."

"Stop talking." He lifted his hand in the air, glaring at his brother with every ounce of anger that he could muster. "We're not letting her die. And I've already thought about her mortality enough for the day. We'll continue this tomorrow while I attempt to understand how my spirit has changed."

Affection cleared its throat, the light sound bubbling through the room until both of them glared at it.

"What?" Lust snapped. "Is there more that you want to reveal?"

"Actually, yes." It floated closer to him, hovering just an inch above the floor. "Selene is still asleep. Her body is fighting very hard to stay alive, but I'm not entirely sure she will win that fight."

"See?" Greed pointed at the spirit. "I'm not making it up to control you."

"But she could have an advantage if I do something to help."

He stared up at the spirit, not following its thoughts. "How could you help?"

"I would rather show you." Affection held out a small pillar of light that looked rather like a hand. "I think she will say yes, but I also think it's very important that we all be there for it."

"She's awake?" He stood as though in a dream, letting the spirit draw him toward the door.

"Not yet. I'll have to ask her in her mind, you see, but I think she'll still approve of it. And I want you to be there when it happens."

Why? What was the spirit intending to do?

He tossed a look over his shoulder and Greed stood as though he'd aged a hundred years in the past few moments. His lion-like brother shook his head of flaming hair and then took off after them.

The three of them meandered down the halls, toward the room where Lust had rarely left. The healer was already leaving, closing the door gently behind herself. She started when she saw the three of them, but relaxed the moment Affection's glowing light touched her.

"Hello," the healer said. "I'm afraid there have been no changes. Her spine is in a state unlike anything I've seen before. Her ribs are shattered, and the back of her skull is no better. I'm shocked she's still alive."

Lust ground his teeth. "She's a fighter."

"Apparently an impressive one at that." The healer gave him one last nod. They'd gotten very acquainted with each other the past week, and he had a significant amount of admiration for the woman who had gone above and beyond what she had to do for Selene.

And then Lust watched as his brother and Affection stepped into the room he hated walking into.

Because he knew what waited for him inside. He knew how horrible it was. She laid on that bed, too pale, like snow. Her dark hair fanned around her head, perfectly smooth because he brushed it every morning and every night. Just in case she woke up, so she'd still be comfortable. Her hands rested outside the blankets, but he tucked them in at night so she wouldn't get cold.

And still, she didn't wake. She was so broken, and there was nothing he could do to fix that.

He strode into his nightmare and stood beside her, looking down at those pale features and the smudges of bruises on her cheeks.

"I'm still surprised she's here," Greed murmured, as though any noise might wake her. "Her sisters were rather rabid about keeping her."

"They couldn't have healed her any better than I could." He brushed the backs of his fingers over her forehead and then arranged a dark curl away from her face. "She's where she needs to be."

Affection's hand laid over his, just above her head. "She said yes."

"What are you even talking about?" he asked. "What is she saying yes to?"

The glowing light receded from his dear friend's face. Affection appeared more feminine in this moment, soft around the edges with a kind smile for him. "It has been a great honor to live with you for such a long time, Lust. I got to see you become this person and I am so proud of you. All that energy given to me from you and her, I've been holding onto it. Just in case. And now is the perfect time to use it."

"To heal her?" He shook his head. "Spirits cannot heal, Affection. We have magic, but not that kind."

A glittering gemstone dripped down Affection's cheek, like a tear. "I can heal if I'm inside her."

"And then what? The wounds will reopen the moment you leave her."

His mind caught up with what Affection wanted to do, and it made his heart squeeze in his chest again.

"No," he muttered, drawing his hand away from them both. "I won't lose both of you. No, you will not try to do this hair brained attempt to save her. Possession? It doesn't work. Two people cannot exist in the same body. It will either be you or her."

"And so it will be her." Affection looked down at Selene's pale face and smoothed its hand over her cheek. "She has always been kind to me. I wish to do this for her now."

"I will not allow it." But he could do nothing to stop it.

Greed banded his arm around Lust's shoulders. He was forcefully held in place as he watched his oldest friend lean over Selene and press its lips to her forehead.

"Please," he tried begging. "Don't make me choose between the two of you."

"It's not your choice," Affection replied with a bubbling laugh. "This has been an adventure. All this time by your side, and I have seen the world with you. I know you don't think you've been given enough time to appreciate me, but none of us ever gets that. I have experienced so much and I have seen you fall in love with her. It's my greatest honor and best purpose to bring her back to you. To show you how much I love you, every day, for the rest of time."

"Affection," he said, his voice catching on a sob. "Please."

But he didn't know if he was asking the spirit to stay or to save her.

Affection smiled and then curled up beside Selene. With a quiet sigh, it whispered, "Give her time. There is much to heal."

Then it rested its head on her chest, gathered her hand up in both of its own, and its glowing light sank beneath Selene's skin.

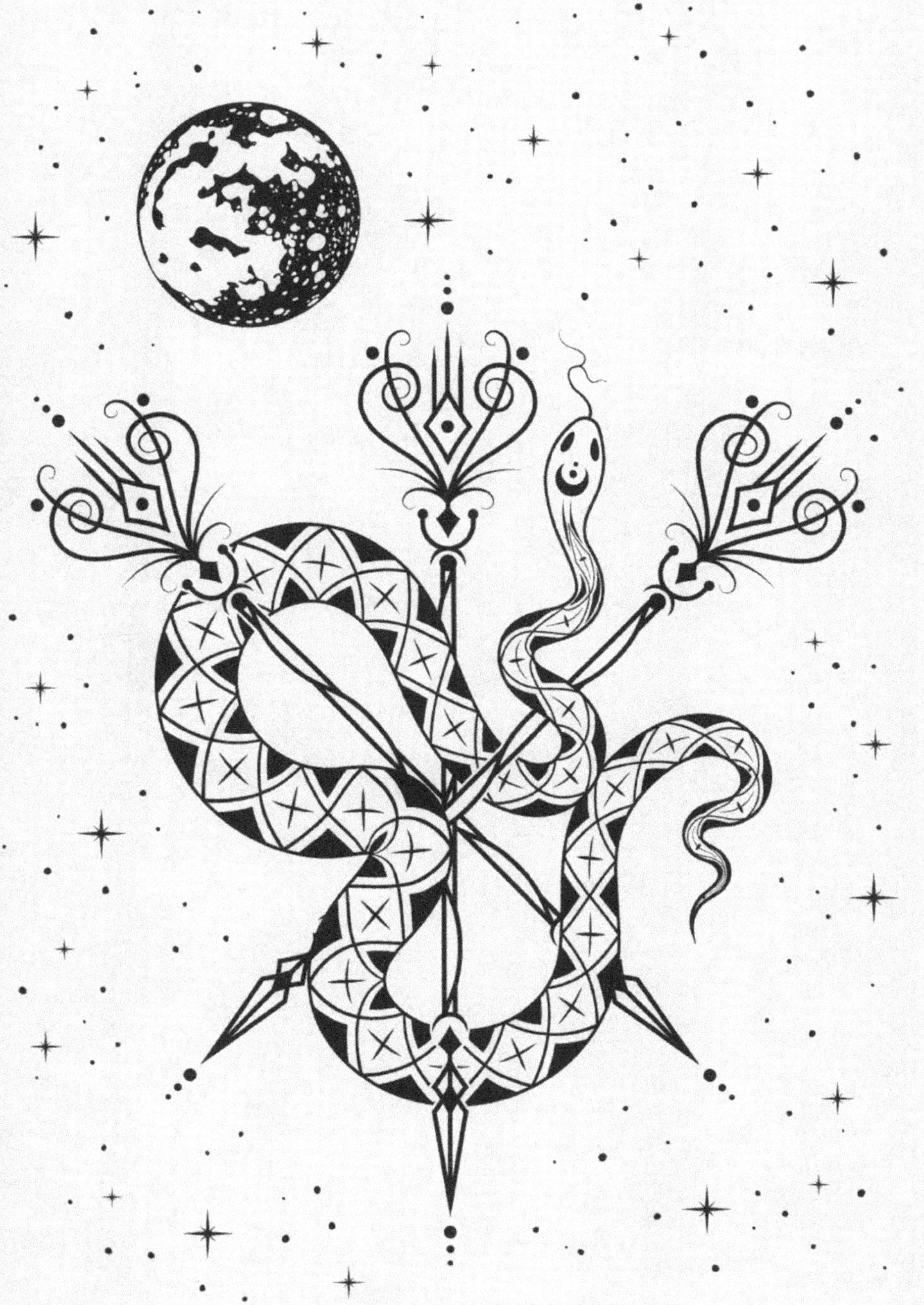

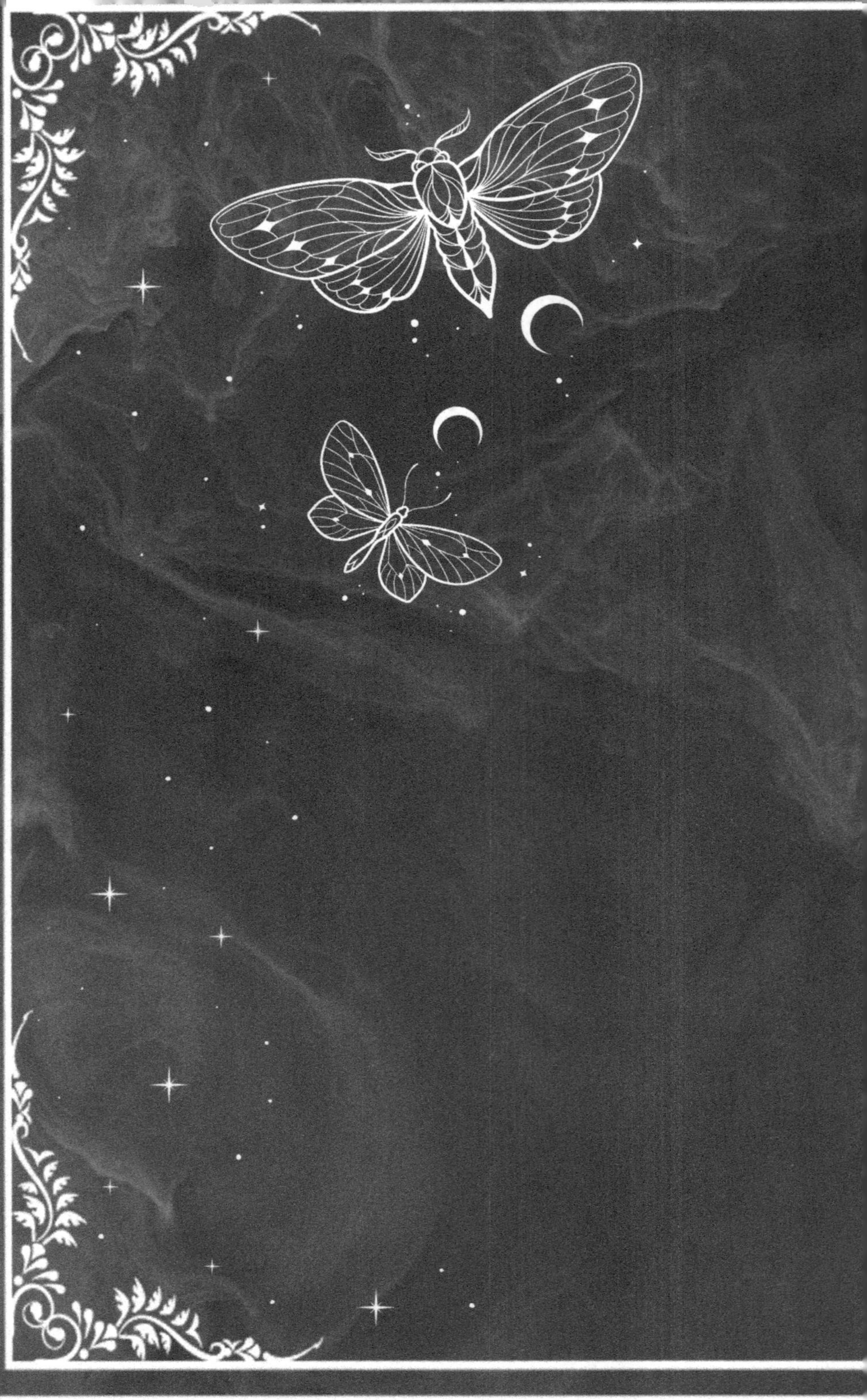

Chapter 46

"You've made a remarkable recovery," Sirona, the healer, said, packing up the last of her things. "When I saw you awake this morning, I have to admit, I was surprised."

"As I am," Selene replied. Her voice was still a little scratchy, but she felt... good. Better than she had in years, which was a strange enough experience after near death.

"I think that spirit inside you has a lot to do with that. But I am not versed in such things."

"I don't think many of us are versed in that." The slight chuckle she attached to the words felt wrong.

She'd only been awake for an hour or so. The healer had been very particular that no one tell Lust until they were certain that

Selene was healed well enough to receive visitors. It was a terrible plan, and she'd told the healer that. Still, the woman was quite firm when she wanted to be.

A good healer always was. Selene suspected Sirona might be the best in the entire kingdom.

Her heart twinged at the thought of Affection inside her. The spirit was visible to this healer, a woman she suspected might be a sorceress of a kind, and apparently had done all the healing necessary for her to wake. Sirona was quite put out when she realized that all her work had been completed in a matter of a few days.

"You've been asleep for nearly two weeks now," the healer grumbled. "All it took was a single spirit two days to fix what I couldn't in two weeks."

"Don't let it bother you too much. Magic is unpredictable."

"At its best." Sirona snapped the last clasp on her bag shut and then nodded. "I do hope we see each other again. Under better circumstances."

"I'd like that." And she meant it. The healer was a very pleasant person to be around.

Then the door to her bedroom slammed open so hard that three paintings on the opposite wall crashed to the floor. Lust stood in the doorway, his eyes wild and his chest heaving with ragged breaths. He stared at her, she stared at him, and then she saw panic start to crawl up inside him.

"I think you should go," she whispered, never taking her eyes off the man she loved.

"I think that's a good idea," Sirona replied before skirting past Lust. He never even looked at the other woman.

His eyes were only for her.

"I'm awake," Selene said when they were finally alone.

His jaw trembled, but other than that, he didn't move. He stood in that doorway with his breath heaving from his lungs, his eyes tracing over every part of her body.

"Are you not going to come here?" she asked, and doubt settled in her stomach. She'd told him that she loved him, but she hadn't been awake for the rest. Had he been terrified that she'd said such a thing? She couldn't take it back.

"You're still hurt." His voice was gruff and deep with emotion.

"I'm not." Selene lifted her arms. "Affection apparently fixed it all before letting me wake."

A small huff of breath erupted out of him before he moved. And suddenly he was at the foot of her bed, crawling up her body with tears streaming down his cheeks as he gathered her close to his heart.

Ragged, uneven breaths fanned across her neck. He'd buried his head there, his lips pressed to her skin as he tried to piece himself back together. A tear trailed down her cheek, and she was already shoving the emotions away before she caught herself. She would not disappear on him. Never again.

Selene smoothed her hands down his back, easing the torment that had plagued the both of them for too long.

"I'm here," she whispered. "I'm okay."

"You weren't."

"No, I wasn't. But I came back." Selene tugged him out of his hidden spot at the base of her neck, forcing him to look at her. She smoothed her thumbs over his cheeks, dashing away the tears. "You've never looked worse."

He laughed, squeezing his eyes shut and shaking his head. "Of course you say that."

"No, really. You look terrible." And he did. With dark circles under his now red-rimmed eyes, gaunt cheeks, and stress lines that furrowed his brow. But he'd never looked more handsome either.

Selene tugged him forward and kissed him. A quiet, soothing kind of kiss that promised she would be here for a while to come. "I'm sorry for worrying you."

"I'm sorry I wasn't faster."

"I didn't need you to save me, or at least, I didn't think I did. I shouldn't have gone without talking to you first. But I didn't want to die in front of you, either."

He nodded, pressing his forehead to hers as a few more tears slid down his cheeks. "Greed told me everything about your conversation. I'll be mad at you later."

Shockingly, heat bloomed low in her belly at his words. Why would she want to sleep with him now? She was hardly awake and she should be tired, exhausted, weak from laying in this bed for two weeks but she... wasn't.

All she wanted was him. To feel that connection between them again and to know that they were both very much alive.

"I love you," she whispered, drawing him down to kiss her again. "I wanted to say it a thousand times before that moment, and I shouldn't have said it when I was dying. But I love you. More than anything else in this world."

He kissed her back as though he were the one in pain. As though without touching her, he would waste away into nothing.

"I was so afraid of losing you," he whispered, drawing away from her lips and peppering her skin with kisses. "The thought of life without you by my side is bleak, my moon, my love."

His love?

She sank back into the sheets as he rolled over her. His eyes blazed and she could see it. The love that burned through him like a star.

"I love you," he said, deep and heartrendingly beautiful. "I love you, Selene, my moon, my sorceress. You wove a spell around my heart and I have no desire to ever break it. Or you. Or this life we will build together."

Every bit of ice that might have remained inside her melted, and she felt it rushing through her. Burning away anything that would ever make her afraid of feeling her emotions again. This was him. Their love that turned her entire world upside down and inside out. It was perfect.

He kissed her again, his hands turning to fists in the sheets. "You are unwell," he whispered, dragging his lips down her throat. "You should rest."

"I have rested for two weeks. What I need is you."

The low growl that came out of his mouth sent her into a near frenzy. The damned blankets were trapping her underneath him, and he used that to his advantage. Lust leaned back onto his heels, his entire body on display for her.

And she had to lie there and watch while he slowly pulled his shirt off. Revealing ropes of muscles that she wanted to lick, flexed abs, and a broad chest that made her entire body heat. She tried to reach for him, but he was just beyond the length of her arms and the blankets pinned her down next to his knees. She had to settle with laying her hands on his thick thighs, knowing that small touch would never be enough.

"Slow," he murmured as he leaned back within reach.

Her hands didn't know what that meant. She wanted to touch him, all of him, without any barriers of feelings or fabric between them.

She wanted to know what sex felt like with someone she was desperately in love with.

But he would not let her.

Lust slowly pulled the blankets back, revealing inch by inch of her naked body. And he took his time with every inch that he found. His lips traced her collarbone, feather light and oh so soft. His fingers moved over the swell of her breast, plucking at one nipple while he only licked the other. Every touch was so delicate and nowhere near enough. His tongue trailed down her belly, licking a path between her legs that had her arching into him.

But he ignored the obvious destination and instead rained kisses down her legs, all the way to her toes.

"What are you doing?" she hissed. "I thought—"

"I want to make sure that every inch of you is healed," he said, his eyes meeting hers as he crawled back up her body. "I want to see every part of you that was wounded, and I want to kiss it better."

Oh.

Well, who was she to complain?

He flipped her over and gave her spine the same treatment as her front. His lips trailed down her back, pressing kisses to every vertebrae that had shattered on impact, every rib that had broken, every bruise that was no longer there.

"I didn't kill her," he whispered against the small of her back, where he had spent time laving each dimple with his tongue. "She's yours to deal with when you're ready."

"Who?" Her mind whirled, trying to think of anything other than his touch.

"Exactly."

With one arm around her waist, he lifted her up onto all fours.

Immediately her pussy clenched, already dripping for him and the sensation of his too large cock sliding into her depths.

But it wasn't his cock that touched her. Oh no, he had other plans.

Gasping at the sensation of him everywhere, Selene held her breath as he licked from those dimples at the base of her spine, all the way down to her pussy, and everything in between.

She'd never... no, had never.... oh god, he did it again.

His tongue trailed over every inch of her until she couldn't think, couldn't breathe, couldn't focus on anything other than his wickedly talented tongue and how it delved into places she'd never even thought a man would want to lick. Except he did. The groans he made as he devoured her were enough to send another rush between her legs.

Her first orgasm hit hard enough to bend her elbows. Her second made her thighs shake. By the third that chased the other two, she was quaking on the bed while he held her hips up for his mouth.

"Lust," she moaned, desperate for more, even though she didn't think she could take another orgasm. "Please."

"You know I love to hear you beg." He kissed her inner thigh before moving behind her. And then she felt him, the wedge of his thick cock against her pussy and how much it would hurt in the best way possible. "Now do it again."

"Please," she whimpered.

"You can do better than that." He dragged his cock up and down her slit, teasing her, making her shiver with desire. "You're so pretty when you beg."

She whined again before forcing her mind back to the present. "Please fuck me."

"With what?"

"Your cock?" It came out as more of a question.

"And?"

"Your fingers."

"And?" The tip of his cock slid inside her, the burn exquisite before she could even think to reply.

"And anything else you want to fuck me with, just please, fuck me already."

He chucked at the growl in her voice and then slid all the way inside her. They both groaned at the same time, their voices mingling as he began to move.

"That's a good girl," he said, his hands grabbing onto her hips so hard she thought he might leave bruises. "Now tell me you're mine."

"I'm yours. I've been yours since the first time you kissed me."

"Well before that." Lust drew back and slammed inside her, hard.

She gasped and braced herself on her forearms, trying to hold herself still for him while he moved in and out at a blinding speed that had another orgasm barreling toward her.

"Go ahead," he said, deep and low in her ear. He bent over her, his hand bracketing her throat as he snarled, "I want to feel you come on my cock, little one."

And she did. So hard that he had to stop moving because she squeezed him too tight. He hissed out a long breath and the moment she was finished, aftershocks still running all the way into her fingertips, he pulled out of her.

A little sound of disappointment was all she could make before he was there again, flipping her onto her back and then drawing her up into his arms. She was suddenly face to face with him, her arms draped over his shoulders and her legs over his hips.

He held her aloft, one arm braced underneath her bottom and the other slowly feeding his cock inside her once again. This angle, the intimacy of it, staring directly into his eyes, almost made her come again within seconds.

Breathing hard, he held her gaze as though his life depended on it.

"I will not lose you again," he said, his voice guttural with every stroke of his body inside hers. "You are mine, just as I am yours. You are everything to me, Selene."

"I will not live without you either," she whispered, pressing her lips to his in a kiss that consumed her entire soul. "I love you."

"Say it again."

"I love you, Lust, my demon king. You have my heart and my soul." She flexed her shoulders, taking over the rhythm as his head fell back. She pressed kisses to the long column of his throat and tortured him for long moments of quiet, slow movements before she couldn't take it anymore.

Selene dragged her teeth down his neck and whispered, "I want to feel you come inside me."

The snarl that ripped out of him was nothing short of animalistic. Hard, rough strokes pounded up into her. They both chased the starlight one more time, rushing toward an end that bound them together even more tightly.

And then she felt him. The magic that existed only inside him, but this time it had changed. It didn't feed her desire for more touching or petting or for a harder orgasm. All it had was the warmth of so much love that her heart thudded harder for him. Only him.

They came together with ragged groans as they fell, tangled limbs and lips pressed to opposite shoulders. She could feel his love inside her. She could feel how much she meant to him and how afraid he had been of every moment without her.

He held her tightly, clutching her in his arms as though he still feared she would disappear or slip back into that coma.

"I love you," she whispered again. He tightened his hold on her. "I will love you forever, my king, my heart."

Selene didn't know how long they stayed like that, her in his lap and his arms woven around her. But she found she didn't care. She'd stay like this forever if she got to be with him.

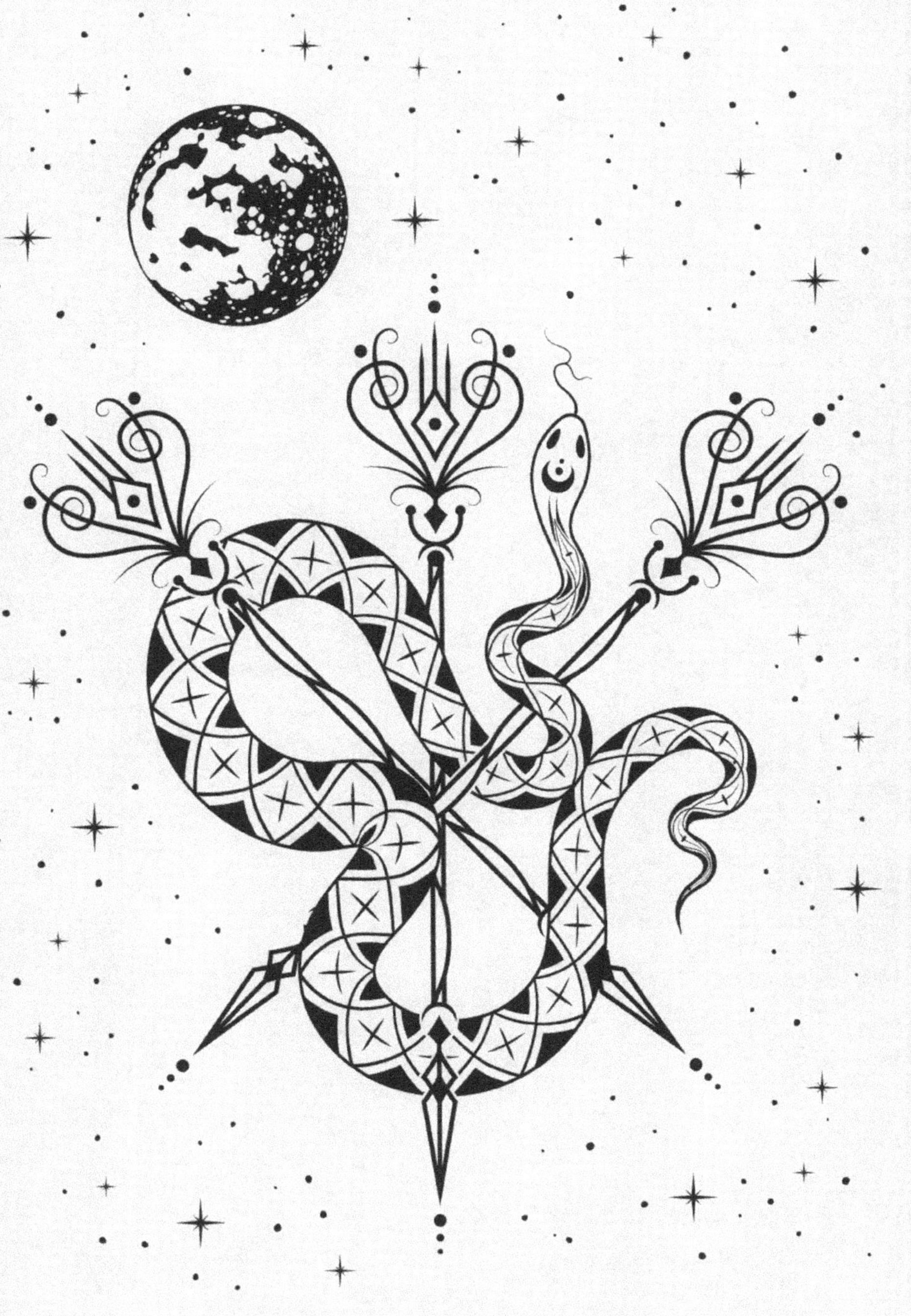

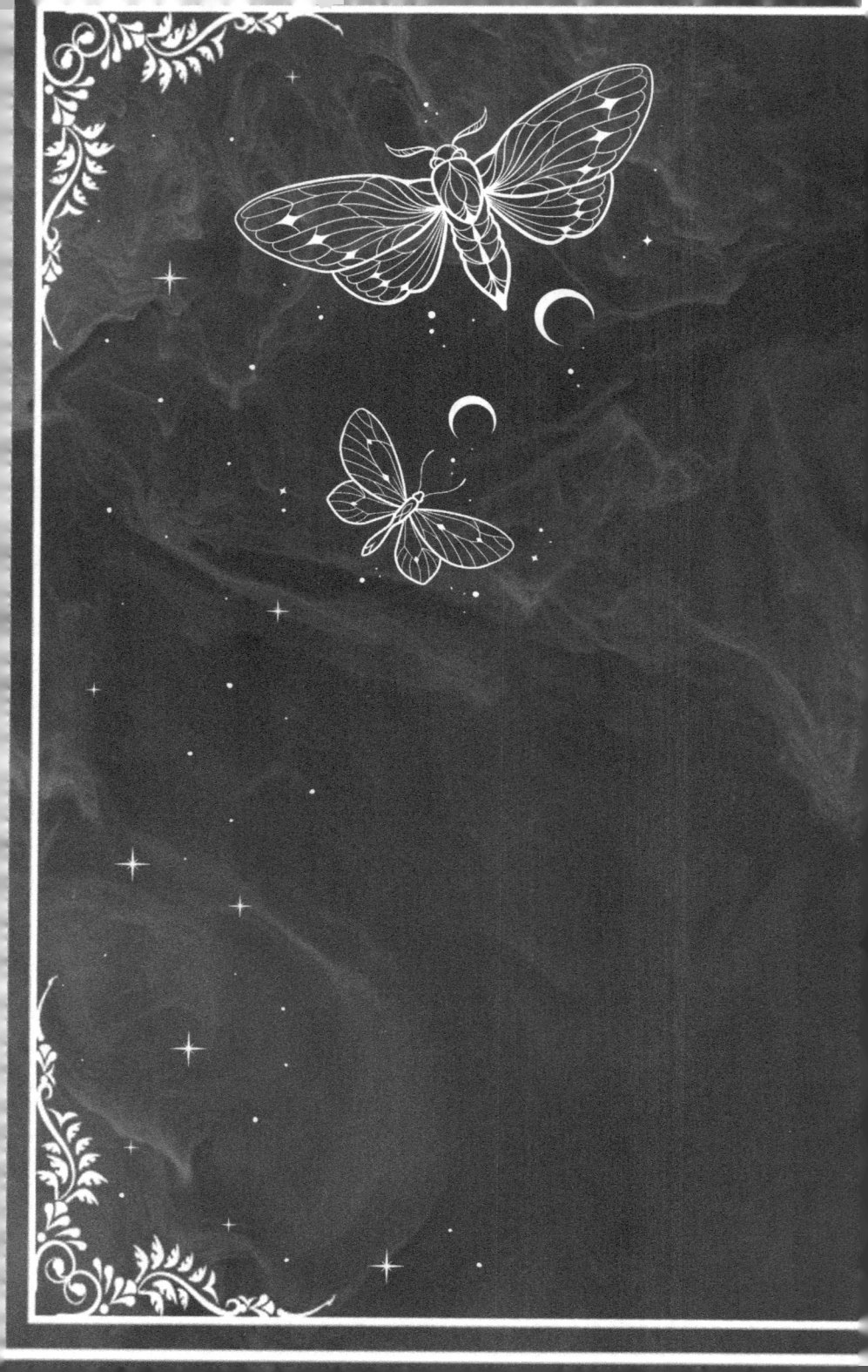

Chapter 47

"Are you sure you don't want to go back?"

Selene rolled her eyes at Lust as he rounded the corner of his desk. Which she was seated at, as she'd taken over most of his office now that she was better. "Yes, I'm sure I don't want to go back to the Tower. They will run it just fine without me."

"They will not run it well without you."

"I trust them to do the right thing."

"The last time you said that, a High Sorceress threw you off the top of the Tower." He rounded the back of her chair and leaned over it, pointing at a line on the letter she'd been reading. "Sibyl doesn't seem all that confident that things are going well."

"Sibyl is annoyed with Ursula for stealing her best quill, and she's angry at Bathilda for claiming to see a future that she doesn't like." Selene shrugged. "It's all entirely normal behavior. They're siblings. They don't get along well."

"I still think we should send someone out there to keep an eye on everything. Greed has offered—"

"Greed needs his people where they belong," she interrupted, trying her best to hide the smile on her lips. "If we want to keep watch over our own sorceresses, we do that without the help of your brother."

"While you stay here, far away from them and their meddling."

"As you wish." She didn't want to go back. That monolith held too many poor memories for her, and she refused to spend even an ounce of energy worrying about her sisters. They would figure it out under her watchful gaze. While she stayed safely in her castle with her demon king.

Sighing, she leaned back in the chair and smiled at him as he pressed a kiss to her bare shoulder. "You look lovely today."

"Thank you. A very talented man picked out my outfit." She ran a hand over her complicated braids, then added, "And he did my hair."

"A man who is obsessed with you, I assume." A low growl rumbled in his chest, and he nipped at her lips. "If you settle for anything less than that, I'll have to take you over my knee."

"You wouldn't dare."

Another voice interrupted them. "You two are disgusting now."

Oh, right. She'd forgotten Greed was here.

Blinking the haze away from her eyes, she smiled at Greed, where he stood in the doorway waiting for them to see him off. "You're sure you'll be all right? It's a long journey back, and I'm sure your brother wouldn't mind sending you rations for the way."

Greed's lips curled in disgust. "As if I'd take anything other than water from here. It's a good place for a vacation, but hardly anywhere to stay for a long time. I'm ready to get back to my own people, my own food, and my own bed."

Lust sat down on the arm of her chair and crossed his arms over his chest. "And here I was, believing your people were nomadic."

"They are," Greed snorted. "I'm not. Besides, there's nothing here for me to take that I can hold over you. Especially now that you're--" He choked on the last word. "Love."

Selene glanced up at the man she adored and smiled. "Ah, well he might be a spirit of that, but he'll always be Lust to me."

Lust's eyes heated as he looked down at her, and a red tinge appeared on the tops of his cheekbones. That was new, now that he'd changed spirits. But she loved knowing what he was thinking. "For you? Always, little moon."

Their romantic moment was yet again ruined as Greed gagged.

"Enough," he said, pressing a fist to his mouth before he shook his head to clear it. "If I have to see the two of you moon over each other for one more second, I will vomit all over your floor and not feel an ounce of guilt. Goodbye. Both of you."

Lust called out, "Be careful with your thief situation! You never know which one of us might fall to the whims of a woman."

The only response Greed gave was to flip his brother off over his shoulder as he disappeared down the hall.

Selene watched as Lust chuckled, the sound music to her ears. When had he laughed so much? Never? She'd only heard the sound a few times before he changed what spirit he was, and now she didn't think she could live without it.

"Thief?" she asked as he picked her up out of the chair and placed her on his lap.

"Apparently, someone is upset. A thief has stolen quite a few priceless objects from outposts all over the kingdom. They're showing back up after being sold or ransomed. Greed doesn't take kindly to someone stealing what he's already stolen." Lust ran his finger over her bottom lip, his eyes tracking the movement. "He needs to deal with that quickly, and not by making an example out of them and killing the person."

"He's going to kill them then, hm?"

"Most likely. But you never know. I wouldn't have thought I'd ever fall in love with a sorceress, either." He leaned forward to follow the path his finger had taken, kissing her lips tenderly with each slow glide. "And yet, here I am. Madly kneeling at her feet and worshiping the ground she walks upon."

"You do not."

"I absolutely do." He leaned back to glare at her, suddenly very serious. "And if, for a second, you do not feel worshiped, then you will tell me. I'll prostrate myself onto the floor and let you step on my throat."

"I don't want to do that," she replied with a laugh.

But then his cheeks flamed again, and oh, that expression. "What if I want you to step on my throat?"

Selene hummed low under her breath before kissing him again, this one lingering a bit more than the first. "Then I suppose we can make that happen."

She let out a little squeal as he gathered her in his arms and leapt up from the desk, rushing back to their bedroom, which they had hardly left for the better part of two weeks. Maybe the two of them would settle down eventually once they'd gotten their fill of each other.

But as she stared up at his beloved face, at his wild grin and eyes filled with love, she rather hoped they wouldn't.

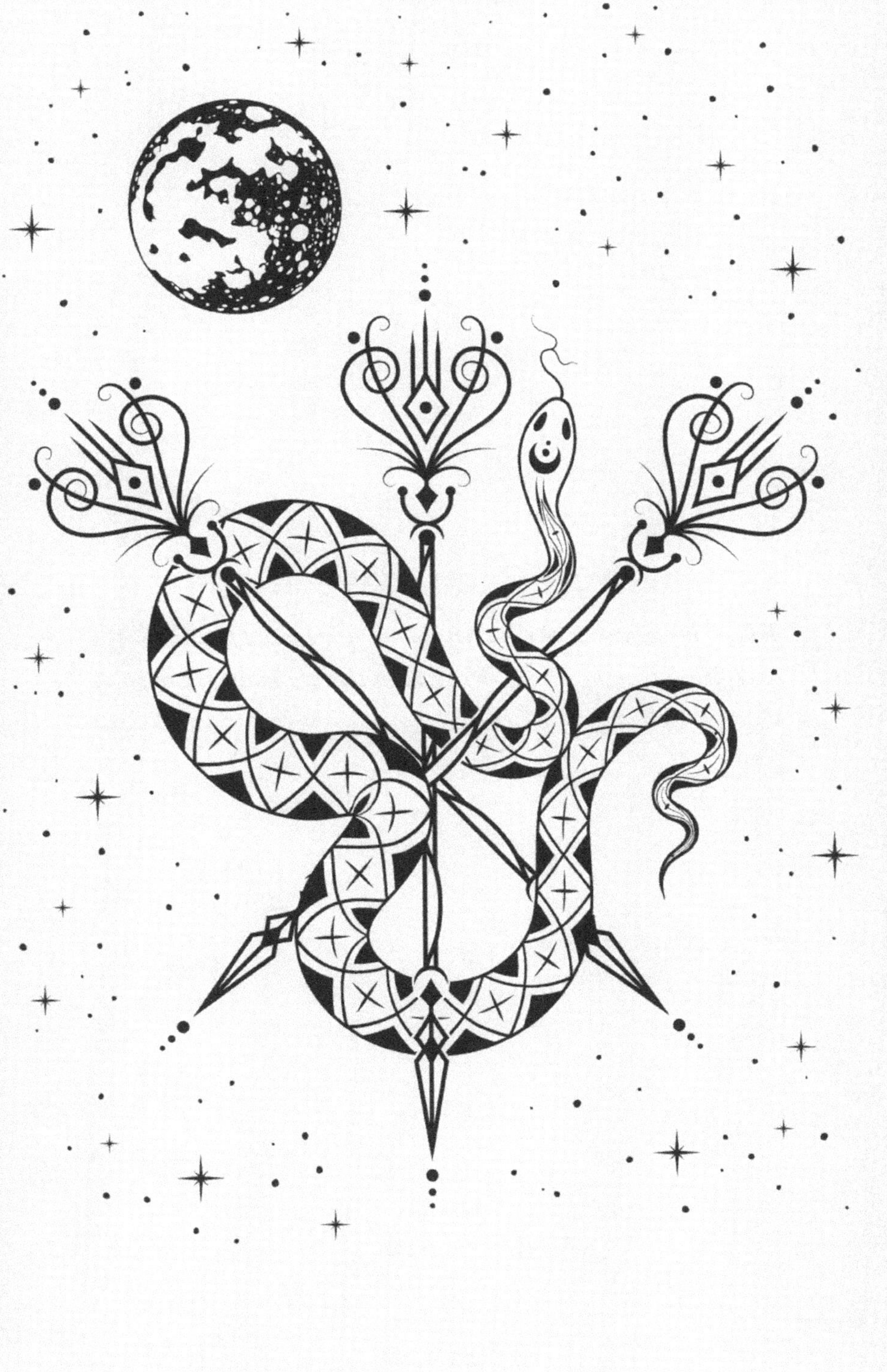

Follow me on socials or Amazon to keep your eye out for the next book. The only thing I'll say right now is that the main guy might be a little.... greedy.

the demon court

ACKNOWLEDGEMENTS

So much of this book wouldn't exist without a very special person in my life. My fiancé regularly gives me all the inspiration I need to write characters that make people smile, who support their partners no matter what oddities that person brings to the relationship, and how to choose each other even through the difficult times.

Thank you to the beta readers who have always sent me notes on each book, and to the new editor who jumped onto my team last minute and provided wonderful edits.

And of course, thank you to all my readers who make these stories a possibility every single day. I wouldn't be doing this without you <3

the demon court

ABOUT THE AUTHOR

Emma Hamm is a small town girl on a blueberry field in Maine. She writes stories that remind her of home, of fairytales, and of myths and legends that make her mind wander.

She can be found by the fireplace with a cup of tea and her two Maine Coon cats dipping their paws into the water without her knowing.

For more updates, join my newsletter!
www.emmahamm.com

the demon court

Ingram Content Group UK Ltd.
Milton Keynes UK
UKHW041055270423
420787UK00030B/147/J